KISS OF
LIFE

Also by Daniel Waters

Generation Dead

KISS OF
LIFE

DANIEL WATERS

SIMON AND SCHUSTER

ACKNOWLEDGMENTS

Al Zuckerman, Arianne Lewin, Jenn Corcoran, Ann Dye, Elizabeth Clark, Jennifer Levine, Angus Killick, David Epstein, Nellie Kurtzman, Christian Trimmer, Colin Hosten, and all of the great people at Hyperion who helped launch *Generation Dead*, and all of the booksellers, librarians, and teachers that we met on our travels. Also Alessandra Balzer, and always, Kim, Kayleigh, and Cormac.

And special thanks go out to all of the book-loving zombies who visit Tommy at his blog *mysocalledundeath.com*.

First published in Great Britain in 2009 by Simon and Schuster UK Ltd
1st Floor, 222 Gray's Inn Road, London, WC1X 8HB
A CBS COMPANY

Originally published in 2009 by Hyperion Books for Children
An imprint of Disney Book Group, New York

Text copyright © by Daniel Waters 2009

The right of Daniel Waters to be identified as the author of this work
has been asserted by him in accordance with sections 77 and
78 of the Copyright, Designs and Patents Act, 1988

3 5 7 9 10 8 6 4 2

A CIP catalogue record for this book
is available from the British Library

ISBN: 978-1-84738-397-6

This book is a work of fiction. Names, characters, places and incidents are either the product of the author's imagination or are used fictitiously. Any resemblance to actual people living or dead, events or locales is entirely coincidental.

Printed by CPI Cox & Wyman, Reading, Berkshire RG1 8EX

For Kim, the story continues

CHAPTER ONE

P HOEBE.
Beautiful Phoebe.
Through the glass watch Phoebe
leave bus walk to house Phoebe green skirt green eyes skirt trailing hair
flowing black and shiny in the sun. Brown leather boots beige scarf wearing colors no black Phoebe beautiful Phoebe. Halloween Phoebe in costume
no costume.

"Hey, Frankenstein. Get away from the window before the villagers
go and get their torches."

Jimmy. Turn. Turn. Want to hit evil stepbrother Jimmy pound Jimmy
turn can't turn. Turn left move right. Left left left.

"Don't strain yourself. It's your special day, Frankenstein! Happy
Halloween!"

Turn can't turn Jimmy shoves fall falling heavy land hard head crack
coffee table loud heavy body crash loud don't feel don't feel anything Jimmy
grinning kicks ribs can't feel get up can't get up Jimmy laughs. Mom yells at
Jimmy Jimmy yells back want to pound Jimmy. Hard. Get up. Can't get up.

1

"I said don't strain yourself."

Standing over FrankenAdam laughing ceiling is the sky get up can't two bulbs in ceiling skylight one burned out out get up Jimmy Jimmy sprays spits when he laughs get up can't.

Jimmy laughing. Mom cries get up can't holds arm pulls can't get up Mom crying can't feel. Feel feelings Phoebe. Get up get up can't get up.

Get up.

Get.

Up.

CHAPTER TWO

ALL PHOEBE COULD think about before going next door to Adam's house was the night he died in her arms. The rose of blood blooming on the white shirt he'd worn to homecoming, his strangled cry as he came back from wherever it was the dead went.

He'd only been dead for a few minutes, but despite the rapid return, control over his body wasn't coming back quickly. Phoebe debated changing out of her school clothes before leaving, but didn't want to waste the time. Since Adam's death she'd become acutely aware of its value.

Other zombies, or "differently biotic persons," to use the politically correct vernacular, seemed able to overcome their physical issues as "life" went on. Tommy, who she had dated, and gorgeous Karen DeSonne walked and talked so well that they could practically pass for traditionally biotic. Even Colette Beauvior had "come back" at a much greater rate than Adam, partly due to her reconciliation with their good friend Margi Vachon. Somehow Margi had even convinced her parents to let Colette move in with them, and now the two were as inseparable as Phoebe and Adam.

Adam, however, didn't seem to be getting any benefit from Phoebe's constant presence, which left her wondering what she was doing wrong.

Phoebe dumped a half inch of sugar into a glass, took the rest of the morning's coffee from the refrigerator, and poured it over the sugar. She stirred it with a spoon, then drank half in one swallow, hoping it would make the world look a little brighter.

It had been nearly a month since Adam's murder. His movements were still random, his speech only occasionally intelligible. Adam, her tower of strength, had been laid low, reduced to the helplessness of an infant. His long, once-athletic body was now awkward and shambling, and his thick limbs jerked as if they were being pulled by unseen strings. His broad shoulders slumped when he walked, which he was able to do only with great concentration.

Phoebe took another sip and closed her eyes, rolling the cool vanilla-flavored coffee on her tongue. When they'd lifted Adam onto the stretcher, he'd looked at her, his arm flailing out helplessly as though he was trying to grasp something that would be forever out of reach.

Phoebe dumped out the rest of her coffee. She scrawled a quick note to her parents and got her backpack, which she'd stocked with a few bags of Halloween candy in case any kids came to Adam's house.

Adam's stepbrother Jimmy was leaving his house as she locked her door. He gave Phoebe a dirty look and muttered under his breath when she waved. She didn't know what it was about Jimmy; he'd been unpleasant enough when Adam was alive, but now that Adam was dead, he was *impossible*.

"Welcome to the morgue," he said, slamming his car door and backing out so quickly his wheels kicked gravel.

Phoebe let herself in. The kitchen smelled of this morning's fried eggs and burned coffee. Dirty plates and pans were stacked up on the counter by the sink, and there were thick yellow smears on the vinyl cloth that covered the kitchen table.

"Don't mind Jimmy, Phoebe," a voice called out from the hall. Adam's mother walked into the kitchen, her once pretty face drawn, her cheeks sunken, and her eyes ringed with gray. "We all deal with life differently."

Phoebe nodded. The phrase was a mantra with the ex–Mrs. Layman, now Mrs. Garrity, and there didn't seem to be an appropriate response to it.

Phoebe watched her walk to the sink, where she moved one of the pans from the stove to the counter. Then she walked to the table with a sponge, went back to the sink and wet the sponge under the faucet. She made a single pass at one of the clotted stains, then dropped the sponge and made a half-hearted attempt to straighten a pile of newspapers that sat on the table.

"Phoebe," she said, "I've got to do some shopping. Some grocery shopping. Would you mind staying with Adam for a few minutes? A couple hours?"

Phoebe tried to keep her smile even as she looked at Mrs. Garrity, whose hands were shaking like leaves. "I'd be happy to, Mrs. Garrity."

"Good. That's great. Adam's in his room. Great."

"Are you okay, Mrs. Garrity?"

"I'm fine," she replied. "Adam had another fall, that's all. I'm okay now. He's fine. I guess it doesn't really hurt him. Falling, I mean."

It took her twenty minutes to find her purse, time Phoebe spent washing the stack of dishes and bundling the papers so they would fit in the recycling bin. She wanted to run down the hall to see Adam, but she wanted Mrs. Garrity to leave first. She was scrubbing the crusted layer of sediment from the table when Mrs. Garrity bustled back into the room.

"Damn that Jimmy," she said, oblivious to Phoebe's efforts. "He took my cigarettes." She walked out the door without saying good-bye to either Phoebe or her son.

When Phoebe was finished and the dishes were left drying in the rack, she walked down the hall to Adam's room. He was sitting on his bed, his back straight against the wall behind him and his long legs stretched out on top of the covers. His large hands rested on his thighs, and although he was staring at her, it didn't seem like he was seeing anything.

"Hi, Adam," she said, aiming for a high level of perkiness, knowing that even on her best days she fell far short of bubbly—and this was not one of her best days. Seeing him there—his face and his big graceful body frozen into immobility—was heartbreaking.

He would have been a professional football player, she was sure of it. Just one summer of karate lessons had given him a fluidity that, combined with his incredible size and strength, made him a force of nature on the field. He'd been the proverbial hometown hero, universally expected to get a free ride to the college of his choice on a football scholarship. All gone. Spent, along with his life.

Because of her.

She sucked in her cheeks and ordered herself not to cry. She'd vowed, along with her promise to bring him back, never to let him see her cry.

"You're looking big, as usual," she said once she had regained control of her emotions. She walked to the bed and bent to give him a kiss on the cheek, letting her lips linger on his cool skin for a few heartbeats.

"I brought bags of candy," she said, "in case we get any rug rats tonight. Hershey's minis, Reese's cups, the good stuff. You know it's Halloween, right? I know we don't get many trick-or-treaters out here; most of the little ones hit either the Heights or Oakvale Manor. But maybe we'll see a few."

He was centered on the bed and there was no room to sit beside him, so Phoebe climbed over his legs and sat across from him, her bent knees tenting over his calves. His head tilted toward her with slow purpose, like a door improperly set in its frame.

She gave him what she thought was her winningest smile.

"Remember that year you and I went out with Margi and Colette? We were all Catwoman and you were Batman? What were we, like, ten? Eleven?"

7

She searched for any sign of remembrance, any flicker of recognition in his eyes, but they were flat and glassy.

"I'll say eleven. We got my dad to bring us to the Heights *and* the Manor that year. What a haul that was! I think Margi and Colette ate about a hundred SweeTarts just going from house to house. I didn't have a single piece of candy until the next day. My parents wouldn't let me have any until they'd gone through it all; they were fanatics about doing an inspection. Like they could detect by sight the myriad of deadly poisons, razor blades, and broken glass hidden in my Charleston Chews."

She thought she saw a faint twitch of his upper lip, but she wasn't sure. The light in Adam's room was terrible and her eyes stung. She slapped his leg, almost knocking one of his hands into his lap.

"You like how I used 'myriad' in a sentence, huh?" It was a game they used to play, dropping little-used words into their conversations to try to get a laugh out of the other. A twitching lip wasn't exactly evidence of high hilarity, but Phoebe chose to take it as a positive sign.

"Then there was the year Margi threw her haunted house party," she said, her voice trailing off as she thought of the other Haunted House, the one where Adam died.

They had been having a party, Phoebe and her friends—the zombies who "lived" there. Karen had hung streamers and a disco ball. The zombies had been dancing and laughing and having fun, able to forget, at least for a little while, that they were dead.

Tommy asked Phoebe if she wanted to take a walk, and

she'd gone outside feeling happy, not only because her friends were enjoying themselves, but because she was with Tommy. Once they were alone in the woods he'd told her that the more loved a zombie was, the more alive they became. He'd been about to test his theory by kissing her, but his chance was ruined when Pete Martinsburg and his henchman, TC Stavis, came crashing through the brush. It turns out they hadn't been alone after all.

Adam looked up at her as though he could sense what she was thinking. His mouth opened and he struggled to speak, a guttural vibration humming up from his throat.

He usually *could* tell what she was thinking, like they really did have the "telepathetic" bond that she had always joked about. Maybe that was why he'd suddenly appeared that night in the woods, as Pete had taken slow and careful aim at the center of her forehead. Pete had sworn to destroy Tommy, but when he'd raised his rifle, it was her that he'd aimed at. When he'd pulled the trigger, Adam was there. Being there for her had cost him his life.

"Ev . . . ry," Adam said, his low, croaking, and dead voice filling his bedroom and calling her back to the present. Phoebe could count the number of words he had managed to say in the two weeks since his return—literally count them—because each night she'd gone home and inscribed them in her journal.

She watched him try to open and close his mouth for the next two minutes before completing his thought for him.

"That's right, Adam," she said, her voice soft. "Every day is like Halloween now."

She took his hand in both of hers and helped him off the bed and onto his feet.

Tommy never got his kiss. Had she been about to kiss him? Among the many things that were unclear in Phoebe's mind, that was chief among them. She'd been attracted to him, but she'd also been worried that he was using her, that it wasn't her, Phoebe, that he'd wanted to kiss, but a living girl. Any living girl.

Even so—what could a little kiss have hurt?

She'd never know, not with Tommy, at least. She'd avoided him since that terrible night, when he'd just stood there like a graveyard statue while Pete Martinsburg leveled his gun at her head. Maybe she would find out with Adam. Holding him as his life drained away, she'd realized what she'd always known in her heart. That Adam Layman loved her, loved her so deeply and selflessly that he was willing to give his life for her, even when, to all outside appearances, she'd chosen another over him.

And she'd realized that she'd loved Adam all along, but she hadn't been *in love* with him. She'd always thought of him as a big brother, someone who was solid and dependable, someone in whom she could confide her deepest thoughts and secrets. Margi was always telling her that it was obvious to everyone in the world *except* her that one day she and Adam would be together. She herself couldn't understand how she'd been able to overlook their connection for so long.

And now?

Adam loved her. He did. And she'd promised herself that

she'd do everything she could to bring him back.

She led him to a seat in the kitchen and started getting things ready for dinner. Phoebe didn't know what she could do to hasten Adam's "return," but she did what she could to keep the Garrity household running as smoothly as possible as each member dealt with their grief.

She cooked spaghetti for Adam's stepdad, Joe, and Adam's other stepbrother, Johnny, when they came home from the garage reeking of cigarettes, sweat, and crankcase oil. Unlike Jimmy, the remaining Garritys were kinder to Adam in death than they had been in life.

Mr. Garrity, Adam's stepdad, who he used to call the STD for short, surprised everyone by the way he'd responded to Adam's death and return. Prior to Adam's death, Joe had treated him with all the affection one reserved for the proverbial red-headed stepchild, seeing him as an inconvenient interloper in a house already cramped with two other teenage male bodies. It was as if Joe did not want to spare the extra percentage of his wife's love. The STD exhibited a complete change of heart after Adam's death, which seemed to galvanize him into a frenzy of parental activity and responsibility. He drank less. He insulted less. He threw reporters off his front lawn, then pursued them in one of the many rusted hulks clustered in and around his driveway, literally chasing them out of the neighborhood.

He began to refer to Adam as "my son" instead of "my wife's moron kid." Adam did not appear to mind Joe's new name for him, but Phoebe wasn't sure if it was because it was something he'd longed for, or because it was too much effort to correct him. Confusing as his epiphany was, Joe's new 'tude was refreshing in an age where many biological parents refused to let their undead youths return home.

"Where's Mary?" Joe asked, a line of sauce trickling from the corner of his mouth like stage blood. He'd gotten so used to Phoebe's presence that the whereabouts of his wife were no longer the first thing on his mind when he got home.

"Grocery shopping." Phoebe refilled Johnny's soda on her way to get herself some spaghetti.

Joe's tanned and weathered face crinkled around the eyes, his fork halfway to his lips, and Phoebe was aware of his scrutiny.

"You're a good girl, Phoebe," he said. "I can't tell you how much we all appreciate what you're doing for my son. He does too."

There it was again. Joe called him "son." Phoebe turned back to the stove and dug her lime green fingernails into her palm until the pain allowed her to push her emotions back down. She couldn't believe this was the same man who used to belittle Adam and push him around.

After dinner, Johnny and Joe lumbered off to watch TV. Phoebe helped Adam down the hall to the kitchen, sitting him where he could see the costumes of any trick-or-treaters. Little kids in costumes could cheer just about anyone up, and if Phoebe's attention couldn't bring Adam further into the world of the living, then maybe candy-snatching children could.

A handful came: a Disney princess, a pirate, a lion in a stroller who giggled without cease when Phoebe dropped a Krackle inside the grinning orange sphere on her lap.

Adam was far enough away that he was hard to see in the dim light of the kitchen, but there was a pint-size vampire who spotted him when Phoebe turned back from the door to get her bag of candy.

"That a dead guy?" he said through the screen door, nearly tripping on his cape as he pointed at Adam with chocolatey fingers.

Phoebe considered her response, wondering where the little boy's parents were. She didn't think that anyone let their kids out without a phalanx of parental guardians swarming around them.

"That's Adam," she explained, opening the door and dropping a couple of Special Darks into his pillowcase.

"Hey, Adam," the kid yelled. The little vampire turned back to her. "He's dead. Like me!"

Then he leaped down the steps, cape flapping behind him.

She looked back at Adam and again she saw the lip twitch, which lightened her heart. The doorbell announced a new group of trick-or-treaters.

Phoebe opened the door, and was startled to see three teenage boys in horrific zombie costumes. Except they weren't wearing costumes.

"Trick . . . or . . . treat," the closest said, a strange mirthless grin on one side of his face.

"Takayuki," she said, taken aback but still reaching automatically for the bag of candy. Takayuki had always gone out of his way to make her feel uncomfortable, and she hadn't seen him since Adam's death. "How have you been?" Her voice broke, betraying her nervousness.

"Dead." The comment put a mirthful, malevolent glint in the dull eyes of his companions. One of them was Tayshawn, who had dropped out of their Undead Studies class, but Phoebe didn't recognize the other two. Zombies were always showing up at the Haunted House, attracted mostly by the writing on Tommy's blog, mysocalledundeath.com. Phoebe hadn't been back to the house since Adam died.

The boy next to Takayuki was wearing a long silver earring and sunglasses with dark lenses. His shaved head gleamed like a second moon in the porch light. When he smiled, he revealed teeth that had been sharpened into rough points. He was wearing a leather jacket similar to Tak's, but the cuffs were stained and spattered with red, as were the tips of the fingers on his bone white hand. There was a very tall fourth boy lurking behind them, his face cast in shadow.

Phoebe reached into the bag and withdrew a few pieces of candy. Tak was the person who had "avenged" Adam, but his presence generated no warmth in her. Whatever it was that drove him to hunt Pete down, his motives were unlikely to have had anything to do with her, Adam, or any of the other "beating hearts" that Takayuki disdained.

"Where are your Halloween bags?" she asked, holding the candy in front of her, feeling foolish. The dead had no use for chocolate. They had no use for her either.

Tak looked over his shoulder. "George," he said, "come trick . . . or-treat from the nice . . . soft . . . beating heart."

Tak and the other boys moved aside so George could ascend the steps. The boy wore a tattered brown jacket, jeans with shredded cuffs, and a soiled T-shirt with holes big enough for Phoebe to see where patches of flesh were missing from his rib cage. He looked at her as he limped up the stairs with a big plastic trick-or-treat bag that had a garish jack-o'-lantern blazing beneath a green and warty witch. The boy was not a pretty sight. He was missing an ear and half his nose, and his hair looked as if it had been washed with sewage. He *smelled* as if *he'd* been washed with sewage.

But the scariest part of him was his eyes. They were like no other zombie eyes she'd ever seen. No matter how flat or glassy the eyes of the differently biotic were, there was always at least a glimmer of intelligence within. Not so with George. There was nothing in his eyes. Nothing at all.

Holding her breath, she forced herself to hold his non-stare. Some of my best friends are dead, she told herself. This boy may be more dead in appearance, but he's no less a person than they are.

He looked at her, or looked through her, she couldn't tell, and opened his bag. She dropped in a piece of candy, but the noise that it made when it landed was not the familiar paper on paper sound wrapped candy made. She glimpsed inside the bag and saw a round wet lump of red and gray fur, and a curling tail.

She shrieked, jumping back.

The dead pretended to laugh. "Can Adam . . . come out . . . and play?" Takayuki asked.

Her heart was beating wildly as she looked over her

shoulder to where Adam sat with his back to the wall. He looked like he was trying, but failing, to speak.

"No," she stuttered. "We're spending the night at home, thank you."

Takayuki cracked his knuckles, making sure she could see the ones that were no longer covered with skin.

"Someday," he said, "he will . . . want . . . to be with . . . his own kind."

"He is," she said, regaining her composure. Tak was just another bully, and she was sick of bullies. "I'm his kind."

"Sure," Tak said as he and his companions began to fade into the night. "Happy . . . Halloween."

CHAPTER THREE

SPEAKING WITH the dead was always disconcerting, but speaking with Karen DeSonne was positively otherworldly. Karen's eyes were like diamonds; Phoebe swore she could see refracted rainbows in them when they were out from under the fluorescent wash of the school's lighting. Even in darkness they seemed to twinkle like far off stars.

Phoebe started eating and was about to ask Margi if she would trade her peach for a yogurt, when she saw Karen from across the crowded cafeteria, her long mane of platinum hair bouncing with each clipped step. Phoebe looked down at her food with sudden interest, even though she knew staring into her salad would not ward off the conversation to come.

"Here's . . . Karen," Colette said, after peering into Phoebe's yogurt as if she couldn't believe she'd ever eaten anything that looked like that. "She's on . . . a . . . mission."

Even with her head down, Phoebe was aware of boys from the surrounding tables craning to get a better look at Karen and her micro skirt and high boots. At one time it was considered impolite to stare at the dead, back in the days where the term of choice was "living impaired." Impaired no longer, the differently biotic could be gawked and leered at just like any other teenage girl. Phoebe wasn't sure if Karen liked the attention or thought it perverse, but if she had to guess, she'd go with liking it.

Halloween had been pretty much a nonevent at Oakvale High. In years past there might have been jokes about the differently biotic already being in costume, but no longer—maybe because Halloween seemed superfluous in an age where the dead walked the earth. But a subtle shift was taking place among the students in adapting to what some called "the second chance" and still others called "the undead plague"—an acceptance. There were still those like Pete Martinsburg who feared or hated the differently biotic kids, but most regarded them with no more interest than they would anyone else.

That was the reaction they had for most db kids, anyway. The reaction they had for Karen was special, and no different than they had for any other girl as flat out *hot* as she was. Phoebe thought of the grisly quartet that had stood on Adam's doorstep last night and couldn't believe how far ranging the differently biotic experience could be.

"Phoebe," Karen said, her voice breathy, as though it had taken her effort to cross the room at such a speed. "Hi, Margi. Colette."

"Hey, K," Margi replied, lifting her diet soda in a silent

toast. The usual clinking of her dozen-odd silver bangles was muted by her newest fashion fad, which was to twist thin wristlets out of electrical tape. Colette waved.

"Phoebe," Karen repeated, and Phoebe lifted her head. "How much longer are you going to ignore Tommy?"

"We're fine, K," Margi cut in. "Thanks for asking. And yourself? Really? No, I didn't watch the game last night. Colette and I handed out six bags of candy. We were both Hannah Montanas. I'm afraid I did not know that you were such a fan of NBA basketball. Isn't that interesting, Pheebes?"

Phoebe watched Karen swivel toward Margi, imagining her diamond eyes flashing into life like twin lasers.

"I'm not in the mood, Margi," she said. "I just had to endure about an hour of . . . interrogation about whether or not I . . . defaced the school last night."

"Did you crack?" Margi said. "Did you sing like a canary?"

"Funny. I don't even know who did . . . it."

"Yeah, you . . . do," Colette said, frowning.

"What did 'they' do?" Phoebe asked.

Karen and Colette exchanged a glance before Karen answered.

"They . . . spray painted the side of the school."

"What did they spray?"

"'Adam Laymon . . . no rest, no peace.'" Karen's crystalline gaze was steady and unflinching. "Over a drawing of a . . . tombstone . . . and an open grave."

Phoebe frowned, thinking of the boy with the stained cuffs and hands.

"Did they use red paint?"

Karen nodded. A tense silence followed until Colette broke it a few moments later.

"I guess they . . . will be . . . talking to me . . . next."

"Could be," Karen said. "They already spoke to Tommy and Kevin. Strange how they don't even . . . consider . . . that a trad may have done it."

"A trad . . . didn't do it . . . and you . . . know it," Colette said. Karen shrugged

"You know who did it?" Margi asked. None of the other girls answered her.

Karen sighed, turning back to Phoebe. The sigh sounded realistic even though Karen didn't need to breathe.

"Phoebe, don't you think you've left you and Tommy . . . unresolved?" she asked. "Don't you think he . . . deserves . . . a conversation at least?"

"Deserves," Phoebe said. She didn't feel good about avoiding him, but that didn't mean that she thought that he "deserved" anything.

"He hasn't . . . been himself . . . since you stopped talking to him."

Phoebe poked at her wilted salad. She didn't like the hitch in Karen's speech. Karen wasn't like most differently biotic people. She could usually converse without any of the pauses and stops that marked typical zombie speech patterns. Phoebe had noticed that with "highly functional" db kids like Karen and Tommy, pauses meant they were feeling emotional, or as close to emotional as the dead could be.

"I've been really busy, Karen," she replied. It sounded lame even to her. "I go over to Adam's every night, and I . . ."

"I know all about Adam, Phoebe," Karen said. "Adam isn't here, and there's no reason why you couldn't give Tommy five minutes of your time. You know, like you used to every day before algebra class back when the two of you were . . . dating?"

Phoebe blushed and set her fork down. She heard Margi tell Karen to take it easy, but she lifted up her hand before Karen could say more.

"I'm sorry, Karen," she said. "It's just really hard."

"It's hard," Karen repeated, her voice growing husky. It was amazing, what Karen could do with her voice, altering the flat monotone that marked the speech of the dead. Phoebe raised her head so she was staring into the blank lights of Karen's eyes. "You think it's hard."

"I know what you're going to say, Karen. I know."

Phoebe knew that the differently biotic had to work at expressing emotions on their faces. She knew from being with Adam since his death that he could have emotions trapped deep within his still heart that his body would no longer convey. She'd spent long hours helping him walk or exercise in the hopes of bringing back a range of motion to his stiff limbs, long hours just sitting holding his hand or leaning against his arm. The time together might make him happy, or grateful, or sad, but Phoebe didn't know. Adam couldn't show it. Yet.

Karen was better at nuance than any of them, as good as some living kids, almost. But if Karen felt any pity for Phoebe, there was no sign of it on her cold, beautiful face.

"Adam needs me right now, Karen," she said. "His mom said he fell again. . . ."

"He fell?" Margi asked. "I didn't think he could, like, walk yet. Without help."

"He can't. He tries, of course. He's stubborn."

"That isn't being stubborn. It's being smart. He isn't going to . . . come back . . . by sitting around on his can all day and night."

Phoebe wasn't sure if Karen was being practical or cruel. "He needs me, Karen. I just don't . . . I don't think I have anything left for anyone else."

Tommy never needed me the way Adam does, Phoebe thought.

Karen put her arms on the table in front of her, palms up. Phoebe couldn't help but notice how smooth and white they were, like she had been carved from a single piece of white stone.

"I know Adam needs you, honey," she said. "He always did."

Phoebe hesitated, then placed her hands on Karen's open palms, relieved that the subject of Tommy was dropped for the moment. Karen's hands felt warmer than hers, which Phoebe could never understand no matter how many times she experienced it.

"Awww," Margi said. "See, we can all play nice."

Karen smiled, looking embarrassed. "I know it's hard, sweetie. I guess I should be asking how I can help instead of bullying you."

Phoebe felt a tear roll down her cheek, but Karen was holding her hands so it made it all the way to her jawline before Margi leaned over and wiped it away with the edge of her napkin.

"I don't know," Phoebe said, crying openly now. "Adam . . . Adam isn't like you, Karen. Or like Tommy. Tommy told me that you and he came back more because . . . because you were loved, and I'm trying with Adam, but it just isn't working."

"He's more . . . like me," Colette said. "It will . . . take time."

The girls fell silent as Principal Kim walked over to their table and asked Colette to follow her. As Colette rose, Principal Kim looked at Phoebe and noticed she'd been crying.

"Phoebe?"

She turned, embarrassed.

"Um," she said, "yes, Principal Kim?"

"Are you all right, Phoebe?"

"Yes. I'm fine, thank you."

Principal Kim gave a slow nod. Phoebe prayed that she wouldn't bring up counseling again: counseling for this and that. Because your friends are dead, because your friends aren't dead. Because they are dead and then they aren't dead and how do you feel about that? How do you feel? How do they feel? How *can* they feel?

Principal Kim's silence was worse even than the mandatory counseling that they'd made Phoebe go to for the first week after Adam was killed. Margi and Karen were looking at the table, compounding the air of guilt that seemed to hang over their lunch.

"Um, is there anything else, ma'am?" Phoebe said, finally.

The principal thought a moment before answering her question. "You wouldn't know who vandalized the school last night, would you?"

"No," she said, the lie passing her lips with surprising ease.

"I know you spend a lot of time with the differently biotic students," she said, looking at Karen apologetically. "With Adam, and with other kids that don't go to our school."

"You don't know that a zombie did it."

"No, I don't," she said. "But I thought you might know if someone was . . . upset with the situation."

"Everyone should be upset." Phoebe's eyes were burning, but she refused to cry again.

"Of course," Ms. Kim's voice was soft. "Understand, I'm more interested in getting people the help they need than I am in punishment. You realize that, don't you? All of you?"

Karen said she did, and Phoebe nodded. She was afraid to use her voice.

Ms. Kim held her gaze. "Well, I'm sure you'll let me know if I can help. Let's go, Colette."

They watched her leave, Karen shaking her head. "You get a few questions, we get interrogated. That's fair."

"I'm sorry," Phoebe said, rubbing at the corners of her eyes. "Thank God, I don't have mascara on today."

"Yeah, what's up with that?" Margi said, as eager to derail the conversation as she was. "And what's with the new wardrobe too?"

Phoebe looked down at her light green blouse, shrugging. "I just thought it was time for a change."

"A change?" Margi said. "I barely even recognize you half the time now. What are those—*slacks*? Blue jeans? And all the colors . . ."

"She doesn't want to look like she's in mourning," Karen said.

Phoebe, her tears under control, pursed her lips. Sometimes it really did feel as if Karen was walking around inside her head, because she'd nailed her motivations exactly.

"Whaaaat?" For someone as fashion conscious as their pink-haired friend, Margi had a tendency to overlook the obvious.

"She doesn't want to look like she's in mourning. When she's with Adam. Out with the blacks and the grays, good-bye gauzy skirts and ruffled sleeves. Good-bye, Morticia Addams, hello, girl next door."

"I didn't think it was that obvious," Phoebe said,

Karen conveyed sympathy with a slight turn of her eyebrows. She really was amazing. Such an actress.

"Don't get me wrong, honey. Earth tones work for you. But you have such nice creamy skin, and that beautiful black hair—you're a knockout in black. White, too. And you could give red a chance."

Phoebe thought of the dress she wore for homecoming, a simple, straight sheath so white it shimmered. She ruined it on the muddy earth kneeling over Adam's body as he died. Tommy knelt with her, and he might have held her, or he might have tried to help Adam. She couldn't remember much about that night except for her dirty dress and the blood spreading across Adam's chest.

He'd said her dress was like moonlight.

She shuddered.

"I'll try, Karen. I'll try to talk to Tommy."

But later, when she saw him lingering by the doorway to their algebra class, the one that they'd once shared with Adam's killer, Pete Martinsburg, and Pete's flunky, TC Stavis, she found she couldn't try at all. He stood so straight and tall, with his shoulders broad and his face strong and angular. He looked like a sculptor's idea of a young god. Like Karen, he looked as though physical perfection could only be achieved through death.

She watched him for a moment. Watching him, with him not knowing she was watching, gave her a weird feeling in her stomach.

You should have saved me, Tommy, she thought. *You.* But you didn't.

Her breath caught as he turned suddenly and saw her, his gray-blue eyes finding hers even through the passing crowd. Her insides did a somersault, and she turned around in a hurry and marched off toward the nurse's office.

But he caught up to her. Even Adam had talked about how quick Tommy was for a dead kid.

"Phoebe . . ."

"Oh hi, Tommy," she said, not stopping. *I'm not ready for this.*

"Phoebe, can we—"

"I'm not feeling very well, Tommy. I'm headed to the nurse's office."

"You're . . . sick?" his said, his face a mask of concern. Literally a mask, as expressiveness did not come as easily to him as it did to Karen.

"I'm sick," she said. What right did he have to be concerned for her?

"I'll . . . walk . . . with you."

"So now you want to move," she said, her anger flashing, the words out before she could stop them.

"What?"

"Forget it."

"No," he said, "what . . . did you mean?"

The anger engulfed her like a hot wave pitched by a boiling ocean. She felt it wash over her and carry her out to sea.

"I said, *now* you want to move! *Now* all of a sudden you can move!"

She was shouting, and everyone in the hall stopped what they were doing to stare. She didn't care. They'd stared when they were dating, when they touched hands in the hallway. The only difference now was that they stared openly, instead of hiding behind books and locker doors. Hypocrites, every last one of them, a world full of hypocrites.

"Phoebe, what . . . ?"

"You didn't move, Tommy! He pointed the gun right at me and you didn't do anything!"

"I . . ."

"All you had . . . had to do was . . . *move*," she said. "It

wouldn't have hurt if he shot *you*. But you just stood there, and
. . . and Adam's *dead*! He's *dead*, Tommy!"

She looked at him, her eyes blurry with tears. He'd stopped
trying to talk, and the mask of concern had fallen away from his
face as he stood there.

Just stood there.

"He'd be alive if it weren't for you, Tommy," she said,
whispering so the gawkers wouldn't hear.

He'd be alive, she thought, and you and I would be together.

Tommy didn't try and stop her as she fled down the hall.

CHAPTER FOUR

"H APPY" BIRTHDAY," Gus Guttridge, the lawyer, said with all of the warmth of a day-old cup of coffee.

"Gee, thanks," Pete replied.

"Cheer up. If you were born a few months earlier you could be tried as an adult instead of a juvenile, and then the circus would really come to town. We're in good shape."

Guttridge sat down at the head of the table facing Pete, his mother and her husband, the Wimp, and the social worker. They were in a conference room at the Winford Juvenile Detention Center where Pete had been living for the past two weeks. There were two wrinkled posters in the room, one that said drugs were Uncool and one that said gang violence was Uncool. Pete didn't mind the detention center. The food was better than what he got at home, and they delivered it right to his room because he wasn't allowed to mix with the other kids being held there. Other kids would probably think that was Uncool, too, but Pete thought it was pretty Cool.

"The downside is I don't think you returning to school is an option at this point," Guttridge said. "The best we can hope for is that you'll be sent home, remanded to your mother's custody, and homeschooled by a state-appointed instructor."

Pete thought the downside was looking up. He ran the tips of his fingers along the scar on the left side of his face, the tips of his index and middle fingers tracing the ragged stitch marks where the zombie had cut him. The wound was still capable of flaring into a sudden pain or a steady dull throb, but Pete didn't mind either sensation. The time when his cheek was numb and he was drooling all over the place was worse.

"Typically, murder by a juvenile offender means you get tried as an adult," Guttridge said. "The fact that Mr. Layman is still able to walk into the courtroom himself means that the court is already thinking that this isn't really a murder. We can work with that."

The Wimp, motivated no doubt by a desire to posture for his wife rather than by any real feeling for Pete, asked a question, but Pete wasn't listening to him. He was listening to the voice of the scarred zombie in his head.

"Did you think I would kill you?" the zombie had whispered, its fetid breath like the air from an open grave. "Death is a gift."

In some ways Pete was glad that the zombie had maimed him, because his scar was visible proof that worm burgers were evil monsters that delighted in the pain and disfigurement of the living.

"Well, Mr. Clary," Guttridge was saying, "the idea is that Pete should not be tried for manslaughter, because Layman doesn't meet the legal definition of 'dead.' He's differently biotic, but if he is still 'biotic,' he's alive and therefore Pete did not commit manslaughter. Assault, maybe. But I think even that's a stretch at this point."

One of the stitches was protruding from Pete's cheek like a small thorn or the sting of a hornet. He worked the stitch back and forth, ignoring the sharp bright pain that accompanied the movements. He realized that the lawyer, Guttridge, was saying his name.

"Mr. Martinsburg? Pete?"

Pete looked up. His mother and the Wimp were sitting with looks of false concern as Gus Guttridge tried to get his attention. Pete leaned forward in his chair.

"Sorry," he said, "what were we talking about?"

"We were discussing what should and should not be said on the stand."

"Right," Pete said. "Right. Just be honest, is what you said."

"Correct." Guttridge said. Pete didn't trust guys with beards, and Guttridge had a hell of a beard, a big wooly thing as thick as the curly hair on his head. But Guttridge was his father's choice, and his father went with the best that money could buy, so Pete went with the flow.

"So, again," Guttridge said, "you understand that when Ms. Lainey asks you a question, it is in your best interest to give her short, succinct answers."

"Succinct, right." Pete felt his fingertips drawn back to the loose stitch like a magnet. They'd come out in a week if everything went as planned, and good old Dad Martinsburg was going to pick up the tab for whatever cosmetic surgery Pete required to get rid of the scars. Pete wasn't so sure he wanted to be prettied up just yet.

"Yes," Guttridge continued, his baggy blue eyes regarding Pete. "So when Counselor Lainey asks you why you went to the property on Chesterton Road, how will you respond?"

"I heard there was a party there."

"Were you invited to this party?"

"No," Pete said.

"Were you under the influence of drugs or alcohol?"

"I had a few sips of schnapps. Peppermint."

"Were you drunk?"

"No."

"So you went to crash the party?"

Pete sighed, his fingertips drifting once again to the cut on his cheek.

"I heard that the zombies were having a party and that some real people were going to be there too, and I didn't like what I heard the zombies were going to do."

Pete watched Guttridge pooch out his lower lip as he peered down at him through his glasses. The glasses were light frames of gold wire, the kind a lot of overweight guys with big faces wore.

"Don't call them zombies," Guttridge said. "Say 'differently biotic.'"

"They call themselves zombies," Pete said, just to see if he could get a rise out of Wooly Face. No luck.

"Doesn't mean you can. Don't say 'real people,' either. If you could remember to say traditionally biotic it would be helpful also. Understand that you may hear *me* use other terms, but that doesn't mean *you* should. You need to project Wholesome and Respectful. Let me do Outraged, if I need to."

"Why should you have all the fun?" Pete tapped the edge of a fingernail on the heavy tabletop.

Guttridge gave him a thin smile. "Because you already had yours. Now, back to business. Did you go to the party alone?"

"No."

"Who were you with?"

"TC Stavis."

"I see. What did you and Mr. Stavis do, once you arrived at the party?"

"We parked the car at a turnoff a half mile down the road, and then we walked through the woods until we got to the house, and then we waited."

"Don't volunteer the info about the car unless asked a direct question," Guttridge said. "Why were you waiting outside?"

"We weren't invited."

Guttridge frowned. "Very funny. Please answer the question."

"We were waiting to see if Phoebe was at the party."

"About Miss Kendall," Guttridge said, shuffling a file to the top of his deck.

"Morticia Scarypants," Pete said, smiling.

But Guttridge's well of patience seemed bottomless, probably because good old Darren paid him by the hour. "Please forget you ever invented that name," he said, "unless you want to be tagged something similar when you get sent to prison."

Pete laughed, and he could feel the skin around his stitches grow taut with the movement. "What happened, Your Honor, is that I saw Julie with the differently biotic boy, and I remembered what he told . . ."

Guttridge lifted his fleshy hand, cutting Pete's thought short. The ring on Guttridge's finger was the size of a cherry tomato, with a large onyx set in the center.

"Another thing," Guttridge said. "You need to stop calling her Julie. There is no Julie I see associated in any way with your case, and the last thing you want is anyone in the courtroom to be confused. Don't confuse them. Call her by her first name. Phoebe."

"Phoebe," Pete repeated. He wasn't smiling any longer, but he wondered if the scar and its stitching made him look as though he was. Julie had been his girl back in California, but she died. She died, and she did not come back. Life wasn't fair sometimes. "Yeah, Phoebe."

They sat there, a patient and concerned audience, and he told his version of what happened on that night.

CHAPTER FIVE

"WE'RE READY, right, Adam?" Joe said. "I mean, you don't want to wait, do you?"

Nod. Nod open mouth no Joe don't ask two questions wait until first answered patience all need patience not ready but ready as can be can't wait around right leg can't stay in room any longer go more insane than already am left leg freaking leg Frankenstein must go to foundation could help mouth open speak speak speak.

"Red . . ."

Speak right leg Joe open the door don't just stand there waiting waiting to speak not used to you paying attention easier when you ignored go see Tommy go see Karen learn learn how they do what they do did what they did left leg goal walk normal one week no three speak speak speak.

"Dee."

Joe opened the car door, frowning. "You sure?"

Speak speak no stop speak nod nod right arm hold door left leg step left knee bend bend push left arm right leg damn body push damn teenage Frankenstein.

"You need some help?" Joe asked.

Help Phoebe help see Phoebe at Undead Studies see Angela Alish move body move left leg see Kevin Sylvia not Sylvia see Thornton see Margi Colette help learn bring back help push Joe yes FrankenAdam am too big heavy push shoulder yes push.

Ignition gear miss driving goal two months no two years driving accelerate stop turn miss friends miss football miss baconandeggs miss karate Master Griffin miss Frisbee God miss Frisbee goal one month no three months.

"Are you nervous?"

Nervous not nervous stop miss Frisbee spinning arc disc flying across surface of the moon topspin backspin overhand underhand Astroturf miss running Phoebe running hold out hand the hand obeys hold out your hand catch spinning floating thing don't let it get away pull it close into the body.

"Phoebe said she'd meet us at the front," Joe said. "I told that girl there, Angel? Angie? I told her I wouldn't be coming in. That okay with you?"

Nod. Nod speak stop speak miss Phoebe miss Phoebe sad Phoebe waste time with teenage Frankenstein myriad of problems heh Phoebe sad said change needs to live not live with teenage Frankenstein miss Phoebe help Hunters help.

"That girl has been such a help to us," Joe said. "Not a bad little cook either."

Miss Phoebe said unsaid pity unsaid too late waited too long to live Karen right too late Phoebe become who you always were not what you are now spinning disc Phoebe why why didn't anyone take the bullet out of my heart?

CHAPTER SIX

"WELCOME BACK, Adam," Angela said as Phoebe led him into the classroom by the hand. Phoebe realized that despite its radiance, Angela's megawatt smile could not bring the dead back to life.

And I had such high hopes, she thought. The Hunters, Angela and her father, Alish, were watching Adam with undisguised interest. Phoebe couldn't help but think that they were wondering how they could use Adam's murder and return from death to advance the stated aims of the Hunter Foundation, which were to "integrate the differently biotic into American society and culture through the application of the sciences." Phoebe knew that Angela had real concern for Adam, but she still found their scrutiny creepy.

She led Adam to the wide vinyl chair he usually occupied in Undead Studies class. She supported him as he bent at the knees, falling back into the chair with a heaviness that drove all the air out of the cushioning. Phoebe didn't let go of his elbow until he craned his neck upward to look at her.

She was aware that everyone in the room was focused on them.

"Thank . . ." he said, and she could feel him concentrating on the word, concentrating on making his lungs move and his mouth open, his tongue like a piece of cold rubber as he tried to form the word. She could feel his awareness of the seconds ticking by into minutes as he tried to complete his sentence. The trad kids in the class were used to being patient with the db kids' mode of speech—Adam himself had been infinitely patient— but she knew that his patience would not extend to himself.

He's so helpless, she thought, and hated herself for thinking it. She couldn't understand why Adam wasn't coming back faster. Even terminally slow Kevin Zumbrowski, who sat next to Colette on the futon, was more "returned" than Adam. Colette was changing, her limbs were more pliable, her skin less ashen. Her hair was closer to the dark brown it had been when she died. Phoebe knew that Margi was spending a lot of her time with Colette. The time together seemed to be doing both girls good. Phoebe was happy for them, and she did her best to tell herself that she wasn't a little jealous too.

In contrast to the slowly returning, there were Tommy and Karen, whose stillness now seemed more like a mark of maturity than a sign of death.

". . . you," Adam said, finally completing his response.

Phoebe sighed with relief. She saw that Angela's smile, at least, was free from the pity she'd seen on so many other faces.

Adam could take the disgust and hatred, but she knew that the thought of someone pitying him filled him with fury he was not capable of releasing.

Angela nodded. "You're welcome."

Phoebe looked up at the sound of a shuffling noise coming from the hall outside, and wondered if a new student was joining them—the ranks were certainly depleted from the last time that Adam had been in class; even with Margi back the class was still down a few people. It was like an episode of some bizarre prizeless reality show; Tayshawn Wade dropped out, Sylvia hadn't come back yet, and Evan Talbot would never be returning again, thanks to Pete Martinsburg and his cronies. They'd reterminated him and got away with it.

Alish Hunter, his lab coat hanging loosely over his spidery, skeletal frame, entered the lounge. The old man's rubber-soled loafers slid along the thin beige carpeting in short, arthritic movements. Phoebe watched his feet and wondered at the static charge the old man must be building; in her mind's eye she could picture him throwing his hands to the sky and shouting "Life!" as he shot Adam with a bolt of pent-up static electricity from the metal head of his cane.

"My boy," Alish said, his bushy gray eyebrows knitting as he stared down at Adam. "I'm glad to see you haven't left us. We can learn a lot from you, Mr. Layman."

Adam didn't even try to respond to that.

"Welcome," Alish said, beaming as though he were reuniting lost relatives over an expansive meal. He led two new students, zombies, into the room. They sat next to Thornton

Harrowwood on the long orange futon. Thorny, who still played on the football team even though Tommy had quit and Adam was no longer able to play, looked especially glad to see Adam back in class. Thorny was the smallest kid on the team, but Phoebe'd heard he was getting a lot of playing time, not only because of the Undead Studies kids dropping out, but because Pete Martinsburg and TC Stavis were kicked off. She was surprised, actually, that Thorny hadn't been injured yet.

"Welcome, students," Alish was saying. "Please help yourself to refreshments. We have coffee and soft drinks."

Phoebe watched the two new zombies. The boy looked typical enough as far as zombies went, a pale, thin kid with gray-black hair, wearing a flannel shirt, jeans, and scuffed work boots. The girl next to him was different, starting with the mass of hair that billowed around her head like a bright red cloud. It reminded Phoebe of Evan, the only other zombie she'd known with red hair. His had been a faded red, but the new girl's was rich and coppery. But that wasn't even the most striking thing about her.

She was wearing a mask. A bone white mask that covered her entire face; it was similar to one of the comedy and tragedy masks that Mrs. Dubois, the drama teacher, had hanging in her office, except this one had no expression at all, the thin lips a carved straight line.

"I'd like to introduce to you Melissa Riley," Alish said. Melissa was wearing a long brown skirt that went past her knees, and a heather green sweater that bunched at her wrists. She sat with her hands folded in her lap and her head bowed, her eyes hidden behind the almond-shaped eyeholes of the mask. Phoebe could see pale beige dots, the ghosts of freckles, on the backs of her hands. Next to her on the couch was a whiteboard the size of a large notebook, and a black marker.

There was a bright chorus of welcomes from the students, but Melissa did not lift her head or respond in any way. Alish waited a moment before continuing, his smile unwavering despite Melissa's apparent shyness.

"And this young man to the far left is Cooper Wilson," Alish said, and as Alish gave a fluttery wave toward the boy, Phoebe noticed that the old man had pale brown spots on his hands as well, but his were liver spots.

"Hey . . . everybody," Cooper said, "call . . . me . . . Coop."

"Hey, Coop," replied most of the class, nearly in unison.

"Yes," Alish said. "You may recall that our Mr. Williams read an article about a tragic fire at a place called Dickinson House, in Massachusetts. Melissa and Cooper were made homeless by that fire. We are thrilled that concerned parties helped them find residence here."

He hesitated. The article that Tommy read indicated that the fire was more of a massacre than an accident, with seven zombies being reterminated in the flames and just the two on the couch surviving. Phoebe looked over at the girl and wondered what the mask hid.

"Well," Alish said finally, "please do what you can to make our newest students feel welcome."

"You are probably all wondering how our fair Ms. Stelman is doing," Alish continued. Phoebe and the other "veterans" of the Undead Studies class snapped to attention. Sylvia Stelman was a zombie classmate who had been taken for a special "augmentation" procedure. All they knew about the "augmentation" was that it would supposedly restore Sylvia to a near-living state. They had no idea how it was performed or what exactly it entailed, and the Hunters refused to elaborate. Sylvia had been gone a number of weeks, and naturally everyone in the class was worried about her.

"I am happy to report that the first phase of her augmentation is complete and that she's doing quite well. If she continues to progress at this rate, we should soon have her back in class."

"That's great," Margi said. Kevin's head lolled forward and back, probably in eager anticipation of being the next in line for an augmentation. "Can we see her?"

"Not yet." Alish's smile remained fixed on his face.

"Well, that's our news," Angela said. "I have a new project, which we're going to have you all work on, but first are there any topics you would like to discuss?"

"There were more killings," Tommy said. "Of zombies. In Texas . . . a mob of . . . people . . . tied two of us to the . . . tailgate . . . of a pickup truck. The killings were . . . soon after . . . a talk given by . . . Reverend Nathan Mathers. They . . ."

Phoebe couldn't look at him as he told the rest of his grisly story. She knew that part of what she was feeling was akin to "survivor guilt," something she'd overheard Angela talking to Margi about: a feeling that one was somehow complicit in acts of violence that one had nothing to do with. Phoebe listened to Tommy talk about how the mob tracked down the zombies and tortured them, and she couldn't help feeling as if she'd helped tie the knots.

She'd certainly tied them around Tommy. Her guilt went beyond survivor guilt, however. There was a hopeless quality to Tommy's reporting today, and she knew it was because of the way she'd treated him.

When he was finished, there was a moment of stunned silence, and then Colette spoke.

"Tommy," she said, "why don't you . . . ever . . . talk about . . . the good news? Your site would be . . . so much . . . better if you had some . . . good news."

Phoebe looked for his reaction, but all he did was blink.

"What . . . good news?" he finally said.

"You never . . . talk about . . . the good . . . things. Like Z," she said. "You . . . wear Z."

Phoebe smiled because Tommy bought a bottle of Z, "the body spray for the active undead male," when they were on their first date. She smiled, despite the conflicting feelings the memory brought up. Tommy started to reply but Colette interrupted him.

"And . . . Aftermath," she said, "you haven't . . . ever mentioned . . . Aftermath either."

Tommy managed a sardonic grin.

"You want me to talk about . . . cologne . . . and dancing . . . when . . . our . . . people are being killed?"

"What is Aftermath?" Alish asked, looking even more confused than usual.

"It's a club," Margi answered.

"A club?" Alish leaned over and put a skeletal finger to his dry lips.

"A zombie club, in New York City," Margi said. "Music, dancing. It's open twenty-four hours a day."

"In New York City?" Karen said. "I've never heard of a club like that."

"Margi found an . . . article . . . in a music magazine," Colette said. "It was started . . . by Skip Slydell."

Skip Slydell was the entrepreneurial founder of Slydellco, the company responsible for launching zombie hygiene products like Z body spray (for the active undead male) and a line of T-shirts with slogans like "Some of my best friends are dead" and "Open graves, open minds." Phoebe had heard Margi refer to the clothing line, which Colette often sported, as "inactive wear."

"I'm kind of surprised you don't know about it," Margi said, probably because there was some sort of relationship between Skip and the Hunter Foundation, as he had been a guest speaker in their class. "He opened it as a not-for-profit, so it's classified as a charity or something."

"Really?" Alish said, intrigued, looking back at Angela, who shrugged. "He made no mention of this. It isn't easy to get the government to recognize the differently biotic as being a group deserving—or even in need of—charity. And what do the differently biotic do there?"

"Dance," Colette and Margi responded in unison.

"Dance?"

"Well, and listen to music," Margi said. "Sometimes Skip gets live bands to play."

"Live bands," Colette said, and Phoebe watched the corners of her mouth twitch upward. Margi busted out giggling, her snorty laughter made musical by her jangling bracelets and dancing spikes of pink hair.

"Amazing," Alish said.

"Skeleton . . . Crew . . . plays there," Colette said. "They have . . . a zombie . . . in the band."

"DeCayce," Margi added, in a teasing voice that made Phoebe think that Colette was a big fan of Skeleton Crew.

"Amazing," Alish repeated.

Angela cleared her throat. "Does anyone else have anything pertinent to discuss before we start today's assignment?"

"I've got something I want to talk about." Thornton 'Thorny' Harrowwood III said. "Something that really made me mad."

"Mr. Harrowwood," Alish said, making a sweeping gesture with his liver-spotted, knob-knuckled hand. Phoebe thought it was kind of cute the way he was enjoying the class so much. It made her wish that he attended more often, but he was probably too busy with all the important lab and scientific work the foundation was doing. "You have the floor."

"I got a detention yesterday for saying the word 'zombie.'"

Everyone in the room, even Tommy, who Phoebe hadn't seen crack a smile since homecoming, seemed to think that was pretty funny. Alish laughed out loud, unmindful of his daughter's warning glance.

"It isn't funny," Thorny said, but a moment later he was laughing too. "Honestly, it made me pretty mad. You guys call each other zombies. We use the word here in class all the time and nobody gets offended."

"Colette said that she didn't like the term," Angela said gently, reminding him one of the earliest discussions they'd had as a group. Phoebe saw Melissa reach for the whiteboard, but she put it in her lap without taking the cap off the marker. She wondered if the girl was able to talk, or chose not to.

"I've . . . mellowed," Colette said. "Like . . . cheese."

Margi cracked up all over again after adding something about how well Colette would go with Thorny's "wine." Phoebe wondered if the two of them had been sucking the air out of helium balloons prior to class.

"Har-de-har," Thorny said. "Go ahead and laugh. We've lost every game since Adam and Tommy left the football team; my girlfriend, Haley, broke up with me because all my zombie—oh excuse me, my—'differently biotic' friends are too creepy; and now I get a detention for saying a single stupid word."

He looked up at his classmates, shaking his head as though overwhelmed by the sheer enormity of ruin that had been heaped upon his bony shoulders.

"Life sucks," he said, and the dead kept laughing.

CHAPTER SEVEN

"THE VAN IS waiting," Phoebe said, taking arm. "Let me help you."

No. No help. Right leg left leg no help Phoebe helpless no help.

"I've got your arm. Lift your leg, the left one. That's it. Almost there. Good."

No help. Phoebe touching holding arm can't feel. Can't feel Phoebe holding arm can't move no helpless baby invalid.

"I'll get in on the other side," Phoebe said, "don't worry."

Worry not worry Phoebe Karen in back Margi Colette. Girls girls not worry speak speak speak not worry.

"Don't . . . worry."

Phoebe smile smile Phoebe Adam two words together pretty good good progress Frisbee in three weeks. Three weeks, final.

"You can't really rush it. It isn't like . . . physical . . . therapy. It will come."

Turn. Turn can't turn. Karen can't see Karen Karen in back. Turn Phoebe leaning leaning on shoulder like she used to Phoebe can't smell her hair her shiny hair smelled like gardens remember hair like lilacs.

"How long did it take you to . . . develop?" Phoebe asked Karen.

Margi giggle Colette giggle in front seat develop heh funny. Phoebe blush heh funnier. Karen's voice from back like music.

"I don't know what's got into those two," Karen said. "Don't go by my experience. The timing is different for everyone. And for some it's overnight, for other it has been years."

"But how long?"

Breathe breathe breathe can't breathe try can't Karen laugh and sigh smile walk and talk. Sigh two weeks. Smile one week. Walk one week no ten days.

"I was pretty close," said Karen, "when I woke up."

Awaken. The great awakening awaken the awakened. Why are we here and why did we come Karen's hand on shoulder can feel it?

"But I'm not saying you should stop . . . trying, Adam sweetie," she said. "Just don't get . . . angry . . . if it doesn't work right away."

Try. Try hard trial in a few days. All in van ready to roll. Thorny and Kevin back with Karen Margi Colette up front Phoebe. All but Tommy look see Tommy walking toward woods Tommy alone. Tommy alone. Van coughs starts Tommy turns waves lift arm lift arm lift arm lift arm!

Wave.

CHAPTER EIGHT

P
HOEBE SMOOTHED out Adam's
tie on his chest and saw him
watching her. She wondered if he
was aware that her fingertips grazed over the bullet hole
through which his life had drained away.

"You look great," she said, going on tiptoes so she could kiss
his smooth cheek. A strange benefit of death was that his beard
stopped growing, even though the hair on his head still did. It
was strange.

She wondered if he could feel her kiss. She tried to imagine
what the kiss would feel like if he were still alive. Did her
mouth feel warm to him? If he weren't dead, would there be
more texture to her kiss, sensation beyond a vague sense of
pressure?

"I bet you'll be glad when this part of it is over," she said,
taking his arm. "I know I will."

He nodded. His answer arrived a few heartbeats later.

"Yes," his voice ghostlike.

She had his arm with both of hers now, hugging it like she was dangling over a cliff and it was the last handhold available.

"He'll go to jail, Adam," she said. "He has to."

She was really putting some strength into her hug. She was beginning to think that no matter how tight she clung to him, it wouldn't change anything.

Her guilt was crippling, sometimes. Standing there, gripping him tightly, she wondered if things would change between them if and when he started to "come back." Would they be more than friends? Did he still want that? Did she?

She rested her head against his arm the way she used to when he drove her home from school and she had had a bad day or there was something that she wanted to talk about. She knew he used to be able to curl fifty pounds with that arm—Thunder, he called it. Thunder was the left and Lightning was the right; he named them just because it hacked his stepbrother Jimmy off so much. Now he was lucky if Thunder obeyed him enough to bend at the elbow.

Phoebe let go of him when Joe called from the kitchen down the hallway to see if they were ready.

"We're coming, Mr. Garrity," she responded.

Phoebe led Adam into the kitchen where his mother and Joe waited, both of them looking stiff and uncomfortable in their coats and ties. Phoebe couldn't help but think they looked like people going to a funeral. Joe's suit looked as though it might have fit him way back in the Clinton administration but was straining at the seams today. He'd tried to clean the grease off of his hands, but Phoebe could still see it embedded in his fingernails and in the ridges of his fingertips. He didn't smile often, but his eyes softened at their weathered and wrinkled corners as she led Adam by the hand into the room.

"Johnny's warming up the car. You look good, son," Joe said, his voice like the starting rumble of the '66 El Dorado parked on the front lawn that he tinkered with on occasion. He clapped a thick, calloused hand on Adam's shoulder.

Phoebe waited for Adam to respond, but he didn't.

"Blue is a good color for you," she said, as much to distract herself from her thoughts as to cover up the awkwardness. She patted his arm, and in doing so was reminded that he was wearing the same suit he'd worn at the homecoming dance on the night he died. The jacket and tie came off sometime at the Haunted House, which saved it from being ruined when Pete Martinsburg killed him.

Mrs. Garrity moved to hug her son. Phoebe turned away, because there was something in the way that Mrs. Garrity hugged him—which she did often—that always brought tears to her eyes. She'd make furtive touching motions on his arms and shoulders, the movements of her hands like the fluttering of butterflies unsure of where to alight, and then she would seem to collapse into his broad chest. Adam was at least a foot taller than his mother, and although his body wasn't fully under his control, Phoebe thought she could see his shoulders hitch forward whenever his mother embraced him, as though he were trying to will his arms to enfold her.

Phoebe stopped watching, because it wasn't her tears that

Adam needed now, it was her strength. Adam had enough people crying and showering him with pity, and he didn't need either from her. She wiped her eyes as Mrs. Garrity's sobs became more audible.

"Let's go," Joe said, shoving open the door. Phoebe followed him down the front steps, noticing as she did that Joe was wiping at his eyes with an oil-stained thumb, flicking away an invisible tear. Johnny saw them coming and turned down the heavy-metal CD he'd been listening to.

Joe turned back to Phoebe and gave a mirthless laugh.

"Every day is a goddam funeral," he said so that only she could hear. Then he called up for his wife and son to get moving, and as he climbed into the front seat of the waiting car, he yelled at his living son to not play his goddam music so goddam loud. There were two groups of people outside the steps of the courthouse. Three, counting the thin row of policemen standing between the two main groups. On the right, a dozen or so people clustered around a middle-aged man in a suit. He was shouting into a megaphone and holding a placard that said "Free Peter Martinsburg." Beside him a woman wearing equally conservative clothing had a sign that said "Pro Life" in bold black letters. There was a biblical quote or two which, bizarrely, were accompanied by a photograph of Reverend Nathan Mathers, who had a number of books out condemning the zombies as evil harbingers of an impending apocalypse. Phoebe wondered if the protestors thought the quotes they bore were actually attributable to Mathers and not the authors of the Bible.

Across from them were a loose collection of mostly young

people, some dead, most of whom were sporting black Slydellco T-shirts, the ones with semi-humorous, semi-political sayings like "Some of My Best Friends Are Dead" or "Got Zombie?" Karen was there, along with Colette and Margi. Thorny and his supposedly ex-girlfriend Haley were holding hands. Phoebe spotted Tayshawn toward the back, talking to Kevin Zumbrowski. The zombie contingent didn't have any signs, unless you counted the slogans on their T-shirts, and spent most of their time watching the more organized, vocal demonstrators along the way. One surprise was that a few of Adam's football teammates were there, wearing their Badger letter jackets.

"Look, Adam," she said, pointing to them, "look at all your friends."

Adam stared out the window. One of the football players was taking pictures of the protestors with his cell phone.

"Get . . . hurt," he said. Johnny had already found a parking spot by the time he finished his sentence.

"They won't get hurt," she said. "The police will keep things quiet." She was trying to believe that, but there was real anger in some of the faces in the "Free Peter" crowd. That killing a teenaged boy could be in any way justifiable seemed an insane concept, but she knew that Pete had plenty of supporters because of his stated intention, of "protecting a living girl" from a zombie.

She didn't know if prison was the right answer, but Pete Martinsburg definitely needed help of some sort.

"There's a side door over here," Joe said. "Let's try to avoid the crowd."

Phoebe looked back, praying that no one on either side would do anything foolish. She was looking at Tayshawn as she whispered her prayer.

She led Adam into the empty courtroom, where a lone, unsmiling bailiff stood by the American flag at the front of the room.

"There's a step," she said, leading Adam toward the front row, just behind the tables where the defense and the prosecution set up. A low hum came from gratings high in the wall where ductwork pumped warm air into the room. Outside, it was chilly, even for a New England November. Adam was still taking his seat when Joe, Adam's mother, and his stepbrother Johnny entered the courtroom in a noisy bustle. They were followed by State's Attorney Lainey, who looked like she already had a headache as she fielded questions from Joe and his wife.

The springs on the stadium-style seat squealed as Adam sat. Phoebe tapped his arm.

"Are you nervous?" she asked.

The shake of his head was barely perceptible.

Tommy appeared at the door of the courtroom with his mother, Faith. His appearance startled Phoebe into giving him a quick wave. She hadn't expected to see him. She should have known, though, that if anything powered Tommy, it was his conscience. He and Faith crossed the courtroom and took seats a few rows from the Garrity family, Faith pausing to say hello to Phoebe with a smile that seemed tinged with sadness. Phoebe felt herself flush.

TC Stavis arrived next, sweaty and uncomfortable in a tight sport jacket and knit tie that was too short for his long, wide body. A large, wheezing man was with him. Stavis didn't look at anyone as he took his seat.

Pete Martinsburg had no problem looking at anyone and everyone. He entered the room with his parents and the rest of the defense team, glaring at Phoebe and Adam as he did so. There was nothing in his expression, not malice, hatred, or regret.

She held Adam's ice-cold hand and prayed that he'd be able to speak when it was his turn.

CHAPTER NINE

LEFT LEG. RIGHT LEG. Joe help don't want help. Light all wrong. Amber. Sick. Light hot can't feel heat Phoebe sweating. Pete not sweating. Like a lizard.

Step. Right leg. Left. Face in mirror one pupil wide one smile. My face not my face right leg. All looking. All watching FrankenAdam right leg left right. Waiting to fall. Won't fall. Staring right leg walk walk.

"Bailiff," judge says. "Please help Mr. Layman to the stand."

Bailiff takes arm can't feel feel only his disgust. Steers pulls right left leg turn. Sit. Sit Sit.

"Please sit, Mr. Layman."

Sit. Sitting.

Right arm. Right arm.

"Please raise your right arm. "Do you solemnly swear . . . Mr. Layman?"

Right arm. Right arm!

"Mr. Layman, please raise . . . thank you. Do you . . ."

Speak. Speak. Speak. Speak.

". . . so help you God?"

Speak. Speak.

"Miss Jensen," said judge, "please enter in the record that Mr. Layman nodded, indicating that he does intend to tell the truth, so help him God. Thank you."

Light all wrong. Amber light. Sick like flypaper film on eyes. Eyes one dilated one not. Fat man approaches bench. Guttridge. Guttridge in suit.

"Mr. Layman," says Guttridge, "please, in your own words, tell us what happened on the night of the Oakvale homecoming dance."

Speak. Speak. Speak!

"Mr. Layman?"

Speak. Speak.

"Mr. Layman?"

Speak.

Guttridge turns. "Your Honor, Mr. Layman is behaving as an uncooperative witness."

Speak.

"He is trying to speak, Counselor. Give him a moment."

Guttridge throws hands in the air. Speak. Speak. Guttridge turns. Looks in eyes.

"I withdraw the question," Guttridge says. "Let me ask something simpler. Mr. Layman, we are here to determine whether or not my client, Pete Martinsburg, is guilty of murder, are we not?"

Speak. Speak. Spoke.

"I'm sorry. I didn't quite understand your comment just then. The question is, are you aware we are here to determine whether or not Pete Martinsburg is guilty of murder."

Nod.

"Do you believe that Pete Martinsburg went into the Oxoboxo forest with any premeditation of killing you?"

"Objection. How could the witness possibly know what was in the defendant's head?"

Guttridge puts on an angry face. "Your Honor, if we have to go through the charade of a murder trial when the supposed victim walked into the room under his own power, can't I at least ask whether or not he felt he was murdered?"

"I think 'under his own power' is an exaggeration," says judge, "but I will allow the question. Mr. Layman?"

Speak. Speak speak speak speak.

Speak. "No."

Didn't sound like "no" sounded like crack crash like explosion deep inside a mountain.

Someone screamed.

CHAPTER TEN

Tak watched George drag his carcass over to a squat mausoleum, following Popeye around the graveyard like an imprinted duck. George held his arms in front of him, his fingers grubby, his nails long and black. He was carrying a box of paper sheets that bore his likeness.

Wind whipped through Tak's smile as he ripped off a thick band of electrical tape and slapped another sheet onto a tombstone. He stepped back to view Popeye's creation.

I WANT YOU, the flyer read, over a murky picture of George he'd taken at the Haunted House. George's head was cocked to the side, his ragged corduroy jacket open, revealing a shredded T-shirt that gave glimpses of his rib cage. The flash of the camera had put a maniacal glint in his eyes, and he looked like he was smiling. He was pointing at the camera, his obviously broken pinky askew at an impossible angle, some of his knucklebones visible beneath skin that looked ready to slide off his hands. The words FOR THE U.S. ARMY! were in the same red, white, and blue lettering below his picture.

And beneath this, in a smaller blocky type, SPONSORED BY THE UNDEAD STATES OF AMERICA ARMY.

Tak thought the flyer was genius. In addition to plasteing the cemetery with the flyers, Tayshawn and other trulydeads— zombies who had no interest in rejoining beating heart society—were putting up still more of the copies at local funeral homes and at Oakvale High.

When they were done, Popeye and Tak met beneath a stone angel, waiting for George to catch up.

"Does he . . . have any copies . . . left?" Tak asked.

Popeye nodded. "We've got a quarter box, maybe. You know, there is . . . a real . . . recruiting station a couple miles up."

"Let's do . . . it," Tak said. Popeye had fewer gaps in his speech when he was in the act of making one of his art pieces a reality. "We have a few hours . . . until the breathers awake."

Popeye called for George, who was rooting around in a pile of leaves that had collected in the doorway of a mausoleum. George lifted his head at the sound of his name and shuffled toward them.

"What has he . . . got there?" Tak asked. George had the box of flyers under one arm and was holding something in his other hand.

George tripped over a low headstone and went face-first into the frost covered earth. The box of flyers tumbled open, some of them blowing across the cemetery. Popeye shook his head.

"We haven't got . . . all night," he said. He and Tak went to salvage what flyers they could as George slowly got to his feet. When he rose they saw that he was clutching a dead squirrel by the tail.

"Nice," Popeye said, smiling. "Did you just . . . catch him, George? Or was he already dead?"

They watched as George brought the squirrel to the ragged slash of his mouth and bit into it.

"Why does he . . . do that?" Popeye asked. George was munching on the creature, bones, fur, and all, with a suspicious, greedy expression on his face, as though he were afraid that Tak and Popeye might want to take it from him.

"He thinks he's . . . supposed to," Tak said.

"Dying must have . . . fried his brain," Popeye said as George looked up at him, the squirrel clenched firmly in his teeth. "Now there's the picture . . . we should have used on the flyers."

"Who's to . . . say?" Tak said. "Maybe . . . George . . . is doing what he's supposed . . . to be doing."

George stared back at him, and Tak thought there may have been the briefest flicker of emotion on his gray, puttylike face as he chewed, but probably not. George was the least expressive zombie that Tak had ever seen. It was almost as if George had no interest in trying to become more like the traditionally biotic boy he'd been prior to death. Tak didn't know if he walked with his arms outstretched because he had to, or because he wanted to. Nobody knew where George came from or how he'd found the Haunted House. He just showed up on the front porch one day, beating on the door with his arms. Tayshawn had called him George, and the name stuck.

The sounds George made as he gnawed on the rodent were not pleasant. Tak watched him eat, and wondered if George would be able to talk if he tried.

"Nice table . . . manners," Popeye said, speaking in front of George as though he were too stupid to understand. Tak held his comments and waited for George to complete his meal. He suspected that George wasn't as stupid as Popeye thought. George could obey instructions for the most part, and seemed perfectly willing to allow any zombie who was around to order him about like a servant. Especially Tak.

George took another bite and flung the broken body over the tombstones. It went surprisingly far. He dragged the muddy sleeve of his jacket across his face and slouched toward them.

"Had enough, George?" Popeye said. He leaned over to Tak. "Can you smell him? I think I can . . . smell him. I think he has actually renewed my sense of smell."

"I can smell him."

"He smells . . . dead."

"It isn't Z, anyhow," Tak said, which Popeye thought pretty funny.

"George," Tak said, "Go back to . . . the house. The sun will be up . . . soon. Go back to the house and . . . wait . . . for us."

They watched him dragging himself over the old graves toward the woods.

"I might be . . . an artist," Popeye said with admiration, "but that boy . . . is *art*."

* * *

Phoebe woke up in a bad mood. She could feel herself emitting a dark cloud of negativity; it poured from her in thick, invisible vapors.

Her terrier, Gargoyle, looked up from the foot of her bed, turned, leaped, and scampered away before her fog swept over him.

She didn't have the energy to argue with Mrs. Garrity when she said that Adam was "too sick" to go to school that day. "Dead kids don't get sick, Mrs. Garrity," is what she should have said, and then she should have asked if she could speak to Adam. Instead she sighed and walked out to the end of her driveway to catch the bus, pushing her hat down lower over her ears against the cold that seemed to be seeping into her.

The bus was seven minutes late. The first thing she heard when she stepped on was Colette's shrill, catlike laughter. Because she wasn't in the mood, she took a seat in the front across from a freshman boy with glasses. He was obviously terrified of her. Phoebe, was self-aware enough to notice that many of the younger kids regarded her with fear. Margi said they gave her the hairy eyeball because of her goth stylings and perfect skin; Phoebe was inclined to think it had more to do with her presence at Adam's murder—either that or being the cause of the murder. She looked over at the boy, who clutched his backpack and stared straight ahead.

Bride of Frankenstein, they called her. She was sure of it.

"Phoebe, Phoebe!" she heard Margi call from the back of the bus.

Phoebe ignored her. She made sure that she was the first one off, sliding into the aisle while the younger boy remained crouched in his seat.

"Where's Adam?" Mrs. Rodriguez asked her at the start of algebra, and if Phoebe had possessed the power to petrify, she would have used it then. She mumbled that she didn't know.

"Tommy isn't here either," Mrs. Rodriguez said. "Do you have any idea where he is?"

Phoebe had to hold back the answer that came to mind, which was to ask Mrs. Rodriguez if she thought she was the den mother for the morgue.

"It isn't like Tommy to miss a day of class," Mrs. Rodriguez said. Phoebe shrugged and went to take her seat. She glanced over to where TC Stavis sat, studious in his attempt to avoid looking at her.

I'm the Gorgon, Phoebe thought, looking over at him, squinting. My stare is death.

TC leaned over his algebra book and seemed to flinch.

Later in the lunchroom Phoebe unwrapped a lackluster lunch of milk, carrots, lukewarm macaroni and cheese, and an apple with a bruise as big as the Tycho crater. Margi came and sat down next to her with such a haphazard flop that she made Phoebe spill milk on the front of her blouse.

"Hey, hey," Margi said as Colette and Karen took chairs on the opposite sides of them. "Baby's in black again."

"Well, I *was* in black," Phoebe said, frowning. "But now I'm in milky black." She rubbed the front of her shirt with a napkin.

"Here, let me help you," Margi said, grabbing another

napkin and thrusting it at Phoebe's chest. Phoebe slapped her hand away, the sharp sound of it making the dead girls laugh.

"Jeez," Margi said, a wry smile on her face, "ease off on the jiujitsu. I was only trying to help."

"Yeah," Phoebe said, "thanks for that 'help.'"

"Still thinking about the trial, huh?"

"No," Phoebe said.

"Adam really freaked, huh?"

"No!" Phoebe said, her voice rising above the boisterous din of the lunchroom. "No, he did not 'freak.' Who told you he freaked?"

"Um," Margi said, looking back to Karen and Colette, but she didn't find any help there. Karen took the lid off a cup of sliced strawberries. "I heard it from Norm. Who heard it from Gary, who I think talked to Morgan Harris, who must have gotten it from TC."

"TC," Phoebe said. "A necessary link in the daisy chain of idiots."

Margi knew that she was being included as a link in the "daisy chain of idiots," so she let the comment slide. "What really happened?"

"I don't know why I even talk to you sometimes."

Margi crossed her eyes. "Because I'm such an insightful listener?"

Phoebe turned to look at Margi, who had now added a wagging tongue to her crossed eyes, completing her performance art piece of congenital idiocy. The dead girls kept their silence, as though they could sense the storm brewing inside Phoebe.

And then a strange thing happened; looking at Margi's display, Phoebe felt the dark cloud dissipate.

"Oh, Margi," she said, laughing.

"See?" her friend said. "*That's* why you hang out with me."

"That must be it."

"Come on, Pheebes," Margi said, leaning over so that Phoebe could feel the points of Margi's spiky hair tickling her cheeks. "Talk about it. Let it out. We're your buds."

"I know you are," Phoebe said. Karen and Colette looked as though they would breathe a sigh of relief if they could. "You really are."

The questions came at a rapid clip, tumbling on each other like a free-verse poem.

"What did he say?"

"Is he okay?"

"What did Pete say?

"Was it really so bad?"

Phoebe held up her hand. "Did they really say that Adam freaked?"

Margi nodded. "Kinda."

"I didn't hear anything," Karen said, holding out the cup of strawberries so Colette could try to smell them. "No one talks to me. I just assumed . . . it went badly because you looked like you wanted . . . to kill everyone."

Phoebe sighed and rolled the bruised apple on the table with her fingers. "He didn't 'freak.' Martinsburg's lawyer asked a million questions, and was being as condescending as he could. Adam tried so hard, but he just couldn't speak."

"Oh, man," Margi said, "poor Adam."

"I felt so bad for him," Phoebe said.

Karen looked like she wanted to say something, but she put a slice of strawberry on her tongue instead.

"What did he do?" Margi asked.

"He tried to answer a question. He did answer it, but his answer wasn't . . . understandable. And it was loud."

"I still . . . do that," Colette said, "sometimes."

"Really?" Margi said. "I thought that was you trying to sing."

"Shut . . . up." Colette shot Margi a dark look.

"It doesn't matter," Karen said.

"What do you mean?" Phoebe was stunned.

"Well, Phoebe," she said, "of course it matters to Adam, and to you. But it wouldn't have mattered how . . . eloquent . . . Adam was on the stand. That boy wasn't going to get punished, no matter what."

"He got community service," Phoebe said. "And he has to get counseling."

"Big deal," Karen said, selecting another slice of strawberry. "Counseling. And they didn't even let Tommy speak. It wasn't . . . easy for him to go, you know."

Phoebe looked at her to see if she was being accused of something, but Karen's strange eyes were guileless. "I would have liked to see him get a tougher penalty too."

"Like a beating," Margi said. "Or worse."

"Some would agree with you," Karen said. "Only they would not be . . . joking."

She smiled and licked the strawberry juice from her lips.

"Are you okay?" Phoebe asked, watching Karen slice into an orange with the edge of her fingernail.

"Well, that's a funny question, isn't it," Karen said, husking the fruit with a sudden violent twist of her hands. "Considering the circumstances."

"You seem like something is bothering you," Phoebe said. "Is it something I said? Or is it the trial?"

Karen looked up at her, and for a moment Phoebe could swear she saw a coppery light in the glittering retinas of her eyes.

Karen lifted the orange to her face and inhaled deeply. She was even weirder than usual, Phoebe thought. She came to school wearing jeans and a heavy sweatshirt with a school logo on it, instead of her usual skirts or dresses. *Short* skirts, and *short* dresses, ones that showed a lot of her ice-white skin, even now when the weather was getting colder.

The light left her eyes. "I'm sorry, Phoebe," she said. "I'm a little off today, aren't I? But why is that, do you think? Don't you need hormones and blood sugar and all those chemically things to be moody?"

"Must be the . . . formaldehyde," Colette said.

Margi's cackle cut across the whole cafeteria.

Karen turned toward Colette and broke the orange in half, offering it to her.

"I'm so glad you're . . . progressing," Karen said. Colette refused the orange, and when neither Margi or Phoebe wanted a piece she set it on the napkin in front of her.

"Speaking of progressing," Phoebe said. "I was thinking that we should do something nice for Adam to try and cheer him up.

Maybe we could have a party for him? At the Haunted House?"

"That's a great idea!" Karen said. "Really, Phoebe. I think having a . . . party for Adam is a great thing. Being surrounded by people who love him . . . can only help."

"I . . . think . . . it is a good thing . . . too," Colette said, "I wish . . . someone . . . had done . . . that for me."

Margi rolled her eyes, reaching for the orange slices. "You *had* to go there again. When will you give it a rest?"

Colette looked at her, the nervous ticking smile pulling at the corners of her mouth. "I will . . . never . . . be . . . at rest," she said, which sent Margi off again. Colette's laughter was a lot different from Karen's, which sounded realistic. Her's sounded more like a choking mirthful hiccup, like the sound someone would make if they started laughing with a mouthful of milk.

"Hey," Colette said, still smiling, "did you guys . . . see the newspaper . . . this morning?"

Margi snickered, but neither Karen nor Phoebe had seen it.

"The . . . boys . . . played another prank," Colette said. "Their idea of . . . reprisal, I guess. Did you bring it?" she asked Margi, who was rooting around in her purse.

"Really?" Karen asked, too innocently, Phoebe thought.

"Yeah. It's . . . hilarious," Colette said.

Margi produced a wrinkly square of newsprint and dropped it on the table. George stared out at them from the photo.

Phoebe laughed. "That's great! Better than marking up the school, anyhow."

"Tak and Popeye can be pretty clever," Karen said.

Phoebe saw right through Karen's enigmatic expression and

was about to call her on it when Margi asked a question.

"Is Tak the guy with the perma-smile? And who is Popeye?"

"You'll meet them when you come to Adam's . . . party," Karen said.

"Ugh," Colette said, "do they . . . have . . . to be there? I like their . . . tricks, but . . ."

"Don't you want to meet the artists?" Karen said. "Besides, it isn't like I can . . . uninvite them. It's their home."

"I . . . know, I . . . know. They're just . . . unpleasant . . . sometimes. Especially to . . . trads."

"They *are* pretty bold," Margi said. "Speaking as a traditionally biotic person."

"I just hope they don't go . . . too far," Colette said.

"At least they're going . . . somewhere," Karen said, waving her hand. "Tak probably won't want to come, anyway."

And that would be just fine, Phoebe thought. "Maybe we could decorate the Haunted House?" she said. "Sort of like you did for homecoming?"

"Okay, Phoebe," Karen said. "That sounds good."

"I'll invite Thorny," Phoebe said.

"What about the rest of the football team?" Margi asked. "All his old buddies?"

Phoebe thought of some of Adam's "old buddies": psychotic Martinsburg and the mindlessly violent Stavis. "I don't know . . . I don't think many of them would be interested in going. Maybe Thorny would have some ideas."

"Let's call it . . . a wake," Colette said. "I really . . . wish . . . I'd had . . . one."

71

"There she goes again."

"I'm choosing to ignore you too, Margi," Phoebe said. "What do you think, Karen? Is Saturday too soon?"

"Saturday is good," Karen replied. "We've got all the time in the world."

"Speaking of time," Phoebe said, looking at Karen and with a nervous pout, "there's something I need you to do for me."

She didn't want to drag the apology out any longer than she had to. If she hadn't put off talking to him for so long, things might not have gone the way they did in the hallway. And Karen was right; she did owe Tommy an explanation, at least.

Even so, she was almost surprised when Karen told her that Tommy would, in fact, meet her after school. She'd been so rotten to him she'd understand if he never spoke to her again.

And she knew, no matter how things turned out, that she didn't want that.

"Hi," Tommy said. He was wearing khaki slacks and a white-and-blue Oxford shirt with the sleeves rolled up. He looked, Phoebe thought, like one of the models out of the L.L. Bean catalogue, but a lot paler. She was in a heavy black padded coat that had fake fur lining the hood. Tommy was never cold.

She knew he'd been watching her from the moment she left the school, tracking her with those clear gray-blue eyes of his, eyes that were the color of an early morning sky before a perfect day.

"Hi, Tommy," she said, and took a seat next to him, even though she could feel the icy cold metal of the bleachers through the seat of her skirt. "Thanks for meeting me. And thanks for going to the trial."

"Glad . . . to go . . . though they wouldn't . . . let me . . . speak." He smiled at her, but it was a sad smile, like he already knew what she was going to say. "Are you . . . feeling better?"

She looked at him, eyes narrowing, wondering if it was going to be *that* kind of conversation.

"The other . . . day," he said, "you went . . . to the nurse. I heard . . . she sent you . . . home."

"Oh. Oh, yeah. I feel much better. Too much Halloween candy, maybe."

She knew then that if it was going to be *that* kind of conversation, it would be because of her. He was way too calm and self-possessed to give into whatever emotions he was feeling.

His eyes—eyes that had such a strange, hypnotic effect on her—were clear. She looked away.

"I wanted to apologize," she told him, and it seemed as if she was swallowing with every third word. "I had no right to say those things, they weren't true, and I'm sorry."

"You were . . . right, though," he said. "If I could have . . . moved . . . Adam might . . . still be alive."

The tears she had been trying to blink back started to escape. Adam might be still be alive, but Tommy might have been irrevocably dead. Or she might be—there was no telling. What happened, happened, and could not be undone.

"I'd have given . . . anything . . . to have been able to move."

"You couldn't have done anything," she said. "I'm sorry I blamed you. I really am, Tommy."

He nodded.

"So we're both . . . sorry," he said, looking up at the sound of the buses pulling away. Soon what remained of the Oakvale High football team would be taking the field for practice.

She hugged her knees, hiding her face so he couldn't see. She wanted to get up and hug him and let him know she really meant it, but she was afraid that he'd get the wrong idea.

She was also afraid to touch him because she was afraid that the "wrong idea" would feel like the right one.

It was Tommy who spoke first, his voice husky.

"You are . . . haunting . . . me . . . Phoebe."

"I'm sorry," she said again. "I'm sorry, I'm sorry, I'm sorry."

"Don't be . . . sorry," he said. "Be with . . . me. Give me . . . another . . . chance."

She sobbed and pulled away as he touched her arm.

"I can't, Tommy," she said, "I'm with . . . Adam needs me now."

He was silent, but she thought she could feel the weight of his stare on the back of her head. She dried her eyes with the back of her sleeve.

"He died for me, Tommy."

He didn't answer for some time.

"You love him?"

Phoebe looked into the trees far beyond the field. She wasn't certain of the answer to Tommy's question, not yet. She had feelings for Adam that she had for no one else. Were those feelings love, or an acute pity wrapped in the guilt she felt over his sacrifice? It was so hard to be sure, especially in Adam's diminished state.

Did she love Adam?

Her heart told her she did, in the rare moments that her brain was quiet, but she couldn't say it out loud. Not to Tommy.

"I . . . he needs me, Tommy. I can't . . . I can't have time for anyone else right now."

She stood up and looked over her shoulder at him, sitting there in shirtsleeves in the chill air, as implacable as death itself. If only she knew—really knew in her heart—that what Tommy wanted was her, Phoebe, and not just any willing, living girl, things could've been different.

But she didn't.

"It's over, Tommy."

She turned away and started walking down the steel steps.

"Phoebe," he said, and she stopped.

"When he . . . pointed . . . the gun . . . at you it . . . felt . . . like this."

Part of her wanted to apologize again, another part wanted to scream. She wanted to scream, "Well, isn't that what you wanted? To feel? This is what feeling is."

But a third part, the part she kept hidden, made her want to give into her other feelings and rush back to him, to take him in her arms and give him the kiss that he imagined would bring him to life.

But she didn't.

She walked away.

CHAPTER ELEVEN

"**D**O YOU KNOW why you're here?" the smiling woman asked. Pete gave two frog-like blinks and waited for his breath to return. Angela Hunter was one of the most beautiful women he'd ever seen, a stunning blonde in a dark blue dress whose conservative style only emphasized her sexy features. Her smile took him back to California, back to the beaches and hanging around his sisters' friends, away from Connecticut, the land of big coats, cold ground, and the dead.

"Mr. Martinsburg?" she said. "Peter?"

"I'm sorry," he said. He couldn't believe this was the same woman who spent her day with the corpsicles in that stupid class of theirs. What a waste of warm flesh. "What was the question?"

Her smile was patient. "Do you know why you're here?"

He nearly laughed. Why are any of us here, he wanted to

say. Why are the worm burgers here instead of quietly rotting in the ground, away from human sight?

"Yes," he said instead. "I was sentenced to therapy and to community service for my involvement in a crime of negligence."

She tapped the lined pad in her lap with a ballpoint pen, and he used the movement as an excuse to lower his eyes to her legs. The blue skirt fell below her knees, but what he could see of them was stunning.

"By crime of negligence, do you mean an accident?"

"Yes," he said, his gaze returning to her eyes. "A tragic accident. I really didn't want it to turn out that way."

"What way did you want it to turn out?"

He started to reply, but the answer caught in his throat. Her beauty was making him dizzy; he forced himself to choose his words with care.

"I don't know how I wanted it to turn out," he said. "I just know that wasn't it."

She nodded. "You know I'm not here to prove or disprove what the state found you guilty of," she said. "That isn't my purpose."

"What is your purpose?" His hands were sweating.

"Just to talk to you," she said. He thought from her tone that she was going to add more, but she didn't.

"Just to talk to me," he said. "Is that what therapy is?"

"It can be. Do you think you need therapy?"

"No."

"Why do you think the state thinks you need therapy?"

"I don't know," he said.

She waited, smiling. He sighed.

"They probably think I'm still a risk to zombies."

"Why would they think that?" she said. "You didn't hurt any zombies."

For a moment he thought of the red-headed zombie, the one that he and Stavis put back in the ground. The look on his face when he saw his second death coming. Pete wasn't sure what that look had meant, but he liked to think it meant "finally." He decided the kid had been grateful in the end.

"No," he said. "But they know I wasn't trying to hurt a real person. Layman got in the way, and then the gun went off. I never meant to hurt him."

"A real person," she said.

"Right."

"So zombies aren't real people?"

Pete looked at his shoes, and then he looked at her legs and up, until his eyes met hers again, taking his time. So she would know.

"I didn't say that."

She nodded. "Well, what do you think? Are zombies real people?"

"No," he said, holding her gaze.

"Did they used to be real people?"

"I don't know." Who cares if they used to be real people? They weren't anymore, that was certain.

"You don't know."

"Nobody knows, do they?" he said, moving his hands fast

to see if she would flinch, and then trying it again when she didn't. "I mean, that's what this whole place is about, isn't it? Studying the dead? I don't know if they used to be people. For all I know they're something else entirely."

"Have you seen Adam since he died?"

Pete looked away in spite of himself. "Yes."

"Is he the same person he was before he died?"

"I don't know."

"You don't? I heard you used to be friends."

"So?" he meant it to sound hostile, but she didn't react.

"Tell me about when you were friends."

"What happens to me if I tell you to go screw yourself instead?"

Her only reaction was a blink, which Pete thought was pretty impressive.

"I'm not sure," she said. "I suppose if you don't participate in the court-assigned therapy, you will be held in contempt and resentenced or something like that. I can find out for you if you want."

"Why do I have to talk about Adam?"

"He's why you're here," she said. "It seems like a good place to start."

"It was an accident. He and I were good friends once."

She nodded.

Pete sighed. "He and I were on the football team together; that's where we met. He was the biggest kid my age I've ever seen. You know. He's in your class."

"Yes," she said.

"We just started hanging out, him and Stavis, lifting weights and stuff. He used to be gawky, a big lummox, but he's gotten really quick since then."

"Stavis was the boy who was with you when Adam was killed?"

He almost snapped at her, but again held his thoughts in check. It hadn't taken her long to get inside his head, but he knew he would have to play along at least a little to keep her happy and get through this.

"Yes. TC. We were the three amigos for a while. We were called the Pain Crew, because when we played football we could dominate the field, especially on defense. Coach played us on both sides of the ball usually, but we were together the most on defense."

"The Pain Crew," she said. "Who called you that?"

"Everyone," he said. "I think I made it up."

She nodded.

"We hung out. Usually at school. We sort of drifted apart at the beginning of this year, though. I came back from spending the summer at my dad's place and we just didn't seem to get along after that."

"Why? Is it because you were apart for the summer?"

"No. We didn't hang out on weekends or anything—just on game days. I made a comment about a girl he liked, and that was the start, I guess."

"You said you spent the summer at your dad's place?"

"Yeah," he said. "My parents are divorced. My dad lives in California, so I stayed with him."

He looked up and saw in her eyes that she thought she had caught something there, some little clue she could use to break his whole head open. And why the hell had he said all that stuff, anyhow, running his mouth like a little girl? He was smarter than that.

"The girl you made the comment about. She was someone that Adam was interested in?"

"Yeah. Tori Stewart," he said, giving her a name of someone that Adam—and half the football team—had casually dated. The lie came easily. "I mean, they went out a few times, but how was I supposed to know he was that way about her? I didn't even say anything that bad, just that I was thinking about asking her to the homecoming dance. He flipped out."

"Flipped out?"

Pete nodded. "Threw his helmet and everything. When a guy that big gets pissed off, you kind of get ready for anything. He said he'd rip my legs off if I so much as looked at her funny. I said, Take it easy, no problem."

"I see," Angela said.

"That was about it, really. We just didn't talk a whole lot after that. I tried, but I think he was jealous or paranoid or something."

"Was this before Tommy Williams joined the team?"

"After. No, before. I'm not really sure."

"What did Tommy joining the team do to your friendship with Adam?"

"Nothing, really," he said. "It was kind of over by then, anyhow."

"What did you think about Tommy joining the team?"

"I can't lie," he said. "I wasn't really happy about it. I don't think it was the right thing to do. I still don't."

"Why?"

"Because," and again Pete chose his words carefully, "because he couldn't play. I didn't think it was fair. Kids work really hard to get some playing time and qualify for the team, and this guy gets to play just because he's dead? Just because the school wants to prove how liberal and politically correct they are? It wasn't right."

"So you're saying Tommy was given playing time just because he was differently biotic?"

"Of course," Tommy said. "He couldn't move, he couldn't run. Last one around the track every single time. No disrespect intended, kids who can't play shouldn't be allowed to suit up. It isn't right."

"Do lots of kids get cut from the team?"

He knew by the way she asked the question that she already knew the answer.

"No. Not really."

"The one game he played," she said, "did he play much of the game?"

"It's the principle," he said. "If you can't play, you shouldn't be allowed to play."

"So it made you angry."

"Sure I was angry," he said. "But he only played the one game, so I let it go."

"Why do you think you were so angry?"

"Because it wasn't right."

"What wasn't right?"

He considered throwing it out on the table. It wasn't right that the dead could pretend they were alive. It wasn't right that Julie was dead and Tommy was not completely dead. It wasn't right that little Miss Scarypants would choose a worm burger over him. None of it was right.

But what he said was just a reiteration of what he'd said before. "Like I said. It wasn't right that he got to play while a more deserving kid had to sit on the bench. People work too hard for that playing time."

"Like you."

"Yes, like me. I busted my ass to make sure I would be on the field for game day."

"You've worked hard today, too," Angela said. "I think this was a good start. Let's go out into the office and I'll call Mr. Davidson so you can start on the community service portion of your sentencing. Wait here a moment."

Pete watched her leave the office, wondering how he was supposed to be able to survive another twenty-three weeks of this. He heard Angela's voice over the intercom asking for Mr. Davidson. He looked around the office—shelves of books, the two chairs, a low table with a pitcher of water and two cups. A print on the wall of a New England coastline, a ship in the distance.

She returned with a tall man who had a bald, lozenge-shaped head. The man looked down at Pete in his chair with all the expression and warmth of the living dead. He was wearing a blue windbreaker with the Hunter Foundation insignia on it, and he wore a belt which had a Nextel clipped on the left hip and a handgun clipped on the right.

"Pete," Angela said, "this is Duke Davidson, the Director of Operations here at the foundation. He will be responsible for overseeing your community service hours."

Pete wasn't sure if he was supposed to get up and shake his hand, but Davidson's narrowed stare kept him in his seat. It seemed like the tall man was licking his lips at the prospect of putting him to work.

Pete considered making a crack about the handgun, but in light of his reasons for being there, it didn't seem well-advised.

"Hi," Pete said, and he said it in a way that he hoped conveyed that he didn't intend to be any trouble.

"Two hundred hours," Davidson said. "The clock starts now."

"I'll see you next week, Pete," Angela told him as he followed Davidson out of her office.

"Thanks," he mumbled.

"The term 'Operations' has a broad context here at the Hunter Foundation," Davidson said, his long strides echoing in heavy, booted footfalls that resounded off the shiny tiled floors and concrete corridors. Davidson liked people to know he was coming, it seemed. "It means security. It means care and maintenance of the physical plant. It means utilities, it means plumbing, it means groundskeeping and whatever else it takes to keep the foundation running as seamlessly as possible."

He stopped at a door, withdrew a ring of keys and keycards

from his belt, and plugged one of the cards into a slot beside the door, which clicked open. Davidson pushed the door open and flicked on the light, revealing a walk-in supply closet, rows of cleaning supplies, lightbulbs, and packs of C-fold towels on gunmetal gray racks.

"It also means janitorial work," he said, wheeling out a yellow mop bucket and wringer. "Especially in your case."

"Pretty high security for some cleaning supplies."

Davidson reached for some of those cleaning supplies. Pete, standing behind him in the frame of the door, looked at the heavy weapon on the man's hip, a single leather strap securing it in place.

"You ever want to cause some damage to a place," Davidson said without turning around, "start a fire in the janitor's closet."

"I'll keep it in mind," Pete said.

"Good," Davidson, pouring some liquid into the bucket. "Use this stuff whenever I tell you to mop out the bathrooms. If you reach for my sidearm I will break your wrist. For starters."

"I . . . I wasn't going to," Pete said.

Davidson looked up at him. "Just so we're clear." There was a sink at the back of the closet with a spray hose that Davidson used to spray hot water in the bucket, sending a lemon-scented steam up from the bucket and into Pete's nostrils.

"A few glugs of the stuff will do it. I don't care how exact you are; we aren't the scientists here."

"Right," Pete said.

"There are cameras all over the facility. Most of them you

will never see, and some of the ones you do see don't really work. I watch the monitors. My staff watches the monitors. Some of your school chums get paid to watch the monitors while they're earning college prep credits. They'll be watching you mop the floors to pay off your debt to society. I'm sure some of them would like nothing better than to catch you doing something that you're not supposed to be doing. I'm sure some of them would like nothing better than to catch you doing something that would actually get you sent to prison, instead of working out your sentence by mopping the floors and cleaning the toilets that the living ones use."

Pete thought that Davidson must hang around dead people a lot: there was sarcasm in his words, but you'd never know it from his inflection.

Pete thought that there was something else in Davidson's words as well, some message hidden beneath his flat stare and deadpan delivery, something waiting for Pete to decode.

"I'll be careful," Pete said.

Davidson tossed a pair of green latex gloves against Pete's chest.

"Careful," he said. "Yes. You be careful. Get that mop over by the wall and wheel the bucket out into the hall. We're going to take a walk to the monitor room so I can get you a jacket."

Pete obeyed without comment. Davidson followed him out and popped his card back into the slot. The lock clicked.

The corridors at the foundation reminded Pete of the corridors at his grade school: long windowless tunnels of gray, the illumination from the fluorescent lighting above dim and shadowy. Every other panel was out, Pete noticed, and he wondered if the foundation was trying to save on its utility bill or that maybe the dead didn't need all that light.

The dead, he thought.

They only passed one office on their long walk. Pete glanced into the open doorway and saw Angela talking to his old pal Pinky McKnockers, the chubby and chesty friend of Phoebe Scarypants. There was another girl in the office, but all Pete could see of her was a billowing cloud of flaming red hair as she sat in front of a computer screen on the wall opposite the door. Pinky's own hair, a thick nest of rigid pink spikes, made it look like a huge sea urchin was sitting on her head.

She looked up as they passed, and he caught the look of sudden recognition under the shellac-thick makeup around her eyes.

He winked at her.

I've still got my list, honey, he thought, remembering the expression on her face as he'd spread out the Undead Studies student list where the name "Evan Talbot" had been crossed out. She looked down at her desk so swiftly that his new boss noticed and glanced up at him. Pete suddenly took a great interest in steering the mop bucket to its destination.

"You aren't listening," Davidson said.

"Excuse me?"

"Cameras everywhere. You think punk stuff like that is going to endear you to anyone?"

"What do you mean?"

Davidson stopped and turned with such abruptness that

Pete almost plowed into him with the bucket. That's all I need, he thought, to slosh my boss's shiny black boots.

"I don't think you're getting it," Davidson said. "Do you want to get away with murder or not?"

Pete looked up at him, not sure how he should respond to that.

"You have an opportunity here," Davidson said. "Don't squander it."

"Okay," Pete said. "Okay."

Davidson regarded him a moment longer before turning on his heel.

CHAPTER TWELVE

WHY DOES HE always have to be the welcome wagon? Phoebe thought, seeing Takayuki perched like a vulture on the railing of the slumping porch. He lifted his head enough to glare at their approaching car, his dark hair brushed back from his face.

"He looks friendly," her dad said.

"That's Takayuki," Margi said from the backseat. "He's not."

"I was being sarcastic."

"I know."

He rolled the vehicle to a stop, then got out of the car to help Margi and her extract Adam from the backseat. Phoebe thought she heard Takayuki make a noise of disgust, but when she turned toward him he dropped to the ground and headed off into the woods, the rusted chains of his motorcycle jacket somehow failing to make any noise as he passed.

"Hey, Adam!" came a cheer from the house, as some of the

zombies—Karen, Colette, and Tommy among them, all wearing absurd pointed party hats—came out to welcome him. Tommy made fleeting eye contact with her, and she recalled their conversation—all of his questions about how she felt about Adam. Turning, she waved at Mal, a zombie who rivaled Adam in sheer size, and he waggled his fingers back at her. She leaned into Adam, wondering if Tommy was still watching but refusing to look at him.

Thorny was already at the house, along with Norm Lathrop—who had been Margi's date on homecoming night—Denny Mackenzie, and Gary Greene. Phoebe saw Gary hide a can of beer behind his back upon seeing her father.

Holding his hand, Phoebe looked for Adam's reaction, and for a long time there was none—but then she saw his mouth tic upward.

She breathed a long sigh of relief. Thank you, God, she thought.

"I didn't know Norm was going to be here," Margi whispered. "We haven't talked much since the dance."

"Hi, Margi!" Norm said, waving at her.

"No better time than the present," Phoebe said, nudging her forward.

"Phoebe," her dad said. "I need to talk to you for a minute."

Phoebe didn't want to let go of Adam, not even for a second, but she joined her father over by the car, watching as Karen and Colette each took one of Adam's arms and guided him up the rickety porch steps.

"Phoebe, was that beer I saw in that boys' hand?"

She held her breath as Adam tottered at the top of the stairs near Takayuki's perch, then let it out when a gentle tug from Karen righted him again. She was about to say "what beer?" But she decided to go with honesty.

"I think so."

"You know how I feel about you going to parties where there's going to be drinking."

"I do. I didn't know that there would be drinking. I really didn't think there would be any trad biotic kids here except for Margi and Thorny."

Her dad looked at her and she could almost hear the wheels of his mind whirring.

"The living impaired kids don't drink, do they?"

"They're called differently biotic now, Dad." she said. "And no, they don't drink, or eat, or sleep. Except Karen. She'll eat a piece of fruit every so often, but I think she does it just to be weird."

Her father opened his mouth and abruptly closed it.

"Do you know that boy?"

"Gary Greene," she said. "Thorny must have invited him— they're both on the football team. I've maybe talked to him twice."

He nodded, looked back at the house, then at the woods where Tak had disappeared.

"Dad," she said, "I'm not going to have anything to drink. I don't drink. I'm here for Adam."

He nodded. "This is where Adam died, isn't it? In the woods here?"

She lowered her eyes, nodding. Inside they cued up an old

Van Halen song in Adam's honor, at a volume that threatened to shake loose the few shingles that remained on the roof.

"Okay," her dad said, and he did something he didn't often do when her friends might be around: he hugged her. "You know I trust you. And I want Adam to have a good time too. If anyone gets crazy you call me, okay?"

She hugged him back even tighter. "Okay."

"Easy," he said, kissing the top of her head. "Aren't you worried that all of your zombie friends will see you hugging your uncool dad?"

"Not worried at all," she said, releasing him, "and you're not uncool. Usually."

He exhaled, and she knew that he would probably drive slow circles on the streets surrounding the Haunted House, just on the chance that there would be trouble and she would call.

She waved as he got back into the car. "We'll be fine."

Most of us, anyhow, she thought, running back to the house. She saw beams of light from inside rake across the cracked windows as the music blared, meaning that the zombies managed to re-rig the disco ball and lighting like they'd done for the homecoming after-party. A chill passed through her and she wondered if Adam was experiencing the same sort of déjà vu in returning there. She ran up the stairs, afraid that she would peek into the open area the zombies used as a dance floor and it would be a bizarre replay of that night—she would see Adam dancing with Karen, his suit jacket off and his tie a lank band of blue silk around his neck.

He *was* dancing, or rather he was standing as others danced near him. Colette and Margi twirled around him like he was a maypole, tugging at his arms and touching his shoulders as they spun.

She watched him turn his head, trying to track Colette as she circumnavigated his wide body. Phoebe couldn't read his expression, and for a moment she was afraid that he felt as if he was being mocked, but then Margi did a pirouette in front of him, her arms high over her head and her flouncy dress twitching. Adam raised his hand as though to catch hers, but she had already spun past. Phoebe decided that the gesture meant that Adam was on his way to enjoying himself, so she went to join them, trying not to blush at the immediate chorus of catcalls from Colette and Margi.

She leaned against him, her mouth close to his ear.

"I'm sorry I was away," she said. "I had to talk to Dad."

The look he gave her was a strange one, and she decided she wouldn't let anything else take her away from him that night.

A few of the other differently biotic kids were doing the zombie hop—a twitchy, jerky set of movements that looked like they were having seizures. Kevin Zumbrowki, who had recently learned how to smile, was a master of the zombie hop, and at times moved as though he was being electrocuted. No one seemed to care if his motions had nothing to do with the rhythm or the tempo of the song, especially not the dead girl beside him, whose entire dance repertoire seemed to be a dip of her right shoulder.

Tommy was talking with Thorny, Denny, and Gary Greene. Denny and Gary were each holding a can of beer. Karen was watching the boys talk, her arms folded and a quizzical look on her face.

Margi hip-checked Phoebe, and because she wasn't paying attention, the sudden jolt almost sent her sprawling to the floor.

"You're going to talk to him, right?" Margi said, her voice a high shout above the heavy throb of the music.

"Talk to who?"

"Tommy, stupid."

Phoebe's eyes flicked up at Adam, who managed to shuffle one of his feet forward. She gave Margi the look of death.

"What?" Margi said, sweat already beginning to wilt her spikes. "*Are* you?"

"I already talked to him," Phoebe said, leaning closer to Margi so maybe, just maybe, every dead kid in Oakvale didn't have to listen in. She felt weird even having the conversation, because these were the sort of details that she and Margi passed to each other almost intuitively prior to Adam dying. Now that she was spending all her time with Adam, they had to play "catch up" more.

"You did? What did you tell him?" Margi, oblivious, shouted, pausing to screech as Colette tried to dance.

"That it's over," Phoebe said, silently cheering Colette on. The upside of Phoebe's absence was the renewed closeness between Colette and Margi. "And that I'm with Adam now."

Margi gave her a quizzical look. "With Adam? Like *with* with Adam?"

"Well, yeah. Sort of." That was how Phoebe thought of her and Adam, anyhow—as a couple. It was like an understanding between them, even though neither had actually said as much out loud.

"Does *he* know that?"

Phoebe started to reply when a shadow fell across her. She looked up, and Adam loomed over her like a tree. She was going to ask Margi what she meant, but she'd already moved away to dance with Colette. Phoebe stepped forward and put her arms around him as the song ended.

"Are you having fun?" she asked. The nod was slow in coming. He opened his mouth to say something but was cut off as another song began tearing through the speakers.

Phoebe put her head against his chest and pretended that the bass was the beating of his heart.

"This turned out well, Phoebe," Karen said.

They were standing in the backyard of the Haunted House, in the shadow of the slouching barn. A few songs ago Adam pointed through the unliving room window at the forest, and Phoebe knew what he wanted. She'd taken his hand and made the laborious process of helping him across the house and out the back door. Karen caught up with them just as they were going outside.

"Thanks, Karen," Phoebe said, pausing as Adam took another lumbering step toward the tree line. Phoebe bit her lower lip.

"It's too bad the new kids didn't want to come."

"Yeah," Phoebe said. "Cooper told me they were still a little nervous about being in crowds of zombies because of what happened at Dickinson House. The fire."

"The massacre, you mean," Karen said, then changed the subject. "Those boys that Thorny brought came to ask Tommy if he wanted to rejoin the football team. They meant it, too."

"Really?" Phoebe replied, swallowing. "Is he going to do it?"

"No," Karen said, "but I think it made him feel . . . good to hear it."

Adam took another step. Phoebe wanted to go back inside the house and tell Tommy that he should rejoin, that it would be good for him and for everyone who looked up to him. She didn't, though, because she had to be with Adam, especially now, especially because of where Adam clearly wanted to go. He took another step and she thought it was strange that the closer he got to his goal the faster he moved. She was frightened; she wasn't sure that she could bear going there, but she knew she had to.

"It's always nice to feel . . . wanted," Karen said.

"What is that supposed to mean?" Was she making some kind of obscure comment about Tommy? Or something else?

"Oh, nothing. Adam, honey," Karen said, "why do you want to see where you died?"

Phoebe's breath caught in her throat, and Adam turned to Karen.

"Don't answer that," she said, "I . . . know why. We can't help it, can we? But it isn't really a good thing. We . . . moved . . . out of my old house because that is where I . . . I died."

Phoebe's grip on Adam's cold hand was tight. She wondered if Karen was going to tell Adam what only she and

Margi knew, which was that Karen had committed suicide.

"When I came back, I . . . would go there . . . everyday. The upstairs . . . bathroom. I'd go and I'd stand next to . . . the tub. For hours. That's where . . . I died. My parents would come home and I'd still be . . . standing there, staring at . . . the tub. Sitting in it, sometimes."

Adam gave a slow blink. Karen sighed.

"It wasn't healthy," she said. "I'm glad we moved."

"Want to . . . see," Adam said.

Karen shook her head. "It really isn't a good idea."

"Maybe we should listen to her, Adam," Phoebe said, holding his arm and looking up at his face for some sign, some expression that told her what Adam wanted from a return to the spot where he breathed his last. "Maybe we should go back to the house, listen to some more . . ."

No," he said, without turning to look at her.

She was hurt, but she managed to keep it from her voice.

"Okay, Adam," she said. "We can go there if you want."

His arm twitched and slid out of hers. "A . . . lone."

She let go of his arm, shocked. She looked at him, wondering why he wouldn't look at her, wondering why he didn't want her with him. She started to protest, but it died on her lips when he finally turned toward her.

"Alone," he said again, and despite the lack of inflection in his monotone, she thought she detected a tone of gentleness there.

He stared at her, his face an unreadable mask.

"Okay," she said after a time. "I'll wait here."

He didn't speak as he began his slow progress toward the woods.

She felt the weight of Karen's arm around her shoulders as Adam's hulking form disappeared into the thick shadows.

"Don't worry, honey," Karen said, her voice a cool whisper against Phoebe's ear. "He'll be . . . fine. Nothing can . . . hurt him now."

Phoebe shook her head, her cheek brushing against the dead girl's.

"That isn't true," she said. "It isn't."

But even as she said it, she knew she was really talking about herself.

CHAPTER THIRTEEN

RIGHT LEG. LEFT LEG. Right hurt saw hurt Phoebe hurt bastard left leg. Right leg hurt Phoebe sad I'm sad too Phoebe is it guilt or is it more there never was more so it must be guilt. Stop. Sad Phoebe.

Stop. Ran down this path That Night. That Night ran and ran like wind ran Phoebe screamed ran saved Phoebe saved my love Phoebe shot shot dead run run left leg right leg run run.

Fall. Get up. Get up.

"How the mighty . . . have fallen," voice said. "Literally."

Get up.

Smiley. Get up. Right arm left arm push right leg push. Right and left arm right leg push.

"Let me . . . help you," said Tak. Tak Smiley.

Speak. Stop speak speak.

"Can't."

"Of course . . . I can," said Smiley

Smiley strong lift help no help haul up Smiley not smile. That Night Smiley found Pete Smiley stopped Pete I stopped Pete stopped Pete's bullet.

"It happened right . . . over there," said Smiley, Smiley pointing. "That . . . is where . . . you died."

Look. Look right leg left leg. Look blood gone leaves and dirt and blood blood gone blood seeped into earth life gone.

"We all . . . do it . . . some time," Smiley said. "Like swallows . . . to . . . Capistrano. Revisit . . . our . . . death."

Look. Look no blood blood in the earth seeped into soil Phoebe's tears seeped into skin dead skin. Phoebe held me she held me and she cried and she cried and I died. Gone gone where one door closing one door opening. Whose hand turned the knob?

"I died on the . . . Garden State . . . Parkway," Smiley said, "truck . . . sideswiped my bike. Broken neck."

Smiley look Smiley crack Smiley's head on shoulder head angle leaning on shoulder Smiley lift head crack crunch head back Smiley smiling.

"They hate us . . . you know," said Smiley. "The beating hearts. Hate."

Smiley lifts shirt Misfits shirt ribs look ribs actual ribs white white bones last cracked flesh gray gray skin hangs.

"They hate us because . . . we . . . remind them . . . of the . . . future."

Look. Look. Smiley lets shirt down Smiley lifts hand

spreads bones spread white bones Smiley dead dead like me like me dead.

"They hate us . . . and they will try . . . to destroy us," said Smiley. "Soon."

Hate not hate. Joe not hate STD not hate Johnny hate not Jimmy hate Phoebe Thorny Margi not hate Phoebe love Phoebe. Speak love speak speak.

"Love . . ."

Smiley laughed the dead can laugh can't laugh Smiley not Smiley dead.

"No," Smiley said, "not love. She . . . doesn't love. She . . . didn't love . . . him . . . and she doesn't . . . love you."

Right arm. Right arm right arm right arm. Miss. Smiley quick Smiley swift Smiley laugh.

"I know . . . it hurts. It hurts . . . being dead. The pain . . . gets worse."

Stop. Speak stop speak stop.

"It gets worse. It gets worse because you . . . start to feel. You start to . . . remember what it was like to . . . feel. Really feel. You can get . . . angry."

Smiley smiled.

"Like you . . . just did. You will feel . . . just a little. You will remember . . . feeling. And you will . . . hate . . . as they hate."

Not hate love not hate love Phoebe love.

"You will . . . hate . . . even her . . . because she will remind you . . . of the past."

Not hate Phoebe love not hate hate.

"There is no past. There is . . . no future," said Smiley, "there is only . . . the . . . endless present."

Smiley walk walk into darkness into forest no path straight into darkness right leg Smiley quick gone in darkness.

"When you are ready . . . to hate . . . I'll be waiting for you . . . in the present."

Gone. Not hate.

Not.

Hate.

CHAPTER FOURTEEN

"**D**ID YOU SEE the plastic surgeon yet?" his father asked from the opposite coast.

Pete sneered into his cell phone. He would rather his dad call up and say, "Does your face hurt? It's killing me," than have one more question about the plastic surgeon.

"No."

"Why not?"

"I just haven't wanted to."

Since his injury, Darren had called almost every other day to check to see if Pete had gotten the surgery. That was the most attention he'd paid Pete since abandoning him and his mother. Even the summers he spent at his dad's place didn't provide as much contact with his father as the scar did.

"You should get that fixed."

"Yeah." But if I got it fixed, you'd stop calling me, wouldn't you?

"Well," Darren said, "I've got a conference call in five

minutes I have to get ready for. How's the community service going?"

Darren never asked about the therapy; just the community service.

"Fine. I'm on my way to work off hours thirty-one through thirty-five," Pete replied. The sound of the admin assistant's voice on Darren's pager told Pete that his father had already mentally disconnected from their conversation.

"That's great," Darren said, with all the enthusiasm of a zombie. "Gotta run. Get your scar fixed."

"Yeah."

"Bye," Pete said, but his father had already hung up. He saw a zombie through the windshield of his car, a pasty-looking freak in a blue jean jacket.

"Was that your father?" Pete's mom asked from the drivers' seat. She hadn't let him drive since his arrest.

"Yes, it was Darren," he said.

"Oh. How is he?"

Pete didn't answer. Duke Davidson opened the front door to the facility as soon as his mother pulled in front of the building. Pete got out when she stopped and said good-bye over his shoulder.

"Ready for more custodial work?" Duke said, smiling thinly and waving to Pete's mother as she drove away. "I'm going to have you do the bathrooms today."

"Great," Pete said. He was looking behind him at the zombie, who seemed to be shambling down the hill toward the security fence. "I have to get my head shrunk first."

Duke laughed. "Don't stare."

"What?"

Duke handed Pete his security badge, which had a small unsmiling photograph of Pete on the right-hand side. "I said, 'Don't stare.' Angela wouldn't like it if she thought you were trying to intimidate the residents."

"Intimidate . . . ?"

"That's Cooper Wilson. He stays here now. He was one of the survivors of a zombie purge in Massachusetts a few months ago. Maybe you heard about it? The Dickinson House Massacre, they call it."

Pete shook his head. He noticed that Duke, who normally kept a brisk pace as he roamed the shiny halls, had slowed to talk to him.

"There's a girl who came from there. Melissa."

"That the one in the mask?"

Duke looked at him, grinning. "See, you do pay attention. She wears the mask because she was horribly disfigured in the fire."

"That's rough." Pete's hand drifted up to the stitching in his face.

"You ever catch up to the guy who did that to you?"

"What?"

Duke stopped, and Pete looked up at him, jerking his hand away from the stitching.

"Do you know who did it?"

"I know who did it."

Duke nodded. "There's some zombies in town," he said,

"they like pulling pranks. Petty vandalism, stuff like that. Some of them are into roadkill."

"Roadkill?"

"They chew on it. Disgusting, huh? But it's the pranks that will get them in trouble."

"I heard about a prank. Zombie recruitment posters, or something."

Duke nodded, his hands on his hips. "That's right. What do you think about that?"

Pete thought that it really pissed him off when he heard about it. Stavis called him up, acting like the posters were a big joke or something, but Pete didn't think it was funny at all. Thinking of Williams and his sick designs on Phoebe, he thought that the posters were too close to the truth—that the dead really were trying to recruit the living for their sick enterprise.

But he didn't know what Davidson was looking for from him, so all he did was shrug. Duke looked at him as though Pete didn't have to say anything, like Duke could see right through into his heart.

"Okay," Duke said, as though satisfied by whatever he saw there.

Pete felt Duke's stare the entire trip down to Angela's office.

CHAPTER FIFTEEN

"I'M GOING OUT, Adam," Mom said. "Do you want me to call Phoebe so you have some company?"

Speak.

"No."

"Okay," she said, "I'll be back in a couple hours."

Left leg. Right leg. Right arm. Through the window Mom looks scared looks relieved to be out can't blame her can't. Phoebe next door with homework with books with music with Phoebe miss Phoebe.

Phoebe.

Phoebe clings needs to live not cling needs to live can't live hurts. Can't live. Phoebe needs to forget forget me can't forget Phoebe needs to forget me. Tak Smiley is right. Forget.

Can't forget Phoebe said Phoebe become who you always were become. Can't become anything. Can't.

Dead.

"Hey, stupid."

Jimmy. Stupid Jimmy. Meet Takayuki Jimmy.

"There's someone here to see you, stupid," said Jimmy.

Right leg. Left leg. Right leg. Moving faster moving better was slug now snail soon be turtle. Hope. Left leg. Hope Phoebe hope not Phoebe Phoebe needs to live can't live with me.

"I'm out of here, stupid," said Jimmy. "Don't let the maggots catch you."

Jimmy out the door past visitor visitor not Phoebe.

Master Griffin.

"Your stepbrother is a rude individual," said Master Griffin. "Not centered at all."

Speak. Speak.

"Come . . . in."

"No," Master Griffin said, shaking gleaming bald head. "Let's go outside. It's almost warm today. I'm very sorry I haven't come sooner. I'm afraid I'm not very big on newspapers or the like, a side effect of being too long on foreign soil. One of the consequences of having a rich interior life is that you can sometimes lose connection with the outside world."

Smiles. "Which is why you need to come outside with me."

Speak. "Glad . . ."

"I'm glad to see you too, Adam. That's right, bend your knees a little more as we go down your steps."

"Can't . . ."

Master Griffin shook his head. "That word is to be stricken from your vocabulary, effective right now. Remember what Yoda said? 'Try not.' The word 'can't' has no place in your recovery. You can and you will. Time is all it will take."

Quoting Yoda? Can't. Can't speak. Speak. Can't.

Master Griffin's eyes narrow, tone serious.

"I know that it is difficult, and I know that your body is not obeying your instructions right now. But it would not obey your instructions when you first began to work with me, if memory serves. You could not do the Bow. You could not do the Crane. There were other forms that you had yet to master. This is no different."

Right leg. Left leg. Master Griffin's hand on my arm pressure is there pressure stars in the sky breeze can't feel no shoes can't feel cold ground beneath my no shoes feet can't feel.

"Good," said Master Griffin. "We are going to relearn the forms, and your body will begin to obey you. The body will remember. You will regain control through the discipline of practice. Do you remember your forms?"

Master Griffin moves moves like water arm rigid crosses body right arm right arm right Master Griffin bends knee drops shoulder arm down lift arm lift arm lift arm.

"Again," said Master Griffin.

Again, again said Master Griffin can't move didn't lift arm lift arm lift arm.

"Again," said Master Griffin.

Lift arm lift arm lift arm look Phoebe's light is on Phoebe books and music Phoebe's hair the memory of the smell of her hair lift arm.

"Good," said Master Griffin, "feel your focus return."

Lift arm. Lift arm move arm focus move arm. Arm, motionless.

"Excellent," said Master Griffin. "Focus. You are the only one that can do this."

Focus. Lift arm. Move arm bend knee bend knee drop fist. Lift arm.

Lift arm.

Lift arm!

Hand moves.

"Excellent." Said Master Griffin, smiling. "Again."

Lift arm.

"You know, I've missed you at the dojo."

Focus.

Lift arm.

CHAPTER SIXTEEN

S HE'D JUST SAT Adam down in the back of the van when she felt a light touch on her shoulder. She turned and saw that Tommy, who, driven by an old-world sense of chivalry, was normally the last one on.

"Hello, Phoebe," he said. "Adam."

Phoebe hesitated. Adam tried to wave in the cramped quarters. He got the arm motion right, but the wrist and fingers weren't really bending just yet. Progress is progress, she thought.

"Can I . . . talk to you?" Tommy said. "Alone?"

He motioned to the pair of seats behind the driver. Looking at Adam, she hoped he'd shake his head, or reach for her hand, but instead he nodded.

"Okay," she said, crouching as she slid into the seat before Tommy. He had to lean so the other students could climb in, and she was acutely aware of her pulse as he pressed against her. He was so solid and unyielding; his arm like a rock against her.

"I've been thinking about what you said . . . Phoebe," he said, shifting back as Kevin climbed aboard.

"Oh?" she replied, glancing over her shoulder as the rest of the class settled in their seats. Her skin was tingling from where Tommy had leaned against her. Karen had taken Phoebe's usual seat and was leaning against Adam, whispering something that brought a phantom smile to the corner of his mouth.

"I've thought . . . about a lot," Tommy said. "I want you . . . to know . . . I still have feelings . . . for you."

"Tommy," she warned, turning to face him as the van started up. "Let's not do this here, please?"

Thorny and Margi were complaining loudly about some experiment gone awry in their biology class. Colette's shrill laughter filled the vehicle.

"I'll be . . . brief," he said. He was whispering, at least. Even so, she couldn't help but risk a self-conscious glance over her shoulder. Karen was still talking to Adam, but he was looking right at her.

"I just wanted . . . to . . . thank you."

"To thank me?" She was conscious that he hadn't taken his eyes off her from the moment they sat down. If he was angered by her darting eyes he didn't show it.

"For trying," he said. "With me. It was . . . a . . . brave . . . thing to do."

"It wasn't an act of *charity*, Tommy," she said, anger raising her voice. "I was just as . . ."

She didn't get to complete her sentence, because Thorny shouted to Tommy from the last row of the van..

"Hey, Tommy!" he called. "What do you think, would

you let us dissect you for a differently biotic class?"

"Why . . . not?" he said, trying to smile. "Learn more than . . . with . . . a fetal . . . pig."

Phoebe looked away, out the window at the trees whose yellow and red leaves were muting to brown. Won't be long, she thought, before they started to fall. Last year there were storms in mid-October that knocked all the leaves down. She remembered raking them up into wet piles, sad that her favorite season had been compromised by the fickle New England winds.

Adam was looking at her. She wished she knew what he was thinking.

The van arrived at the same time as a sputtering compact car that followed them around the turning circle in front of the foundation. Phoebe could see Melissa riding along in the passenger seat, her coppery hair high enough to press against the car's roof. The girl turned toward the van. She had a different mask on today, still a blank white but this time with the corners of the mouth turned up in a slight smile.

The car pulled to a stop, and the driver got out of the still-running vehicle to trot around to help Melissa out. Phoebe could see that it was Father Fitzpatrick, the Catholic priest that had performed the funeral service for Evan Talbot. She would have liked to have said hello to him, but by the time she'd helped Adam out of the van, he was back in his car, speeding off. Must have some souls to save, Phoebe thought.

Melissa waved to her, holding the whiteboard in front of her like a shield.

"Hey, Melissa," she said, watching the girl hitch from side

to side as she walked to the doors. Father Fitzpatrick was late; usually Melissa was already in her seat by the time they arrived at the class. The girl walked with great difficulty; her left leg especially seemed unwilling to move at the appropriate pace or bend at the appropriate angle.

Adam took a shuffle-step forward, and Phoebe tried her best to steady his massive frame.

"Good job, Adam," she said.

He looked down at her, his expression unreadable.

Cooper Wilson, Alish, and Angela were already seated as the students went through the motions of retrieving assignments and notebooks, stowing gear, and, in the case of the few traditionally biotic ones, helping themselves to the refreshments from the back table. Angela spoke over the din.

"Cooper has asked for class time today," she said. "He'd like to tell everyone the story of the Dickinson House fire."

"I've been . . . waiting for a chance . . . to tell . . . this story," Cooper said, managing to look shy as he brushed a lock of gray-black hair out of his eyes, "to . . . people . . . who will actually . . . listen."

Melissa, her arm swathed in loose green fabric ending in a tight cuff at her slender wrist, raised her hand.

"Yes, Melissa?"

The girl wrote on her board with as much alacrity as she could muster.

MAY I B XCUSED?

"May I ask why?" Angela asked.

"Mel," Cooper said, "they've got . . . to . . . know. It's why

. . . we . . . came here." He was tall, rail-thin, and usually had a clownish half smile on his face, but Phoebe could see that his goofy demeanor masked a more serious nature. Melissa's presence in the room was very important to him.

Melissa shook her head, her hair bouncing as she erased and wrote.

"Mel . . ."

CANT.

Angela said that she could leave. "I understand, Melissa. I'm sure all your friends do too. You can do work in my office for now, if you'd like. I'll come get you at the break."

Melissa rose, with effort, and dragged her feet across the carpet and out the door. Cooper didn't look like he understood.

"She should . . . hear . . . this," he said to Angela.

"She isn't ready."

"What is she . . . scared of?" he said. "She's already . . . dead."

"Cooper," Angela said, her voice as close to reproach as it ever got.

"Okay . . . okay. Dickinson House," he said, and everyone was rapt. A few weeks prior Tommy had read a news article he'd found on the torching of Dickinson House, which was a sanctuary for the differently biotic, similar to St. Jude's mission, but secular. According to the article, the fire had destroyed seven zombies and taken the lives of two employees.

"The article that you . . . saw . . . was a bunch . . . of crap," Cooper began. "Almost nothing in it . . . was . . . right except . . . that . . . there was a fire.

"The body . . . count . . . for example," he said, "ten

zombies . . . burned to . . . a second death. No . . . trads . . . died. Amos Burke . . . was the alcoholic . . . janitor . . . and the only one . . . who talked . . . to the press."

"How did the fire start?" Tommy said.

"Oh . . . yeah," Cooper answered. "That was the other . . . thing in the article. . . that was right. There were . . . white vans."

Phoebe was a little shocked. She'd heard of the white vans so often without seeing any actual evidence of them that even she had begun to think that they were Tommy's personal conspiracy obsession, like the single gun theory or the alien autopsies at Roswell.

Cooper spoke to Tommy. "I know . . . people . . . think you are . . . nuts. Even zombies . . . I've seen them . . . call you a crank . . . on your own . . . Web site . . . but it is true."

If she expected Tommy to look smug or self-righteous, she was disappointed. He looked intent and serious, maybe a little sad. But Cooper was right, there were a number of surprised faces in the room, including, for a moment, Angela's.

"Tell us what you saw, Cooper," she said, covering well.

"I was in . . . the house," he said. "Because I didn't . . . feel . . . like dancing."

He must have noticed the looks of confusion. He closed his eyes and continued.

"There was a . . . dance. Miss . . . Mary . . . she was a volunteer . . . from the college . . . who spent . . . a lot . . . of time . . . with us . . . had arranged it. Miss Mary would bring . . . art supplies . . . puppets . . . and scripts from . . . plays. She was always . . . trying to get us . . . to have 'fun.' Her idea of fun, anyhow."

The voice was a dead one, but Phoebe could hear a note of sadness there.

"She brought . . . a radio . . . and CDs and hung . . . ribbons . . . in the barn. The other . . . employees . . . did not . . . like her. Or . . . us. We were there . . . to work. On the . . . farm.

"I . . . wasn't going . . . to dance. But Melissa . . . came to . . . the zombie . . . room . . . and . . . asked me. Told her . . . I'd think . . . about it.

"I read . . . a comic book. Batman. Then . . . went . . . upstairs. Saw the vans. Two vans, white. Four men . . . the men . . . wore sunglasses and white suits . . . Tyvek suits. Two had shotguns like . . . Burke . . . said. I saw them shoot . . . inside the barn. The others had . . . Super . . . Soakers . . . not . . . flamethrowers."

"Super Soakers?" Thorny said.

Cooper nodded. "Filled with . . . gasoline. They sprayed . . . inside . . . the barn . . . I couldn't see . . . inside . . . where I was but . . . Miss Mary . . . came out. She was . . . screaming. Covered in . . . gasoline. One of the men said . . . she should . . . shut up . . . unless she . . . wanted to . . . burn . . . with the dead."

"She wasn't mentioned in the article," Tommy said.

"Conspiracy," Cooper said, something like a rueful smile on his face. "The other . . . employees . . . had . . . mysteriously . . . vanished. One of the . . . men . . . punched her . . . in the stomach and . . . threw her down. Then his . . . friend . . . threw . . . the bottle . . . with the rag . . . in it. It went up . . . so quickly."

"So it was the . . . barn . . . not the house?" Tommy asked.

"The house . . . is still there," Cooper answered. "Free of . . . zombies."

"What happened then?"

"The killers . . . watched. The flames . . . threw . . . shadows . . . across the lawn and I heard . . . silence. Nothing but the . . . roar and . . . rush . . . of the fire. My . . . friends . . . didn't scream"

He looked at the floor, his eyes unfocused, as though he was staring at the ashes of his friends. "Later . . . there were . . . sirens. The men . . . got in . . . their vans."

"How did . . . Melissa . . . escape?" Tommy asked, his voice low, almost a growl.

Cooper looked at him a moment, and Phoebe felt like something electrical was passing in the air between them as he answered Tommy's question.

"She . . . didn't."

No wonder the poor thing couldn't stay, Phoebe thought. She felt her fingernails biting into the skin of her palms.

"Miss Mary . . . got up.. The flames . . . were covering the . . . barn like . . . a coat of paint. A part of . . . the roof . . . gave way. She . . . ran in . . . used her jacket . . . on Melissa. I helped . . . drag them out. None of . . . the . . . others . . . made . . . it."

"What did the police . . . do?" Tommy asked.

"They took . . . a statement . . . from . . . Miss Mary. And from . . . Burke . . . who was . . . passed out . . . in the . . . supply room."

Thorny was incredulous. "They didn't talk to you?"

Cooper shook his head. "One of the firemen said . . . 'they missed . . . one.'"

"How did you get . . . to the foundation?"

"Miss Mary . . . drove us. She was . . . afraid . . . they would try . . . to kill us . . . again. She was . . . arrested . . . for helping us."

"Really? For helping you?" Phoebe could almost see the wheels spinning in Tommy's mind; Cooper's story was hitting him on a number of levels, all of which he would be compelled to write about and act upon. Maybe it was hearing the story firsthand and not through the filter of a computer screen that made a deeper impact. That and seeing the evidence of the atrocity—Melissa—with his own eyes.

"The owners . . . of the farm . . . claimed we were . . . their property. An . . . asset."

"Because you worked there?"

"Because they . . . housed us," he said, looking at his hands. "I don't even know . . . if my friends . . . tried to get away. Or if . . . they let the gasoline . . . and then the flames . . . hit them. I don't know . . . if they tried."

He didn't take his eyes off Tommy as he spoke. "Melissa was almost . . . happy . . . before they came. All they wanted . . . was to dance. That's . . . all."

Angela suggested that they take a break after a moment of silence. Tommy volunteered to go get Melissa. When they returned ten minutes later, Tommy was guiding her gently by the elbow. Angela spurred on a discussion about an article that had appeared in *Time* magazine about Slydellco and Aftermath, trying gamely to steer the class in a more upbeat direction, which worked for a little while until Tommy pointed out that the magazine had given equal time to Reverand Nathan

Mathers. Melissa sat quietly throughout their discussion without making a single mark on her whiteboard.

There was less than a half hour to go when Angela brought the class to a halt.

"Tommy," she said, her voice soft, "don't you think you should make your announcement before the end of our session?"

Tommy looked up at her and Alish, as surprised as the dead could look.

"I am . . . leaving . . . the class," he said.

There was a moment of protracted silence in the room, like that after a prayer at a funeral.

"Mr. Williams," Alish said, leaning forward on his cane and clearing his throat "has stated his intention to pursue his studies elsewhere." He smiled, in what Phoebe thought was supposed to be a reassuring manner. "Fieldwork, if you will."

"I'm leaving school," he said. "Dropping . . . out."

Thorny was the first student to speak. "Aw, man," was all he said. "Dude," Cooper said, "I am . . . bummed. I . . . am a . . . big . . . fan. I read . . . My So-Called . . . Undeath . . . every . . . day . . . even before . . . we came here."

"I'm really sorry," Tommy said. Phoebe was aware of her own breathing, how fast it had become. "I . . . really am. I will . . . keep writing . . . though."

Kevin was looking at the floor, which is as close as his dead face could come to crestfallen. Margi and Colette watched Phoebe, afraid she was going to freak, but she remained calm.

Karen was another matter.

"Tommy," Karen said, an edge to her voice. "I'm mad at you."

He tilted his head in response.

"I . . . am . . . very . . . mad at you," she went on. "Very. Don't you think . . . you should have . . . discussed this with us?"

Tommy's lip curled up in a fair approximation of sarcasm.

"It's my . . . life," he said.

"It is . . . a lot more . . . than that . . . and you . . . know it," she said.

"Karen, maybe this isn't the best time to discuss this," Angela said.

Karen's eyes flashed as though there were a flurry of hot responses blazing up inside her.

"May I be excused?" Karen asked. "May I go . . . to . . . to the bathroom?"

Angela sighed and gave her permission to go.

Phoebe watched her short blue skirt waving like a flag as she hurried away. Margi raised her hand.

"Can I . . . ?"

"By all means," Angela said, fluttering her hands in frustration. "Maybe the rest of you would like to start discussing how differently biotic people are represented by the entertainment industry today. Would that be okay?"

There were a few nods. Phoebe watched as Alish made his way over to a wide square table that the students used to complete written assignments. He sat in one of the padded rolling chairs, leaning his cane against the table, and tapping his smooth chin with one long and wrinkled finger.

CHAPTER SEVENTEEN

"SIT . . . BY . . . MY . . . SELF," Adam said, just before he preceded Phoebe on the bus.

As slow as his words were, it took them a moment to register.

"Oh," Phoebe said. "Oh. I'll just sit over here, across . . ."

"No," Adam said. She realized he was trying to point. "Sit . . . with . . . friends."

Phoebe looked at his pale gray face, searching for the meaning that he used to be able to convey with the slightest movement of his eye or mouth. Now he was an enigma, as unreadable to her as an ancient Aramaic scroll.

"Oh," she said, knowing that he could still read her feelings and there was nothing she could do to hide them. Was he mad at her for talking to Tommy? Is that why he wanted her to go away? His stare was impassive and cold, and she couldn't help but shrink from the blankness of it. She let go of his arm.

"Okay, then," she said. "I'll catch up with you later."

She turned and walked toward the back where the Weird Sisters held court, their voices audible over the dull rumble of the bus engine.

Margi and Colette were in the last seats of the bus, and Margi stepped out of her seat to let Phoebe slide in. Margi was already into full monologue, so if she noticed that Phoebe and Adam weren't together she didn't say anything.

"I am *so* glad to be out of the lab," Margi said, her hands a blur of motion as she went on. Colette winked at Phoebe, her mascara'd eyelid dropping and raising lazily, at half speed. "I just thought that was the creepiest thing in the world. Sorry, Colette, but it was. Batty old Alish sticking you guys with pins like you were life-size voodoo dolls or something, that was totally nasty. Totally nasty. Not that the letters are much better. Hell this and hell that, monster this and evil that. Can you believe some freaky mortician is *marketing* to the foundation? Every week we get an e-nouncement where he sends us pictures of all the coffins he has on sale. Phoebe, why didn't you warn me about stuff like that?"

Phoebe shrugged, her gaze drifting outside as the bus rolled to a stop in front of the Oakvale mobile home park, where Tommy usually waited for it.

"Probably . . . could not . . . get a word . . . in . . . edgewise," Colette said.

"Har-de-har," Margi said, "you are such the little comedienne. She should have said something, though. I haven't read that much profanity since I had to use the bathroom at El and Gee club when we went to see the Shadowy Organization last month."

Phoebe listened to Margi laugh and Colette pretend to laugh. She forced herself to smile, but she wasn't quick enough. Margi looped her metal-sheathed arm around her shoulders.

"Aw, what is it, Pheebes? Are you still upset about Tommy?"

"I am not upset about Tommy."

"Is it because he's leaving? Or because you still have feelings for him?"

"I am *not* upset about Tommy!"

"Okay, okay," Margi said, squeezing her tighter. "Jeez, sorry I mentioned it. Bite my head off."

"I didn't bite your head off," she said, knowing that she did. Margi was right on both accounts.

Margi looked at her, pink lips wrinkling. "Clearly, I have erred. There is obviously nothing bothering you, so let's just move on, shall we?"

"I'd appreciate it."

"Good."

"Because it isn't like it's my fault or anything," she said, but her hands were shaking in the frilly sleeves of her blouse.

"That's right. We all agree that it wasn't your fault. Don't we, C.B.?"

Colette was also wearing her hair spiked lately, but no matter how much product she and Margi put into it, the lank strands wouldn't stand up like they did on Margi's head. Margi's spikes swayed, Colette's gave a limp bounce.

"We . . . agree."

"Good," Margi said. "See? We agree. What exactly are we agreeing on?"

Phoebe blew the bangs out of her eyes with a huffy breath. "That it isn't my fault. Tommy leaving."

"Ah. No. No, that definitely isn't your fault. You breaking up with someone is not to say you are responsible for them going on a zombie vision quest."

"A zombie vision quest?" Phoebe said. "So you *do* think I'm responsible."

"Didn't I just say the opposite?" Margi looked out the window, then she asked, "Are you and Adam fighting?"

"Why? Just because I'm not sitting with him you think we're fighting? Am I such a terrible monster that you think I just go around picking fights with people?"

"You mean like you're doing now?" Margi said, poking her in the ribs as though trying to puncture Phoebe's cloud of gloom. "No. It's just when you turned away from him, he reached for you, like there was something else he wanted to say. But he was too slow, and you kept moving."

Phoebe looked at her friend. "He reached for me?"

"Yeah," Margi said, "like he was afraid you were upset or something. It's so hard to tell what he's thinking now, he just hasn't got the 'expression' thing or the 'inflection' thing down yet. What do you think he was doing, C.B.? Can you give us a little help with the zombie-to-English translation?"

Colette tried on a smile. "I think . . . he was . . . going Romero."

Phoebe, being a great fan of *Night of the Living Dead* and all of George Romaro's movies, couldn't help but smile even though she knew what was coming.

"You mean he was reaching for her brains?"

"Yes," Colette said, "delicious . . . brains."

Margi giggled.

"There's a flaw in your thinking, C.B. Even Adam is smart enough to know Pheebes doesn't have any."

The Weird Sisters cackled.

"You guys really need to take this act on the road," Phoebe said, but was suddenly serious again. Margi and Colette caught the vibe as well.

"Like Tommy," she continued, leaning her head against Margi's shoulder.

"Aw, Pheebes," Margi said, kissing the top of her head. "He's coming back, right? This is probably just something he needs to get out of his system."

"I don't know." She thought about how solid he'd felt leaning against her. Tommy wasn't one to change his mind easily.

"I think so," Margi said. "I heard him talking to the Hunters. It sounded to me like he was coming back."

"What was he talking to the Hunters for?" Phoebe asked, sitting up.

"I was working a shift in the office and they were talking to him about the Web site, and how important it was for it to continue. They said that the foundation would pay for the site and for the hosting. Tommy said that was cool, but that he wouldn't let Skip Slydell put banner ads for Z on it."

"You're kidding."

"No, really," Margi said, "they said Slydell wanted to do . . ."

"No," Phoebe said, "I meant about the foundation funding it."

"For real. They said that the site was critically important

for the survival and advancement of zombie rights and culture. I remember because I thought it was weird that they said 'survival.'" She thought for a moment. "They didn't say 'zombie,' though. 'Differently biotic.'"

"That is really weird. What did Tommy say?"

"He said he would still write for the blog, but that he couldn't manage the site anymore. He said if the Hunters could ensure that the people he chose to run the site for him got paid for their work, he would consider letting them fund it."

"Wow," Phoebe said. She had so much going through her head just then it was difficult to focus on one thing. She wasn't so certain it was a great idea to give the foundation or Slydellco access to mysocalledundeath.

"I know," Margi said. "Pretty cool, huh? I guess that would make Tommy the first zombie entrepreneur."

Colette shrugged one shoulder as though to say "imagine that."

"He said he was coming back, though?" Phoebe said.

Margi gave her a quizzical look. "Not exactly. Not in so many words. It was sort of implied."

The bus rolled to a stop at the curb, and the students, some of the living as sluggish as the dead with morning fatigue, began piling out of the bus. Phoebe watched Adam rise from his seat and shoulder his way into the line. He didn't look back. She slipped past Margi with the intention of talking to him before he entered the school. She caught up to him on the second short flight of steps.

"Hi," she said, taking his arm.

"Hell-o," he replied without breaking ponderous stride.

"I haven't seen you in *forever*?" she said. "I missed you."

She was pleased to see the corner of his mouth twitch upward.

"Phoebe," he said.

"I know," she said, "I'm clingy. I'm hovering. I'm altogether a huge pain in the butt."

"No," he said, almost managing to shake his head. He was walking, talking, and trying to shake his head at the same time. This was good, she thought. This was very very good.

"No?" she said, giving him a gentle nudge. "No? Don't tell me we're going back to the old days where you were afraid your friends were going to see you with me. I don't know if I could take that."

They reached the doors, and she sprang ahead to open them for him.

"No," he said.

"Thank goodness. You just want a little space, is that it?"

He stopped, and Phoebe could see a whole flock of emotions lying below the dead skin of his face. He opened his mouth and she thought he was going to say yes, and then she thought he was going to say no, and then she had no idea what he was going to say at all. He reached out a hand as heavy as a ten-pound weight, and clamped it on her shoulder.

"Phoebe," he said, the effort appearing painful. "Live."

He released her, staring down with glassy, lifeless eyes.

She thought that was his way of pushing her away, but then he held out the same hand for her to take. She walked him to his locker, holding his hand on the dial of the combination lock so he could feel the movement of her fingers.

CHAPTER EIGHTEEN

ANTED TO TEACH her, not Joe teach her.

"Let up on the brakes, kid," said the STD not the STD Joe. "You don't want to hit the brakes when you're going into a curve. If anything you want to give it a little gas."

"I feel like I'm going too fast, Mr. Garrity," said Phoebe. Phoebe's eyes in the rearview mirror look scared but excited too.

"Nah. You're fine."

"Phoebe live," said to Phoebe not sure Phoebe understood. Don't understand. Joe the stepfather formerly known as the STD teaching Phoebe to drive now that's living. Now that's entertainment.

"I can't believe my dad is letting me do this," said Phoebe.

Joe laughed. "I just told him I had plenty of cars, so it wouldn't matter if you crashed one. And if you did I could fix it."

"He's so uptight when he tries to teach me," she said.

"Stop sign coming up. That's it. Ease on it. Good."

Good. Phoebe driving good, Joe acting good. Franken-Adam moving not good not good but better. Better. Turtle. Turtle not snail.

Dojo ahead. Phoebe parks like FrankenAdam gets into the car; slow, sloppy, and with sixteen-point turn. Gives up, parks at entrance.

"Thank you, Mr. Garrity," said Phoebe, handing keys.

"Least I could do," said Joe. Said Joe warmly. Actual warmth. Joe human. Adam not.

"Let . . . me . . . out,"

Phoebe laughed. Phoebe laughed like music, Phoebe live. Live.

"Come on, Adam," Phoebe said, "I wasn't that bad."

Speak. Speak.

"Yeah, son," said Joe. So weird name son. "She's doing all right."

Speak.

"Life . . . flashed."

Phoebe laughs hugs FrankenAdam, Phoebe lives. Her black hair perfect shiny black hair underneath my nose lungs breathe breathe breathe maybe flowers. Maybe. Miss flowers.

"Thanks for the vote of confidence, Adam," said Phoebe, laughing. "That helps."

"See you in forty-five," said Joe, waves. Phoebe waves. Wave.

Walking. Walking with hitch but walking. Phoebe skips

ahead, holds door. Hold door, one week. No, one day. Tomorrow at school.

"Adam," said Master Griffin, bowing. Bald head shining, beacon. Bow. Bowing.

"And you are Phoebe Kendall."

"Yes," said Phoebe, looking at walls. Photos of Griffin in ghi, in tournament, in Gulf. Had hair. Photos of Griffin kicking ass.

"Would you like to work out today as well, Phoebe?" said Master Griffin. "First trial session is free."

Smiles. "I'm not really dressed for it."

Phoebe in black. Boots and all. Phoebe is back in skirts and ruffles and frilly lacey cuffs. Filled with life.

"You can borrow a ghi," Master Griffin said, "no shoes required."

"Maybe next time," said Phoebe. "I'll just watch if that's okay."

Griffin nods, light reflecting off bald dome head. Turns, bows to the dojo. Walk. Bow.

"We will do the basic forms again, Adam," said Master Griffin. "Please do not be shy in front of your audience."

"No."

"Maintain your focus," he said.

Nod.

Move. Moving.

See Phoebe, in mirror. Phoebe happy and sad. Both.

Moving.

Phoebe loves. Love Phoebe.

"That's it, Adam," Griffin says, "Focus. Try to feel your body as it moves."

Phoebe loves, but doesn't *love*. Loves Tommy?

"Focus."

Live, Phoebe. Forget. Just forget the dead and live. Forget, Phoebe. Phoebe, forget.

"Again."

Forget Phoebe. Try.

"Ha . . . iiiiii,"

"Good," said Master Griffin.

CHAPTER NINETEEN

"Y OU'RE DOING really well," Phoebe told Adam. He walked to the refrigerator, opened it, then withdrew the creamer, which he set on the table in front of her. "I can't believe how mobile you're getting. It was so much fun watching you."

He half smiled at her, then slumped into his chair with enough force to bump into the table and spill her coffee, sending beige liquid onto the plastic tablecloth.

"Oops," she said, and he smiled instead of getting frustrated like he would have a few weeks ago.

He'd made the coffee almost entirely himself, needing her help only to spoon enough of the grounds into the filter. He poured the water and added the sugar after getting her a mug from the cabinet.

"It's good," she said after taking a sip. "Master Griffin has really helped you."

Adam nodded. "More . . . focused . . . already"

"He's an interesting guy," she said, taking another sip. The coffee was actually a little weak because Adam's hand shook when he poured the water. She set her cup down and got up. "How long was he in the military?"

"Five . . . years," Adam said. She went over and stood behind him. "He was . . . wounded."

She started kneading his shoulders, which felt like tractor tires beneath her hands. "I didn't know that."

"Just . . . told me," he said. "Shot . . . in the . . . leg."

"You'd never know," she said. His shoulders weren't budging, so she ran her fingers through his hair. It was dry and crackled under her fingertips. She scratched the back of his neck with her fingernails.

"He told . . . me . . . because . . . thought . . . would help . . . rehabilitation."

She leaned in close, so close that her mouth was near his ear.

"Something's helping," she whispered.

There was no reaction. She hadn't really expected one, but she'd been hoping.

Time to test Tommy's theory, she thought, and kissed Adam on the neck, just below and behind his ear, where a pulse would beat if he were alive.

It was like kissing a rock, she thought. Then she thought about how much Adam loved her. He loved her so much that he suffered in silence while she was dating Tommy.

He loved her so much that he *died* for her.

She kissed him again, lower on the neck, stifling a giggle as she thought about how she could help him with his "rehabilitation." Her hand rubbed his broad shoulders and she turned and slid into his lap, kissing him on the cheek. She felt his arm and it was like steel.

He turned toward her and she looked up at him, smiling, then kissing his cheek. It would be so much easier if he could just grab her and hold her and plant his mouth on hers. Maybe he couldn't now, she thought, but perhaps with proper encouragement, he would, soon.

"Phoebe . . ." he said, his voice a husky rumble.

He died for you, she reminded herself, lifting her lips to his open mouth. *First kiss.*

"Stop!" he said, his voice loud enough to rattle the dishes in their cabinets. His arm uncoiled like a spring as he tried to stand up, shrugging Phoebe out of his lap. She fell on the floor with a loud bump.

"Stop," he repeated, looking away.

Phoebe was stunned. She sat there on the floor in the Garrity's kitchen, looking at Adam, not knowing what to say.

"I thought," she said. "I thought you . . ."

Adam shook his head, unable to meet her eyes.

She stood up, got her bag from the corner of the kitchen, and went home, her cheeks burning.

CHAPTER TWENTY

"YOU WANT ME to go in with you?" Margi asked as she parked.

Phoebe shook her head and opened the car door. She still wasn't entirely comfortable with her friend's relative lack of driving experience.

"No thanks, Margi. I really appreciate this."

"No worries," she said, "I need the practice. Buzz my cell when you want me to get you, I'm only fifteen minutes away."

"Okay. Thanks."

She waved good-bye, wondering if she'd even be here if Adam hadn't dumped her. Literally.

Phoebe's heart was in her throat as she walked up the narrow steps, too afraid to knock on the door. She knocked anyway.

Faith answered a moment later. "Oh hello, Phoebe," she said, somehow managing to look and sound happy and sad at the same time. "Please come in."

"I wanted to talk to Tommy," Phoebe said, stepping into the mobile home. She was annoyed at the hint of apology in her voice. She had nothing to feel sorry for.

"Certainly," Faith said. Then she hugged her.

When Faith released her she stood back and Phoebe thought that she was on the verge of tears. Her sudden show of emotion made Phoebe feel like crying too.

Faith brushed at the corner of an eye. "He's in his room. Karen's already there."

"Karen?" she said, an unexpected jealous flash bringing warmth to her skin.

Faith nodded. "Trying to talk my son out of his quest, or something," she said. Her next smile brought real warmth to her worry-lined face. "But you know Tommy's mind can't be changed once it's made up about something."

Phoebe smiled. She knew. His singularity of purpose was one of the things she most admired about him.

"Sometimes I think what makes these kids come back from the dead is just plain stubbornness," Faith said, laughing. "Do you want something to drink?"

"No thanks." She could hear Karen's voice from down the hall.

"Well," Faith said, getting out the milk and a bottle of chocolate syrup for herself, "if you change your mind, help yourself."

Phoebe said she would and walked through the living room to Tommy's room. Karen was standing by Tommy's desk, her hands waving, telling Tommy that he was wrong. A hot spike of anger bloomed inside her as she watched Karen berating Tommy, who sat in passive stillness on the edge of his bed. Despite the harshness of Karen's delivery, Phoebe felt as if she was intruding on a moment of deep intimacy between them, and almost stepped away. Before she could, Tommy saw her in the doorway and the blue of his eyes seemed to brighten. A moment later he willed himself to smile. Phoebe knocked lightly on the doorjamb.

Karen turned. "Phoebe," she said after a pause. "Thank heavens, another sane person in the room. Will you please help me talk some sense into him?"

"I don't think I could do that," Phoebe said. Tommy rose from his seat. He was wearing faded blue jeans, a dark blue T-shirt, and battered white high-tops. His room smelled like Z. Phoebe liked it.

Karen grunted in frustration and turned away.

"I was afraid you'd go without saying good-bye," Phoebe said, holding her left elbow in her right hand. Tommy looked at her, and she was having a difficult time looking back, not because he was dead, or because he could stare without blinking for hours at a time. She had trouble returning his stare because there was something there, something that wasn't longing exactly, but longing and love and sadness and understanding all wrapped together. No one ever looked at her with quite that combination of emotions. It was this look and the feelings it caused in her that first attracted her to him, but now she found herself wilting before the intensity of it.

"I . . . will never . . . say . . . good-bye . . . to you," he said.

Phoebe held out her hand. He took it.

"But I thought . . . you said . . . good-bye . . . to me."

Phoebe was aware of Karen taking a seat on the edge of Tommy's computer desk, her arms folded across her chest and a chagrinned expression on her flawless face. But Phoebe didn't care.

"I did," she said. "I did, Tommy, but . . . but I didn't want it to be forever."

Tommy looked away. "But you . . . don't know . . . what you . . . wanted it to be."

"No. No, I didn't. I don't."

He let her hand slip from his. "I don't know when I'll be back."

He looked sure of himself again, Phoebe thought. It was something that was missing in the weeks since Adam's death, that sense of purpose.

Phoebe bit her lip.

"I know," she said.

"You know?" Karen said. "You know? What is the . . . matter with you, Phoebe? He can't . . . leave. He's our . . . leader . . . for heaven's sake! King . . . Zombie. Baron . . . Samedi."

She took Tommy's arm, and Phoebe's. Her grip was cold but insistent.

"You can't . . . go, Tommy. I'm . . . sorry it didn't work out . . . between . . ."

Tommy raised his hand, cutting her off. "I have to go," he said.

"They all . . . look up to you, Tommy. They . . . *need* . . . you. They . . ."

Horrible choking sounds came somewhere deep within Karen. Her grip on Phoebe's arm tightened painfully.

"Karen," she said, reaching for her with her free arm as the other went numb in Karen's unbreakable grip. Karen's eyes looked pained and scared—lost, the lights behind the crystals fading. Phoebe ignored her own pain and stroked Karen's cheek.

"Shhhh," she said, and repeated it until Karen focused on her. She began to calm down, finally releasing Phoebe from her death grip.

"You . . . can't . . . go . . . Tommy," Karen said, her "breathing" ragged, the sound of a slow fan with a piece of paper caught in the blades. "I . . . they . . . need you."

Tommy took her face gently in his hands.

"Karen," he said, his voice a calming whisper, "that's why I need to go. Because you need me."

And Phoebe knew, watching him, that that was the truth. If he really was "Baron Samedi, King of the Zombies" as they all suspected, he wasn't going to be able to rule his kingdom from Oakvale, Connecticut. He'd have to go elsewhere— Washington, probably. Somewhere he could get government recognition for the undead. The guilt lifted from her shoulders. He wasn't leaving because of her.

Faith appeared in the doorway. "Is everything okay in here? Karen, honey, are you—"

"We're fine, Mom," Tommy said, still holding Karen, still looking at her as though he could pour his own strength into her simply by staring. "Thank you."

Faith looked at Phoebe for confirmation and received it.

"Okay, then," she said. "Can I get anyone anything?"

"We're fine, Mom. Really."

When she left, Karen sat on the edge of the bed. "I can't," she said. "I can't do it, Tommy. I'm not . . . you."

"You don't need to be," he said. "Just be . . . yourself."

She gave an ironic laugh. "Sure."

"They look up to . . . you," he said, "and the living too . . . more . . . than me."

Phoebe saw an odd expression cross Karen's face.

"For all the right reasons, I'm sure," she snapped, running both her hands through her long platinum hair, which seemed to frizz out in her distress. "What about . . . the Web site? How are you going to do the Web site?"

"I'm not," he said, a smile stretching one corner of his mouth. "You two are."

Karen looked at Phoebe and back again.

"What?" they said in unison.

He smiled. "You are. It will be part of your work-study credit at the foundation. They are going to . . . pay . . . for everything. The hosting, the fees. Advertising, even, so we can reach more of . . . our people. They are going to pay . . . you . . . for your work."

"Tommy," Phoebe said. "We can't do that. It's your site."

He shook his head. "That is . . . the problem. It needs to be . . . more than that. You are a . . . great writer, Phoebe. I think if . . . you . . . did a blog, it would be as helpful for . . . the dead . . . as it would be for the living."

Phoebe thought of the poems she'd written for him, and let

the full weight of the compliment settle upon her. Tommy used the moment to turn his attention to Karen.

"And you . . . could be too . . . Karen. If you bothered. You are one of the most . . . gifted . . . people I've ever known. In every . . . sense of the word."

"But mysocalledundeath, Tommy," Karen said, ignoring him. "You can't stop . . . doing that."

"I won't," he said. "The foundation bought me . . . a laptop. Wireless . . . Internet."

"Wow," Phoebe said. "What will you do for power?"

"Libraries, bookstores. Bus stations. Wherever I can find . . . an outlet. I'll e-mail the . . . road reports . . . to you . . . and you . . . can post them."

"So we are going to be your employees?" Karen said. "I've already . . . got . . . a job."

"This is . . . more fun . . . and it will get . . . you out of the lab. Or Davidson's . . . office."

"Well, that's pretty . . . cool," Karen said. "But . . . do you really think it is a good . . . idea for the foundation to fund this? And have access to all of your subscribers?"

Tommy sat on the bed next to Karen. "I . . . put a lot . . . of thought into that question," he said. "It is . . . a risk. But I think the benefit . . . of the risk . . . is great. I think with their . . . backing . . . we can really reach a lot of people. Traditionally biotic, too, especially with Phoebe . . . writing. The foundation has resources to get the site more . . . media . . . attention. We have an opportunity to make . . . our cause . . . a real youth movement."

"A youth movement," Karen said with a wry smile. "In this country, only the young die good."

"That's funny," Tommy said. "You come up with that one yourself?"

"Pretty clever, aren't . . . I?"

"Yes, Karen. You . . . are." Tommy said, and again Phoebe felt like an intruder.

As though he could sense this, Tommy turned toward her. "What do you . . . think, Phoebe? Will you help . . . us?"

I'll help you, Tommy, she thought. "You know I will. I joined the program so I could learn more about the differently biotic and how I could help."

They talked a little more after that, about what needed doing and how it could get done. Tommy spoke with unrehearsed passion about how good this project was going to be for the community of the dead. He was leaving in the morning.

She and Karen left into the chilly night air after hugs all around. Phoebe had on her puffy black coat with fake fur; Karen wore her usual uniform of short plaid skirt and white blouse. "I'm sorry I freaked out on you in there," she said.

"Oh." Phoebe was amazed at how her friend seemed to shimmer and glow in the moonlight. "I'm a little freaked out too."

"He's still totally in love with you." Karen said. "Adam too. You get all the good ones."

Karen wouldn't have believed that if she'd seen Phoebe flat on her butt in the Garrity's kitchen, she thought.

"No, I . . ."

"Shh. Denying it will only make me more jealous. You know it's true and it's okay. They aren't wrong to fall in love with you. I'm a little in love with you myself."

A reply caught in Phoebe's throat, and her cheeks went warm in the cool air. She wasn't sure if Karen was kidding— should she make a joke of it, or tell Karen not to worry, there was someone out there for her too and all that jazz? She hadn't told anyone what had happened between her and Adam. She wasn't at the point where she could talk about her relationships with anyone, because she felt so many conflicting things.

"Oh, I know what you're thinking," Karen said. "Someone's out there for me too. Don't worry, I've got plenty of them chasing me. Just not the right ones. Hey, looks like your ride is here."

Phoebe looked over at the entrance of the trailer park, where the headlights of Margi's mom's car swung a wide arc and cut through the darkness to illuminate the patch of dirt where Phoebe and Karen were talking.

"So, we partners on this?" Karen said, holding out her hand.

"Partners." Phoebe clasped it.

"You want a ride, Karen?" Phoebe asked as Margi gave the horn two quick beeps.

"No, thanks. It's a beautiful night and I promised Mal I'd go over and read to him for a little while. I want to say hey to Margi over there, though."

Phoebe thrust her hands into her pockets as Karen skipped over to the car, smiling as an old Echo and the Bunnymen tune from back in the day wafted out along with the heat that Margi kept on full blast whenever she drove.

How does she keep those patent leather shoes so shiny? Phoebe wondered, her hands seeking warmth in her pockets but finding only a scrap of paper. She withdrew it and saw that it was a carefully folded piece of lined notebook paper, the paper on which she had written her first poem for Tommy. He had written a note at the bottom of it, his words a squat and blocky blue print. He must have slipped her the note when they hugged good-bye.

HOLD ONTO THIS FOR ME, he wrote, I'M GOING TO WANT IT BACK SOMEDAY.

Margi and Karen were chattering away, and neither noticed as she folded the note back into a tight square and put it back into her pocket. She decided she was not going to be sad about this; Tommy was going out to make the world a better place for zombies everywhere, and she would be helping him to do it. Getting the note back only meant that he intended to return someday.

But I miss him already, she thought, getting into the sauna that was Margi's car.

"It's pretty late," Margi said after they said good-bye to Karen, who headed straight for the woods.

"It is," Phoebe agreed.

"So Karen was already over there, huh?"

"She was."

Margi sighed. "You aren't going to tell me what happened, are you?"

"I'm not," Phoebe said, "at least, not tonight." She knew

she'd tell Margi in time, but right now she felt too raw, with Adam rejecting her and Tommy going away. Margi, like Karen, was always joking about her many options—and now she had none. She just didn't want to talk about it,

Margi shook her head.

"Phoebe Kendall, Queen of the Mysterious Silences. Can you at least tell me if you and Tommy are okay? I mean, it kind of ended quickly between you two, and I know I was weird about it, but he is a really nice guy, and . . ."

"Yes," Phoebe said, the paper smooth and cool in her hand. "Yes, we're okay."

CHAPTER
TWENTY-ONE

PHOEBE, LIVING. Watched, waited. Margi came driving shock fear Margi driving! Margi and Phoebe left, gone who knows where. Live, Phoebe, live.

FrankenAdam trying. Walking. Talking. Opened door yesterday and this passes for thrills in realm of the undead. Turning a doorknob not so easy. Thinking. I'm thinking. Thinking more clearly, more quickly. Why?

"Are you okay, son?" said Big Joe. STD gone, Big Joe. Watching television, hockey. Like basketball Joe likes hockey we watch basketball. Don't mind. Joe on third beer. Brought him third beer walked opened door got beer closed door walked could not pop tab. Oh well. Next time.

"Okay." Dead but okay. Can do most of Master Griffin's forms. Can bow and raise.

"You seem awfully quiet tonight," he said.

Laugh! Laugh! Laugh!

Can't laugh. Yet. Turn. Look. Joe watching game, sipping beer. Intent. Comedy unintended. Speak.

"Okay."

Much later, knock on window. My window. Bedroom window. Drop book, get up.

Tommy.

Walk to the door. Kitchen door. Walk to the door on quiet feet. Tommy makes me feel stronger. What he accomplished. Braver.

Open door. Cold night, no coat. Don't feel it. Join Tommy in backyard. He's got a backpack, looks heavy. Moonlight. Feel smarter, faster around Tommy. Tommy or the night air.

"Adam," said Tommy. And then remember: Tommy is leaving.

"I'm leaving tonight," said Tommy. "I wanted to come to say good-bye. And to . . . thank you."

"Thank . . . you?" Speaking. A hitch but not a pause. A gap but not a chasm. Night air. Will miss Tommy. Will miss Tommy even though Phoebe is in love with him, not FrankenAdam.

Probably still be alive if never met him. Miss him, maybe. Maybe not.

Tommy nods. "For being my friend, Adam. For accepting me on the . . . football team. For standing up for me in the woods . . . twice."

Smile. "Phoebe."

Tommy smiles too. "Yeah, I know it was for Phoebe. Mostly. I know what she means to you."

Do you? Think about it. Do you know how much love have

for her and how much it hurts? Thinking this. Thinking that maybe he does.

"But I know it was for me too. I appreciate it. Which is why I feel . . . guilty . . . for the favor . . . I'm about to ask of you."

"Favor?" Can speak more quickly if just repeat the last thing everyone says. Tommy looks at Phoebe's house, the house where Phoebe is Living. Do you know the feeling, Tommy?

"A favor. I'm asking you . . . to watch out for them. Our friends. The . . . people . . . at the Haunted House. The kids in the class. Watch out for them for me."

"Real . . . useful." When alive and "watching out" for people managed to get clobbered with a baseball bat and then next time managed to get killed. Unqualified when alive. Now? Have trouble getting in and out of a car and wants to "watch over" people? Maybe not so smart.

"You are really useful, Adam," he said. "You've got a strength to you . . . not just physical. You do what's right. You could really . . . help people."

Waited. Wait a lot now.

"What I'm really asking, Adam . . . I'm asking you to step up. It's not just because I'm . . . leaving. The dead kids . . . need strength. You have it. Step up and let them see it."

"Trying."

"I know you're trying," he says. "Sometimes trying is enough, and sometimes it isn't. You need to step up."

Want to argue. Throw a punch even. Sort of. Don't.

He's right.

"You can do it, Adam," he said. "I know you can do it. But

more . . . important . . . we need you to do it. Things are going to get . . . rougher . . . for our people, Adam."

Saw something in his eyes that scared me, scary as the thought of Phoebe living her life without me. Reminded of Smiley.

"We won't be able to . . . live . . . at the fringe much longer. They won't let us."

"They?" Doing it again. FrankenAdam.

"The trads," he said. "The 'beating hearts.' But also our own people, Adam. Most don't want to stay in the shadows forever, and the others want to see shadows covering everyone."

"Tak." Thinking out loud. Thinking, like the brain energy or whatever making body bend its knees or swing its arms was freed up, free to think higher thoughts and larger concepts. Saw that Tommy agreed.

"Yes, Takayuki," he said, "and he isn't alone."

"I'll step."

"I know you will, Adam. She'll need you to. We all will." He clasped my shoulder.

Shook hands, wished him well on his travels. Watched him walk down the road until the moonlight didn't touch him anymore. When he was gone thought of Phoebe looked up at her window hoped her bed was warm and her dreams untroubled and was thankful very thankful that she was alive. That she was living. Thankful gave my life for her and that despite all the heartache and frustration would do it again in a heartbeat if had a heartbeat to give. Even if she loved but didn't *love* me.

Worked out practiced forms until the sun came up, until red fingers of light reached over frost-covered skin.

CHAPTER
TWENTY-TWO

"SO," PETE SAID, "do you have a big holiday planned?"

Davidson didn't look up from his magazine. He'd brought in a large stack, which he'd been reading in silence the entire three hours that Pete had been watching the bank of monitors continue to reveal nothing.

"Holiday?" Davidson said, turning a page. *Time, Newsweek, Psychology Today*—Davidson was a magazine-reading fiend.

"Yeah. Thanksgiving, in a couple days."

Davidson looked up, his pale blue eyes empty of expression. "Oh," he said, "I'm working."

"That sucks," Pete said. "Will your family send over some leftovers, at least?"

He didn't know why he was bothering; talking with Davidson was like talking to a tree stump. But the boredom of staring at the monitors had grown to soul-crushing proportions; the only movement of the whole day was the geek zombie from the dormitory taking a short walk from his room outside. Pete had watched him walk twenty paces toward the fence, stop, walk ten paces to his left, stop, and then walk back to the dorm. This took the geek twenty minutes.

"I don't have a family," Davidson said. Pete wondered if he was just pretending to read, because his eyes didn't seem to move at all while the magazines were in front of him.

"That sucks." Pete said. "I feel that way too."

He didn't know why he was running his mouth, anyhow. Davidson didn't give a rat's heinie about his personal problems, and Pete wasn't used to sharing. Thanksgiving at Casa de Wimp was a theater of pain to him; the Wimp had his parents over—they showed their gratitude for his mother's efforts in the kitchen by criticizing every little thing, right down to the way she'd organized the pickle tray.

"You have a difficult home life," Davidson said. Pete couldn't tell if it was a statement or a question.

"Not difficult," Pete replied. "I just hate it."

"Your mother? Your stepfather?"

"My mother's second husband," Pete said, aware of how churlish he sounded.

"Why don't you like them?"

Pete wanted to tell him to forget it, to just read his stupid magazines. "They're weak," he said.

Davidson flipped another page.

"He's the biggest wuss on the planet. An accountant that wouldn't ask for his money back if he found rat turds in his dinner at a restaurant. And she's weak for being with a loser like him."

"And you're strong."

Again, Pete couldn't tell if it was a statement or a question, nor could he tell if Davidson was mocking him.

"Strong enough," he said.

Davidson looked up again.

"Strong enough to go mop the lab," Duke said.

Pete wheeled the mop bucket down to the lab, gaining access to the room via the keycard that hung on a clip from his uniform shirt. The keycard had his name and a mug shot.

The lab was full of odd sounds, random blips, and tones from a host of indecipherable computerized machines that were conducting experiments while the experimenters themselves were at home baking pumpkin pie. Pete wondered briefly what Thanksgiving was like at the Hunter home. Did pretty little Angela make a big bird for her scarecrow of a father? Did they invite a bunch of dead friends over for a gnaw on a turkey leg? Did she sit around psychoanalyzing everyone at the table?

What a fraud, Pete thought as he wrung out his mop and started in the far corner of the lab. He hip-checked a table on which a machine that looked sort of like a coffeemaker was humming, a beaker of greenish liquid cooking or electrolyzing or whatever behind a glass door. He hoped the jostle ruined whatever mad science Alish was trying to conduct, just as he hoped tripling the amount of bleach he normally used on the floor would cause some of the findings to go awry.

When he really thought about it, none of this stuff made any sense to him. The lab wasn't climate controlled—Pete knew from experience that it was normally much warmer; today the lab would seem cold if he weren't moving around. He thought that if it was really a scientific lab, people would be here in masks and hairnets and clear plastic gloves and all that, instead of just the too-big stained lab coats that the scarecrow gave to everyone. It didn't make sense.

He mopped a section, then went to work on one of the stainless-steel tables, using a laundered white cloth and some spray cleaner from a bottle he hooked on the edge of his bucket. He spritzed the table in three places, then aimed a forth spritz at a rack of open test tubes before making lazy circles on the table with his less than clean cloth.

"Take it your father didn't call," Davidson said from the doorway.

Pete grunted with surprise, wondering if Davidson was onto his little acts of scientific vandalism. The baleful eyes revealed nothing.

"Isn't anyone worried about these cleaning products affecting the experiments?" Pete asked, ignoring Davidson's question/statement. Of course Darren hadn't called. All Darren called about was to see if Pete had gotten his scar fixed yet, and Pete was pretty sure he'd even lost interest in that.

"I don't think you could ruin any of the experiments if you tried," Davidson said, the ghost of a smile on his bloodless lips. "None of the real experiments are done here."

Pete leaned his mop against the wringer. "What are you talking about?" he asked. "I've seen the . . . I've seen Alish take blood or whatever it is from the zom . . . from the living-impaired kids."

"Would people know that you're a murderer just by looking at you?"

"What?"

"Or would they have to talk to you a little? Watch you. See the look on your face when a zombie walks into your field of vision, like the look on your face when Cooper takes his pointless stroll? I wish I could hold a mirror up to you every time you see our resident zombie leave his room on the monitors."

"What the hell are you talking about?" Pete said. His palms were sweaty, his mouth dry. His heart was racing and the lab equipment chirped like a field of crickets on a hot day late in the summer.

"Sometimes you have to peel the skin back," Davidson said, and now he really was smiling. "Sometimes you have to go beneath the surface. Sometimes you have to dig."

Pete opened his mouth and then closed it. The look on Davidson's face was like the look on the half-faced zombie just before he'd cut him. It was a look that held nothing, not hatred, not anger, nothing.

"I'm not sure what we're talking about right now."

"You will," Davidson said. "Keep the cleaning chemicals out of the experiments. We wouldn't want you accidentally discovering anything."

He left, leaving the sliding lab door open behind him. Pete heard the arrival of the Undead Studies students down the hall; Pinky's voice was shrill enough to grind steel.

Pete didn't realize he was shaking until he took hold of his mop again.

CHAPTER
TWENTY-THREE

"MS. HUNTER?" Margi said, "I really, *really* have a problem with Pete Martinsburg doing his community service here."

Phoebe stiffened on hearing his name, but Adam remained motionless on the seat beside her. Margi had pointed out Pete lurking in the shadow of one of the labs, leaning on his mop and looking at them as they entered the building. She'd wanted to take Adam's arm and rush him down the hall before he saw Pete, but she'd been too embarrassed after her smooth moves in the Garrity's kitchen to do much more than say hello to him when he climbed into the van.

"I can understand that," Angela said. "And I'm sure you're not the only one here who feels that way. The court thought that it was a good way to bring him face-to-face with the consequences of his actions."

"He threatened all of us," Phoebe said. "He said he

was going to hurt everyone on the Undead Studies list."

"He . . . killed Evan Talbott," Colette said. "And . . . Adam."

"We don't really know about Evan, Colette," Angela said.

"He *told* me he did it," Phoebe said. "When they asked me for a statement after Adam was murdered, I told the police. I told the prosecuting attorney. I told everybody who would listen, but they all said there was nothing anyone could do about it. There isn't a law to prevent someone from killing the dead. The attorney actually told me it might hurt their case against him for Adam's murder if she were to bring it up."

"He winked at me when he walked by the office," Margi said. "He's dangerous, Ms. Hunter."

Angela frowned and made a notation in her pad. "I'll try to see that he's kept away from the students."

"Is it true that he is getting counseling?" Margi said. "With you?"

"It is."

"What are you talking about with him?"

"I can't tell you that, Margi."

"Sure," Margi said, shifting her seat. "It wouldn't be proper for poor Pete's rights to be infringed on."

"Margi . . ."

"He killed Adam!" she said. "It doesn't feel safe to be in the same building as him! What about our rights? Why can't dangerous kids just be taken away from the rest of us?"

"I'll do what I can, Margi," she said. "I'll see to it that he only works and does his therapy here when you're all out of the building."

"How can you do that?" Phoebe said, wishing that Tommy was there to fight this. "Sylvia is still here in the building, isn't she? And Cooper, you're staying here too, aren't you?"

"I don't . . . know the guy," Cooper said. Beside him Melissa, her mask incongruous with the heavy weight of the conversation, began writing on her whiteboard.

"You didn't know those white van guys, either," Thorny said.

"Watch out for him. I think he would find you . . . guilty . . . by association," Karen said. "Angela, you know that this is a big part of the reason why Tayshawn refused to rejoin this class, don't you?"

"Because he was worried that Pete would be coming here?"

"He wasn't worried," Karen said. "He was furious. In his words, it was the biggest display of hypocrisy that he'd ever seen, an organization supposedly . . . created . . . to help the undead harboring someone who has sworn to destroy them . . ."

"We aren't *harboring* him. We're—"

". . . and has acted upon his promise."

Angela held her hand up. "I understand why you're all so upset. I really do. We agreed to assist with Martinsburg's sentencing because, frankly, we thought we were better qualified than anyone else. We also thought it would be an opportunity to really dig at the roots of the prejudice that all differently biotic people experience. If we can get him to articulate the reasons why he has so much hatred inside him, then maybe we can fight it. If we understand it, maybe we can find a way to help people, traditionally and differently biotic alike, to find common ground."

"So you think you can . . . reason with him?" Karen said.

Angela nodded. "We're hoping. I think we can learn something from people like Pete. I think at the very least we may be able to find ways to prevent others from becoming like him."

"Good . . . luck," Cooper said. "My experience . . . says . . . otherwise."

Phoebe thought of Tommy. Everyone in the class seemed out of sorts and lost without his leadership.

"Look," Angela said. "The way to deal with prejudice isn't to ignore it, or worse, to bury it under a rock. It's to deal with it head-on."

"Tayshawn would agree with you there," Karen said. "He would just have a . . . different . . . definition of 'head-on.'"

"Karen," Angela said, "I would like the chance to talk to Tayshawn. I'd really appreciate it if you would let him know."

Karen paused deliberately before answering. "I will."

"Thank you. Now . . . I'm sorry, Melissa. Did you have something to add?"

Melissa's arm was raised, and her comedy mask seemed nearly sinister beneath the coppery mane of her hair. When she nodded, her puffy green velvet sleeve drooped a few inches from her wrist, revealing patches of cracked, raw, curling skin that resembled the pages of a book thrown into a fire. She turned her board around.

ANGELA IS RIGHT, she'd written, WE ALL NEED 2 UNDERSTAND EA. OTHER

"Come . . . on . . . Melissa," Cooper said, leaning toward her. "You really . . . believe that . . . would work? You think the people that . . . burned . . . Dickinson House . . . can under-stand us? Or we understand . . . them?"

She rubbed the board clean and her marker squeaked as she wrote.

I'D ♥ 2 TRY

"Give me . . . a break."

I'D ♥ FOR THEM 2 C ME

"They'd be . . . glad, Mel!" Cooper said. "They'd . . . be glad! They wouldn't feel guilty . . . at all."

Phoebe watched Melissa drag the white cloth back and forth over the white board, erasing the heart, erasing her words. The room was silent as they all waited for her to write another line.

TOMMY WOULD AGREE WITH ME

"Good for . . . Tommy," he said. "Easy to do . . . when he isn't . . . here."

"Hey!" exclaimed Thorny, whose idolization of Tommy was only exceeded by his idolization of Adam.

"She's right," Phoebe said. "Tommy would meet the situa-tion directly. That's why he did things like join the football team and start the Web site. It's why he's going on this trip." She wondered if that was why he dated her, "He's going out to confront the world with his existence."

"You think he'd be okay with Pete Martinsburg working right down the hall?" Margi asked. It was one of the first ques-tions that anyone had posed today that sounded more like a question than a condemnation.

"I think he would, Gee," Phoebe answered.

"You're right. He *would*," Karen said. "He thinks that safety is an . . . illusion, anyway."

"Well . . . he got that one . . . right," Cooper said.

"There's only so much you can do to take precautions these days, I think," Phoebe said. "I know not everyone is going to accept the fact that I want to hang out with zombies. Some people just get so crazy . . . it's like there's so much pressure on everyone in our society, no matter what age you are. People break under that pressure. And when they break, they either give up or lash out. Until everyone is okay with the differently biotic, and I don't think that is going to happen for years, a generation, maybe, we're going to be dealing with violence."

"We're zombies, sweetie," Karen said. "Forget . . . differently biotic."

Phoebe shot her a look and would have thrown a pen if she'd had one handy.

"Great," Margi said, "the crazies will hate us, and safety is an illusion. That doesn't mean I have to go playing with rattlesnakes."

"I'll talk to Mr. Davidson," Angela said. "He'll keep Peter out of sight, if not out of mind. I'll understand if any of you are still uncomfortable with the situation and want to withdraw from the class. I'll see what I can do about getting you partial credit."

She was looking at Margi when she said it, and it was Margi's turn to shy away.

"Nobody's quitting," Thorny said.

"I wouldn't blame anyone if they wanted to withdraw,"

Angela said, as though he hadn't even spoken. "Margi and Cooper both have a point. The path we're on isn't without risks. "

"Nobody's quitting," Thorny repeated. Phoebe was about to say something when Adam's spoke.

"Want . . . to . . . kill . . . him," he said. His slow, uninflected voice lent an even greater degree of menace to the word "kill." The word cleaved through the conversation. Somehow as the debate about Pete went on, everyone had managed to forget that his victim was sitting right in the room with them, and that he might have an opinion on what should or should not be done with and for his murderer.

"But . . ." he said, and though it took him some time to finish his sentence, everyone waited without interrupting. Phoebe watched him struggle to form the words, and she was close enough to hear the raspy wheeze that preceded each sound as he tried to work his lungs to force air through his voice box. She wanted to hug him, but knew that to do so would be a betrayal, a public admission of his debilitated state. He was having a hard enough time forgiving her for the kindnesses she did show.

"Would . . . do . . . no . . . good," he said.

Phoebe allowed herself to smile. Because she was so proud of Adam, both because of the effort it took him to speak and because of what he was saying. More, she was smiling because Adam was choosing to follow Tommy, and not Takayuki.

"Tommy . . . is . . . right."

It was Adam's big moment, but again Phoebe found herself thinking of Tommy, and wishing he was with them.

CHAPTER
TWENTY-FOUR

ALISH WAS muttering to himself as he stared at the computer, where long chemical equations scrolled to the bottom of the screen. Thorny, looking like the bass player in an eighties synth band with the cuffs of his lab coat rolled up, sat on the edge of his desk, checking the time on his cell phone every few minutes. Colette sat in a chair, no doubt wondering if Alish would require another hank of hair, vial of fluid, or patch of skin. Phoebe wondered if she would be as compliant if she were differently biotic.

"Correlations," Alish muttered.

"Did you find something, sir?" Phoebe asked, trying to make sense of the strings of data on his screen. She'd been allowed to skip the last couple shifts of the "work" part of the work study requirement of the Undead Studies class, and was confused by what it was Alish was trying to accomplish.

"What? What?" he said, his wrinkled face far more corpse-like than Colette's in the white-blue glow of the screen. He looked up at Phoebe and pushed his wire bifocals up the length of his aquiline nose.

"Well, yes," he said. "But in the fields of scientific inquiry finding 'something' may mean that what you have, in fact, is 'nothing,' as in, the something you thought was something really turned out to be nothing."

"Huh?" Thorny said, dropping his phone into the deep pocket of his coat. He had a game later in the day—the upside of all of the stars of the team either being injured (permanently, in Adam's case) or under house arrest meant that Thorny got a lot of time on the field.

"In this case," Alish continued, "there does not seem to be a correlation between the presence of formaldehyde in the body and a return to existence."

Phoebe thought his choice of words was interesting, not to mention the course of his study. Adam hadn't been dead long enough for a trip to the morgue, never got the ole formaldehyde inoculation, so ruling out formaldehyde as being a "causal agent" of the whole undead thing seemed self-evident.

Dallas Jones, the first known zombie, was killed on camera while robbing a convenience store, then arose a few hours after his death with no visit to the mortician either. Sometimes Alish's "science" was pretty suspect.

"Isn't formaldehyde a compound?

"What? Yes. Yes, Ms. Kendall. It certainly is."

"Is there something in the compound that could be causing the return?"

He frowned, the skin of his face sagging down as the muscles around his mouth pulled. "My studies would indicate no, that that would not be the case."

"This is going to sound rude and I don't mean it to be," she said. "But what have yours, or anyone's, studies indicated?"

Alish smiled, his long fingers tapping on the edge of his desk. "Not much, I'm afraid."

"Can I go, sir?" Thorny asked. "I've got to get to the game."

"Certainly, Mr. Harrowwood," Alish said. "Score seventeen touchdowns for us."

"I'll try, sir," Thorny said, sprinting past the lab equipment.

Alish turned back to Phoebe. "What we know," he said, "is that there are at least fifteen hundred and sixty-three differently biotic persons in this country."

Fifteen hundred and sixty-three seemed like such a small number, especially when she'd met at least twenty of them. She'd never counted the pictures on "the wall of the dead" at the Haunted House but estimated that there were two hundred.

Tommy once told her he had over six hundred subscribers, but didn't know how many of them were dead.

"Of that number, we have some type of reliable documentation on half. All of those we have good documentation for died between the ages of thirteen and eighteen. The verifiable period of 'true death' has been between two minutes, fifty-seven seconds and eight days, three minutes."

"Eight days?"

Alish nodded.

"I was gone five . . . days," Colette called from her chair. She looked bored, but most of the dead looked at least a little bored if they weren't trying to emote.

"Yes. There does not appear to be a relationship between the time spent dead and the amount of functionality the person has. There also does not appear to be a relationship between the time period one exists as differently biotic and the amount of functionality they have."

"Time is not on their side," Phoebe asked. "In increasing functionality."

Alish took his bifocals off and closed his eyes. "It does not appear that way, no."

"What helps?" Phoebe said, thinking of Adam trying to will his body into a karate stance.

"We have not found anything that helps," he said.

"Music," Colette called. Alish opened his eyes and looked back at her. "Hugs."

"I interrupted you," Phoebe said to Alish. "What else do we know?"

"Not much, I'm afraid," he said. "Nothing conclusive. Our friends Ms. DeSonne and Mr. Williams—no offense, dear Miss Beauvoir—appear to be on the higher end of the functionality scale. There is a girl in California who only blinks. Some of the dead appear to regain senses beyond sight and sound. The degree of touch sensation appears to differ among them. We know that if the brain is destroyed, functionality ceases. We know that traditional biology does not seem to apply."

"What do you mean?"

"No heartbeat, no circulation, no respiratory activity," he said, and there were teeth, faintly yellow and crooked, in his smile. "They're dead, Ms. Kendall. It just doesn't make any sense."

"I can . . . smell . . . that perfume . . . Margi wears now," Colette said. "I . . . couldn't do that . . . before."

"Interesting," Alish said, smiling at her. He looked like he wanted to figure out how to fit her inside a petri dish.

"So what are you trying to find?" Phoebe asked.

"Oh, a lot of things," he said. Then he leaned forward and motioned with a crooked finger for her to lean in.

"Miss Kendall," he said, his voice a dry whispery rasp, "I'm trying to find the secret of life."

He laughed then, and lifted the hooked finger he'd beckoned her with to his lips, as though it were their little secret.

"What a . . . weirdo," Colette said from the front seat of Margi's car, "a total . . . creepy weirdo."

Margi was clapping her hands to try and warm them up while waiting for the heater to kick in, her bangles muffled by her mittens and her coat.

"Who?" she said. "Alish?"

"First . . . guess," Colette said. She turned on the radio so that they could listen to the Restless Dead CD that they had listened to only fifty-three times that week.

"Ugh . . . I hated it working in the lab," Margi said. "But Angela is more than a little creepy too."

"What do you mean?" Phoebe said, leaning forward so she could hear over the bass-heavy drone pouring from the speakers behind her head.

"Well, she's perfect," Margi said. "Just look at her. Nobody is that perfect."

"Except . . . me," said Colette.

"I stand corrected. But really, how could she possibly be the daughter of leathery old Alish? He must have conceived her in his sixties."

"Conceived her . . . in a state . . . of scientific inquiry," Colette said. They all broke up.

Phoebe was the first one to control her giggling. "I just don't know what he's really trying to do. It seems so random."

"He told Tommy once that he was looking for a cure," Margi said. "Tommy got pretty mad. He said he didn't have a disease."

"I don't . . . know." Colette's expression was wistful. "I . . . wouldn't mind . . . being . . . cured."

Margi put the car in gear and rolled down the hill to the gate.

"Okay, Duke," she said, waiting for him to trigger the release so they could leave the compound. And then whispering, "Speaking of creepy."

"Yeah," Colette said, "if anybody should be . . . a zombie . . ."

The gate clicked open and began to separate in the center.

"Creeeeeeeeeeeak," Margi said. "So Pheebes, are you hanging out with us today? It's a beautiful gray Saturday. I had my mom buy some expensive coffee, which is perfect for a day like this. We can go through my recent MP3 downloads."

"I can't, Gee," Phoebe said.

"Can't, or won't?" Phoebe knew that Margi had been

aiming for a gentle chiding tone, but she could hear the irritation in her voice.

"I've got to check in on Adam," she said. The silence from the front seat told her how everyone felt about that excuse.

"He's . . . moving . . . better," Colette said after a time.

"Yes."

"And talking . . . too."

"He's really making some progress," Phoebe said.

"Well." Margi pressed the accelerator a little too hard. "How about I pick him up too?"

"I . . . I don't think that is a good idea right now," Phoebe said, wishing that Margi would back off, knowing that she wouldn't.

"Why not?"

"He's still very self-conscious," she said. "Can we take a rain check?"

Margi looked at her in the rearview, and it was obvious she didn't buy it. She opened her mouth to reply, but Colette beat her to it.

"I was . . . that way . . . at first . . . too," she said. "Tell him . . . when he is . . . ready . . . he's always . . . welcome."

"Thanks," she said, deciding that she'd go see Adam when she got home and maybe talk to him about what had happened. Putting off the inevitable hadn't worked so well with Tommy, and she didn't want a replay of that scene.

She regretted her decision soon after knocking on the Garritys' door. Jimmy opened it.

"He's at karate, pretending he's a real person," Jimmy

said, his contempt for her clear in his dark eyes. "Go the hell home."

"Tell him I stopped by, please?" she said.

Jimmy's laugh matched his personality. "Yeah, right," he said. "I don't talk to corpses."

He slammed the door, and Phoebe could hear Adam's mother yelling at him from a room deeper in the house. She sighed and crossed the short stretch of lawn that separated their houses, then went inside hers. Her mother, still in a sharp, blue business suit, was moving around the kitchen and pulling things from various cabinets and drawers.

"Hi, honey," she said, reaching high into the cabinet where her father—who did most of the cooking—had arranged the spices. "How was your day?"

"Filled with wonder," Phoebe said, giving her a kiss on the cheek. "How about yours?"

Her mom smiled and leaned into her daughter's hug. "I don't know about 'filled with wonder,'" she said, "but it could be worse. Your father is going to be a little late, so I told him we'd get dinner ready."

"Sure," Phoebe said, looking at what her mother had spread on the counter: bread crumbs, heavy cream, tarragon, egg noodles. "Tarragon chicken?"

"Tarragon chicken," her mother replied.

"That's fowl," Phoebe said, continuing one of the little goofy family traditions that seemed to hold the internal world together while the external world was making no sense at all. Her mom smiled.

"I know," she said, "and no fuss about it being Thanksgiving in a couple days. More bird won't kill you."

"Unless, of course, it is avian flu–rich bird."

"Miss Morbid," her mother said, "you mind getting things started while I change? Or do you want to change first?"

"I never change, Mom," Phoebe said. She meant it as a joke, but she could tell by the look that crossed her mom's face that she didn't take it that way.

"Is something wrong, Phoebe?" her mom asked, stopping her bustling to move loose strands of ink black hair out of Phoebe's eyes. "Are you okay? Was it the article?"

Uh-oh, Phoebe thought. "What article?"

"It was in the paper. Some undead people went around Winford last night killing people's pets."

"Can I see?" Phoebe asked. She didn't bother to correct her mother's terminology.

Her mom opened the recycling bin and withdrew the paper for her.

"I'm going to get changed," her mom said. "The chicken breasts are in the fridge. They might need to be defrosted a little more."

"I'm going to read this first, okay?" Phoebe said, scanning the front page of the *Winford Bulletin*. ZOMBIES KILL PETS, the headline read, and Phoebe was glad that she hadn't corrected her mother. There was a photograph of a young mother holding two distraught children. The caption beneath the photo said that the Henderson family was mourning the loss of the Airedale Brady, who was "attacked and killed by zombies" sometime during the night.

There was also the photo of George from the Undead States recruitment flyer.

"Oh my," Phoebe said.

The article suggested that the zombie in the poster was considered the primary suspect in the rash of pet killings that had happened over the past few weeks, and she instantly thought of the wet furry lump that had been in George's trick-or-treat bag on Halloween.

Her mother's voice startled Phoebe. "Terrible, isn't it?"

Phoebe looked at her mom, who'd changed into jeans and a loose T-shirt. "I can't believe it."

"Do you know that boy? You know so many of the living impaired people in Oakvale."

Phoebe looked back at the paper; she thought she knew *all* of the living impaired people in Oakvale.

"Yes."

"Really?" her Mom said. "Shouldn't you go to the police?"

"I . . . I can't believe he would do this, Mom," she said, although she really could.

Her mother got the chicken out of the fridge, cut the plastic wrapping, and slid the three split fillets onto a white cutting board. She began trimming them with a knife.

"Is he a friends of yours?" she asked. She wasn't looking at Phoebe when she said it.

"Not really, no," Phoebe said.

"Well," her mother said, plating the breasts and covering them to prep them for a brief spin in the microwave, "let's hope that it wasn't really him, and that something else is going on.

Coyotes, maybe. It wouldn't be good for your friends if this crime was committed by living impaired kids."

Phoebe wanted to argue the point. She wanted to say how stupid society was if they would blame a whole group of people for the actions of a small minority, but in the end she held her tongue, because she knew her mother was not speaking judgmentally, and that she was right. This was going to make trouble for differently biotic people through out the town. Phoebe had visions of a parade of cop cars leading up to the Haunted House, their lights flashing on the dead faces that gathered at the cracked windows to watch their approach.

"What goes better with tarragon chicken?" her Mom asked. "Carrots or peas?"

"Dad likes peas," Phoebe said.

"Peas it is."

Phoebe had trouble sleeping that night, so rather than fight it she lit incense and a few candles, then straightened her room. Her restlessness annoyed Gargoyle, who raised his furry eyebrows as she bustled around.

"Oh, Gar," she said, sitting down on the edge of the bed to mollify him by scratching behind his ears. "I would never let mean old George eat you."

Gar's eyebrow twitched once, then he settled back down to sleep. Phoebe went and sat at her computer. The article, and its accusations really bothered her.

She set the media player on her desktop to cycle randomly

through the thousands of songs stored on her hard drive. The first one that came up was by the Restless Dead, a group that always made her think of Adam.

She had three real e-mails among the advertisements and spammage. One from Margi, exhorting her to not be a lame-o and go to Aftermath. The second one was from Margi, telling her not to be a lame-o, and to go to Aftermath with them. The last one was from Margi, and it asked her to *puh-leeze* not be a lame-o and go to Aftermath with them.

> *Hey, Margi,*

she typed in reply to the third e-mail,

> *I'm sorry I have been such a lame-o. I'd love to go*
> *to Aftermath with you tho I wish that the train could*
> *pick me up at my house becuz in truth yr driving scares*
> *me to death. True and final death. See you in school*
> *Mon. and we'll make plans. Say hey to Colette fur me,*
> *love Pheeble.*

She surfed for a while, popped on and off MySpace addys of bands as the media player selected them. The Restless Dead appeared again after about a half hour, and Phoebe wondered how the "randomizer," or whatever it was, could pick two songs from a band that maybe had twenty total among thousands in such a short span of time.

She popped onto mysocalledundeath.com and reread

Tommy's last entry, the one where he gave a mission statement of sorts. He talked about hitting the road in an effort to "advance the cause of zombie rights." By traveling, he said he had hopes of connecting with zombies who might not have access to technology, and sharing their experiences with the "wired" readers of mysocalledundeath.

He didn't mention Phoebe by name, but he did say that a "traditionally biotic friend" was going to be assisting with the management of the Web site in his absence, and he expressed a hope that "subscribers of mysocalledundeath would join her, Karen, and himself in expanding both their online community and their presence in the world at large." Phoebe thought about the word "presence" and what Tommy meant by it. He chose his words so carefully; she often suspected that the pauses in his speech weren't due to typical zombie lack of control but because he wanted to make his meanings clear to his listeners. She was thinking this when a hand fell on her shoulder, statling her so much she almost knocked one of her lavender-scented candles over.

"Easy," her dad said. She could smell the wine that he and her mother had been sharing in the living room earlier that night. "Didn't mean to scare you."

"Okay,"

"It's pretty late," he said.

"I know."

"You okay?"

"I'm okay. Just can't sleep. Nothing to worry about."

"Okay, then."

"Really."

"I believe you."

"Dad?"

"Yes, Phee?"

"Is it okay if I go to a club in New York with Margi and some girls?"

Her father's sigh sounded like one of those forced sighs that Karen made when she was trying to show how trad biotic she could be.

"New York, as in New York City?"

"Yes, Dad."

"I don't know. Let me think about it. It's an underage club, isn't it?"

"Absolutely," she said. "You trust me, right?"

"Absolutely." He leaned over and kissed the top of her head. "Hey, it's that undead club, isn't it? Afterbirth or something like that?"

"After*math*, Dad!"

"Oh yeah. So you're bringing Adam and Colette there, is that it?"

"Just Colette," she said. "And Karen. Girls' night out."

"No Tommy either?"

"No Tommy. How did you hear about Aftermath, anyhow?"

"I read too, you know. Like I read about what happened to all these pets that disappeared."

"Oh."

"Pretty scary," he said. Across the room Gar buried his

muzzle into his forepaws as though he understood the jist of their conversation.

"The world can be a scary place," she said, "but that doesn't have anything to do with how much you trust me, right?"

"It has everything to do with how much I trust you," he said, kissing the top of her head. "I'll need to talk it over with your mom. I can think of a thousand reasons why it is a horrible idea to have a group of sixteen-year-old girls going to New York City by themselves."

"All of which are overcome by your trust for me, right?" She debated telling him that Karen would actually have been eighteen or nineteen if she were still alive, but decided it wouldn't help.

He patted her shoulder. "I'll let you know in the morning. Why don't you get some sleep?"

"I will. I just want to finish something first."

"Okay. Good night."

When he was gone she focused again on her computer screen. Someone with a screen name she didn't recognize had tried to instant message her, and she told the service to block them. She read a few of the comments on the bulletin board regarding Tommy's last entry, and most of them were very encouraging and supportive of his "quest."

She minimized the online service and opened up her word processing program. She stared at the blank screen for a moment and then typed in a title.

Words From a Beating Heart

She thought a few more moments and then started to type with increasing rapidity. The sound of her fingernails tapping on the keys was always a special music to her, especially when it seemed to match the rhythm of the music she was listening to.

Hello, she typed, my name is Phoebe. My friends call me Phoebe or Fee or Pheebes or, my favorite, Pheeble. That's what my friend Adam called me. You know, I typed "called" just then instead of "calls." Sometimes I get confused in my mind over Adam, because Adam is dead. Since Adam is dead, I sometimes think of him in the past tense and it makes me crazy that I do this, because he's dead but he's come back. He's a zombie now. We still spend a lot of time together, but the time that we spend is different from how it was. A lot of things that we used to do, like talk, and drive to Honeybee Dairy to get hot fudge sundaes after tossing a Frisbee around (my favorite thing to do with Adam) are all things we can't do anymore—not yet, anyway. All those things occurred in the past tense, so, as wrong as it seems, I sometimes think of Adam in the past tense as well. I feel really guilty about that. I feel guilty about it because Adam died saving my life.

I have one other nickname, one that was given to me by the boy that killed Adam. He called me Morticia Scarypants. I wear black clothes and have long black hair and am very pale, and so I'm Morticia Scarypass. I listen to goth and darkwave and trance and horror punk and even a little heavy metal. I write poetry and at the time I was dating a dead boy—I was dating Tommy, actually. I think this really made the boy that gave me my nickname angry with me. I think that's why he tried to kill me—although I'm not sure if he was trying to kill me or Tommy, or if he really meant to kill Adam.

They call me the Bride of Frankenstein now, since I still spend so much of my time with dead guys.

Tommy asked me to help with mysocalledundeath when he was gone, and he thought it would be good if I wrote a blog, that it might help connect trads like me with the zombies who read the Web site daily, and vice versa. I know that it's a risky thing he's asking of me, just like it was risky for me to type the word "zombies" just then. I'm sure there are those of you who will read my words and think, "how dare she, a trad girl, call us zombies." I could say in my defense that my friends use the word zombie all the time, but that won't do anything to justify it if you feel that it's a word that no trad person should use.

The thing is, most of my friends are dead. Just like the shirt says.

Again, this doesn't give me free license to say or do anything I want just because I'm friends with dead people. I mention it only because it's the truth, and because my friends and I are still trying to work through the issues that friendship present us.

When I started dating Tommy, I had no idea that people would hate me just for dating him. I had no idea that friends and family might react differently than I would have expected from them.

I had no idea that some of Tommy's dead friends would object to it either. All I knew was that I was interested in

Tommy, and he seemed to be interested in me, so I thought it would be fun to spend time with him.

When I first saw Tommy, he was so confident. He knew that he was taking risks. And I knew soon after meeting him that the risks he was taking were not for his own benefit but really for the benefit of undead people everywhere. I'd never met another boy who was as selfless as Tommy. I admired him greatly for it.

There I go, writing about my friends in the past tense again.

I already miss Tommy even though he hasn't been gone very long. I hope the road is smooth and safe for him. If you see him on his travels, thank him on my behalf for giving me the chance to "speak" to all of you. Tell him that I hope he was right, and that I hope that the words that I write will help all of us, living or dead, understand each other a little better.

When she was done she leaned back and stretched. She tried to imagine how some of the zombies she knew—Colette, Mal, Takayuki—Tommy even, would react to what she'd written. What would Adam think, and would he even tell her?

She hovered for a moment—like she did with everything she'd ever written that was of a personal nature—over the thought of deleting the whole thing. Tommy this, Tommy that. She sounded like a mopey schoolgirl. Oh, wait, she thought, I *am* a mopey schoolgirl.

If you missed Tommy so much, she thought, why did you blow him off, practically chase him out of town? If you were so guilty over Adam getting killed, why didn't you go see him tonight after he was done with karate? Just because you tried to kiss him and he pushed you away?

The zombies who read this would probably think she was the worst sort of hanger-on, the sort of kid that's so screwed up and lonely and cut off from her own kind that she was trying to glom onto the little community that Tommy built. But isn't that what all lonely kids do in some way?

She highlighted the entire text and right-clicked "Cut." The thoughts were out of her head, she told herself, that was the important thing.

Her computer told her that she had mail. She maximized the screen and there was an e-mail from WILLIAMSTOMMY @MYSOCALLEDUNDEATH.COM. "The Long and Unwinding Road" was in the subject header.

Tommy.

She clicked the e-mail open; there was an attachment called ROADBLOG1, and she started downloading as she began reading.

Hi Phoebe—

I'm almost in New York and so far the trip has been going well. I walked alongside of 95 for a little stretch and saw about four thousand white vans, but am happy to say none of them stopped with nets and flamethrowers. I've attached my first blog for you or Karen to post on the site. I'm sending this from a church, if you can believe it. With so many religious types of all denominations out there wanting to burn us like a stack

of Harry Potter books, it continually amazes me how many of
the clergy reach out. Actually, so far the kindness of people—
well, you can read the blog. Have you started writing yours yet?

I miss you already. Say hi to Adam and the gang.

T.

She clicked reply and keyed in a quick response.

Hi Tommy—

Glad to hear you're safe, everyone here misses you too.
We—the Weird Sisters—are going to NYC later this week, on
the day after Thanksgiving to go to Aftermath. Want to meet
us there?

Love,

Phoebe

Despite her sign-off, she thought the e-mail was a little impersonal. She was about to hit send when at the last second, she tapped

PS: What do you think of this?

And then pasted the "Words From a Beating Heart" text she had cut into the body of the e-mail. She immediately felt embarrassed and closed out her Internet service, as though by turning it off she could recall the e-mail she'd just sent.

She looked at the clock and was thankful that to-morrow was Sunday. She opened Tommy's blog and began to read.

* * *

The hour was now so late it was almost absurd, but Phoebe went back online. She saw that WILLIAMSTOMMY had beaten her to the punch.

> *Phoebe—*
> *This is beautiful. I think the zombie community is really going to respond positively to what you've written.*
> *Love,*
> *T.*

Love, she thought, he'd typed "love" just as she had. A multifaceted word, *love*, there probably wasn't another word in this or any other language that had so many shades and degrees. She knew that he loved her and she loved him, just as she loved Adam and Adam loved her. But with love, theirs or his, it was always a question of degree, and what one was willing to do to express that degree.

She wondered what Adam was doing right then, and her breath caught in her throat. But then again, it did the same thing when she thought of Tommy. Shades and degree.

She signed off without replying, turned the volume of the speakers down another notch or two, then blew out the sputtering candles. Only then did she crawl into bed and pull the blankets close to her.

CHAPTER
TWENTY-FIVE

T RIED TO WORK the remote
but the remote was slippery like
a fish slipped out of hands once
twice three times on the third Jimmy yells from the kitchen will
you stop it you stupid ass and Mom yells and Joe yells and
Johnny yells and they're all yelling but this is a pretty typical
Thanksgiving.

Mom wanted me at the table but Jimmy freaked said it was
bad enough he had to look at me and it ruined his appetite are you
trying to make me puke. Felt kind of sad looking at all the food
can't eat looked at the table for a minute before they sat mashed
potatoes stuffing turnip. Never thought would miss turnip.

Johnny's brought a girl with him for dinner Susan and
Susan seems nice but she's scared. Scared of FrankenAdam.
Should be. Reached for the remote got it changed the channel
the Patriots are winning the Jets are losing and wish wish wish
could play.

Next year. Next year. If Tommy why not FrankenAdam? Could play again.

Sure.

Jimmy yells again and storms out and Mom starts crying didn't even know dropped the stupid remote again. Think can smell turkey for a little while but maybe it is really just wishful thinking. Talked to Karen and to Colette about this for a while and they both say it will come. Karen says she can smell just about everything and maybe more. Don't know what she means but Karen isn't really on the same playing field as most zombies anyway. Then Karen started talking about how she thinks she can taste some things and Colette makes a stupid joke about how Karen tastes and then Phoebe came over and for some reason we all stop talking.

Phoebe.

"You okay, son?" Joe asks, florid from holiday wine Hey, Phoebe florid does that count? He reaches for the remote but FrankenAdam is quicker. Quicker!

"I'm . . . fine, Joe." Shorter pause maybe.

He nods, goes back. Johnny is telling Mom that Jimmy is just an a-hole like he thinks that will get her to stop crying and Susan is crying too. Wishing could play some football when there is a knock on the door and Joe lets Phoebe in. Saw Phoebe at school walked with Phoebe to classes sat together on bus but different now. Doesn't touch, doesn't hold my hand.

Phoebe apologizing. FrankenAdam should apologize. Scared shamed Phoebe should apologize.

"Is this a bad time?" she said.

When is it not. Johnny tries to be gallant and introduce crying girlfriend Mom runs to bedroom and slams the door. Fridge opens and another beer is cracked.

"Hi, Adam," says Phoebe, Phoebe so pretty in a silky blouse, light green, shiny, reflecting perfect skin and eyes two shades darker and green, the color of her skirt. Soft suede boots, chocolate brown, just below her knee, with heels. Phoebe.

"Hi, Fee . . . bull." Nervous or dead? At least always have that excuse now.

She sits on the sofa across, green eyes turned toward the game for briefest of seconds. "Holidays can be fun, can't they?" she says. "We have Gram over, that can always be a trip."

Gram is Phoebe's grandmother. Remember she made good pies, pumpkin pies. Used to have a piece of pumpkin pie with Phoebe and her Gram in her kitchen Thanksgiving night.

"Fun. Did . . . Jimmy . . . run you . . . over?"

"He tried," she said, "I'm too quick."

"How . . . was . . . dinner?"

"Oh, it was good," Phoebe said she eats like a bird. Not like Margi that girl can really pack it away but Phoebe always quit before she got full. She'd eat a hot fudge sundae but that was about the only thing. Sad. Sad remembering thinking about all the time wasted with airheads like Holly when could have been having sundaes with Phoebe.

Joe stands in doorway with his beer and that is his way of telling to vacate his seat, so vacate his seat. It takes a little time but almost got it when Phoebe reaches out to help. Wish she wouldn't do that and tell her so. Somehow can't move or talk fast enough unless it is to say or do something that hurts her.

"Why don't you two go for a walk?" Joe says. Johnny and Susan are already leaving and Mom is down the hall with the door closed. Joe pouring beer onto a fire that he does not want to get out of control.

"Let's go . . . for a . . . walk."

"I . . . I just came over to say hi," Phoebe said. "I'm going to go back."

See the hurt in her eyes, hurt that FrankenAdam put there. Don't do much right anymore.

"I'll . . . walk . . . you . . . out."

"We're still planning on going to New York tomorrow," said Phoebe. "If you want to come."

She's not looking at me when she says it. Phoebe was changing right in front of me, I realized.

Realized that finally might have pushed her away.

"No . . . thanks."

She knew anyhow. The wind is sweeping her hair up and can imagine the scent of flowers being drawn forth by the breeze. She doesn't have jacket on and she is shivering. Want to tell her to go home but guess already done that really.

"'Bye, Adam," she said. "I'll see you Monday."

Monday, three days away. The longest gone without seeing Phoebe since death is about twenty-four hours.

"Bye . . . Pheeble,"

Watched her walk away but turn before she gets to the door because don't want her to see watching her. Suppose should be happy, because have been trying to get her to leave alone and live for weeks now, been trying and finally succeeded but no sense of triumph. Could have apologized at least.

Inside the house Joe is watching some team, Patriots or Jets or Giants achieve some objective; scoring of a touchdown or completion of a pass. Feel no sense of accomplishment for achieving my objective, only a pervading sense of loss. Objective of finally pushing her away.

Pervading. Didn't think dead body possessed sense motor impulses but turned reflexively back toward her house. She was already inside.

God, I thought. God, I love her.

Spent the rest of Thanksgiving doing karate in the backyard, barely noticing when a light snow began and stopped a few hours later.

Snow began to fall. Couldn't feel it.

CHAPTER
TWENTY-SIX

"WILL YOU STOP . . . apologizing?" Colette said. "And please
. . . watch the . . . road? I don't
want to . . . die . . . again."

"Okay, okay," Margi said. "Chill out. Is that truck still
behind me?"

Phoebe watched the conversation from the "safety" of the
backseat, trying not to be distracted by the big pink bubbles that
Karen was blowing, or by the other cars on the highway that
Margi seemed to be in perpetual danger of drifting too close to.

Margi's parents had given her an eight o'clock curfew, so
the girls' decided to go to the city during the day, something
that Margi felt compelled to apologize over ad infinitum.

"Don't worry about it, Margi," Karen said, snapping her
gum. "I have to work tomorrow morning anyhow. And I need
my beauty sleep."

Colette turned around in her seat—Margi had done

189

an exceptional makeup job on her.

"Do you really . . . sleep . . . Karen?"

Karen reaches over and patted her hand. "No, sweetie. I was just kidding. Your eyes are really pretty, BTW."

"Really? Thank . . . you. I . . . do . . . sometimes. Sleep . . . I mean. Not sleep really . . . more like . . . hibernate."

"Really?" Karen said, sucking in a bubble. "Mal does that too. I zone out sometimes, but it isn't really like . . . sleeping."

"I don't know . . . what it is . . . it's weird. It's like I'm . . . awake . . . but dreaming . . . at the same time."

"Weird. George was talking about that the other day."

"George? Old-school George? He . . . talks?"

"Mmm-hmm," Karen replied. "He does to me."

"Ick," Margi said.

"George isn't so . . . bad," Karen said. "I think the . . . old-schoolers . . . are just . . . misunderstood."

Phoebe was about to comment on the fact that they were currently being misunderstood by the local police, but Margi beat her to it.

"Isn't George the one gnawing on pets?" Margi asked. "I haven't let Familiar out of the house in a week."

"What do you mean?" Karen said.

Phoebe realized that Karen was wearing Lady Z; she could smell it mixing with the scent of bubble gum.

"You didn't see that article in the paper?" she asked. She gave a summary of the article when Karen gave her a look of confusion, ending with the photo of George.

"You're kidding," she said.

"That's what the paper said."

"No way. George wouldn't hurt a fly."

"Tak would," Colette and Margi said in unison.

"So would . . . George," Colette added. "He probably . . . thinks . . . he is . . . supposed to."

"I don't believe it," Karen said. "There's no way. No way. George is a little too interested in roadkill, but there's no way he'd do this. He's not *fast* enough. He'd get . . . caught . . . the moment he tried."

Phoebe thought that Karen was trying to convince herself, which made her want to drop the subject. The other girls in the car must have had their telepathetic powers working, because they let the matter rest.

"And Tak wouldn't . . . *kill*," Karen said again. The next bubble she blew made a noise like a gunshot as it popped. "Not even an animal, no way. No . . . way."

"There's the . . . train station . . . exit," Colette said. Everyone seemed glad for the interruption.

New Haven was the first stop, but there were plenty of people who stayed on, wanting to get into New York City for the holiday weekend. Margi ushered the girls into a quartet of facing seats.

"Oh, I can't ride . . . backward," Colette said, "I get . . . motion . . . sickness."

Only when she forced out a laugh a moment later did the other girls realize she was kidding.

She was wearing a black Restless Dead sweatshirt that

Phoebe had given Margi for her birthday a year or so ago. The sweatshirt had a hood, which Colette pulled up so no one could see her face. Phoebe knew that her constant wisecracking was just a cover for a deep-seated self-consciousness.

Karen, her platinum hair trailing down the shoulders of a smart, black leather jacket that tapered at the waist, was sometimes not self-conscious enough. She would look into the eyes of anyone who passed, drilling into their souls with her bizarre diamond eyes. Phoebe watched a young woman pushing a stroller freeze in her tracks before turning around to find a seat in a different car. Beside her, Karen gave the impression of being oblivious to people's various reactions, but Phoebe thought she could see a light dancing in the diamonds whenever she provoked one, good or bad.

And there were other reactions besides the fear. A pair of boys hopped on to the train just before it left the station. One of them had long black hair and a leather jacket, and for a moment Phoebe felt her heart beating in her chest because she thought it was Takayuki, but when the boy looked up she saw that he had blue eyes. His companion was dressed in a similar fashion, with ripped denim jeans and a faded Zombie Power! T-shirt on beneath his motorcycle jacket.

The blue-eyed boy saw Karen and smiled.

"Hey," he said.

"Hello," Karen answered, her voice cool, bordering on blasé.

The other girls, even Margi, who had been chattering away, fell silent when the conversation began. Colette wouldn't even peek out from beneath her hood.

"I like your eyes," he said.

"Thank you," she said. "Yours are nice too."

His buddy thought that was pretty funny, but Phoebe could tell he was also trying to decide which one of them he would try and talk to now that his friend had engaged Karen. He stared past Colette to Margi, who managed to affect a glare that was three parts contempt and one part provocation. Phoebe knew from seeing the look in action that it turned off most of the boys she met, but a certain segment—like poor Norm Lathrop—fell for it utterly and completely.

The train jerked into life and the boy introduced himself as Dom and his friend as Bee.

"Where are you ladies headed?" he said, including the rest of them in the conversation. When his eyes met Phoebe's she felt her heartbeat again; his facial features were angular and handsome, his smile the only soft thing about him.

"We're going to Aftermath," Karen said, sounding both matter-of-fact and bored. Phoebe thought of a cat batting around a ball of string.

"No kidding," Dom said, flashing white teeth. "We are too. Are you looking forward to dancing with the dead?"

He was smiling when he said it, his voice free of sarcasm. Was he unaware that Karen was a zombie?

"Sure," Karen said. "We like to dance. There are a bunch of db kids at our school who go to the club, so we thought we'd go out and have some fun."

"Yeah? What school do you go to?"

"Oakvale High," she said, and there was a momentary

pause. "We're graduating . . . in the spring so we want to make sure we're having as much fun as possible . . . in our last year."

A look passed between the boys. "Seniors, huh?"

Karen nodded.

"Yeah," Margi challenged. "Where do you go to school?"

"Yale," Dom said, sighing like he was ashamed of it. "We're only freshmen, though."

"Oh," Karen said, "are you in . . . the Skull and Bones society?"

Dom and Bee laughed along with them.

"Something like that. We're in a band called Skeleton Crew, so that's pretty close."

"Skeleton Crew?" Margi said, interest suddenly replacing abrasion in her voice. "So you sing 'Living is like Dying'?"

In response, Dom started to sing, "Living is like dying, all over again, all over again, like dying, all over again . . ."

"You're not the singer," Karen observed.

Dom ran his hand through his hair, revealing that it had been razored to a thin dark stubble over one ear. "Boy, you're tough. No, I'm the guitarist. Bee plays bass."

"And your singer," Margi said, "DeCayce. He's a . . ."

"Zombie," Dom finished. "Yep. A dead guy sings for us."

Even Karen seemed intrigued by that.

"So listen," Dom said. "I don't even know your names. How can I get you on the guest list if I don't know your names?"

"You're playing today?" Margi asked.

"You bet. If DeCayce and Warren manage to get our equipment there, yeah."

"I'm Margi Vachon."

"Who's your shy friend?"

"Colette Beauvoir."

Dom withdrew a small wire-bound notebook and a black pen from a pocket inside his jacket. "Hold up. Is that spelled B.E.A.U.V.O.I.R?"

"Wow, you really do go to Yale," Karen said. "I'm Karen DeSonne. D. small e. capital S.O. double N. E."

"French girls," Bee said, grinning.

"I'm Italian," Karen said with a withering glare.

"I'm Phoebe Kendall," Phoebe said. Dom looked up at her with something like interest for the first time.

"Phoebe Kendall," he said, writing her name in the book and then flipping it closed before withdrawing a cell phone from his other pocket. "Hey, Serena?" he said into the phone. "Hey, it's Dom. I've got a few people I want you to add to the guest list for today." He read off their names, starting with Margi and ending with Phoebe. Something Serena said must have been funny because he was still laughing when he said good-bye and hung up.

"Well, Bee," he said once the phone was away, "let's go grab a seat. Hopefully we'll be seeing you girls later today. I'm glad I met you."

Colette peeked out of her hood to watch them swagger down to an empty pair of seats in the back, and retreated like a turtle back into her shell when Bee waved at her.

"I've never been on a . . . guest . . . list . . . before."

"Oh, honey," Karen said, reaching over and tapping her

knee. "That's just because you haven't met enough people yet."

"You're amazing, Karen," Phoebe said. "You were so confident. No wonder they were crazy about you."

"Me?" Karen replied, and when she turned toward Phoebe, the diamonds glittered. "You didn't say a word, but you're the one who has all the boys back home chasing you."

She knew Karen didn't mean it to hurt, but Phoebe couldn't help but feel stung. Currently there were zero boys chasing her. The one she wanted to chase her, she chased away. Actually, she'd chased both of them away.

Karen must have sensed everything that was roiling in her mind because she gave her a gentle push.

"Hey, I didn't mean anything by that. Nothing other than you're hot, that's all."

The train pulled into the next station

There was traffic on the street and sidewalk in front of the squat building where Aftermath was housed, but none of it seemed to be leading to its single door, a massive gray-green slab of metal that looked to Phoebe as though it could withstand a direct missile assault. There were only two decorations on the windowless building: a sign that hung from a metal pole recessed into the building's concrete about twelve feet off the ground bearing the name of the club, and a second sign in the same white script on a black color scheme that read, ENTER FREELY . . . AND OF YOUR OWN FREE WILL. This sign was secured to the door with four heavy bolts.

"Nice," Margi said upon reading the "welcome."

"It looks . . . closed," Colette said. She hadn't taken her hood down the entire time they had trekked through Grand Central Station and into the street where Margi finally got a cab to stop for them. Phoebe didn't think she looked much different from many of the younger people they'd passed.

"I hear music," Karen said.

Phoebe listened. She may have heard a low bass throbbing, but it could have just been the breath of the city, in and out, the sounds of thousands of cars rolling on the streets, the rushing of liquids through thousands of underground pipes, the sounds of a million words being spoken at once.

"Do we just go in?" Margi asked, looking around as though expecting a list of instructions to appear, like the menu boards of a drive-through.

"I think we do," Karen said, tugging the handle of the blast door open. What they saw inside Aftermath was not at all what Phoebe had expected.

The door opened into a sort of lounge area that had been covered floor to ceiling with vibrant swirls of color: a bright, kaleidoscopic display that was a far cry from the featureless dank warehouse Phoebe had been expecting. She followed a flaring curve of yellow ribbon that began somewhere on the plush shag carpet up one wall and then onto the ceiling, where it's varying thickness gave it the illusion of undulating over their heads before curving down the opposite wall. There were symmetrical bursts of multiple colors atop some of the curving bands; they looked like tie-dye designs pressed onto the wall. The riot of color distracted her, momentarily, from the dozen or so people in the room, some of whom were sunk into formless plush furniture that floated like giant amoebas on the swirling sea of color.

Phoebe looked at Colette, a dark black blot against the brightness of the walls. She watched her lower her hood, and then she watched as the color seemed to flow into her rapidly blinking eyes. Her look of astonishment morphed into a wide smile.

"Welcome to Aftermath," a dead girl said, hopping up from a counter near the door in a way that reminded Phoebe of the baristas at the local coffee franchise whenever a quiet customer disturbs their study time—half-embarrassed, half dutiful, and trying their best not to look wholly annoyed. "We have a . . . ten dollar . . . cover charge."

Phoebe was already opening her purse when Karen stepped forward and said she thought that they were on the guest list.

The dead girl gave a fair approximation of a smile. Her hair was stylishly cut, a soft-looking blond that had been chemically enhanced, probably to hide the gray streaks that were sometimes a natural consequence of death. Colette's hair had been streaked with gray for quite a while, but was now closer to the dark brown it had been when she was alive. The dead girl was wearing a white tank top with the Aftermath logo in black, black jeans, and boots. Her bare arms were pale and smooth.

"Let me check . . . the list," she said. While she was checking, Phoebe took a quick scan of the people hanging out in the lounge. There were a couple of zombies, two boys, playing one of those fantasy card games across a glass table with silver legs. Phoebe never quite grasped how to play beyond the basic concept that whoever could afford the most cards usually won. A girl sitting beside one of the gamers on the pillowy futon gave a bemused whoop when her companion played a card, flipping it with decisive vigor. His zombie opponent leaned back in his seat and gazed up at the Technicolor ceiling, his mouth open and gray-pink tongue lolling out in a half comical re-enaction of his death.

"Are you . . . Karen?" the zombie hostess was saying.

Karen said she was, and then she introduced the other girls, adding, "I really like your belt."

The girl looked down, as though surprised by the strip of silver studded leather around her waist.

"Thank you . . . Karen DeSonne," she said, extending a hand that ended in long white fingernails. "I'm Emily."

She's pretty, Phoebe thought, watching them shake hands. Colette and Margi drifted toward the hallway where the music would periodically blast forth as people opened the glass door.

"There are . . . lockers . . . in the locker room," Emily said. "For your . . . coats and . . . things. Five dollars . . . to rent. Dancing, down the main hall." She pointed with both arms as she gave the directions, like she was trying to bring an airplane into the gate. "There is a . . . snack bar . . . and vending machines . . . upstairs . . . next to the gift shop," she said, giving a final wave at a garish lavender stairwell. "The bathrooms . . . are down the hall . . . past the locker room. Have . . . fun."

"I need to use the restroom. Thanks, Emily." Phoebe said.

"I'll go with," Karen said. Phoebe didn't realize it, but she must have given her a funny look because a moment later Karen added "to check my makeup, silly!"

"Oh," Phoebe said, feeling foolish. "I'll see if the girls want me to put anything in the lockers."

She came back with Margi's coat and ten-pound purse and Colette's black hoodie.

"We're going to need two lockers," Karen said. She nodded back over Phoebe's shoulder. "Look how happy Colette is."

Phoebe looked back. Colette and Margi were on the periphery of an animated discussion occurring at the entrance of the hallway that led to the dance floor. One of the zombies was waving his hands in the air in front of his face to illustrate his point. His left hand was not as obedient as the right. Regardless, one of his companions, a trad boy holding a bottle of energy drink, laughed loud enough for them to hear even over the hivelike buzz of music and conversation.

"Just look at her . . . smile," Karen said. "Could you hear what they're talking about?"

"Books," Phoebe said.

"Books?" Karen shook her head. "Cool."

They started toward the locker room, the swirl of colors abruptly ending at the mouth of a long gray corridor lined with framed posters.

"The guy talking said the best thing about being dead was that he had tons of time to read. He said the worst thing was that the dead can't get library cards."

"That's pretty funny," Karen said. "So is that."

She pointed at the first of the posters, which was for *Night of the Living Dead*. Facing it across the hall was one for *Dawn of the Dead*, beside it the grinning skull from the first *Evil Dead* movie

"Wow," Phoebe said. The next one in line was a promo for a video game entitled *Zombie Apocalypse,* which depicted a man wading into a mob of zombies with a chainsaw. A severed arm went skyward in a spray of dark, ocher-hued "blood."

"You don't find it offensive?"

Karen shook her head. "I like irony. Oh, look, *Return of the Living Dead.* That was always my favorite." She started singing. *"Do you wanna paaaaaarty? It's party time!* Remember that scene?"

Phoebe blushed. She remembered. "That's a 45 Grave song."

Karen was less interested in music trivia. "How could I get offended by this?" she said, pointing at a pair of greenish zombies, the male Mohawked and skeletal and wearing a dog collar, standing over a gravestone, with the movie title being sprayed on it in red by a third zombie burrowing up from the ground beneath. "It's like the music you listen to, right? Zombies and monsters and whatever else, being hunted down by you trads?"

"The monsters usually win in the songs I listen to," Phoebe said. The last poster was the front cover of *And the Graves Give Up Their Dead,* by Reverand Nathan Mathers. The girls stopped and looked at it a moment, and at the photo inset of the author whose severe ice-blue eye gazed at them without pity.

"As long as they don't win in real life," Karen said. "Speaking of . . . monsters."

The zombie staffing the locker room gave them a bored wave as they entered.

"You'll . . . need . . . two," he said, looking at the mound of stuff in Phoebe's arms. He'd had a weight problem in life that had followed him into death, the stool he was perched upon creaked in protest as he leaned over to pluck two keys from the Peg-Board with his stubby fingers.

"Ten . . . bucks," he said. "Or . . . no lock . . . and take your . . . chances."

"Thanks," Karen said, handing him the money and a bright smile. "I'm Karen."

"B . . . Billy," he said.

"Thanks, Billy," she said, taking the keys, and leading Phoebe through the numbered rows of lockers.

"Let me give you some money for the lockers," Phoebe said, once their coats and bags were stowed.

"Don't worry about it," Karen said. "I've got that highly lucrative second job at the mall. I'm flush." On their way out she favored Billy with another killer smile. "Bye, Billy!"

Farther down the hall they found the bathrooms. There were four doors, two on the left that said "Boys" and two on the right that said "Girls." The word "Dead" was above one of each, and the word "Trad" was above the other two.

"More irony?" Phoebe said.

"At least I didn't have to sit in the back of the train."

They pushed their respective doors open, and stepped into

the same room. There were a row of stalls and a row of sinks. A dead girl was applying lip gloss from a black tube that had the distinctive Z logo that appeared on almost all of the Slydellco Zombie cosmetic products.

"Hi," the girl said, looking at them in the mirror. Phoebe thought that maybe she stared at her a beat too long, and it made her uncomfortable as she went into one of the stalls. She heard Karen ask her a question about the lip gloss.

"'Kiss of Life,'" the girl replied. "Sometimes . . . Skip is . . . so corny."

Phoebe heard the dead girls' laughter echoing in the tiled room.

When they returned to the lounge, Margi and Colette were nowhere to be seen.

"Probably burning up the dance floor," Karen said. "Let's go."

The sound hit them like a physical force when they stepped into the club proper, as did the assault of color and light strobing and flashing.

"I'm glad I don't have epilepsy," Phoebe said, blinking against a red strobe that seemed to be aimed directly at her retinas.

The dance hall was smaller than she expected, but only because every other dance she'd ever been to was in a school gymnasium. The dance floor here was far smaller, it looked like a sheet of opaque white plastic beneath which lights of green, yellow, blue, and red glowed with muted color. Margi and Colette were indeed burning up the dance floor, moving in rapid time with the Guy Who Can't Get a Library Card and his friends.

The floor was packed. There had to be thirty people on it, jumping and swaying with the music. Karen leaned over Phoebe's shoulder, her breath cool on her ear.

"We're here to dance, right?" she said, taking her by the hand and leading her down the carpeted steps to the floor. Colette gave an off-note cheer as they joined them, and Phoebe laughed when the eyes of both the deads and the trads bugged out as Karen twitched her short leather skirt.

The smell of Z hung heavy on the air as spotlights from above raked the crowd. Phoebe gave herself into the music, a heavy industrial song by a band she liked called the Seraphim. Then the lights cut all at once, plunging the hall into total darkness for a moment before hot white strobes flickered from all sides. Phoebe couldn't tell who was living or dead in that light; the rapid flashing made everyone's movements appear stiff and jerky. The room went dark again and then the floor lights returned, as well as the overhead spots. Lifting her arms above her head and laughing as Margi executed a few gypsy-like steps, she saw that some of the lights playing on walls and skin were butterflies, or flowers or stars.

She realized a zombie boy was mumbling something at her.

"What?" she yelled.

"I said," he screamed back, "loud enough for you?" Looking closer she realized he wasn't dead after all, he just had bad skin. She nodded and spun away.

The machine-heavy track segued into a crunky rap song

that Phoebe didn't recognize but could understand instinctively, the bass and drum wash infusing her limbs with their energy.

Is this what it's like for them? she thought, feeling the rush and watching Colette laugh at something the Library Card Guy said. She found that she could use music as fuel, like a candy bar or an apple. Without the latter two options, was sound what the dead needed to power them? She thought of Kevin and his jerky scarecrow dancing at the homecoming dance. Here, even the most sluggish of zombies in the room appeared to be moving at normal speeds.

Above the dance floor was a sort of catwalk that led to a perimeter of booths with more of the pillowy blue furniture that was scattered around the club. There were dozens of people loitering around, many watching either the dancers or the pretty colored lights that played across them. There was a DJ in an enclosed booth at the far end of the catwalk, and below that was a platform raised up from the rest of the dance floor that had a drum set and a few stacks of amplifiers. There was a yellow smiley skull—a giant emoticon—on the bass drumhead with the words "Skeleton Crew" written in letters made out of bones.

"Oh, man." Margi slumped onto a futon after a third extended club remix song ended. "I'm all out of breath."

"Me too," Colette said. The people that could hear her over the music thought that was pretty funny.

Margi led a haphazard parade up to a ring of couches on the catwalk. She and Colette introduced Karen and Phoebe to some of their new friends.

"I can't believe how many people are here," Phoebe said.

"How many dead people, you mean?" the boy on her left said. This was Trent, the Library Card Guy.

"No, just people," she said, not sure if he was trying to be confrontational or if he just wanted to start conversation. "We thought the club was closed when we first got here."

"Ah."

Colette said that it was sort of overwhelming, being around this many zombies. "I think the most we've ever had at the Haunted House was twenty-three," she said.

Phoebe turned toward the dance floor. She spotted one of the zombies out there looking as though he'd just crawled out of a three-year-old grave; his clothes were shredded and stained and the skin on the side of his head looked like it was flaking off. He was the only old-school zombie she'd seen, the only one that would not have looked out of place on one of the posters in the hall by the restrooms. Like George.

When she turned back, everyone was leaning in their chairs a little closer to Colette.

"The Haunted House?" Trent asked.

"Um . . . yeah," she said. "That's just . . . just what . . . we call this house we . . . hang out . . . at."

"Where did you say . . . you were from?"

"Connecticut?" she said, like she was being quizzed. "Oakvale?"

"No way!" Trent said, excited now. "Tommy Williams? Mysocalledundeath.com?"

Colette, suddenly a celebrity, smiled at him without answering.

"Wow, that's . . . incredible," Trent said. "Do any of you . . . go to . . . the Hunter Foundation?"

"We all do," Margi answered. She was trying to look like she wasn't interested in Trent's living friend, but she *was* interested in Trent's living friend.

"Unbelievable," Trent said. "Skip has . . . told us . . . a lot . . . about what you are . . . doing there." He paused for a moment, looking at each of them with new interest, which made Phoebe want to sink into her plush cushion until it enveloped her completely.

"Did . . . Tommy . . . really leave . . . like it says on the site?"

"He did," Margi answered.

"Wow," Trent said. "It isn't . . . easy . . . being young and . . . undead . . . in America. Lots of the . . . kids . . . here had a long . . . distance . . . to travel."

"I came here from . . . Iowa," one kid said.

"I'm . . . sorry," Colette said, making him smile.

"Hey," Trent said, "that stuff about . . . dating . . . a trad chick . . . was that true?"

You would think that someone like Colette, who had to make a conscious effort to speak and move their limbs, wouldn't have been so quick to give Phoebe up, but not so. The smile left her face as Colette looked right at Phoebe. Bad enough, but Margi and Karen did the same.

Phoebe made a clicking noise with her tongue and looked away.

"Oops," Trent said. He had trouble cutting off the "oo" sound.

"Um, yeah." Margi seemed to notice Phoebe's discomfort.

"Maybe we could talk about something else? Where are the rest of you from?"

Most, like Trent and his pal who hailed from Staten Island, were from New York City or the environs.

"But who . . . cares about that," he said, even though Phoebe did. "What's going to happen to mysocalledundeath . . . without Tommy? Do any of you know? Just about . . . everyone . . . here reads it."

"How?" Karen asked.

"Computers, upstairs," he answered. "Skip prints out the blogs and . . . hands them out."

"It'll still happen," Karen answered. "Tommy is going to be sending his blogs in from the road. Phoebe and I . . ."

The music cut out and the room went black. Phoebe shrieked.

"Some of you have been waiting an eternity for this, I know," the brash confidence of the voice cut through the darkness. "And you will now know that eternity was not spent in vain. Marking their record seventeenth appearance at Aftermath, please join me in putting claws and paws together in welcoming the band that you've been clamoring for, dead or alive. . . . Skeleton Crew!"

At the stroke of a razor-sharp opening chord, lights came back on. Phoebe looked below and saw Dom standing in front of a microphone. Next to him stood a short, shirtless, rail-thin boy who wore bright orange surfer shorts that ended below his knees. The thin boy was leaning on his microphone stand like he needed it to prop him up. Bee stood on the other side of the stage thrumming the low string on his bass guitar.

"Aftermath! Make some noise!" Dom yelled as Warren, hidden somewhere behind a ring of cymbals, began to play an escalating roll on his snare and double bass. Phoebe thought the greeting uninspired, but it provoked a healthy reaction from the crowd.

"Good . . . day . . . .everyone," the thin boy said, his voice somewhere between the somber intonations of Peter Murphy and Morrissey, "My name . . . is . . . DeCayce . . . and we are . . . Skeleton Crew."

He's the dead one, Phoebe thought. Dom hit another blaring chord and the dead boy leaped three feet in the air without flexing his legs as Bee and Warren erupted into song.

Phoebe was dead tired on the ride home, although Margi was still bopping around in the driver's seat, reliving each moment of their club adventure with minute detail. On the train she was a bundle of energy, even when Karen and Colette seemed to be holding their strength in reserve.

"He was so totally into you, Colette," Margi said. This idea more than anything else seemed to be the wellspring of Margi's energy, and as such Phoebe didn't get tired of hearing it, even though she'd already heard it at least two dozen times.

"I . . . don't . . . know," Colette said. Her denials became weaker each time Margi repeated the statement. Phoebe smiled; it was good to see Colette so moony.

"Yeah, you do," Margi said. "Totally."

The "somebody" was DeCayce. When their set was over

Dom had brought his band over to talk to the girls. As raw as DeCayce was onstage, he seemed very shy in person, and barely added to the conversation—which was mostly Dom bantering with Karen. Trent and his crowd drifted over, and the more people that were around, the more Phoebe noticed DeCayce retreating into himself. Trent was going on and on about what a groundbreaking band Skeleton Crew was, as Colette leaned over and said something that only DeCayce could hear. Whatever it was, it must have been pretty funny, because DeCayce laughed like the idea of laughter was new to him. They were inseparable for the rest of the night; Phoebe would catch glimpses of them talking animatedly, off by themselves in the hidden corners of the room.

Animatedly, Phoebe thought. Wrong word. Definitely the wrong word.

"Hey, Colette," she said. "What was it that you said to DeCayce that made him laugh so much?"

Colette turned back to her, smiling. "That . . . annoying boy . . . kept saying the word . . . 'groundbreaking.' Not good . . . word choice . . . for a zombie."

"We couldn't even find you when it was time to go," Margi said, her pink-shadowed eyes glancing up at Phoebe in the rearview. "Just what were you doing, huh, kid?"

"Stop it," Colette said. She was smiling. "We were . . . dancing."

"We were," and here the pause Margi took was three times as long as any that the New Improved Colette took, "*Dancing*. Is that what you call it?"

"Stop it!" Colette said, nudging her.

"Careful, Colette." Karen said. "She's liable to . . . kill us all. Besides"—and here Karen leaned forward in her seat—"she's just jealous."

"Of course I'm jealous," Margi said. "Who wouldn't be jealous? Did you see the way he was looking at her? Just once, I'd like for someone to look at me like that. Just once."

"I don't know," Phoebe said, "Bee seemed pretty interested in our pink-haired girl."

"Sure," Margi said, "all I get is the bass players."

"Big Christmas sales at Wild Thingz ! tomorrow," Karen said as Margi pulled into the driveway of the DeSonne home. "A great chance to stock up on all of your Z brand cosmetics."

"Colette will be needing some of those now that she has a boyfriend," Margi said, pretending to think aloud. "But I just don't think Santa is coming for her. She's been naughty."

"Will you . . . stop," Colette said, clearly not wanting her to.

On their way to drop Phoebe off, Margi and Colette started making plans about going to the mall, the people they needed to buy Christmas presents for, and what those presents would be. Phoebe sat in the backseat and willed herself invisible just so she could listen in on their conversation and the easy friendship it represented.

"What about . . . Norm?"

"What about Norm?" Margi replied.

"Don't . . . snap. And don't be . . . mean . . . to Norm."

"Being encouraging would be mean."

"You know he's going to get . . . you . . . a present."

"Tell him to save his money."

"It doesn't . . . work that way."

Phoebe was happy for them, but she was a little sad too. It sounded a lot like the conversations *she* used to have with Margi.

"Well, it needs to work another way. Norm is a really nice guy but I don't feel *that way* about him. I don't feel the way DeCayce, the sexy undead rock star, feels for you."

"Don't change . . . the subject."

"Who's changing? It's the same subject."

"I just . . . think . . . you might want to get him . . . something. Something . . . small. A CD."

"Then he'll read all sorts of deep meaning into the song titles and it'll be even worse than it is now."

"No love songs."

"All songs are love songs," Margi said. A car passed them going the other way and Margi checked her rearview to watch it recede. "What do you think, Phoebe?"

"Colette is right," she said, shocked that her veil of invisibility had been penetrated so easily. "A CD. No love songs. Maybe the Skeleton Crew CD?"

"Great idea!" she said. "Colette can probably get me a case of free copies!"

Adam was in the yard working out when they rolled up the driveway. She saw him revealed briefly in the bright swath of light beaming from Margi's headlamps, turning on his heels from left to right, his fists rotating from his hips to strike unseen assailants.

Margi had seen him too. "You going to go practice your ninja skills with Adam now?" she said.

Phoebe started, but it was just a question. Sometimes she forgot that she hadn't told Margi what had happened. She got out of the car and watched her frosted breath curl in the air before her. Adam was just a vague shadow in the darkness, a flickering ghost half seen through the ambient glow of Margi's headlights.

"No," she said after a time. "I think he's probably pretty deep into it by now. You know how intense he gets."

Margi rolled down her window as Phoebe slammed the door.

"You guys are okay, right?"

Please, Phoebe thought, let's not spoil the evening. "We're fine."

Margi looked at her a long moment. "Thanks for coming today," she said, finally.

Phoebe leaned down and gave her an awkward half-hug through the open window, reaching over to grip Colette's shoulder as well.

"Thanks for having me after all," she said. "You guys are really good friends."

Margi waited until she was on her steps before backing out. Phoebe waved to them from the steps, and then she waved to Adam, but she couldn't tell if he waved back through the darkness.

CHAPTER
TWENTY-SEVEN

"SOME OF THE Undead Studies students said that they've seen you working here at the foundation."

Angela had this trick she did when they were in session, where she sort of cocked her head while brushing her long hair behind her ear with her fingers. Pete thought it was supposed to signify how interested she was in what he was saying.

"Am I supposed to start talking about that?"

She smiled at him.

"I don't know what to say. Am I supposed to hide or something when they come?"

She shifted in her seat. "I don't know. Do you think you should?"

He sighed. "No."

"Don't you think your presence might be . . . upsetting to some of them?"

"Maybe. So you think I should hide."

"I don't think we're talking about hiding. I think we're talking about not making yourself so . . . conspicuous."

He hated the pauses in her speech. It made her sound like a worm burger. "Conspicuous."

"You were staring at them when they arrived at the foundation the other day, Pete. I would call that . . . making yourself conspicuous."

"Fine. I'll make myself scarce when they're here."

She held his gaze. "Why were you staring at them, Pete?"

He shrugged.

"Is it because you want to say something to someone?"

"Like who?"

"Adam? Or Phoebe?"

"What would I say to either of them?"

"I don't know. What would you?"

He shifted in his seat. "What, you think I should apologize or something?"

She didn't answer, her smile and gaze remained steady.

"If you are asking me if I feel bad about what happened to Adam, if I'm, like, *remorseful*, the answer is yes. Yes, I'm sorry he died."

She nodded.

"I wasn't trying to hurt him. Her, either. They were just in the way."

"In the way?"

"Yes, in the way." He looked right at her. "In front of the corpsicle."

"Tommy."

He shrugged.

"Why do you think you're so angry with Tommy, Pete?"

"We've already been through all this."

"Please sit down. Let's go through it again, okay?"

"Okay." He sat down. He hadn't really been aware of standing in the first place. "Okay, fine. I don't like zombies. I hate zombies. We talked about a girl I used to know, Julie, and how she died and she didn't come back and that probably fuels my anger. We talked about how my parents are separated and my father doesn't have any time for me and how I don't approve of my mother's choices or her second husband. These facts, or so you seem to think, contribute to what you consider to be my irrational hatred of zombies."

She nodded, her smile widening, as though they were getting somewhere. Pete couldn't wait until his six months were up.

He sighed. "So now we know . . . we sort of know . . . why I hate zombies. But I don't know what to do about it. I see them and I start getting angry all over again. I know it isn't rational. I know that they—the zombies, I mean—aren't really responsible for what happened to Julie. But I don't know what to do about it.

He looked back at her, afraid he'd laid it on too thick. He knew it was important for Angela to think her ridiculous "therapy" was rehabilitating him. Duke had been right, it was stupid for him to try and intimidate the necrophiliacs like he had been; Angela must have seen him on one of the security tapes. Stupid.

He looked at her, affecting a hangdog, contrite expression while trying not to overdo it.

"Pete," she said, "I think it's time we start discussing some coping strategies for you to deal with your feelings about zombies."

He made as if the tension was slowly going out of his shoulders.

"I'd like that. I really would."

He hoped that she didn't notice him gritting his teeth the moment the words were out.

Pete cursed under his breath as some of the bleach slopped over the sides of the mop basin. The wringer didn't want to slide onto its mounting. He kicked it and it clattered to the ground.

"Tough session?"

Pete started. Duke stood behind him, his large frame leaning against the wall. Normally the echo of Duke's heels filled the corridors he patrolled, but when he wanted to, the big man could move in total silence.

"Oh, it was great."

Duke laughed. He reached for the mop wringer and planted it effortlessly in place on the side of the rolling bucket. "I can tell. Isn't head-shrinking fun?"

"I'll be done with it in a few weeks."

"Sure." Duke pushed the bucket to him with the toe of his boot. Bleach water sloshed over the sides and onto Pete's shoes. "Oops, better mop that up. So you think you'll be all done hating zombies when it's over?"

Pete dunked his mop, then wrung it out. "I love zombies."

"I can tell."

Pete let the mop fall against the cement wall. "Look, is there a point to all your insinuations? Every time I come out of my sessions, I try to get to work right away and not bother anybody. And every day, you have something to say to me. Except I never know what you're saying."

There was a flicker of amusement on the pale man's face. "No?"

"No, I don't. Except you seem to be interested in what goes on in there." He ducked his head in the direction of Angela's office down the hall.

"True, very true."

"Well, why the hell should you care? Don't you have anything better to do than mess with me?"

"Sure I do," Duke said. "Like hunting."

"Hunting? What do you mean, hunting? Like, animals?"

"Domestic animals, mostly."

"Domestic . . . ?" Pete stopped. He'd heard about the recent pet disappearances around town. The papers had been quick to blame the zombies.

Duke's smile had grown wider. "A whole bunch of them have died in town recently."

"What are you saying? That you . . . that you killed them?"

Duke shrugged.

"*You* killed those dogs? Not the zombies?"

"Dog. One dog. A couple cats. Mostly it was just creative use of roadkill."

"You're serious? You killed them?" Pete laughed. "Why?"

Duke shrugged, a gesture of false modesty. "Doesn't matter who kills them. It matters who gets blamed."

Pete couldn't believe what he was hearing. He knew Duke was sick, he just didn't know how sick.

"The zombies. The zombies get blamed."

Duke clapped his hand on Pete's shoulder and squeezed. "Of course the zombies get blamed. They're already out there causing trouble, acting clever with these little pranks they're pulling, the graffiti and the stupid posters. They think they're being cute, "raising consciousness" or whatever, but that kind of activity just scares decent living folk. It isn't that much of a stretch to picture them killing the family pet, is it?"

"I don't even believe it. I don't even believe you're the one."

"Believe it." Duke let go of his shoulder. "Even better, it's your good buddy that's going to be left holding the bag on the crimes."

"My good buddy?"

Duke brought his hand up to his cheek, a gesture Pete instinctively copied, and he felt the rough threads of his stitches beneath his fingers.

"Yeah, your buddy. He's the main prankster."

"Good," Pete said, lowering his hand, "I'd love to see that scary dead bastard get his."

Duke raised an eyebrow so high it was almost comical.

"You would?" He leaned in close enough for Pete to smell the spearmint on his breath. "How badly?"

CHAPTER
TWENTY-EIGHT

From: WilliamsTommy@mysocalledundeath.com

To: KendallPhoebe@mysocalledundeath.com*

Hey Phoebe—

Here's my latest "adventure." I'd really appreciate
it if you could check it over for mistakes before posting it.

How is everybody? Still dead?

Love,

Tommy

DEATH ON TWO LEGS: Aftermath

I stopped at Aftermath during my stay in New York City,
which I'm told has more zombies per capita than any other
place in the country. If that rather unscientific statement is
true, they must all stay in the club itself, because I didn't see
any zombies on the streets of New York. Either that or the
zombies I did see were indistinguishable from the traditionally
biotic people.

Readers of this blog know that at times I have been critical of Skip Slydell and his company, Slydellco, who I have seen as profiteering off the undead without regard for the repercussions of that profiteering. I've been concerned that his cosmetics and clothing trivialize our cause rather than advance it, but after meeting Skip in his club I'm convinced that that isn't his intention. I won't go as far as to say that I am a supporter, but he isn't the greedy robber baron I originally pegged him for. His methods may be suspect, but I do think he has undead interests at heart.

Aftermath is in an unassuming three-story building off the Bowery. In much of his media material, Skip calls the club evidence of a "cultural revolution." Typical Skip, he goes too far with his own hyperbole—but it's hard to deny that some form of cultural change is taking place there.

The club departs from the typical cavelike, warehouse decor of most clubs, favoring instead bright primary colors that cover every visible surface (with the exception of the corridor to the bathrooms, but I'll get to that later).

"You have to go with what's stimulating to people," Skip told me as we sat on leather chairs in a small office he keeps above the DJ booth. "Dead kids like light, they like color, they like three hundred beats per minute. We've done theme parties, ones where we keep the houselights on for the whole dance. Living kids, they dance in the dark. Why? The dark is exciting to them. It's thrilling. Dead kids, some of them spent too much time in the dark, alone. They don't want to be back there. I went to a rave in an old brick warehouse a few weeks ago

looking for ideas. I looked around and said: I'm in a crypt.
Some of these kids have actually been in crypts; who wants to
dance in one?"

"Take our furniture. All overstuffed, comfortable. Velour.
Fake fur on a lot of the pillows with nice bright colors. Soft
things, comforting things."

I ask him how the club makes any money when it runs
twenty-four hours. Earlier in the day I talked to Simon from
White Plains, a zombie who told me he'd been at the club for
"at least six days."

"Yeah, we have about twenty-five people living here," Skip
said, and for a moment I think he's going to dodge the question.
"I have outside funding," Skip tells me. "You'd be surprised how
many people, people with means, are sympathetic to the plight
of the undead. I get money from Hollywood, I get money
from Washington. I kick money from my product line into
the kitty; we're set up as a not-for-profit. The labor is all
volunteer; the expenses are low. Electricity and rent are our
biggest headaches."

"What do you do if a dead kid can't pay the cover?" I
asked.

"We let him in," Skip said, smiling. "Living or dead. We'll
take a partial donation if they can't pay up in full.
The living kids always, always have the money, though.
And they all buy T-shirts and snacks while they're here.
It works."

We watched a band called Skeleton Crew performing
from the window of his office. The members all hail

*from New Jersey, and, their lead singer, DeCayce,
is dead.*

"I don't pay the bands either," Skip said, as we watched
Skeleton Crew launch into the first of a set of
eight songs, which were an interesting mix of the bands'
competent speed punk with DeCayce's slow, dirgelike
vocals that hover like the wings of bats. "They play for
exposure."

I ask Skip if there's really that much exposure to be found
within the walls of Aftermath, which some people may never
leave.

He thought the question was funny.

"It's an investment," he said, "I think it's a good one.
Cultural credit is different from financial credit; you build
cultural credit by trading credit with other brands and
products in the hopes that they add to your own."

I'm told I have a good poker face, but Skip could see my
confusion.

"Look," he said, "did Michael Jordan make Nike, or did
Nike make Michael Jordan? And does it matter?"

Skip has a real Michael Jordan fixation, I've noticed, even
though the man has been retired for years. He pointed
out a few kids in the audience who were wearing shirts
that had the Skeleton Crew symbol, a yellow smiling skull
emoticon.

"It's like when certain designer clothes started appearing in
retail stores, the stuff was getting shoplifted by the closet load.
The designers thought they had a real problem, but then they

realized something. The clothes were getting boosted by
fashion-conscious gang kids, and every one of those hip
gangsters was like a walking billboard for their product.
So the designers said, let 'em steal. They did subtle things to tie
their brand into what was happening with urban chic; they did
some branding with the rap stars of the day, and pretty soon
the clothing was in such demand it wouldn't matter how many
outfits they lost from their retail outlets.

"Aftermath is going to be like that. Undead culture is
going to be the next pervasive phenomenon in the United States
and the world. Six months from now this band is going to be
able to tell all the people that want their songs for movies, for
television, for commercials, that they were once the house band
at Aftermath. And Aftermath is going to be able to say they
put Skeleton Crew in the public eye. It's like that skull T-shirt
you see everywhere, the Misfits one? Where were the Misfits
until Metallica started wearing their shirt onstage and talking
about what a "seminal influence" they were? They were a small
local band with a small cult following, right up until Metallica
went crazy and became one of the biggest music acts of all time.
And then the Misfits were cool because Metallica wore their
T-shirts. And Metallica was cool because they were part of
that select cult following of the Misfits. It's all about cultural
cred."

Skeleton Crew was a good band, the flat, pause-heavy
intonation of DeCayce an element unique enough to set them
apart from the dozens of bands that played in the same style.

"You don't know how lucky you are," Skip said, and unlike

the songs that DeCayce sang, his words were free of irony, "To be dead in America at this point in time. This is your time."

I didn't know how to respond to that, so I just stood in his high office and watched all the lucky people on the dance floor below as they tried to have some fun.

I spoke to DeCayce sometime later, long after the rest of his band had left, presumably to get some sleep, to dream of being the vanguard of a new cultural revolution.

We talked about many things—how we died, how those around us reacted to our returns. I think it's funny how we rarely reveal the circumstances of our deaths to trad people we meet, but it is usually the first thing we exchange with fellow undead, and I said so.

DeCayce picked up on this instantly: "It's sort of the 'what do you do for a living' for the dead set," he said. "Instead, we ask, 'So, how was it that you stopped living?'"

He told me that the other members of his band were his best friends, and had been prior to his death.

"They all stood by me when I came back," he said. "My family had a much harder time of it—they still do. My friends, though . . . they were there through it all."

I asked him how long it took him to get the control over his speech and body.

"I'm still trying," he said. "I'm better onstage than I am one-on-one, as you can probably tell. Something about the crowd, maybe."

My last question was whether or not he thought there was a message in his music.

"No," he said first, but then thought about it. "Well, I guess there is, but not an overt one. I guess the message in the songs is that it shouldn't matter if someone moves differently, or looks differently, or talks differently. Is biotic differently. What matters is that we're all thinking beings, and if we are thinking beings we ought to be able to find common ground somewhere. Maybe if people can see us playing, three beating hearts and a dead guy, it will inspire a little more tolerance in the country."

Tolerance. I thought that his statement was similar in sentiment to the ideals of the Hunter Foundation. And I wondered, as I did when I first heard the Hunters speak of it, if tolerance was going to be enough.

Phoebe read the blog a second time before typing a reply.

Tommy—
Everyone here is fine. Except for George, who might be in some trouble. Something or someone has been killing animals in Winford and the police are blaming him. Karen says there's no way he would do something like that. What do you think?
When were you at Aftermath? Was it on the 28th? That was when we were all there. Margi, Colette, Karen and I. We had such a great time dancing and meeting so many people. I couldn't believe how many trads were there!
Did you see us?
Phoebe

CHAPTER
TWENTY-NINE

KAREN CALLED HER the next day and asked if she wanted to work on the Web site with her after school on Monday.

"I'd love to," Phoebe said.

"Great. You can come over after Undead Studies. You can eat here. I'll watch you, living vicariously the whole time."

Phoebe smiled. "We have the field trip tomorrow, right?"

"I know. I've got a bunch of . . . work to do for that . . . too. We're going to have an action-packed day."

"Okay," Phoebe said, wondering what a meal at the DeSonne household would be like.

"Sounds fun."

"I got Tommy's e-mail last night," Karen said, "the little . . . creep. Sometimes he makes me so mad."

"It was a good blog, though," Phoebe said.

"I can't believe he didn't come talk to us," Karen said. "Don't tell me it doesn't burn you up."

"A little." She was more sad than angry, though. Tommy was avoiding *her*, not them. She'd hurt him deeper than she'd realized.

"Well," Karen said, "I've got to get back to work. I'll see you at school tomorrow."

"You're still at work?" Phoebe said. "How late is the mall open?"

"Until ten, even on Sunday," she said. "This is my second double shift. Craig asked me to stay because two people called in. I figured it was the least I could do after going dancing on the biggest shopping day of the year."

"I should get a job," Phoebe said, thinking out loud. Really the work-study hours were enough; she could wait until the summer.

"Wait until I open up my business," Karen said. "I'll hire you."

"Your business?"

"Tell you later. Craig is giving me the . . . evil eye. I have to go. See you."

"See you," Phoebe said to dead air.

"Field . . . trip!" Cooper said as he took a seat in the back of the bus. Phoebe thought he was pretty pleased with himself for having arranged it.

Cooper claimed to have suggested the field trip so they could get out of some class time, but Phoebe suspected that he'd really done it because he knew Melissa wanted to go to the Haunted House, but had difficulty getting around. She'd worn her comedy mask today, and almost looked happy as she lurched into a seat. Alish and Angela were the last two to get on the bus, and they took the seat directly behind the driver. Phoebe figured that they would be the first adults ever to be invited to the Haunted House. Unless you count the police, who were called there on the night of Adam's murder.

She slid in the seat next to Karen, after a quick glance back at Adam, who sat in the back with Thorny and Kevin.

"Do you really think this is such a great idea?" she asked. "Inviting Angela and Alish?"

"I don't know, really," Karen said. "I don't know if I trust the foundation completely. I e-mailed Tommy, though, and he thought it was okay."

"You e-mailed Tommy?"

"Yes. That was okay, right? Me emailing . . . Tommy?"

Phoebe whirled to face her. "Of course it is. Why should I care?"

"I don't . . . know," Karen said, and Phoebe thought she was using more speech pauses than usual just to be irritating. "Why . . . should you?"

"Should I find another seat?" Phoebe asked.

"No," Karen replied, patting her on the shoulder. "I still love you. We're going to have . . . a blast tonight, aren't we?"

The bus pulled away from the curb, and the chatter grew in volume to compete with the dull growl of the engine. Thorny was telling Adam and Kevin about some phenomenal play he'd made on the football field, practically shouting about his gridiron prowess even though the dead, despite their many issues, were not hard of hearing. Margi was laughing about an e-mail DeCayce sent to Colette with an MP3 attachment of a song they'd added to their live show, a cover of "So Alive" by Love and Rockets, a band they'd known from Colette's brothers' vast record collection.

"He's totally singing about you," Margi said.

"Is . . . not."

"Is too!"

"Is . . . not!"

Melissa was sitting alone a few seats behind them, looking out the window. Karen called over to her.

"Hey, Melissa," she said. "Are you excited?"

Melissa scribbled on her board and held it up. She'd drawn a large and blocky exclamation point.

"There are lots of kids there. Hopefully you'll get to meet Mal. He's one of my best buddies. He used to stay at St. Jude's too."

Melissa erased and wrote.

FR. FITZ TALKS ABOUT MAL

"He does? Father Fitzpatrick seems to be a pretty nice guy, for a beating heart," she said, nudging Phoebe with her elbow. Phoebe nudged back.

I ❤ FR. FITZ

"Tayshawn was at St. Jude's for a while," Phoebe said. "Will Takayuki and his boys be there, you think?"

"I think so," Karen said, "They live there. So to . . . speak. I think it will be more . . . interesting . . . for everyone if they are."

A banner that read WELCOME ALISH AND ANGELA hung from the slouching porch of the Haunted House. It was Karen's idea, executed by some of the zombies with black paint on an old sheet. Alish took Thorny's arm as they went up the rickety steps of the front porch.

"Amazing," the old man said. "Simply amazing."

There were about twenty zombies waiting for them in the foyer. Phoebe watched Karen move to the front of the group, where she asked for silence even though none of them had made a sound. She did a quick scan for Tak, but didn't see either him or Popeye, although there were a handful of the other old-schoolers around, George among them. She was surprised and happy to see that Tayshawn had stuck around to see his old classmates.

"Hello, everyone," Karen began, "I'd like you all to meet Alish and Angela Hunter, who began the Hunter Foundation for the Advancement and Understanding of Differently Biotic Persons. That means us dead folk."

Karen smiled, and Phoebe was gratified to see more than one stony face twitch in an attempt to smile along with her. As irritated as she was with Karen, Phoebe had to admit she'd put a lot of planning into the event. Now that they had chosen to fully accept the Hunter Foundation as a source of funding and support for the Haunted House, she'd thought it made sense for them to try and cement their relationship in a way that went beyond the typical student/teacher relationship. To schmooze them, in other words. Skip Slydell would be proud.

"I would like to introduce each of you . . . to the Hunters," Karen said. "One at a time. We've also brought some new friends along from our class, Cooper Wilson and Melissa Riley."

Cooper waved, but Melissa looked like she was trying to hide behind Adam. Karen didn't force the issue.

"I appreciate your patience . . . in advance for helping make everyone feel at home. And for you . . . living . . . folks, we have some refreshments in the . . . unliving room. Soft drinks and chips."

"Really?" Thorny asked, suspicion evident in his voice. "Where did you get the snacks?"

Karen gave him a droll look. "From the cemetery, Thornton," she said. "Where do you . . . think?"

Karen stood by the Hunters and introduced them to each zombie in turn. Phoebe could tell that Alish wished that he was able to take notes to record his impressions, his hand shook as he clasped each cold, dead hand that was offered to him. His eyes kept drifting to George, who was shambling around the periphery of the gathering like a boy at a party too shy to ask a girl to dance. George made no attempt to hide the physical aspects of his death, the rents in his skin, his missing ear, the ribs visible beneath his ripped and muddy clothing. The funny thing about George was that, unlike zombies like Tak and Popeye who used their scars for effect, it didn't even occur to him to cover them up.

"This is Jacinta," Karen said, introducing a young girl who was still wearing the pink dress she was almost buried in. "She's a newlydead."

As Angela shook the blankly staring girl's hand, Phoebe took another quick scan of the room. Kevin and Thorny were looking at the CD rack by the stereo, and Margi and Colette were already making a loud nuisance of themselves with a small cluster of zombie girls in the corner. George had stopped his circumlocution of the room and was staring openly at Melissa. He took one dragging step toward her, then froze when she looked over at him.

Oh no, Phoebe thought, hoping that the shy girl wasn't spooked by the most zombie-esque of all zombies. They couldn't be more different. George, in truly dead fashion, had no compunction at all about revealing the evidence of his death; she took as much care as possible to hide her own scars, even from herself. Phoebe wondered how many people had figured out she was wearing a wig.

Melissa wrote something on her board and held it up in front of George.

"And how long have you been dead?" Phoebe heard Alish ask Jacinta. Karen and Angela exchanged a quick look, as though neither could believe the question he'd just asked.

"Three . . . weeks . . . sir," was the slow, slow reply.

George was staring at the whiteboard, his tall gangling frame like a six-foot-tall undead question mark.

"What was it like?" Alish asked. Jacinta didn't answer right away, either confused by the question or by its inherent rudeness.

Tak and the rest of his crew made an appearance just as the party was winding down. Phoebe watched Karen fix Tak with a withering glare.

"Nice of you to show up," Karen said to Tak.

"We've been . . . busy," he said. Despite his promise to "be good," he made a point of not shaking hands with Alish. He looked at the Hunters as though the sight of their living flesh was repellent to him. He did his stupid little trick with his cheek too, keeping it hidden from view until he was a couple feet away from them, brushing back his lank black hair with a bare-knuckled hand so they could get a good up-close view of his teeth. The Hunters both flinched, and Karen told him how clichéd he was becoming.

Phoebe noticed something in Angela's expression, though: recognition. Angela, unlike Alish, did not offer her hand to be refused.

"You aren't . . . doing enough," Tak said.

Alish asked him what he meant, but Tak had already turned away. Karen was about to apologize for him when Popeye pushed his way over and thrust one of his recruitment posters into Alish's shaking hands.

"Be all . . . that you . . . can be," he said. He lifted his right hand, the one with all the skin removed from knuckle to wrist, and reached for his glasses.

"Thank you, Popeye!" Karen said, trying to interpose herself between him and the Hunters.

Alish didn't notice her alarm. "This is wonderful!" he said, looking at the poster.

Popeye stopped. "What?"

"This poster," Alish continued. "It's brilliant. The way it captures the grim reality of the undead experience."

Popeye removed his hand from his glasses and peered over Alish's shoulder. "Really?"

"Oh, yes," Alish said, his bony fingers passing along George's image. "The colors, the way it shows the boy's obvious pride in being a zombie . . . even the font and the fine print. It is a remarkable composition."

"You really . . . think so?" Popeye said. "I . . . created it."

"Really? This is a fine piece of work. A fine piece. Such a powerful message. May I keep it?"

"Yeah! I mean . . . sure. The more people that see . . . my work . . . the better."

"Would you do me a favor?" Alish said, gazing intently into Popeye's dark lenses. "Would you inscribe this for me?"

"Um, yeah!" Popeye said, patting the pockets of his leather jacket. "I think . . . I've got . . . a marker . . . upstairs."

Phoebe watched him rush away, in search of his marker. When she turned back to Alish and Karen she almost laughed out loud at Karen's expression.

"Mr. Hunter," Karen said. "That was . . . that was . . ."

"Ms. DeSonne," he said, "in my position, I have to deal with bullies of all stripes. He smiled at her, his eyes twinkling beneath their furry brows. "It gets easier and easier each day."

She smiled back at him, but Phoebe thought she looked uneasy.

"Phoebe, would you come with me a minute?" Karen said, leaving the Hunters socializing with Tayshawn, who had reluctantly promised to talk to them. "I want you to hear something."

Phoebe followed her over to Takayuki.

"Do you have a minute, Tak?" Karen asked with mock sweetness.

"For you," he said, "I have an . . . eternity." Phoebe couldn't tell if he was trying to be charming or sarcastic.

Once they were in the kitchen Karen asked him about George, whether or not he could be responsible for the animal slaughters in Winford.

"George?" he said. "Impossible. George is not . . . fast . . . enough. Just to get to . . . Winford . . . is a major . . . ordeal."

"One of your other . . . pals?

Tak shook his head. "The Sons of Romero . . . would not . . . butcher . . . house pets."

"Sons of Romero?" Phoebe said, wondering if being a Son of Romero meant they were going to act like movie zombies. Tak pretended that she hadn't spoken, that she wasn't even in the room.

"That's cute," Karen said quickly, as though trying to defuse the tension between them. "You think of it . . . all by yourself?"

He shrugged, only one shoulder raising. "Of that crime . . . we are . . . innocent."

Tak was a lot of unpleasant things, but Phoebe didn't think he was a liar.

"Karen," Tak said, "why don't you . . . come with us . . . next time?"

"Please. I have a . . . job. Two jobs."

Tak showed his teeth. "We'd love . . . to . . . have . . . you."

Phoebe watched Karen cast her diamond eyes toward the heavens, but again she had the feeling that Karen was amused, maybe even charmed, by Tak's actions.

She herself was less amused when she saw Tak and his cronies leading Adam and some of their guests upstairs.

CHAPTER THIRTY

HAD TROUBLE WITH the stairs right leg left but made it. Made it in time for Tak Smiley's speech.

Cooper whispers. "Is that . . . Tak? Is that the . . . guy . . . Karen talks about?"

"Smiley." Last stair.

"This is . . . the wall," Smiley said, waves bare knuckle hand at the photographs. Cooper, Melissa, Smiley, Popeye, George, Thorny. Popeye stands next to Thorny shows knuckles shows ribs looks dead. Deader than dead. Thorny leaves.

Smiley continues. "These are . . . your people."

Hundreds of photos. Zombies, deadheads, corpsicles. Poloroids, jpeg printouts. Kids looking scared. Step. Cooper and Melissa looking.

"Our . . . people. The . . . returned dead. Zombies." Dragging the "Z" like drag left leg. *Zzzzzombies.*

"Here . . . I am," Cooper said, pointing at a curling sheet

238

of computer paper. Smiling at Smiley.

"Thought you . . . looked . . . familiar," Popeye said, Popeye clapping Cooper on back, all smiles and light now.

"The beating hearts . . . want us . . . gone," Tak said. "The ones . . . downstairs . . . are no . . . different."

Melissa, writing.

"Not all trads are . . . bad." Cooper said, shaking his head. "Alish and Angela . . . are good to us."

"Like they are . . . good . . . to pets." Tak tapped on the wall.

Melissa writes, holds up: LIKE U?

Tak smiles. "We had nothing . . . to do . . . with . . . the incidents . . . you refer to. All part of the . . . bioist . . . conspiracy . . . to destroy us."

Tak waited, no reply. Turned back to the wall. "Half . . . of these . . . kids . . . have been returned to death. True death. And what . . . have they done?"

Melissa crossed-out writing, started again. Cooper's answer never came.

"You know . . . zombies . . . that have been destroyed. You . . . lived . . . with them. Does the . . . foundation . . . protest? Do they . . . demand justice? Do they do anything more than . . . hold you captive . . . and stick you . . . with needles?"

"I'm not . . . a captive . . . I'm . . ."

Melissa flips sign. George stares so hard, almost funny.

FATHER FITZPATRICK

Tak shakes head, lank long hair flicking against leather, tendons creaking. "You can't look to . . . the beating hearts . . . for sanctuary. In the end . . . they just make it easier . . . to round us up."

"What about the work . . . that Tommy . . . is doing?" Cooper said. Strength there beneath goofy exterior.

Tak looks at Cooper. "I wish . . . Tommy . . . well. My hope . . . is that . . . he reaches . . . Washington. I fear . . . he will not."

"What do you . . . think . . . we should do?"

"I think . . . you should be . . . with your people. With . . . us."

Popeye put his arm around Cooper's shoulder, squeezed. George reaches out, touches Melissa's mask. Gently. She doesn't flinch.

"We will be . . . ignored . . . by our country . . . no longer. We will . . . continue . . . to make noise," Tak said, "until . . . they . . . can no longer . . . destroy us . . . at will." Taps wall. "For . . . them. For our . . . people."

Want to clap. Don't. Look at wall instead. Have no idea what Tak thinks he is accomplishing.

Call from below, time to go. Popeye and Tak thank Cooper and Melissa for time. George waves. Follow them out. Smiley stops at top of stairs, turns.

"You, Adam . . . you should . . . be with . . . us."

Contact. Eye contact. Smiley doesn't look deranged. Looks concerned. Earnest.

"I'll think . . . about it."

Smiley nods, claps arm. Small gesture, big impact. Tayshawn at bottom of stairs like standing guard. Angela waiting, says van has to go.

See Phoebe in doorway. Phoebe turns away.

CHAPTER
THIRTY-ONE

PHOEBE WENT over to Karen's house when Undead Studies was over. She was fairly exhausted after the Haunted House event, but Karen was still in go mode, talking about all she felt they had accomplished with the visit. As she watched the dead girl talk about how important it was that the Hunter Foundation spent its money on the right things, all Phoebe could think was how wrong Karen had been when she told Tommy she didn't have any leadership skills.

Dinner at the DeSonne household was strange indeed. Karen's father did most of the cooking, although Karen helped him chop vegetables for a salad. Mr. DeSonne insisted that Phoebe not help them but instead "relax" in the living room, where Karen's little sister, Katy, was playing with a trio of small stuffed bears.

"Mommy has to work late," Katy told her. "Can I touch your hair?"

"Sure," Phoebe said, leaning forward so Katy could drag stubby fingers through her hair. Her mother would be eating at the office, her father said, and would not be in until later.

When dinner began, Karen sat at the table watching them eat spaghetti and salad, listening without comment as her father asked Phoebe some questions about school and the work study, which he referred to as the "special class." Karen would lean over to wipe her sister's face with a napkin whenever the tomato sauce threatened to cover it.

When they were done eating, Karen helped her father clear the dishes, another activity he forbade Phoebe to help them with. Phoebe noticed that Karen didn't speak much as they worked, and her motions were almost mechanical as she moved around the kitchen. Maybe she was reading too much into things, but Phoebe thought that Karen's father was doing everything he could to keep from touching her.

Katy used their absence to lean over and touch Phoebe's hair again.

"They say my sister's dead," she whispered, "but I think she's the prettiest girl in the world."

When the dishes were away, Mr. DeSonne had Katy say good night, which for Katy was a gentle hug and a kiss on the cheek for her sister and for Phoebe.

"I like you," she said, her breath warm against Phoebe's neck. "Come back and play with Karen?"

"I will," Phoebe promised, and Katy bounded down the hall after her father.

"Cute kid," she said to Karen when her chores were done.

"The best," Karen replied. "She was born nine months after I died. Kind of weird, huh?"

Phoebe didn't know what to say to that. She followed Karen to her room in the basement. The room was colder than upstairs, and the cellar floor was hard beneath the thin carpet. There was a musty scent in the air that Karen had tried to cover with various scented candles and plug-in air fresheners.

"The basement used to flood," she said, reading Phoebe's mind. "Sorry."

"No worries," Phoebe said. "It's a little dark down here for work, though. We don't want to go blind."

Karen turned on a few lights, and they sat on the edge of her bed. She saw Phoebe staring at a small silk pillow atop a pair of normal pillows.

"Yeah, it's the one from my coffin," Karen told her.

"I'm sorry, Karen. I . . ."

Karen waved. "Don't worry about it . . . really. My parents bought me a really nice one, lacquered wood with a white satin lining and pillow to match. I came back before I got to use it. And guess what? The funeral home had a 'no returns' policy! So I kept the pillow. Sometimes I lie down on the bed and put my head on the pillow, and I daydream about dreaming."

"What did you do with the coffin?"

Karen shrugged. "I wanted to keep it, but my mom thought it was too morbid. She didn't even want me to have the pillow, but I was . . . insistent. I think they sold the coffin on eBay."

Phoebe took her printed copy of "Words from a Beating Heart" from her bag.

"Karen," she said, "I'm sorry I was so cranky with you today."

Karen smiled. "You wouldn't be saying that . . . just because I'm about to read . . . your story, would you?"

"No."

"Hey," Karen said. "Don't worry about it. You've got a lot on your mind. You're entitled to be cranky."

She nudged Phoebe with her shoulder. "I remember what it was like to be alive too."

"Karen . . ."

"Kidding, I'm kidding. Now are you going to let me read that, or . . . what?"

Phoebe reluctantly handed over the papers. She looked around the room while Karen read, trying and failing to keep from looking for Karen's reactions to her words, and then trying and failing from being disappointed when there weren't any.

"I really like this, Phoebe," Karen said finally. Phoebe let out her breath, realizing how much Karen's approval meant to her.

"Really? You think so?"

"I really do. I wasn't...sure if Tommy's idea of having a . . . living . . . person write for the site was such a hot idea. After reading this not only do I see why it was a good idea—but I think you're the perfect person to do it."

Phoebe thanked her and paused.

"I wrote Tommy a poem when we . . . when we first really became friends."

"I know. He had it in his locker."

"You knew?"

"Everybody knew, honey. The community of the living weren't the only ones scandalized at first, if you must know. Tommy had dead people calling him a sellout even then."

"Tak."

"Not just Tak. Not everyone is as moderate as you think. There's a lot of jealousy and bitterness among 'my people.' And Tak isn't really such a bad guy."

"He's not?"

"No. He can be quite . . . sweet . . . sometimes."

Something in Karen's tone stopped her. Karen was rereading her blog entry, her smooth white skin spectral in the glow of the computer.

"Karen?"

"Mm-hm?"

"Did Tommy talk about it with you? About me, I mean?"

Karen turned toward her, her eyes seeming to hold the glow of the monitor a moment too long.

"He did."

"And?"

"And what?"

"And what did you think?"

"About him dating a beating heart?" Karen said, her pale lips in a thin smile. "I didn't have a problem with it, actually. And that was before I really knew you, even." She shrugged, her shoulders rising and falling in perfect sync. "People should be happy."

"And once you did get to know me? What did you think then?"

"I thought he had great taste." Karen looked at her, and

Phoebe had the same sensation of falling that she'd experienced when looking into Tommy's eyes that first night in the woods.

"Why do I feel like I'm not really answering . . . your question," Karen said, lifting her hands in exasperation. "What is your question, Phoebe . . . Hello, Phoebe?" Karen said before realizing why Phoebe had hesitated. She lowered her arm, too slow a gesture for it to be reflexive.

"Karen, I . . . did Tommy tell you how he felt about me?" she said, stumbling.

"Yes, he did." Karen said, crossing her arms in front of her, picking at the cuff of her sleeve with her fingers

"He told me he was in love with you, Phoebe," she said, her expression not changing, making Phoebe wonder if the subject was causing a rare emotional retreat in her. Then her face softened and her diamond eyes sparked and flared with a sudden and momentary white light.

"I think he meant it too."

Phoebe turned away. "Sometimes I thought . . . I thought that it wasn't *me*, you know? It wasn't *me* but the idea of me. Like I wasn't really important. What was really important was that I was alive."

She looked back, feeling shy and self-conscious, and Karen's pursed lips did nothing to relieve those anxieties.

"Because you were living," the dead girl repeated. "Phoebe, maybe that was . . . part of it. Is part of it. But the two of you had just met, right? You're sixteen. Didn't you ask yourself the same question yourself?"

"What do you mean?"

"Well, how do you know you weren't going out with him just because he was a zombie?"

"I wasn't."

"Are you sure? Dating a zombie really takes the whole edgy goth chick thing up a whole new level, don't you think? How many of the other little goth girls can say that they dated a zombie?"

"It wasn't like that," Phoebe said defensively.

"I know it wasn't, honey," Karen said. "Tommy's a loveable guy. He's brave, he's handsome—if he were still alive he'd be every girl's dream. And you're pretty lovable yourself, you know. I sometimes wonder if you have some kind of chemical or mutant pheromone or something you put out that drives everyone crazy."

"A mutant pheromone?" Phoebe smiled.

"Hey, stranger things . . . But look: you took interest in him as a person, Phoebe," Karen said. "Sometimes that's all anyone really needs to fall in love. Wasn't that what you were trying to say in your blog?"

"I guess so."

"I think it was, Phoebe."

"What else did he say?" Phoebe asked, hoping she didn't sound too eager .

"Not much else," Karen said, but Phoebe thought she could detect a far-off twinkle in her crystalline eyes, like the flare of some distant sun. "He's a very private person despite that . . . blog. Plus he probably didn't want to hurt my feelings."

"Hurt your feelings? Were you in love with him too?"

"All of us dead girls were a little in love with Tommy," she said, "but how do you know I wasn't in love with you?"

They both laughed at that. At least, Phoebe thought Karen was laughing. Phoebe's cheeks felt warm.

"Anyway," Karen said after a time, "I wish I could write like you. I think that was part of why Tommy is so into you. He likes the arty types. Music and poetry, deep feelings."

"You aren't arty?"

"Not very . . . creative, I'm afraid."

Phoebe caught a hint of sadness in her voice, ever conscious that whatever inflection and emotion she saw was a conscious decision by Karen. Looking at her, at her platinum blond hair swept over her shoulder, her diamond eyes sparkling above pale high cheekbones, Phoebe wanted to tell her that it didn't matter if she was "arty," because she was *walking* art. But she wasn't sure how Karen would take the comment, so she kept it to herself.

"Tommy wanted me to kiss him," she said instead.

"That would be a typical thing, yes."

"He thought it would bring him back to life. Or partly back, or something."

"Well, you did, I hope."

Phoebe looked up at her with confusion.

"Kiss him?"

"Oh. No, I didn't."

"You're kidding."

"No, I didn't kiss him."

"Why not?"

"I don't know."

"Why? Because he's a zombie?"

"Well, yeah. That's part of it. But it was just weird, anyway," Phoebe said. "I've never kissed a boy. Not really."

"You're kidding."

Phoebe bit her lip, thinking about her botched attempt with Adam.

"Phoebe," Karen said, her eyes glittering, "you had a boy believing that your kiss would bring him back to life, and you didn't kiss him? That takes playing hard to get to a whole new extreme."

Phoebe started to laugh, and when she did, Karen leaned in and kissed her on the side of the mouth: a cool, feathery kiss that was over before Phoebe could react. "There," Karen said, sitting back. "You kissed a zombie and survived. Next time you see Adam give him one of those, but with more feeling. Who knows? You might even bring him back from the dead."

"I didn't kiss a zombie," Phoebe said, resisting the urge to wipe her lips. Karen wore peach lip gloss. "A zombie kissed me."

Karen thought that was hilarious. "Whatever," she said. "I'll let Adam know he'll have to make the first move." Phoebe could no longer hold her gaze, and turned away.

"I don't think so."

She said it softly, because she wasn't really sure that she wanted Karen to hear her.

"What do you . . . mean? Adam is absolutely crazy about you—you must know that."

Phoebe shook her head. "No."

"Phoebe." Karen gripped her arm. "He's been all puppy dog . . . for you since . . . forever. You're joking, right? He told me . . . he was."

"He told you? When?"

"The night he . . . died." She didn't look away when she said it. "He was going . . . to tell you."

Phoebe's breath caught in her throat, the only reply she could manage was shaking her head.

"What . . . is it? Did something . . . happen?"

When words came, they did so in a rush and a sob. "I tried to kiss him! He . . . he pushed me away! Tommy told me . . . he told me a kiss would bring him back to life, but I tried, and Adam . . . Adam pushed me away!"

Karen's arms were chilly around her. "Oh, honey." Karen rocked her, and Phoebe felt so stupid and helpless.

"I guess he'd rather be dead than be with me."

Karen held her up straight. "No, sweetie. Don't you think that at all. That isn't it. He loves you, I'm sure of it."

"Then why would he *do* that?" She looked around the room for some tissues, but Karen didn't really have a great need for them. Finally she found a package in her backpack. "If he's so crazy about me, why would he practically *shove* me on the floor when I tried to kiss him?"

Karen smiled at her as she wiped tears from Phoebe's cheek with her cool fingers. "Phoebe, you have to think like a guy for a minute. Worse, a zombie guy. One of the most confused and . . . confusing . . . beings on the planet."

"What do you mean?"

"Look at it from a guy's point of view. Here's . . . Adam, superjock . . . extraordinaire . . . and not only can he barely walk, or talk . . . or anything. Even when he was in . . . full command . . . of his game, he couldn't express his feelings, could he?"

"He always had girlfriends."

"Yeah, he was really serious about those . . . airheads, too, wasn't he?"

"I think he was expressing himself pretty well when he pushed me onto the floor."

Karen's look was so deadpan at the bitterness of Phoebe's words that Phoebe couldn't help but giggle. Karen laughed with her.

"Phoebe, does Adam know about what Tommy said to you? About kisses bringing the dead back?"

"I don't know. Maybe."

Karen nodded. "That might be it too. He might not believe that you really . . . love him. He might think you're just going through the motions to try and resurrect him. He might think that what you feel is guilt, not love. Think about it—he's loved you for a billion years, and you never seemed to notice until he . . . died."

"How do you know he's loved me for a billion years? Did he tell you that?"

"Not with words."

Phoebe was skeptical. And, she realized, a little jealous. What did "not with words" mean?

"Phoebe?"

"What?"

"Do you . . . love him?"

She had an answer prepared for that question; she knew it would be coming as a normal part of the conversation they were having, but as soon as the question was asked she forgot the answer.

What she remembered instead was the way she felt when Adam appeared out of nowhere to save her life. She remembered what it was like when they were together, when they were younger, reading comic books or going swimming at the Oxoboxo. What she remembered was how strong he was, what he looked like in his suit, and how he was always, always there for her when she needed him.

And then she remembered how she felt when she was with Tommy, and confusion crept in.

"I . . . I don't know," she said. "I think so . . . I really think so, but I'm not sure."

Karen nodded. "I think maybe you are."

"But I'm not sure. How can I be sure?"

"You'll get . . . a chance. Adam will . . . come around. He just needs to get . . . his confidence back."

"You think?"

"I'm sure of it. And forget . . . about kisses and all that stuff. That isn't really what's going to bring him back. Love will bring him back. Love works."

"You seem to know a lot about guys."

"I know some things." Karen winked, and it was a perfect,

flawless wink, as if she'd been practicing. It startled Phoebe so much she laughed out loud.

"Karen," she finally said, to break the awkward silence, "we were supposed to be working on the Web site, weren't we?"

"Oh yeah," Karen said with an exhalation that was very much like a sigh. "Maybe we should just wait until our next work study at the foundation," she said. "At least then we'd get paid for it."

CHAPTER
THIRTY-TWO

"AGAIN," MASTER Griffin said. Did same form one hundred and seven times, counted. One hundred and eight.

"Again."

One hundred and nine. "When . . . will . . . I . . . be . . . ready?"

Griffin squints, reaches, adjusts arm. Lift arm.

"When you can grab the pebble out of my hand. Again."

One hundred and nine. Stare.

"I'm kidding, Adam. Is something the matter? You seem distracted today."

Distracted, he said. Not distracted, dead. Been a zombie for weeks and can barely move. When living, mastered this form on day one, two or three tries. One hundred and ten.

Griffin crosses arms. "Adam, let's take a break."

One hundred and eleven. Look at Master Griffin never

took a break not once in whole year of practice. Griffin sits on the mat, motions to sit in front of him. Griffin crosses legs, lotus. Can't do that. Can't even sit. Sort of flop.

Griffin waits, stares. "Adam, something is troubling you."

No joke, sensei. Dead, or hadn't you noticed? Griffin smiles. Everyone's a mind reader these days.

"The girl who brought you to the dojo," he said. "It's her, isn't it?"

Stunned. Stunned so only the truth will come out.

"Yes."

Griffin nods. "You have had feelings for her for a long time."

Not a question. Statement. Griffin looks, laughs.

"Don't look so surprised. You've studied with me for months now, and I've heard her name a dozen times. 'I played Frisbee with Phoebe.' 'Phoebe likes milk shakes,' 'Phoebe likes strange music.' When you are quiet, you hear things that other people don't actually say out loud."

Shut my mouth. Master Griffin not a talker. Says "again," "again," "again." Higher, faster, use the instep. Quiet.

"Listen more. I haven't heard you say her name since she brought you here last, and today you have trouble with the most basic forms. And not because you are a zombie. Because your mind is elsewhere. With her."

With her. Yes, with her.

"I listened to her when she was here, also, Adam. I watched you both."

Breathe. Tried to breathe.

"What . . . should . . . I do?"

Griffin shakes head.

"I don't know. You made a choice on the night you died, no? A choice for her. You cannot let the results of that one choice absolve you from choosing for the rest of your life."

Smile.

Griffin returns smile. "Sorry. Existence, whatever we term it. I am glad you are listening!"

"She . . . needs . . . to . . . live."

Griffin sits, patient and frowning, waiting for me to finish.

"She . . . needs . . . to . . . forget . . . me."

Griffin inhales. "Is that what she wants, Adam? More importantly, is that what you want?"

Don't answer. Can't

Griffin, serious. "You have a choice to make. Your heart, beating or not, will tell you what to decide. Keep listening."

"How was karate?" Joe asks, driving home.

"Good."

Choices. Pushed Phoebe away. Hurt her. *Chose* to hurt her. Chose to die for her. She chose . . . what? Chose to waste time on FrankenAdam.

"Phoebe hasn't been around a while." Just drive, Joe.

She chose, why? I thought guilt. Think guilt. Who am I? *What* am I?

"Kind of strange, when she was over every day."

Won't quit.

"Hurt . . . her . . . feelings."

"You hurt her feelings?"

Nod. Manage smooth nod.

"Well, you better apologize, and quick."

Joe's right, Master Griffin's right. FrankenAdam's wrong.

Choice would be Phoebe. Choice always was Phoebe.

"You listening to me? You need to apologize to her right away."

"Miss . . . her . . . cooking?"

"Do I *what*? Do I miss her *cooking*?"

Joe hits, actually hits, with knuckles on my arm. Don't feel it. Funny.

"You love her, you big idiot!" Ramped up, now. "And she loves you! You're smarter than that."

Real smart.

"Was . . . joke."

"Real funny. You better apologize to her."

Apologize. Choice always was Phoebe.

"I . . . will."

"You better."

"I . . . will."

Phoebe was surprised to see Adam at the door. He hadn't crossed the thin patch of grass that separated their yards since falling on Mischief Night. "Hey . . . kid," he said, "can . . . I . . . come . . . in?"

"You never had to ask before," she said, holding the screen open for him.

"We need . . . to be . . . invited," he said, his hand slapping at the screen and stepping inside.

Phoebe turned so that he couldn't see her smile.

"So," he said, "what are you . . . up to?"

"Just getting ready for school, same ol' same ol'."

"Doing anything . . . after . . . school?" he said.

"I'm supposed to have a driver's lesson," she said. "But I'll be home around five. Why?"

"Funny," he said, "I always thought . . . I'd be the one . . . teaching you . . . how to drive."

"Me too," she said, sitting down at the kitchen table and taking her bowl-size mug in both her hands. "The gearhead next door."

"Me," he said, pointing at himself, his thumb about even with the bullet hole over his heart. "Want to . . . toss . . . the disk around . . . sometime?"

He stopped his shuffling to look at her.

"I'd love to," she said. "Getting a little cold, though."

"Good," he said, "that's really . . . good. Frisbee . . . I mean . . . not . . . the cold."

She sipped her coffee. "Taking the bus today?"

"Yep."

"Can I sit with you?"

"Well," he said. "I . . . guess . . . so."

"It doesn't have to be in the same seat. If you're afraid of your dead friends seeing you."

"You know . . . how they can get," he said, smiling at her. She thought that even his smile looked more like it had in his pre-death days, much less a rictus. "All bent . . . out of . . . shape."

"Okay," she said, "I'll try to be discreet."

There was a lot they could say there, she thought, in the quiet kitchen, a lot that had gone unsaid and a lot about what had been said, but for the first time she felt that nothing needed saying. The link, the bond—call it friendship, call it telepathetic—that had been broken was there again, radiating in the air between them as palpably as the aromatic steam rising from her cup.

"It is . . . almost . . . time," Adam said. "Can . . . I take . . . your . . . bag for you?"

Her negative reply was reflexive, but the bond enabled her to catch it before it was out of her mouth. Adam, who in a hundred small ways, through opening doors and driving her to work and carrying bags and holding coats and letting her pick songs on the stereo, had not been able to do a single thing for her in the past two months.

"That would be great," she said, nudging her heavy bag from its place beside her chair with the toe of her boot, "because it is pretty heavy."

"Good . . . thing," he said, "that I am . . . pretty . . . damn . . . powerful."

"Good thing," she said, and excused herself to get her coat, hat, and gloves.

"Phoebe." He touched her arm.

She turned, and when she did, he leaned forward and he kissed her.

Kissed phoebe gently gently didn't want to hurt her. Can't hurt her hurt her enough already. Kissed her. Long but not too long.

Steps back is she angry is she horrified is she happy?

She's shocked.

"Adam," she says, and she's sad. Made her sad crying tears and then "Adam" again and she hugs, her arms are tight around and she's holding like she doesn't want to let go. Like she never wants to let go.

Hug her back. Gently.

She looks up. Kiss.

No magic. No instant resurrection, no return from the dead. No bolt of lightning that starts the heart and pumps the blood. Can't move faster, can't speak more clearly.

But

Oh the kiss.

CHAPTER
THIRTY-THREE

H E KISSED ME, Phoebe thought, as they walked to her locker. It's all she could think about.

Adam had to duck beneath some poorly hung strands of garland as they walked. Phoebe again fought the urge to mother, to take the bag from him at the door so he would have time to shuffle (walk, she reminded herself, *walk*) down to his own locker and have a chance at getting to class on time. But she didn't. Adam was a big boy and being dead made him slow physically but not mentally. He wanted to do this for her and she needed to let him.

"Company," he said. She looked through the puffy-coated crowds milling through the hall and saw Margi waiting for her at her locker. She waved and Margi blew them both kisses.

"Thanks, Adam," she said, accepting the heavy bag back. He nodded and blew a kiss back to Margi, managing a fair approximation of a sneer as he did it.

They watched him walk back down the hallway, where he was joined by Thorny, whose red-and-green elf hat looked oddly appropriate on his curly head.

"Hey, Pheebes,"

"Hey, Gee."

"Good to see you and the Lame Man all chummy again."

"Yep. We're chummy."

"Did he ask you to the Winter Jubilee yet?"

"No," Phoebe said, a quip about Adam probably having a healthy aversion to school dances dying on her lips. "Where's Colette?"

Margi sighed. "She didn't finish her algebra assignment last night, so she got to class early to work on it."

"She doesn't have to sleep, but she still didn't finish her homework?"

"I know, kind of crazy. If you didn't have to sleep you'd probably have a sequel to *War and Peace* written by Thursday," Margi said. "But we got to talking last night, and you know how that goes."

Phoebe paused in the careful stacking of her textbooks to look at Margi and saw that the darkness around her eyes wasn't all eyeliner.

"Uh-oh," she said.

"Nah, it was good," Margi said. "Deep but *sans* drama. We've all had enough of that lately."

"Mmm. So what did you spend all night gabbing about then, if I may ask?"

"Well, we started off by talking about you and Adam, if you really want to know."

"Margi," Phoebe said.

"No, hold up, it wasn't like that either," Margi said, leaning into her and giving her a nudge. "It was all hugs, smiles, kittens, lacy underwear."

Phoebe slammed her locker and waited for her to finish.

"And then Colette said, 'You know, Gee, you haven't spent any time with Phoebe lately. Just the two of you. We've gotten together, the three of us, and that's been a hoot, and we've gotten together with the Dairy Queen—'"

"The Dairy Queen?" Phoebe said.

Margi bit her lower lip. "That's what we call Karen."

"The Dairy Queen? Margi, that's terrible!" Phoebe said, but she was laughing. "I know. I know, I know. It's wrong. We don't mean anything by it, other than she's well, a little frosty. And very, very, white."

"Terrible."

"I know. We're just evil. Well, C.B. is more evil than I am ' 'cause she thought it up. Anyhow, she was saying how we all get together, but you and I never get together anymore, just the two of us. And how, before she, like, died, and Adam died, you and me used to hang out all the time."

"Colette is a good friend," Phoebe said.

"She really is, Pheebs," she said. "And she's sharp. She said that you and I ought to go out and do something together, you know, and not bring her along."

"That would be great," Phoebe said. "I mean, it's great when she's along, too, but it would be fun to be just me and you."

"Yeah," Margi said, taking her arm, a bauble from one of her bracelets snagging on the frilled cuff of Phoebe's blouse. "Us beating hearts need to stick together."

Phoebe tried to detach the charm, a gloomy-looking pewter teddy bear. "Not tonight, though. Adam and I are going to play some Frisbee."

"Holy crow," Margi said, "you guys are really back on track, then?"

"We're back on something," she answered, smiling.

"That's great!"

"Yeah, it really is."

She could feel the weight of Margi's stare upon her. "What?"

"You tell me what. You've got this goofy, faraway look on your face. You look like you just landed on the moon."

"Oh."

Margi stamped her foot. "Come on, Phoebe! Give!"

Phoebe lowered her voice. "He kissed me, Margi. Adam kissed me."

Margi shrieked and clutched her arm. "Adam *kissed* you?"

"Shhhhh!"

"What was it like?" A little thrilled, a little scandalized, a lot curious. "Come on, Phoebe, tell me!"

There was so much that Phoebe thought she could tell her. How different it was when Adam kissed her than when she had tried to kiss him.

Phoebe was going to tell her, but then the bell rang, and the girls ran down the hall to their class.

There was little of the sense of moral outrage that had followed the news of Tommy and Phoebe's relationship once word about her and Adam got out, at least at school. Phoebe thought there were a few reasons for this, the first being that she and Adam were friends, and people were used to seeing them together.

Unlike Tommy, who was an outsider, an alien, Adam had been a favorite son of the community prior to his death, and as such, was exempted from the hatred that many people reserved for the undead. He was also exempted from blame, as it was common practice for bioists to blame zombies for the "crime" of being undead, as though they'd chosen such a fate. They knew Adam had been killed, and many people, while not knowing who specifically he was trying to protect, knew that he died trying to save someone.

Even when Phoebe and Adam chanced a trip to Winford to see a movie, people mostly ignored them, which was about the best reaction that a mixed living/dead couple could hope for.

"I'm amazed no one is saying anything," Phoebe said. "The popcorn guy didn't even blink when you handed him the money."

Adam was having a difficult time folding himself into the narrow theater seat, and Phoebe was glad the movie they'd chosen was sparsely attended.

"Played . . . football . . . against . . . him."

"Really? Maybe that's why."

"Maybe . . . people . . . are getting . . . used . . . to . . . us."

She wasn't sure if the "us" meant "zombie" or "Adam and Phoebe." They stopped by the food court after the movie to check in with Mr. Kendall, who was sipping a soda and reading a paperback, ready to spring into action if any of the traditionally biotic denizens of the mall chose to make trouble for his daughter and her date. Phoebe tried to talk him out of staying, feeling both foolish and guilty that her father should feel he had to chaperone them in such a manner. Not so foolish and guilty that she didn't ask for more time.

"Hi, Dad. Can I bring Adam over to Wild Thingz! before we go?"

"Did you have any trouble?" he asked.

"No . . . trouble."

"We'll only be a few minutes, Dad. We'll be done by the time you get the car."

Her father bent the corner of his paperback down, a practice Phoebe hated. "Okay. Ten minutes, okay?"

"Thanks, Dad."

The main reason that she wanted to bring Adam to Wild Thingz! was so he could see the line of Slydellco zombie hygiene products. Body spray, lip gloss, hair gel—she always got a kick out of the display, even though Tommy was the only zombie she'd known who actually used any of the products, most of which probably went home with trad kids trying to be edgy. She herself had a tube of Kiss of Life, a dark crimson lipstick "especially formulated for the differently biotic."

She had just begun showing him the rack when she noticed

Karen standing behind the cash wrap, apparently working.

"Oh, my gosh," she said, gripping Adam's rock hard bicep. "It's Karen! I totally forgot she worked here!"

Karen saw her and held up a finger, asking for a moment. She spoke to a frowning, acne'd guy with a ring through his eyebrow who Phoebe assumed was her boss, and a moment later Karen joined them at the display.

"Hey, guys," she said, "don't you look cute together. Off . . . on a date?"

Phoebe blushed without knowing why. Adam's "yes" sounded like a tire slowly deflating.

"Listen," Karen said, drawing close. "Don't let on . . . I'm dead. They don't know."

The news stunned Phoebe, but Adam seemed to take it in stride.

"Does this . . . stuff . . . work?" he asked, holding up a can of aerosol zombie deodorant. "I don't . . . smell . . . do . . . I?"

"Of course not," Karen said. "It's really an . . . antibacterial spray. If you've been in the ground too long, I think. Try the Z if you want a . . . cologne."

"You didn't tell them you're a zombie?" Phoebe noticed that her eyes were blue instead of their usual diamond color. Was she wearing contacts?

"We all have secrets. Don't . . . out me, though, okay?"

"I wouldn't do that."

"I know you wouldn't, sweetie." Then, loud enough for her scowling boss to hear at the cash wrap, "We also have the Z in a six-ounce bottle if you'd rather, sir."

Adam smiled.

"Perhaps a T-shirt, then?" she continued, her voice ringing out over the loud horror-punk music playing from the store's sound system. "We have, just in, baby doll tees with the 'Some of My Best Friends Are Dead' logo. Very . . . popular."

Phoebe couldn't keep herself from laughing, and she held on to Adam for support. Karen smiled sweetly at her grumpy boss, fluttering her long eyelashes as she did so.

Phoebe thought it felt very natural, very real, to be having fun with her friends. Very normal. She looked at Adam and he was smiling at her, and she squeezed, not wanting to release him, not wanting to let that feeling go.

CHAPTER
THIRTY-FOUR

DUKE SHOWED UP at exactly two a.m., as promised. His huge black truck, sleek and reflecting moonlight, was almost soundless as it rolled up to the curb.

"Hey," he said as Pete climbed in. "Have any trouble getting out?"

"Are you kidding?"

Duke smirked and gave him the once-over. He'd worn exactly what Duke had told him to—black sneakers and jeans, a dark, hooded sweatshirt. Duke was dressed almost the same.

"So where are we going? You know you have to go back the way you came, right? This just goes into the development."

"I know." Duke slowed down a few streets away and pointed at a house near the end of a cul de sac. "Is that where Evan Talbot stayed?"

Pete noted he didn't say *lived*.

"Yeah."

"Got away with that one, didn't you?"

Pete didn't reply. Duke smiled at him, and then gunned the engine, and soon they were on the back roads of Oakvale.

"Did you know that there are twenty-seven cemeteries in Winford? And another seven just in Oakvale?"

Pete shook his head. "No, I didn't know that."

"True fact. That's almost three times as many cemeteries as liquor stores. That's a lot of dead people."

"Are we going to a cemetery?"

"We certainly are. There's a bag under your seat. Open it up, would you? I brought you a present."

Pete found a green canvas bag by his feet. He opened it and a pair of rubber masks fell out.

"You get the one with the long black hair."

Pete spread the mask on his knee.

"Zombies? We're going to pretend to be zombies? In a cemetery?" His mask had a long slash on the left cheek that exposed cracked yellow teeth along a gray gum line. The eye-holes were cast to make the mask look faintly Asian. It was a cartoonish likeness of the zombie who had maimed him.

Duke was smiling. "Fun, huh? Go ahead and try it on."

Pete held the mask stretched out before him a moment longer, then he pulled it on his head. The latex was moist and cool against his skin.

"That looks great." Duke reached over and ruffled the long black hair. "You, son, have just joined the ZLA."

"What's the ZLA?" Pete's voice echoed against the mask

and he adjusted it slightly. Already the trapped heat was making his stitches itch.

"The Zombie Liberation Army." Duke grabbed his own mask and pulled it on with one hand. Pete looked back at a bald zombie with pockmarked skin and round, crazed eyes, its mouth drawn back in a wet looking snarl.

Liberation, Pete thought, excitement and nausea welling up within his stomach in equal amounts. "We're going to dig up some graves, aren't we?"

The mad, slavering zombie face turned toward him.

"Oh yeah," it said.

There were three other vehicles at the cemetery, two white vans and an American-made sedan. Pete saw a half dozen or so figures milling about in front of one of the white vans, each with a shovel.

"Holy crow." He lifted the neck of his mask up because he thought he was starting to hyperventilate in the latex. "We're so close to the main road. What if the cops come?"

"The cops won't come." Duke brought the truck to a halt on the shoulder of the gravel path.

"How do you—"

"I know. The cops won't come. I've got a shovel for you in the back. And put your mask back on, we don't like to show each other our faces."

Pete scrambled out the door and joined Duke at the back gate of the truck.

"What about the zombies? Isn't this the place they put all those posters up?"

Duke unlatched the gate; the shovel he selected rasped against the bed as he drew it out, like a sword. He handed it to Pete.

"I like you, kid. You're observant."

"But what if they show up?"

Duke paused, and Pete could almost picture his bemused expression beneath the garish zombie mask.

"You aren't afraid of some zombies, are you? Big Pete, zombie killer?"

Duke's words made his stitches itch even more. "No, I'm not afraid. I just don't want to get caught."

Duke slid his own shovel out. "Quit acting like a girl. We know where the zombies are. They're busy with their own pranks tonight, so don't worry about them."

He dropped his free hand on Pete's shoulder and pulled him close, so that their masks were almost touching.

"Don't think we're a bunch of stupid rednecks going off half-cocked, Pete. Don't confuse our actions with yours. This is a very carefully thought out operation. The key to destroying your enemies is knowledge and planning. We've got both."

"Who's we?"

Duke let him go and rose up to his full height. He was bigger than any zombie Pete had ever seen.

"Just keep your mouth closed and your eyes open, Pete. I'm giving you a great opportunity here, but you're the one that's got to take advantage of it. Now don't say a word."

With that, Duke called over to the men from the other vehicles, shouting naturally, as though they weren't about to desecrate a cemetery at two thirty in the morning.

"Gentlemen," he said, as they formed a loose ring around him. Pete counted seven other figures, all men by the looks of it, but he wasn't entirely sure because they were all wearing zombie masks. Each mask was designed to frighten, each having a macabre or grisly detail like a severed ear, missing nose, or wild pop eyes to make the wearer look insane or dangerous, or both. Someone made a comment about the long hair on Pete's mask, another whistled. The weight of the shovel felt reassuring in Pete's hand.

"Hey," a "zombie," definitely male, his large gut hanging over the waistband of his black jeans on all sides, called. "Who's your date?"

Duke pointed a finger at the fat man. "Shut up. We don't have time to be screwing around. Everyone know their parts in this?"

Zombie-masked heads nodded.

"Just to be sure, I'm going to break it down."

The respect that Duke commanded from these men was obvious, even through their disguises. When he spoke, all chatter and joking ceased, and they all milled in a little closer as Duke began to break down the plan. Pete gathered that he was supposed to dig graves along with the men while Duke supervised and took pictures.

"Read the tombstones before you dig," Duke said. "What we want is people with families, hopefully with one name on the marker not yet buried. Kids are okay, but stay away from teens."

"Don't want to catch a live one?" the fat man said. "I mean, a dead live one?"

No one laughed, maybe because Duke leveled his shovel at the man's protruding gut.

"That's the last time I'm warning you. You want to see if you can be the first person over eighteen to come back from the dead?"

The fat man shook his head, his zombie mask twitching back and forth so fast it would have been comical if it wasn't abundantly clear that Duke thought the time for jokes had passed.

Duke lowered the shovel and nodded at another zombie-masked man. "What do you have for us?"

He came forward with a large duffel bag. The man unzipped it and withdrew a stack of paper sheets similar to the "Undead States" posters that the real zombies had used when they decorated the cemetery. They had the same picture of that really, really dead-looking zombie, but the words had been changed to "ZLA—Rise up and Destroy the Living!"

Duke nodded. "Nice."

The man with the duffel took out an old grayish bedsheet. He unfolded it completely until it lay atop a grave like a picnic blanket. The words, "Zombie Liberation Army—Destroy the Living!" had been painted in dripping crimson letters.

Duke laughed. "Put that bad boy up on that mausoleum over there. Okay, people. Let's dig."

The men, even the fat comedian, rushed to obey. A few had already picked out their graves; Pete heard the unmistakable sound of blades biting into the frosted turf. He was aware, suddenly, of the crazy eyes of Duke's mask staring down at him. He almost flinched.

"You okay, son?" he said softly.

Pete nodded, hefting his shovel.

"Attaboy. Why don't you get started on that one over there?"

Pete walked over to the grave Duke had indicated. There were two names on the headstone; the woman had died last year, in her forties. Her surviving husband, a few years older, was still out and about.

He looked back at Duke, who was leaning on his shovel to balance the camera he pointed at him.

Pete started to dig.

CHAPTER
THIRTY-FIVE

TAKAYUKI LOOKED back to the edge of the parking lot, where Tayshawn stood under a high streetlight. Tayshawn's job was to watch the mall entrance for prowling police cars, and signal the remaining Sons of Romero with an air horn that he had "liberated" from the hardware store. They had been in the mall lot for an hour now and not a single cop car had swung by. Tak couldn't believe their luck.

He looked back at the mall entrance, where Popeye was putting the finishing touches on his latest art installment. George and Karen stood with four mannequins propped up on the front steps under the unlit neon sign, each bent into stiff, awkward poses meant to parody the languidly unnatural poses of fashion models. Popeye had used papier mâché to give the mannequins a rough, old-school zombie appearance; one even had a strand of latex skin hanging down from its cheek in what was perhaps a sly tribute to Tak himself. Tak thought it looked like someone had plastered shredded wheat to its wooden face.

"Move her over . . . to the left . . . George," Popeye said. "Just a . . . hair. No, my . . . left."

The mannequin had one of the newest shirts from the Slydellco line, the words "Just Dead" in block letters on a white background. The zombie mannequins were all smiling, and all of them sported Slydellco shirts that Karen had picked up for them at her job. The two girl mannequins were wearing cosmetics from the Z line; Tak had watched Karen apply "Kiss of Life" lipstick to one of them from her own personal tube. Tak thought that the crimson lips and the other liberally applied cosmetics—the eye shadow and blush—combined with the grayish papier mâché made the figures look like garish undead clowns.

He thought "Kiss of Life" looked really good on Karen, though. He wasn't sure but he thought she used the eyeliner as well, and he once thought he smelled flowers when standing next to her—his sense of smell was so tricky, and he was never sure if he wasn't imagining scents rather than experiencing them.

George knocked off the zombie's wig as he moved the mannequin.

Tak wished they would work faster, but he was also glad that Popeye took things so seriously; his creativity had been a real boost to the Sons of Romero, who responded to the various projects with eager enthusiasm. And there wasn't much that any of them were enthusiastic about.

"Let me help you, George," Karen said.

Tak watched her bend down to retrieve the wig, her short plaid skirt hiking up on her thighs. She glanced back at him and a wry smile crossed her lips.

"Here we go," she said, straightening the wig on the mannequin. George gave her his version of a smile, and the result was horrific.

"There," Popeye said. "It's . . . perfect. Let me take . . . a few . . . pictures."

He withdrew a camera from his backpack and urged George and Karen to stay in the frame for the first few shots.

"Why don't you . . . join them . . . Tak?"

"No."

Popeye's eyes were unreadable behind his thick wraparound glasses. He turned and snapped a few pictures with Karen and George in the background.

Tak watched her pose, and he could tell she was aware of his attention. She leaned over and mimed a kiss to the mannequin with the slashed cheek. Popeye snapped a few more with them out of the frame, then popped out the memory stick.

He held it out to Karen. "Do you have . . . pockets . . . in that skirt? It's . . . awfully . . . small."

Karen took the stick and dropped it into the pocket of her white blouse. "Don't be cheeky."

Tak watched the exchange, wondering if Popeye got away with his innuendoes because he was gay. He looked back at Tayshawn, still under his spotlight.

"Are we . . . done . . . here?"

Popeye cast his hands heavenward. "Are we done . . . here,

he . . . says. Not . . . 'Popeye, you . . . genius! You've . . . done it . . . again!'"

"Popeye, you genius, you've . . . done it . . . again. Now . . . can we . . . go?"

Popeye shook his bald head and shouldered his bag of supplies, muttering about the lack of respect. Tak watched Karen help George down the stairs; fearsome as the boy looked, he was easily defeated by a simple staircase. His left leg just wasn't working the way it was meant to.

They started across the lot.

"I'm really . . . glad . . . you came with us, Karen," Tak said, once they were out of the spotlights and into the woods. "Thank . . . you."

"Why, Tak. You say the . . . sweetest . . . things."

Tak looked over his shoulder, making sure that George wasn't lagging too far behind. He felt Karen's hand brush against his, and wondered if she'd felt the hard bones of his knuckles where they protruded from the skin. His sense of smell may have been dull, but his hearing was excellent—he could hear the rattling of the equipment in Popeye's bag, the scrape of George's step as he dragged his foot along the trail, and above it all the swish of Karen's skirt as she kept pace beside him.

He cleared his throat. "Will you . . . be late . . . for school?"

She shook her head, and he was almost certain he could detect floral traces in the air around her. "I'll walk . . . straight there. It's . . . closer . . . than home."

"Karen . . . I . . ."

He didn't get to finish, as Popeye trotted up beside them, angling his thin body between them.

"I can't . . . believe . . . no cops . . . the whole night," he said. "We were . . . wicked lucky."

Tak wasn't so sure. "Yes . . . lucky."

"And Karen, thanks for . . . getting the . . . shirts. That really made the . . . piece . . . I thought."

"Sure, Pops. Anytime."

Tak wanted to trip Popeye, who stood between him and the memory of flowers. "You risked . . . your job . . . for us."

Karen smiled at him. "You mean you aren't still . . . mad at me . . . for taking the job?"

Tak looked at the ground before their feet. He'd argued with Karen when she told him about how she was passing, going as far to say that she was setting their cause back to the days of Dallas Jones, the original zombie, by her actions. But the more he thought about it, the more he realized that Karen had a right to live her own undead life. Besides, he'd thought, there were ways that her actions could be useful to everyone.

"I was . . . wrong," he said. "It . . . happens."

Tayshawn, who had stayed back with George, called for them to wait up, and the trio stopped at an intersection of paths.

"Was it hard . . . stealing the shirts?" Popeye asked.

Karen looked offended. "I didn't . . . *steal* . . . them, Popeye. I . . . *bought* . . . them. I have two . . . jobs, you know."

"Really? You . . . bought . . . them?"

"Yes, really."

Tak frowned. "At the same . . . time? I would . . . hope no one connects . . . your . . . purchase . . . with . . . the installation."

Karen looked unconcerned as she took a seat on the remains of a stone wall that had once marked off some Connecticut landowner's plot. "We sell so many . . . of them," she said, "and I've bought . . . a bunch more. I think I'm . . . safe."

"Good," Tak said, watching her smooth her skirt on her pale legs. "We want you . . . to be safe."

Tak knew that that was what had fueled his initial rage when she told him about her job at the mall. Working in a public business was different from her working at the foundation, where there's at least the pretense of a shared beating heart/zombie worldview. If her zombie nature was to be discovered while she was working at the mall, Tak thought she ran the risk of being dragged out into the parking lot and destroyed. It had happened to zombies across America for lesser offenses.

"Does this mean . . . you are . . . a Daughter . . . of Romero . . . now?" Popeye asked.

Tak thought he detected a slight note of jealousy along with the excitement in Popeye's voice. He knew Popeye was fond of him, but he also knew that what drove Popeye's train most of all was his "art," and if Karen was on the team he'd be able to accomplish a lot more because of her access to computers, photocopiers, and things that could be bought in stores. And besides, Tak had made it as clear as he could without saying it out loud that he thought Popeye a trusted friend, but that was as much as he'd ever think of him.

Popeye, he knew, wasn't really deterred. That was one curse that didn't leave when you died. The curse of hope.

"I don't think I'm . . . ready for a . . . commitment yet," Karen said, her eyes that flashed in the darkness still locked on Tak's.

"Your presence is . . . enough," Tak said, "for . . . now."

Karen smiled, and in her smile Tak realized that he was still cursed as well.

Tayshawn and George caught up a moment later, and then they continued through the dark wood.

CHAPTER
THIRTY-SIX

UNDEAD STUDIES. Alish looks grave (ha) when class enters. He and Angela are talking to a pair of tall men in suits, some type of law enforcement. Duke Davidson was there as well, his expression and pallor could make him and the gray cop cousins. The men both have zombie eyes. Gray Suit turns, and although Thorny spends much of his day around dead folks, the man's stare is enough to kill the laughter in his throat. Feel Phoebe's hand on arm, her touch a vague sense of pressure. She could be gently resting her hand or squeezing with all her might. Touch could be one of compassion, or affection, of alarm—can sense none of these gradients.

"Guest speakers?" she whispers. Try to shake head. The presence of men like these indicates that Something Has Happened. First thought is of Tommy. Sitting—unaided—can see by the way Karen goes to the beverage service that she is having similar thoughts. Wonder what it is about the presence of certain types of authority that triggers a rebellious response in her. The fact that she can drink liquid, and does so to distract the living people around her, is something of a defense mechanism. She does it in the same way that a juvenile delinquent would clean his nails with a knife.

Angela speaks to us first. She looks as though this class has aged her; the radiance in her smile has diminished.

"Class," she tells us, "this is Detective Gray and Detective Alholowicz. They are here to talk to each of you. About . . ."

"Ms. Hunter, if I may?" the gray one, Detective Gray, said. It wasn't really a question. "We're here to talk to you about a crime." He looked at everyone in the room, but he seemed to find me particularly interesting.

"A terrible crime. A felony. Grave desecration."

"And you think one of us . . . did it?" Karen asked, pouring at least an inch of sugar into her coffee cup.

Gray turned toward her. He was a thin guy; the suit jacket made him look bigger, but when he turned you could see how thin he was.

"We know at least one of the perpetrators of this heinous act was dead," Gray said, and for the first time I saw a flicker of reaction in his pale eyes. I think it was because he'd assumed that Karen was alive when he first walked by. "Ms. Hunter, I think I'd like to begin the interviews right away. Adam Layman, you're up first."

Might have blinked.

* * *

In Angela's office, a little room off the clerical offices that had a couple leather chairs and shelves filled with books. Three chairs stood on a red oriental rug.

Alholowicz kept dabbing at his left eye with a handkerchief. The eye was tearing and glassy looking. He was lumpy around the middle in contrast to his partner, and there was a coffee stain on his white shirt that his tie almost covered.

"You want to stand?" he asked. "You guys don't get tired, right?"

"I want him to sit," Gray said before I could answer, pulling the office door closed with a little more emphasis than what I would have thought necessary. He waited, then he took the other leather chair, pulling it a little closer.

"Do I . . . need . . . a lawyer?" Probably sounded guilty, or worse, scared.

Gray didn't blink. "You don't have any rights," Gray said. "You're dead. You're not even a citizen."

"Jeez, Louise," his partner said. "Give the kid a break, will ya Steve?" Good cop said. "It doesn't have to be like that, does it?"

Gray's eyes were like drills as he reached inside his suit jacket. Inside was a gun in a holster and for a moment I thought he was reaching for the gun and now I'm sure that is exactly what he wanted. Instead he took out a photograph.

"You tell me," he said, holding it out in front of me. "You tell me how it should be."

Looked at the photograph. It was of a murky dark hunched figure heaving a shovelful of earth from a grave.

"Real nice, huh?" Gray said, slapping the photo on the table beside us so hard that Alholowicz had to steady the lamp before it fell to the ground. There was another chair behind Angela's desk, but he remained standing. "That's Chesterton Cemetery, right over the Winford line. You want to tell me who that is in the photo?"

"Have no . . . idea."

"Do you always talk that slowly, or just when you have something to hide?"

"Don't . . . have . . . anything . . . to hide. Didn't . . . do it."

"You didn't do it. He didn't do it, Agent Alholowicz." Gray leaned forward, his elbows on his knees and his hands tented as though to keep them from shaking. "I guess we can just go. He didn't do it."

He got up quickly, his whipcord body brushing against the table. Alholowicz replaced the lamp again.

"Look, kid," he said, "we know you didn't do it. Agent Gray has a niece that's a whatchacallit, a zombie, and he gets really angry when a zombie does something like this because he knows you all don't have, um, any constitutional rights."

"Every time one of you maggot brains screws up like this," Agent Gray said, "you get that much closer to sending people wild in the streets. We're talking chains and torches, smart guy. Eighty percent of America is just waiting to light you guys up in one big bonfire, you hear me? And what do I got if they do? What can I arrest people for? Public disturbance? Fire code violations? I do not want some crazy mob burning up my sisters' kid."

He slapped the table in case I didn't understand how passionate he was about the subject.

"You . . . are in . . . the FBI?" It took a while. Gray, undead niece or not, wanted to hit. He turned away, thrusting his fists on his narrow hips.

"Yeah, we're FBI," Alholowicz answered. He walked over to the shelves of books and tried to look like he was scanning their spines. "We're a new task force, actually. Undead Crimes. No disrespect intended if that isn't, whatchacallit, politically correct. You know better than anyone that people don't really know what to do with you fellers."

"Undead . . . crimes?"

"Yeah," Alholowicz said, lifting a glass paperweight off the bookshelf with one hand while dabbing at his eye with the other. "Yeah, absolutely. Lots of undead crimes. We started out investigating crimes *against* you people, you know? The burnings and the lynchings and the getting dragged behind cars. We cracked this one case where this group was actually crucifying dead folks. Nailing 'em up on crosses and leaving them there. Didn't kill 'em or anything, but left them hanging there in fields for days. Remember that, Steve? That case in . . ."

"I remember," Steve said.

"Anyhow, that's how it started. The Bureau figured that even though you people were dead already and didn't have any legal rights or anything, it wasn't exactly something we wanted to condone. I mean, crucifixions! Jeez, Louise!"

"Can we get on with this, please?"

"Sure, Steve, sure. Take it easy. Anyhow, kid, that's what we were supposed to do. Investigate groups of people that were getting together and committing acts of violence on dead people. But then a funny thing happened. Not so funny, really. More and more we got called upon to investigate crimes of violence committed *by* dead people."

Agent Gray turned around then, no longer looking angry, but just looking tired. "And that isn't good, Layman," he said. "It isn't good, because like it or not—and I don't like it—you and your friends don't have any rights. Zero. The laws aren't there to protect you. Which means that the laws aren't there to protect *from* you either, and the last thing we want is people going to look for some street justice.

He leaned close again, but this time his intimacy was free from rage.

"I don't want to see that happen," he said. "It's wrong."

"Steve's a patriot," Alholowicz said, fumbling the paperweight before navigating it back to the shelf. "He really is. And he loves that little niece of his."

Gray leaned in a little closer, close enough to count Adam's eyelashes

"So let's cut the crap," he said, "Tell me about this guy with half a face."

The dead were always given some distance in the halls of Oakvale High, but once the news of the grave desecration came out, students were literally turning around and running the other way. The incident was all over the news, with the families of the people whose graves had been disturbed making tearful pleas for the police, the government, anybody to do something about the "evil zombies" who would commit such blasphemy. One man, the scab of his grief not yet healed from having lost his wife to a drunk driver the year before, was stone-faced as he called for "the eradication of the zombie menace" on national TV.

The fear the incident had caused was so disruptive that a notice was posted mandating that all differently biotic students needed to be escorted from class to class by a teacher.

"Come on, Layman," Coach Konrathy said, meeting him at his locker before the first bell. "Show some hustle." Phoebe couldn't decide who looked more pissed off about the arrangement.

Some trad students, ones that had been in the pink of health just twenty-four hours before, were absent from school entirely. Norm Lathrop told Phoebe that there was a petition going around school to ban undead students from common areas like the foyer and the cafeteria.

"Boy," Karen said to Phoebe in the hallway as she waited for her to retrieve her books. "Dig a few . . . graves and the whole world comes down on your head. Could I get . . . arrested for digging out of my own grave?"

"Don't even joke. This is too weird," Phoebe said. The flow of traffic had moved all the way to the other side of the hall to keep from getting too close to Karen. "We're getting together at Margi's after school. You want to come?"

Karen shook her head. She was staring over Margi's shoulder, as though her diamond eyes were recording each and every one of her classmates who was now shunning her.

"I'm going to try to . . . talk to Takayuki . . . and the boys. Find out what the story is. Tak swore that George didn't hurt the animals. Maybe they didn't do this either."

"Karen, they were showing pictures of someone that looked a lot like Tak."

"The pictures were grainy. And I know the boys had nothing to do with those flyers."

"How do you know that?"

"Because I didn't make them." Karen's expression went blank. "This time."

"Karen! *You* made those flyers?"

"The first ones, yeah, I . . . used the computer and the . . . photocopier at the mall, when I was on break. It was . . . a joke. A funny one too. This wasn't . . . funny."

Phoebe didn't know what to say, she just stood there with her mouth hanging open.

"Miss DeSonne!" Principal Kim called. "You have a date with history!"

"There's my escort. At least she doesn't . . . pretend these new rules make sense. See you."

"See you."

Phoebe was halfway to her own class when she saw a group of boys standing around Kevin Zumbrowski. His books were on the floor, his shirt was untucked, and one point of his shirt collar pointed at the ceiling. His cheek looked dark, as though it had just been slapped, or punched.

"Hey!" she said.

The boys, she was surprised to see, had Denny Mackenzie

and Gary Greene among them. She heard someone make a joke about the B.O.F.: Bride-of-Frankenstein.

She took Kevin's arm.

"Are you okay, Kevin?" she asked. "Where's your escort?"

He shook his head from side to side violently, like a dog with a new chew toy.

"What is it, Kevin?"

"He . . . wouldn't . . . take . . . me," he said, making a noise like a sob.

She put a steadying hand on his shoulder, shushing him. He looked so pitiful leaning against the wall, unable to cry real tears.

"We're going to be late, honey," she said.

"Don't . . . leave me!" he wailed.

The final bell rang, and for a moment she didn't know what to do.

But then she hugged him, holding him until he calmed down.

"I won't leave you," she said, holding him tight. "I won't."

"They actually gave you a detention?" Margi said, incredulous. Phoebe had gone over to Margi's after school to vent her rage. She hoped some time with Margi and Colette would help her feel sane again. "And Kevin too? That's the stupidest thing I've ever heard."

"I know," Phoebe replied. She was thinking about Kevin. One of the teachers had started yelling at them when he'd discovered them in the hall, and had already vowed to have them both expelled, when Principal Kim arrived and told the teacher to get back to his room and shut up. "It was stupid."

"Principal Kim is making you serve the detention?"

Phoebe nodded. She said that it would be in everyone's best interest if Phoebe accepted the wrist slap, as a complete lack of punishment might be perceived by the student body as special treatment for differently biotics. She didn't actually come out and apologize, but Phoebe could tell from her tone that Principal Kim wasn't happy about the decision. Phoebe accepted the punishment without comment. Kevin didn't say another word the whole time they were in the office, even when Principal Kim called the Hunter Foundation and asked that they send a van.

"That is so unfair."

"I regret nothing," Phoebe said. She was worried about Kevin, worried he'd go to the foundation and shut down, fearful of trads. He'd made some gains over the past few months, and it would be a shame for all his progress to be erased.

"My only great . . . regret . . . in life," Colette said, "is that I was not able . . . to get . . . my brothers' LPs before . . . my parents threw me out of the house."

Phoebe smiled at her from her seat on the floor, at the exotic way "LPs" sounded in her whispery voice. Colette was stretched out on her stomach and hanging over the edge of Margi's bed, a glossy black LP jacket in her hands. The gray was all but gone from her hair, but Phoebe thought that might have been because Margi was dyeing it.

"Why?" Margi asked, taking the jacket from her. She'd bought it at a yard sale ages ago because she liked the cover. "We don't even have a record player, and I've probably got his stuff on MP3."

"I'm feeling . . . retro," Colette said, reaching for Margi's cat, Familiar, who shied away from her.

Phoebe thought it didn't have anything to do with her records but instead had to do with her brother himself,

"Have you heard from him?" Phoebe asked. "Your brother, I mean?"

Colette shook her head. "I don't even . . . know . . . where he . . . is," she said. "He's probably . . . still on . . . foreign soil. He could be . . . dead, for all . . . I know."

"Oh, Colette."

"Well, he could. He's past the age of resurrection too. I think he turns . . . twenty-five . . . this year."

"Twenty-five?" Margi said. "Might as well be dead."

Colette threw a pillow, but it went wild and knocked an unlit candle off Margi's shelf. The clunk it made sent Familiar into a corner, and the much heavier clunk that Colette made when she slid off the bed sent the cat into a frenzy.

"Will you quit it?" Margi said. "My parents are liable to think you've finally turned into an eighties horror movie."

Colette's fall had been way more than awkward; the akimbo way she lay reminded Phoebe of a big Raggedy Ann she'd had as a child, and the boneless contortions it would make when thrown. Colette was not quick to untangle the knot of her own limbs, and she was more than a little disturbing to look at, especially given the unnatural angle of her neck.

"I've got . . . no . . . strings," she said, finally rolling onto her back.

"Couldn't you find him?" Phoebe asked, managing to get skittish Familiar to come into her lap, where he perched with his eyes bright and focused on Colette. "Through the Web, or something? A government agency?"

"No rights," she said, "and my . . . parents . . . don't, do not . . . ack . . . knowledge . . . my horrific existence."

"We're going to see them this summer," Margi said without looking up from her computer screen, where she was scrolling through her playlists. A song from Skeleton Crew was playing at the moment. "They still live in Tennessee. I checked."

"Sure . . . we . . . are," Colette said, looking away. Phoebe could feel Familiar tense up under her hands as she rose to a sitting position.

"We are," Margi told her. "I've got my license and we're going. That's final."

Colette looked back at Phoebe, rolling her eyes up in their sockets until only the white showed. For a terrible moment, Phoebe thought they wouldn't return to normal.

"Whatever."

"You want to talk to your brother, don't you?" Margi said.

"Of course . . . I do," Colette replied.

"How else are you going to do that? The rest of your crackpot family has already written you off. Your dad is the weak link and we're going to get him to talk."

"What if . . . Cody . . . doesn't want . . . to talk to me . . . either?"

"He will."

"How do you . . . know?"

"I know all," Margi said.

"Sure . . . you do."

"I think it's worth trying too," Phoebe said. "I think Cody would want to see you."

"He thinks I'm . . . dead," Colette said, and than tried to giggle. "Oh, wait."

"I've Googled the guy a bazillion times," Margi said. "Nothing. There's some Cody Beauvoir that I guess is a lacrosse hotshot at some high school, that's all I get when I Google him."

"I wonder if Cody . . . ever Googled . . . me."

"He wouldn't get anything but your obituary," Margi said.

"Hey," Phoebe said, "what if we put you up on mysocalledundeath? A picture and a request that if anyone knows Cody to have him contact you through the Web site."

"That's a good idea," Margi said. "Let me get the digital camera."

"Oh . . . no," Colette said, "can't we use a pre-death photo? I want him to . . . recognize me."

"Anyone who knows you would recognize you," Margi said, but even as she said it she was reaching for a photograph that was framed and sitting on her shelf. It was the same photo that Phoebe had hanging in her locker, the three of them standing outside the Cineplex in Winford. Colette's eyes had a thick streak of dark eyeliner in the corner, so that she looked like an Egyptian princess, her arm was gauntleted in a dozen or so shiny bracelets. Her mouth was open in laughter.

"We should Photoshop us out, Pheebes," Margi said, sliding the photo free of its frame.

"Then I . . . would look . . . like an insane . . . freak," Colette said.

"Welllll . . . "

"Look how I'm . . . laughing."

"Okay," Margi said. She found her digital camera and took a photo of the photo, "the Weird Sisters stay together, then. I'll e-mail it to you, Pheebes, and you can put it up on the site, okay?"

"Absolutely."

"Do you really think . . . he'll see it?" Colette said.

"Someone will," Phoebe said.

CHAPTER
THIRTY-SEVEN

WALKED THROUGH the door into a hug from Mom. So worried, she says. Always worried, but what is the worst that could happen now?

Okay, Phoebe okay, everybody okay. Don't worry so much.

"The school called," she said. "I spoke to Principal Kim and she told me what happened. About the graves."

Bananas in a bowl, cookies in a jar on the counter. Used to come home and make a sandwich. Sandwiches and ESPN after school. Miss many things, but miss sandwiches most of all. Since making up with Phoebe, anyhow.

"Adam," Mom at arms length, squeezing shoulders as though checking if real. Real or unreal? Fingers kneading, flesh unyielding. Hard. Stone cold, like rock.

"Adam, do you know who vandalized the cemetery? Was it your friends?"

"Don't . . . know."

Looking like she can't believe her son is in the room with her. Maybe not wanting him in the room with her.

"You didn't have anything to do with it, did you?"

Stop, look. Words take time take longer when emotions come first.

"No."

Smiles nervously. Lets go of shoulders, hands shaking as she lights a cigarette.

"There was a boy here to see you earlier, Adam. At least I think he was here to see you; he left when he saw me looking at him through the window. A boy with long, black hair and a terrible scar. He was just standing at the edge of the woods in our backyard and watching the house. Do you know who I'm talking about?"

Nod. Nod.

"Is he a friend of yours, Adam?"

Says name over and over, like she's afraid to forget it. Or afraid that son will forget it. Is he a friend? Complicated. Not friend, but he is a zombie. That makes us something. Decide to assent.

Nod.

Exhales, smoke leaving lungs like the soul leaves the body. What replaces?

"That boy scares me, Adam."

"Me . . . too."

After, left leg right walk to bedroom, think about Phoebe. Phoebe has the night off, going with friends. Margi and Colette, Weird Sisters. Good. Glad. Glad for Phoebe, happy happy glad. Happy.

But worried too. Killing house pets, digging graves. Dangerous activities sure to end in tears.

Like dating the dead.

Right leg left hoof it outside to practice. Around car on blocks, across grass. Practice, practice, focus. Forms coming easier now bend leg flex wrist. Focus.

Phoebe almost died because of date with a zombie. Became zombie because of Phoebe's date.

Forms. Concentrate on the forms.

Phoebe. In danger all over again.

Takayuki doesn't wait long. Comes out of woods like he's made of collecting shadows. Wastes no time.

"Adam. I wanted . . . you to know . . . we did not . . . desecrate . . . the cemetery."

"Didn't . . . think so." Didn't, really.

Tak, nonplussed. "It is . . . part of their . . . plot . . . to destroy us."

"Stop . . . helping them. No . . . pranks."

Tak would spit if he could. Can't. "The 'pranks,' as you . . . call them . . . are our way . . . of telling . . . humanity . . . we will not . . . go away."

"Not . . . working."

"You haven't a right to . . . accuse." Leather creaks when he walks. "You, who . . . fraternize with . . . the living."

"My way . . . of . . . telling . . . humanity . . . I . . . won't go . . . away."

Lie. No politics. Just love. Love Phoebe.

Tak looks, doesn't answer. Scared? Not scared. Shrewd.

"Regardless. I didn't come . . . to argue . . . but to . . . ask."

"Ask . . . away."

"You should . . . be with us . . . Adam. The others . . . would welcome . . . your presence. Your . . . strength."

Very shrewd.

"It does not . . . matter . . . that we . . . disagree. It's . . . healthy. I disagreed with . . . Tommy. But in the end . . . we're both . . . zombies."

"In . . . the . . . end."

Stands, folds arms. See his teeth moving. "I'm not . . . looking for a sidekick. Most people . . . zombie or beating heart . . . want to follow. I'm looking for . . . a partner."

"Flattering."

"Think about it." Eyes are dark but clear through his straight hair. "Decide . . . before . . . the living . . . decide for you."

Gone, back to the woods. No trace, never a trace.

Decisions. Master Griffin encouraged decision, best ever. Or is it—Phoebe in danger? Bend knee, arms out.

Decide.

CHAPTER
THIRTY-EIGHT

"DID YOU KNOW the real witching hour is at . . . three a.m.? That's in seventeen minutes," Margi said, looking back at one of the few light sources left in the room. Colette's face looked smooth and flawless in the spectral light as she leaned against the foot of Margi's bed. There was only room for one and a half people in the bed, so in a show of solidarity the girls joined Phoebe on the floor with sleeping bags.

Familiar meowed, content to have the bed all to himself.

"But really it feels like . . . any other . . . hour . . . to me."

Phoebe yawned. She had started to make a comment about how nice this was, how long it had been since the three of them had a Dawn Patrol, but then she realized that Margi and Colette had done it every single night since Colette moved in, although only one of them slept.

"I don't know," Margi said. "Some hours seem a little more magical than others."

"If you . . . say so."

"You aren't getting depressed again, are you?" Margi said. "I'm fresh out of zombie Prozac."

Colette tossed a pillow at the burrito-like shape Margi represented in her sleeping bag, where it landed with a soft plop.

"We used to play board games," Phoebe said

"And make . . . s'mores." There was a hint of sadness in Colette's voice.

"God, we were corny." Margi wriggled in her sleeping bag. "Hey, C.B., you up for a game of Life? We'll spot you a couple of those little peg-people."

Colette stuck her tongue out at her. "And then Margi . . . would tell us about all the boys she was crushing on."

"I did not!"

"And that would take up half the night," Phoebe said, stifling a giggle as Margi popped up, her spiky hair matted and flat on one side.

"Which would end . . . the Dawn Patrol," Colette said, "because she would . . . put us . . . to sleep."

"Har har," Margi said. "You used to fall asleep before eleven o'clock anyhow, so what would you know?"

"Remember the time . . . we each drank . . . like . . . a pot . . . of coffee?"

"Phoebe's dad actually yelled at us," Margi said, laughing. "*Phoebe's* dad. Mr. Low-Key himself. He had his pj's on."

"'I have . . . to give a . . . lecture . . . tomorrow,'" Colette said, in a fair but off-tempo rendition of his speech.

"We used to tell ghost stories," Phoebe said.

There wasn't any immediate reply. Phoebe wondered if there would ever be a time where she could get through the night with Colette or Adam without every other thing she said being ironic or tragic.

"That was . . . fun," Colette said, letting her off the hook in her soft, gentle way. "You always had . . . the best . . . stories."

"Aw, thanks."

"Mine were . . . boring. And Margi's always had . . . a guy with a . . . hook . . . and too much . . . sex."

"A matter of taste."

"I liked Margi's stories," Phoebe said. "Yours too."

"Hey, C.B.," Margi said, "why don't you tell Pheebes about dying?"

Phoebe tensed up while waiting for a reply. Tommy had shared the manner of his death with her on the night Adam had been shot. He died in a car crash that also killed his father—only his father didn't return. The fact that Margi already knew Colette's story caused the sadness to flare in Phoebe's chest; it was another reminder of the closeness her two best friends shared, and how she was on the outside of that closeness.

"It was . . . weird," Colette said. "The after part. The death itself . . . was stupid. I drowned. I might have . . . had a seizure . . . or something. Who knows. One minute I was breathing . . . the next I . . . wasn't."

"You were wedged in a branch," Margi said. "That fallen

tree we used to jump off. You already weren't moving by the time I got to you."

"Yeah. Stupid. Anyhow . . . I was floating after that. I mean I was . . . already dead . . . but it was like I was floating. Well, sinking. There was this blue light about . . . a mile away . . . and I was just sort of sinking toward it. I remember I . . . looked at my hand and it was . . . blue . . . too . . . but I could see . . . through it."

"Were you scared?"

"No, not . . . really. The water was cool . . . not cold but cool . . . and I was going down to this . . . blue light."

"I read this thing about how when people die and come back—not zombie people but like heart patients and stuff—the light is really this chemical thing in your brain," Margi said.

"Now why would you . . . even say . . . that?"

"Sorry, I just thought it was relevant."

"It's my . . . story. I'll decide what's . . . relevant."

"Jeez. Don't get huffy."

"Anyway," Colette said, her eyes tracking the arc of Phoebe's throw pillow to Margi's head. "This . . . floating . . . to the light took about a day. But I wasn't . . . impatient. It was weird, because it . . . wasn't boring . . . either. But the closer . . . I got . . . the faster . . . I sank. And when I was near . . . the light . . . my grandmother . . . floated up to me out of . . . the light."

"Really?"

"Really. You wouldn't . . . have recognized her . . . because she was young . . . and made of light. But I did. She hugged . . . me."

"No way."

"Way. But not really . . . hugged . . . because our light bodies kind of . . . *mixed*. There were other . . . people . . . around. . . . too. One of the things . . . she said . . . was that I couldn't stay. She was . . . sad. I asked her why I . . . couldn't stay, but then . . . she disappeared. The light disappeared, every-thing. All . . . at once. And then I was . . . going up. Like I was dust being . . . vacuumed. It . . . hurt. I was losing . . . pieces . . . of light."

"What do you mean?"

"It was like . . . I was shedding . . . beads . . . of light. It was . . . freezing. And then I was . . . back."

"You were back. As in, back in your body?"

"Yes. And I . . . was . . . naked. In the dark. On a long . . . metal . . . table. It was dark . . . and I could . . . see. I tried to . . . move . . . and I couldn't. At first. It took . . . hours . . . I guess. I got . . . off . . . fell . . . off . . . the table. There was another . . . body . . . under a sheet."

"You were in a morgue?"

"Funeral . . . home. I got up . . . took one step . . . toward the door. And then . . . someone . . . came into . . . the room."

"Oh, God," Margi said. "I hate this part."

"He . . . started screaming. He was young. College boy, maybe. He was screaming so . . . shrill. I wanted to ask . . . for help. My mouth opened and . . . water came out."

"Ugh."

I've never . . . heard . . . screaming . . . like that. He grabbed a . . . push broom . . . and started hitting me . . . with it. Like I was a . . . monster. He broke it . . . on my . . . back. I couldn't even . . . feel it."

"Oh, Colette."

"He . . . jabbed . . . stabbed, really . . . me with the broken handle . . . in the side. He was still . . . screaming. He was going . . . to do . . . it . . . again . . . when a man . . . in a suit . . . ran in . . . and . . . pulled . . . him away."

"Welcome back," Margi said.

"It was horrible . . . the way he screamed."

Phoebe didn't know what to say.

"The man in the . . . suit . . . put his coat . . . over me. He tried to help me . . . sit."

"And then it sort of went downhill from there," Margi said.

"Colette," Phoebe said, crawling out of her bag and over to her. "I'm so sorry. That's terrible." She sat next to her and put her arm around her shoulder, and Margi came over and did the same.

"Not . . . fun," Colette said. "But I'm here . . . now. With my . . . friends."

"Better late than never," Margi said, yawning.

Phoebe thought Colette's smile was tinged with sadness, as though she was leaving a part of the story out, but it was hard to tell in the green light.

They were quiet for a few moments. They were well into the witching hour by now, and Margi had closed her eyes and was snoring softly against her dead friend.

"Colette," she said, "do you ever think of the blue light?"

"Every . . . day."

"Do you think it was heaven?"

"I don't . . . know," she said, "but I know . . . my grand-mother . . . was there."

After getting Colette her iPod so the music wouldn't disturb their sleeping friend, Phoebe checked her e-mail on Margi's computer.

"I've got one from Tommy."

Colette was so intent on working the selector wheel to queue up a new playlist that she didn't hear her. Phoebe turned back to the screen.

From: WilliamsTommy@mysocalledundeath.com
To: KendallPhoebe@mysocalledundeath.com
Dear Phoebe—

 I wanted to let you know that I really loved your second "Words from a Beating Heart" column. I've talked to a number of people our age, living and dead, about the site, and everyone was very excited about "Beating Heart." One dead friend I met while I was staying in New Jersey said that your voice has really done a lot to "humanize" the Web site. A funny comment, considering.

 BTW, I sympathize with you about trying to get Karen to contribute a little more with the site. Her "I'm not creative" schtick is really tired. I've sent her some harassing e-mails, but I don't think I'll be any more successful at getting her to do it than you were.

 I'm not so sure about her T-shirt idea, though. Did she

talk to you about that? While I think she's right about it
helping get the message out, I'm really not sure the db
community needs any more Skip Slydells. What do you think?

Anyhow, the story that follows is about a side trip I took
to Scranton, Pennsylvania. It's a little rough. Please don't be
worried after you read it, and please tell all "the kids" not to
worry. This stuff is still happening in the world and they need
to know.

I miss you.

Love,

Tommy

Phoebe read the attachment, which was a long report from Tommy about a "station" somewhere in Pennsylvania for a sort of underground railroad for the differently biotic. Tommy stayed with a young couple who would pick up zombies that were fleeing Pennsylvania and points south and drive them to undead-friendly locales in New Jersey. They drove some of the zombies straight to Aftermath in New York.

Phoebe's mouth went dry when Tommy wrote about a side trip the couple took so they could bring him to a fire pit surrounding a row of stakes in a field outside Scranton. Phoebe knew what the purpose of the pit was even before Tommy started to write about finding bone chips among the ashes. When he mentioned finding a melted locket it became too much for her, and she had to put the story aside for a moment.

I worry about you, Tommy, she thought, picturing him hitchhiking down into Maryland, slowly working his way to the state capital. Reading about the horrors that people could enact on the zombies—their *children*, for God's sake—it made her worry about all of them. Colette, Karen, Melissa.

Adam.

She read the story, which ended with Tommy talking at length about the kindness of the young couple, a testimonial that not all traditionally biotic people were madmen bent on the destruction of zombiekind. She set it aside and started typing a reply.

From: KendallPhoebe@mysocalledundeath.com
To: WilliamsTommy@mysocalledundeath.com

Dear Tommy,

Your story is absolutely terrifying and sad. I'll post it immediately; I think anyone who reads it will be sympathetic.

I'm very worried about you. Please take care of yourself.

A little news: we brought Alish and Angela and the Undead Studies class over to the Haunted House so they could meet everyone. I'm sorry if Karen already told you all of this. I know earlier you guys wanted to keep the HH a secret, but the secret was pretty much out anyway after Adam was killed. The visit seemed to go really well, even Tak and Popeye were polite. Well, actually, polite may be a stretch, but they weren't as offensive as they usually are, so that's a plus.

Tak is still bringing the old-schoolers out on little prank missions. They did the recruiting posters that you know about, and they did another one where they took store mannequins and zombified them and left them out in front of the mall entrance in Winford. Pretty funny.

Not so funny is that someone dug up some graves in one of the cemeteries in Winford. Tak insists "his people," as he likes to call them, had nothing to do with it. Karen believes him, and I sort of do too. It makes me nervous, though, because whoever did it really did a good job of throwing the blame on Tak— there were photos in the newspaper that looked like him digging. The article made it sound as if zombies were taking "recruiting" to a new level by digging up the graves. It seems like someone is spending a lot of time thinking about how to frame them.

Which reminds me, Pete Martinsburg is working off his community service at the Hunter Foundation. I think it's the most idiotic thing possible, but Angela thinks the best way to overcome "the enemy" is to include and educate them. Most everyone seems to agree with her, and Karen says you would too. Do me a favor and don't tell me if you do.

Also, Tommy, I wanted to let you know that Adam and I are dating. I guess you probably figured that we would, but it's official now. We get the same reaction from people that you and I did for the most part, except in school. I guess people are a little more used to seeing Adam and me together. Except for his old girlfriend Tori Stewart, who I'm told became physically ill when she saw us in the hallway. We're actually going to Aftermath again tomorrow, with Margi and Colette. Karen couldn't make it, she's working (that's another story entirely, but I'll let her tell it). I can't believe Adam is going dancing, *but we've seen all the movies in the theater, and it doesn't really make sense to go out to dinner. We tried bowling but that was a total fiasco. Not much else for a girl and a zombie to do on a Saturday night, is there?*

I don't know where it's going—you never really do, do you? But it feels right. I'm happy and Adam seems the happiest he's been since his return. I just thought it was fair to let you know.

Stay safe, please! We all miss you.

Love,

Phoebe

Phoebe looked at what she'd written for a long time before deciding to delete the two paragraphs about Adam. She told herself that if Tommy was still depressed about their breakup she didn't want to add to his misery. Then she changed the "Love" to "Best," because writing "Love" made her feel unfaithful to Adam. Then she decided that she was being ridiculous and changed it back to "Love."

She hit "Send," and then went to her sleeping bag praying that she wouldn't dream of fire pits.

CHAPTER
THIRTY-NINE

"So," DAVIDSON said, his large feet up on the desk, while Pete stared at the monitors, especially the one that showed the Cooper kid in his room. Cooper watched television round the clock, except for the twenty minutes each day when he walked to the fence and back. Just about every time Pete looked at his monitor, Cooper was watching television, usually Cartoon Network. SpongeBob and old Tom and Jerry cartoons.

"So, what?"

"So what do you think?"

Pete looked over at Davidson and felt a flicker of anger spark within him. "Are you a head shrinker now too?"

"Not me. I'm a mind expander. What do you think about our prank?"

Pete wasn't sure what he felt. He'd dug the grave all the way down to the casket liner when Duke finally told him to stop.

He wasn't sure what he'd have done if Duke *hadn't* told him to stop.

"Does it bother you, what you did?"

"I don't know. I don't think so." The truth was he'd felt sick to his stomach standing there in front of the headstone, but the feeling went away the moment the edge of his shovel bit into the earth, because he pictured it sinking into the Japanese zombie's—Tak's—chest. It was unnatural to be digging up a grave, but each shovel of dirt felt like a blow against Tak and his kind.

Duke slid his feet off the desk. "Good. It shouldn't. You've got to keep our goal in mind at all times. As long as we're focused on the goal, we'll be all right."

"The goal," Pete repeated. "The goal of killing all the zombies."

"Destroying the zombies." Duke's tone was firm, that of a teacher correcting a promising student. "Destroying them. Some of the things we do will seem a little unpleasant."

"Yeah, unpleasant." Pete smiled.

"Hey, it isn't like we killed anybody." Pete shot Duke a look and Duke covered his mouth with his hand.

"Oops," he said. "Look, to me your only crime is bad aim. If you'd shot Williams they'd be giving you medals instead of making you scrub my floors."

Pete looked back at the monitor. The zombie hadn't moved from his chair. He only had another twenty hours left on his community service, but he spoke anyway.

"Why are you riding me?"

Davidson laughed, drained the last of his coffee. "Don't be so sensitive. If I were 'riding' you, you'd know it."

Pete didn't reply. He looked away but could feel Duke scrutinizing him.

"Are you worried they'll come after you?"

"Who? The zombies?"

"Who else? They're going to be pretty upset when they realize they got punked in the graveyard."

Pete looked away. "No. I'm not worried"

"Really? I would be, if I were you."

Pete shrugged. Part of him wouldn't mind seeing Tak again.

"In fact, I'm worried it's only a matter of time before they come after me too."

"Really?" Pete said. "Why would you worry about that, when you work for this wonderful zombie-loving institution?"

"Things aren't always what they seem," Duke said.

"I'm kind of tired of this cryptic crap," Pete said. "I've got that blond whore trying to shrink my head, and you keep saying this crazy *X-Files* stuff. Like you want to tell me something but you never tell me. I dug up somebody's *grave* last night and I don't even know why, except you think it's some practical joke to play on the zombies. I can't figure it out and I don't want to try anymore."

Davidson stood up. "You're a smart kid, Martinsburg," he said. "A really smart kid. Let's go."

"Go?" Pete said. "We're going to fight?"

Davidson shook his head. "You're a really stupid kid, too. No, we're not going to fight. We're going to discover why things aren't really what they seem. Turn the monitors off."

"Turn them off? But . . ."

"Just turn them off. The fifteen minutes they aren't recording is going to be an equipment malfunction. It happens. Now
move your ass."

He followed Davidson to Alish's lab. Davidson checked his
watch.

"We have eleven minutes. Don't dawdle."

He waited until Pete caught up before walking to the door
in the back of the room.

"You know what this room is?"

"I thought it was Alish's office."

"You ever see Alish go in there?"

"No."

"You ever wonder why Alish's office is the only place on the
entire grounds that doesn't have a camera on it?"

"Yeah," he said. The thought had occurred to him.

"Well," Davidson said, smirking, "here's why."

He keycarded the door, which made a sound reminiscent of
the vacuum tubes they use at the bank drive-through. The lights
in the room triggered automatically and revealed a small, dingy-
looking lab.

There was a girl, part of a girl, strapped to a vertical table
that faced the door. Another part was attached to a machine on
a counter by the sink on the wall, a few feet away.

"Meet Sylvia," Davidson said.

Pete didn't scream until she opened her eyes.

* * *

Pete's hand shook as he lifted Duke's coffee cup to his lips. Duke hadn't bothered to wash it and Pete was too numb to care.

"Fourteen minutes, thirty-seven seconds," Duke said, turning the monitors back on. "Equipment back online."

Pete, shivering in Duke's chair, watched him as he took his seat on the edge of the desk. The smirk was gone.

"Are you okay?" Duke asked. He poured the last of his coffee from the Thermos into the cup Pete held with two hands.

"She was . . . she was trying to talk," Pete said. He didn't even remember his flight back to the monitor room. He'd dug up a grave the other night, and he'd been ready to open the casket if that was what Duke had wanted, but all he'd felt was numb. But seeing the girl . . . he thought it was far worse than desecrating a grave. It was like desecrating a grave where the person inside knew you were doing it. Knew it, and couldn't do anything about it.

"She does," Duke said. "You could hear her before Alish went to work on her lungs. She used to say, 'Help me.' You ever see the movie *The Fly*? The original one?"

Pete couldn't focus fully on what Duke was talking about; the image of the girl in pieces filled his brain.

"What," he said, "what is he trying to do with her?"

Duke laughed. "He's trying to cure death."

"Cure death?" He thought of Julie, somewhere deep in the California soil.

"Sure. Why not? The dead are up and walking around, aren't they? Maybe, just maybe, we can cure them."

"Cure death." Pete said.

Davidson grunted. "Don't hold your breath. Alish is crazy."

Pete leaned back in his chair. He drained the last of the coffee, hoping the dark liquid would untangle the images of Julie and Sylvia from his mind.

"He is?"

"Of course he is. You saw that mess down there. He thinks he's going to put her back together again and everything will be all peachy keen. But he needs to get some results pretty soon or he's going to have the plug pulled on his funding. And then things would get really messy."

Pete didn't know what he was talking about. The girl had brown eyes. She had looked right at him and moved her lips.

"Alish thinks he's being clever," Duke went on. "He thinks we don't know what he's trying to do. He's a scared old man who wants to stay alive, and he thinks he's going to find the answer in the dry veins of one of the worm burgers. But the cure he's looking for is not the one that we are looking for."

"It isn't?"

"No," Duke said. "He's trying to treat a symptom. We're looking to cure the disease."

Duke must have seen the confusion on Pete's face. "He wants to cure death," he said. "We just want to cure the dead. Like polio and smallpox. That's what Alish is *supposed* to be looking for."

"We," Pete said.

"We," Duke repeated, nodding. "You and me." Duke clapped his shoulder with a firm hand. "There are some people who want to meet you, Pete. And you will want to meet them. You have a lot in common."

Pete didn't say anything. Duke's hand was on his shoulder, and Duke's pale eyes stared at him with almost fatherly affection. The girl in the laboratory was like a squirrel that Pete had backed over a few weeks after Darren had bought him the car. Clipped by a tire, it's back half was crushed and it flopped around in the pine needles and dirt of one of the make-out spots around Lake Oxoboxo, not aware that it was already dead. Although Pete's date begged him not to, Pete got out of his car and put the little rodent out of its misery with the heel of his high-top sneaker. It took a while, but it was his responsibility to make sure the job was done right.

He'd been to the spot many times since, although never again with that girl. Looking up at Davidson, he realized that his hands had stopped shaking.

CHAPTER FORTY

"ARE YOU . . . SURE . . . this . . . is a . . . good . . . idea?"

Sitting in the bleachers above the field. Phoebe said it's cold outside can't tell too cold for Frisbee another bright idea. Phoebe wears heavy coat with the fake fur lining on hood and cuffs, black mittens hard-to-play-catch-with mittens. Hood up, black fur framing white face. Like snow. Her eyes. Her pretty green eyes.

"What do you mean? Our big date?"

Hard coming to the field. Don't need to close eyes to imagine the snap of the ball and the crack of hitting shoulder pads. Can hear the crowd, smell the turf and sweat. Shake head, shake.

"You . . . and . . . me."

Phoebe takes hand. Strokes cheek with other mitten.

"Adam, you aren't going to break up with me, are you?"

"No," too quickly. "Don't . . . want . . . to."

"Then what is it? Are you afraid of what people would think?"

Hardly. "Afraid . . . of what . . . people . . . will do."

Phoebe turns thinking. Looks at field into the past sees Adam running blocking winning. Looks at field sees into the future sees what?

"Adam," holding arm, huddling against as though for warmth no warmth to give. "Are you happy?"

"Happy as . . . a dead . . . guy . . . can be."

"Being with me, I mean?"

"Being . . . with . . . you." Only with you. Feels more than happy. Feels like life.

"I'm happy too. Happier than I've ever been, I think."

Crow flies across field. Ungraceful but swift.

"It won't be easy, Adam. It never is."

"Scared."

"You're scared? Of what? Me getting hurt?"

"Yes."

Had to say it. Didn't want to say it admit it but Phoebe needs to know. Phoebe thinks fearless but not true. Terrified.

"I'm scared for you too, Adam. The way the world is now there is a much better chance of something happening to you than to me."

"Not . . . true. Worst . . . already . . . in past."

"No." Wish could feel mittens as they hold cheeks. Wish could feel smell her breath as she looks into eyes. Cinnamon. Phoebe liked cinnamon gum. Can only imagine. "The worst would be that I lost you, really lost you, without having given us a chance."

Kiss, light. Close eyes and alive again, Phoebe alive in my arms and hold her and kiss back and breathe her and don't let her go.

Open eyes, still dead.

"Okay?" Light snow starts to fall, tiny flakes settle in fur lining.

Nod.

"O . . . kay."

Pats hand, gets cell phone from deep pocket. "I better call Margi. I don't want her to have to drive us when this starts to stick. Good thing we all live so close."

"Good . . . thing."

"I hope this lets up by tomorrow, otherwise Margi's parents won't let her drive to the train station." Brushes hair back. Pretty. Listens to phone, Margi's voice. Margi's loud voice. Be there in five, hang up. Quick call.

"Wish . . . wish could stay . . . longer."

"Me too," Phoebe, snow melting on cheek, catching hair. Shivering. "I wish it wasn't so cold."

Wish.

Wish could warm her. Wish could chase the shivers away.

Can't.

CHAPTER
FORTY-ONE

"CAN'T . . . BELIEVE . . . I let . . . you talk . . . me . . . into this." Phoebe leaned against Adam in the backseat of Margi's car, resting a cheek against his unyielding arm. They were just outside of New Haven on their way to the train station for another trip to Aftermath.

"I can't either, but I'm glad I did." She was nervous, though, because Adam hadn't gone any farther than Winford since becoming a zombie. "You'll have fun, you'll see."

"Too bad . . . Karen . . . couldn't come," Colette said from the shotgun seat as she toyed with the radio dial. Margi snorted.

"Less competition." Margi gave Colette a wicked grin. "Not that *you're* worried about that."

"Is Karen working today?" Phoebe asked.

"Christmas . . . season. Never get . . . away . . . now."

Margi ignored this thread and addressed Phoebe and Adam in the backseat.

"Did you guys know that DeCayce has e-mailed Colette like seventeen times since they met? Which was what, three weeks ago?"

"Seventeen times?" Phoebe leaned over and caught Colette smiling.

"Who's . . . DeCayce?"

"Just . . . ignore her, Adam," Colette said. "Besides, it was . . . nineteen . . . times."

"Oh, excuse me, nineteen times. Colette's getting ready for some zombie lovin'."

Colette slapped her arm, and Margi looked into the rearview at Phoebe and mouthed the word "sorry." Phoebe stuck out her tongue at her and squeezed Adam's arm more tightly by way of reply.

"Are Skeleton Crew playing tonight, Colette?" She'd noticed that Colette was wearing makeup and a new-looking silky blouse. Her hair was brushed back and had a glossy shine—Phoebe wondered if she was using products from the Z line. Whatever she was using was working. She looked great.

Margi answered before Colette could get a word in. "Are you kidding? Do you think we'd be going if they weren't?"

"They are . . . playing. Last night . . . before . . . road trip."

"Send him off smiling, C.B.," Margi said. "Send him off smiling. Are you going to dance tonight, Lame Man? Or are you going sit in the corner like a giant wallflower?"

"He'll . . . dance . . . won't you, Adam?"

"I'm a . . . dancing . . . machine." He looked at Phoebe and tried to smile.

Phoebe was thinking that he didn't really get a chance to dance at homecoming, having ditched his date to take her and the rest of the crew over to the after-party at the Haunted House. But then she remembered that he did dance—with Karen, once they'd arrived.

"You'll dance with me, won't you, Adam?"

"You'll . . . owe . . . me," he said.

She leaned her head back down against his hard shoulder.

"I already do," she whispered.

The club was jumping when they arrived, the dance floor packed with what looked like twice the people than had been there on their previous visit. The increase in population was due almost completely to trad kids—there were loose groups of trads dancing by themselves without any zombies in their midst. The zombies, she noticed, also had a tendency to cluster together. She held Adam's hand as they walked in. Margi and Colette brushed by them, looking for DeCayce.

"Wow. Look at all . . . the zombies."

"Isn't it amazing?" Phoebe squeezed his hand, and leaned closer so he could hear her over the loud trip-hop that pulsed from invisible speakers. "I can't believe what Skip has done here."

"Skip? That's right . . . this is . . . Skip's . . . place."

She nodded. "Tommy did a nice interview with him. I posted it on mysocalledundeath."

Adam looked up, scanning the room and taking in the sights and sounds. A trad couple walked by and gave them an odd look, which Phoebe decided to take as "good for you!" She felt Adam's hand tighten over hers.

The lights were like blue and white rain splashing on his skin.

"Want to . . . dance?"

"I'd love to," she said, and let him lead her out into the throng on the dance floor.

They were joined three songs later by Margi and Colette, who had managed to find DeCayce and Bee. Bee paired off with Margi, although neither of them looked thrilled. Colette and DeCayce, on the other hand, were dancing with their faces only inches apart, although the song that was playing wasn't a slow one. Phoebe watched them, fascinated by their obvious chemistry. She wondered if the people who stopped to watch her and Adam did so for the same reason.

"They look . . . happy," Adam said, reconfirming her belief in telepathetic bonds.

"I think I look happy," she replied, stepping into him for a hug. His arms were slow in enfolding her, but she knew that wasn't the same thing as hesitation.

"I think . . . you look . . . beautiful."

"Aw, I bet you say that to all the trad girls."

She was always amazed by how his embrace was firm yet gentle at the same time—she knew he couldn't really feel how tightly he was holding her. He was probably strong enough to snap her spine or crush her ribs; his arms felt like steel clamps as they went around her waist.

A song or two later, Dom, the guitarist for Skeleton Crew, came over to tell DeCayce and Bee that they were on in ten minutes. The boys said their good-byes, DeCayce with a quick kiss to Colette's cheek and a promise to see her after the show. Dom, turning, caught sight of Phoebe and asked her how Karen was doing.

"She's great." Phoebe replied. "She got a job at the mall, if you can believe it."

Dom looked puzzled. "Why wouldn't I believe it?"

"Well, not a lot of zombies work at malls." When Dom just stood there looking stunned she realized she may have said something she shouldn't have. "You knew she was a zombie, right?"

"She said she was," he said, his voice barely audible above the music. "I thought she was kidding." He shook his head, his thick hair waving as he stared at the floor. "Wow."

"I'll tell her you said hi?" Phoebe asked, hoping Karen wouldn't want to kill her.

"Oh, yeah, absolutely! Would you do that for me? That would be great," he said, answering the question behind her question.

"You know, she has e-mail too."

"Yeah," he said, gathering himself as though suddenly realizing how cool he was. "I'm not much on teledating."

"Seems to be . . . working . . . for your . . . singer," Adam said.

"Yeah, well. Tell her I said hi, though, okay?" Dom said, and then started angling through the crowd.

When Skeleton Crew hit the stage, they hit it hard. They led off with a new song DeCayce announced as "The Dead Living," and Dom's shredding opening riff could blow the dust off a tired soul. The drums came in a moment later like a nest of machine guns, and Bee's bass line was a cavalry charge. The crowd's response was immediate. Phoebe looked around her to see dead bodies pogo-ing and slamming into each other, although with considerably less velocity than their living friends could muster. She saw a girl lifted up over the crowd, her body rigid, as many dead hands passed her to the stage. She looked like she had rigor mortis. Phoebe felt the tug of the music on her body, but when she looked at Adam he seemed to be unmoved, even when DeCayce's chorus sailed out over the fast rhythm of his band.

> *"We are the dead living*
> *Up from underground*
> *Went through hell getting out*
> *You won't put us back down!"*

Other bodies were borne aloft, and the whole crowd was singing along when he repeated the chorus a second time.

"There's . . . Margi," Adam said, pointing at a body bobbing like a cork on the sea of hands.

Phoebe squinted against the glare of the stage lights.

"Colette too! See her, just stepping onto the stage?"

Adam nodded. DeCayce, his sinewy body twitching as if he were being electrocuted, waved at Colette and then Margi to join him at the front of the stage where they sang the next chorus with him, Colette almost managing to sing the words in the proper time with the music. When the song was over they both returned to the crowd, and the lights were cut to a single spot that bathed DeCayce's bare skin with a bluish glow.

"Thank . . . you," he said to the cheering crowd. "And thank you to our . . . beautiful . . . backup singers, Colette . . . and Margi."

Adam bellowed an incomprehensible cheer, which pleased Phoebe to no end.

"This is our . . . last night . . . at Aftermath . . . for a while," DeCayce said. He folded his skinny arms to his chest, hugging himself while the crowd moaned in disappointment. "But we'll be . . . back. Hell, if I can return . . . from death . . . I can make it back . . . to Aftermath."

He was a natural performer, Phoebe thought. The melodrama of his movements, the easy banter with the crowd—she couldn't help but wonder what he'd have been like onstage when still alive.

"We've got to hit . . . the road," he continued. "We've got to bring . . . our music . . . and our message . . . to the rest of the country. So that trad people will know . . . we're not . . . monsters or . . . grave robbers. We're not what that old gargoyle . . . Mathers . . . says we are. We're just . . . people, man."

The crowd settled into a disgruntled mumble at the mention of Mathers's name, and DeCayce used the lull to deliver his message full force, his voice rising in tone and timbre to match the best of the fire and brimstone preachers, to rival even Reverand Nathan Mathers himself.

"We've got to let people know that . . . what they are saying about . . . our brothers and sisters . . . in Connecticut...that they are . . . killing pets and . . . wrecking graves . . . is a bunch of bullshit, man! Straight up . . . bullshit!"

The response was thunderous, and the stage lights returned as Dom hit a random chord.

"This one is for . . . Tommy Williams," DeCayce said, pacing along the lip of the stage. "It's called . . . 'Headshot.'" Skeleton Crew kicked in with a brutal wave of noise that sent the club dwellers into another frenzy of motion and screaming. Phoebe started dancing in place, her skirt and long hair whirling as she thrashed. It was some moments before she realized that Adam was standing still beside her, watching.

"You really . . . like this . . . stuff?" he said, something like a wry grin on his face.

She slapped his unyielding bicep. "Don't be a lump, Adam. Move that body."

His response was to start headbanging. Adam headbanging was funny enough, but because his body couldn't quite master the motion, he looked more like a chicken pecking for loose grain in the barnyard than a metalhead. Phoebe thought it was absolutely hilarious.

"Here," she said, taking his hands in hers. "Move with me."

Skeleton Crew wasn't exactly playing dance music, but there was enough energy in their playing to get her hips swaying and her shoulders rocking. She held Adam's hands and swung his arms from side to side, but beyond that he didn't move—he just watched her moving in front of him.

Phoebe thought that was just fine.

* * *

They found the girls by the stage after the show. Colette was deep in conversation with DeCayce off in a corner, and Margi was with a few people Phoebe remembered from their last trip to Aftermath.

"Hi, Trent." The boy looked thrilled that Phoebe had remembered him. "How's it going with the library card?"

His grin was charming, if lopsided.

"No . . . go. I haven't left . . . the building."

"We need to get going soon," Margi said, pushing herself up from her perch at the lip of the stage. "There aren't a lot of trains later in the day, and my mom will kill me if we're not home by midnight."

"Ready when you are." Phoebe had laced her fingers with Adam's, which were pleasantly cool. The air in the club had grown warm and humid, which meant that there had to have been quite a few trads jumping around on the dance floor during the show. "What did you think, Adam? Did you have fun?"

"Had . . . fun. Could watch you . . . all . . . night." Phoebe thought his smile had become more natural, his face more boyish as the night went on—but maybe it was just the heady club atmosphere playing tricks on her.

Phoebe, blushing, was glad for the dim lighting of the club. She was also thankful that Margi didn't comment beyond a loud "Awwww."

Colette and DeCayce walked over, also holding hands.

"Ready to go, C.B.?"

Colette looked at DeCayce, who tightened his grip on her hand. She looked like she was about to cry, if she could still cry.

"I'm not . . . I'm . . . not . . . going back . . . Margi."

"What? What do you mean?" Margi said, but Phoebe could tell from the quaver in her voice that she knew exactly what their friend meant.

"I'm not . . . going back," Colette repeated. "I'm going with . . . Skeleton Crew . . . on their . . . tour. With . . . DeCayce."

Margi looked like she was going to cry too. She lifted her hand to her mouth like she was trying to hold her words in, and Phoebe, as happy as she was for Colette, suddenly felt terrible for Margi. She looked so forlorn standing there, with her hair matted and her shirt clinging to her skin with sweat. She looked like a puppy that had been abandoned in the rain.

Colette felt the same way, Phoebe could tell. She was crying in every way except producing tears when she spoke again.

"We might . . . try . . . to find . . . my brother . . . or my parents. Or . . . or . . . I'll just . . . travel, I don't . . . know."

The silence grew awkward, and the zombies Margi had been partying with started to drift away to give them their moment.

"Wish me . . . luck . . . Margi . . . .please."

Margi nodded, but she didn't remove her hand from her mouth. Adam was the first to speak.

"Good . . . luck." The low rumble of his voice seemed to kick Margi into action, because she ran to Colette and wrapped her in a forceful hug, finally releasing the emotion she was trying to hold in. Colette hugged her back, making strange hiccupping sounds as Margi poured out her grief.

"I will take care . . . of her," DeCayce said, turning to Adam and Phoebe like they were Colette's parents on prom night. "I'll make sure . . . she's safe. We don't take chances when we are . . . on the road."

"We know you will," Phoebe said, watching her friends. She looked at Adam, who released her so she could join their embrace. When they got control of themselves, Margi dried her tears and forced herself to speak, her voice choked with emotion.

"I'm happy for you, C.B. I really am."

"Thanks . . . Margi. You know . . . you know . . . how much . . ."

"Shhh." Margi put her finger to Colette's lips. "Don't say it. Don't make it feel anymore like a good-bye than it has to."

Margi released her and went to DeCayce, kissing him lightly on the cheek.

"Good luck," she said. "Both of you. Good luck."

DeCayce looked relieved. Actually, Phoebe thought, everyone looked relieved.

They said their farewells, made promises to stay in touch, then said some of the things people wish they said to loved ones while they were still alive. Margi managed not to cry again until their train was pulling out of Grand Central Station, but even then it didn't last long. Phoebe offered to drive once they were back in New Haven, but Margi said she could handle it.

"Aren't you a needy little boy tonight?" Phoebe said, picking

Gargoyle off the floor and squeezing him to her. Gar licked her cheek and then her ear. She dropped him on the bed, where he curled up on her favorite pillow.

She walked to the window and looked down to where a large shadow was moving through the Garrity's backyard. Adam, doing his exercises again. Her lights were out, with only the soft spectral glow of the computer behind her casting any illumination. She didn't think that he'd be conscious of her—the night was practically moonless, so she could barely see him. But she waved anyhow.

Her room had grown chilly, and she had put her terry cloth bathrobe on over her pajamas. She sat down at her computer and went online. There were a number of e-mails to mysocalled-undeath.com, one of which had "RE: Colette Beauvior" in the header line, and also one from Tommy. She knew she was being selfish when she chose the one from Tommy, but Gargoyle was her only witness, and he wasn't going to tell anyone.

Hi Phoebe,

he'd written,

> *"I've made it safely to DC. I think I'm going to be staying at least until springtime. There's a lot I want to do here.*

Great, she thought, one line and I'm already starting to tear up.

I wanted to let you know I think you guys are doing a great job managing the site. I also think it is a great idea having the "I'm back" section. I had no idea that Colette had a brother and that he might not be aware that she's differently biotic. I saw that you had two more postings from db people the next day. I really hope someone figures out a way to get the picture uploaded for the girl in Omaha. I'm really, really excited about the things you're doing with the site; I'm leaving stacks of the cards we printed up everyplace I think people might use them.

She whistled for Gar, and when he wouldn't come she got up and captured him, sitting down with him on her lap. He gave her a grouchy look but didn't move, probably because she started scratching behind his ears.

I have a list of people I want to talk to and places I want to go. Most of my agenda involves talking to people who could help us, or talking to people who refuse to help us, but there's also some other things I want to check out. On my way down from Pennsylvania I met a zombie who told me that there's a zombie gang—as in actual criminal street gang—who gets recruits by encouraging trad kids who want to join to shoot each other. If you come back, you get to be in the gang, and if you don't, game over. I can't see why anyone would willingly choose this existence over real life, but the kid I met insisted it was true. He said his cousin tried to get him to join, but he turned him down. He said

*they're "crazy fearless" because they're dead, and apparently
they have all the other gangs scared witless of them. Do me a
favor and don't tell any of this to Takayuki or the other
old-schoolers, because I think he'd come down here and be leading them within a few weeks. How is Tak and the whole dead
crew, by the way? Is Karen keeping everyone in line?*

Phoebe smiled at the thought of Takayuki and George and
the rest of his crew catching a bus down to DC so they could
join the fun. But Tommy's next line erased the smile: *Phoebe,* he
wrote, *I wanted to let you know I've met a girl.*

She read the line a second time. Gar had begun to growl
because she had stopped scratching his ears. He had written
Phoebe, as in "Phoebe, listen up, because this next bit is serious.
Very serious."

> *Phoebe, I wanted to let you know I met a girl. A zombie
> girl. I don't know if it's going to go anywhere, but since I met
> her here we've been spending a lot of time together—time is
> something we've both got a lot of—and I like being with her
> and I think she likes being with me. Her name is Christie
> Smith.*

I don't want to know her name, Phoebe thought. Tommy,
why would you think I would need to know her name? Christie
Smith, Christie Smith. Sounds like a weathergirl. Or a porn
star.

Why do you even care? she thought. You're happier with Adam than you ever would be with Tommy. With Adam, you never have to guess how he really feels about you.

She pushed up and away from the desk with an abruptness that surprised Gargoyle, who let out a little yelp of surprise. She went back to the window. Adam was still working in the gray grass below.

Christie Smith, she thought. And then: wasn't it *you* that broke up with *him*? *Adam needs me. I don't have any time for you,* you said, or something equally stupid. *I don't have time* to a boy who has nothing, nothing in the world *but* time, an eternity of endless sleepless hours waiting, like waiting for the phone to ring when you know it never will.

After a while she sat back down at the computer. There wasn't much left to read, and she was determined to get through the rest of it even though her hands were shaking and she could feel a rush of tears ready to spill from her eyes. She didn't know if she was angry or sad or both. Probably both.

I still think of you a lot,

he wrote,

all the time, really, except some times when I'm with Christie. I haven't talked to her about you yet, but she's been to the Web site, so she knew that I had feelings for a living girl.

A living girl. Not a Traditionally Biotic Girl or a Beating Heart, she thought. For someone who chose his words so carefully, how could Tommy not know that each one he wrote was like a razor blade being dragged slowly across her heart.

I feel like you're still in my soul, Phoebe. And I haven't told her
about you because I feel like in doing so I would be
letting you go, and I'm just not ready for that yet. It probably
isn't fair to her, or to you, even, because I know how you feel,
but just not ready.

He thinks he knows how I feel, she thought. She closed her eyes and was more than a little surprised when the rush of tears subsided.

Anyway,

began his final paragraph,

I hope you aren't mad at me for writing about this. I just
wanted you to know that I really am trying to let go like you
wanted, so you don't have to worry that some creepy, love-
struck dead kid is going to show up under your window some
night playing a mandolin. I'm trying, Phoebe. But it isn't easy.
Love,
Tommy

She was hot all of a sudden, and she wriggled out of her bathrobe and threw it onto the bed, where the belt fell across Gargoyle, whose ears pricked.

"I know," she said, "you're wondering what's gotten into me tonight. I'm sorry, baby boy."

Somewhat mollified, Gar put his doggy chin on his forepaws. He was too dignified to try to move the belt.

"So you think you know how I feel," Phoebe said, the fingers of her now-steady hands tapping but not depressing any of the keys on her keyboard. She looked back at Gar, who seemed to raise one fuzzy, questioning eyebrow at her. "Well, how about I tell you how I really feel?"

Her fingers were like long, vicious knives stabbing at her keyboard.

> *"Dear" Tommy,*
>
> *I'm so, so glad that you have met someone new. And I'm so, so glad that you made the brilliant decision to tell me about her, but not tell her about me, because that once again under-scores what a self-centered, manipulative jerk you can be. I'm still "in your soul," am I? Well, let me out, please. Evict me.*
> *Adam and I*

She stopped typing a moment, suppressing the cry of frustrated anguish that was welling in her chest.

Eyes burning, she resumed typing with a steadily increasing rapidity.

CHAPTER
FORTY-TWO

"SO THIS IS IT," Duke said. "After tonight your debt to society is paid. What do you think about that?"

Pete shrugged. "I've still got to do the counseling for the rest of the year."

"Cry me a river. You really aren't glad you don't have to work here anymore?"

"I don't care about it either way." Which wasn't exactly true; being home-schooled was duller than actual school, and he hadn't seen or talked to TC since the trial. He didn't think Stavis's parents would let TC talk to him anymore.

"Really?" Duke said. "That surprises me. I'd think you'd be pretty eager to get away from all of these dead people. All of these insane experiments. You must be completely rehabilitated."

Pete didn't answer, nor did he return Duke's disturbingly reptilian smile.

"Buck up," Duke said. "What's the matter?"

"Nothing."

"Nothing, huh? Are you thinking about that creature in the lab? Thinking you want to put her out of her misery?"

Pete looked at the monitor screen where Alish was bustling back and forth between what looked to be a microscope and another machine that looked like a microwave. After he'd thought about it a bit, he realized he had no wish at all to end the zombie's misery, if that is what it was. The disgust he'd felt when he initially saw it there gave him a reflexive urge to destroy it just like he would any other aberration of the natural world, like finding a bug as big as your hand, or a green mold covering the last piece of cake. He hadn't really thought that the zombies could feel anything, but that one looked as if it was in pain. And that was just fine by him.

"No."

"No?"

"No."

"Hmmm. What did you think of that book that I gave you?"

"I liked it," Pete said. Duke had given him *And the Graves Give Up Their Dead*, by Reverend Nathan Mathers. He hadn't much cared for the biblical references that backed up Mathers's arguments, but he definitely enjoyed reading the sections where Mathers urged his readers to "send the dead back to hell." There was a whole chapter on why it was necessary to burn the corpses, even if they had become inanimate after a head shot.

"You liked it? You didn't think he was a little too over the top?"

"No," Pete said. "He didn't always go far enough. He gives an awful lot of Biblical evidence and warnings, but he never actually recommends an action."

Davidson laughed out loud. "You are an odd duck, Peter Martinsburg," he said, "an odd duck."

On the screen before him, Alish was closing up an experiment and dousing the lights. He walked past the door to his "office" four times, but never went in.

"Alish is coming," Pete said. For some reason Duke always wanted to know when Alish was getting ready to check out. Probably because Duke was supposed to be doing something other than hanging out, drinking coffee, and having study groups with Pete.

"You want to meet him?" Duke asked.

"Who? Alish?"

"No, stupid. Reverend Mathers."

Pete looked back at Duke, trying to see if he was serious. He looked like he might be.

"I don't know," Pete said.

"The Reverend is an amazing person," Duke said, "absolutely amazing. A man of intelligence as much as faith."

"You've met him?"

Duke nodded, with what Pete thought was exaggerated solemnity. "Oh yes," he said, taking a swig from his Thermos cup.

"Really? Where did you meet him?"

"I've seen him a couple times, actually."

"You're kidding. The foundation know about this? I wouldn't think they would be too happy knowing you were hanging out with 'The Scourge of the Undead.'" Pete had done more than read the book. He'd gone online and read some other material about Mathers, his church, and his activities.

"Oh, they know," Duke said, taking another swig.

Alish arrived at the door to the monitor room just then, and he paused, as though aware of the sudden silence that greeted his arrival. His gray eyes regarded Pete the way they always did, which was as if he wasn't—or shouldn't be—there.

"Hello, Mr. Hunter," Duke said.

"Hello. I will be teaching with Angela today. Please vacuum the carpets in the encounter room before the students get here, and see to it that the lab floors are cleaned. Those shoes that the Wilson boy wears leave black marks all over the tile."

"Will do, Mr. Hunter," Duke said. "Pete here will take care of it. It's his last day, you know. The last of his two hundred hours of community service."

"Really," the old man said. He looked at Pete for a moment, but didn't say anything. Then he turned and started back to his daughter's office.

"He's not using a cane today," Pete said. "Why doesn't he need it every day?"

"You're pretty observant," Duke said. "Listen, I'm giving you a going away present. I'm going to talk to Alish. He and I need to meet about a couple of things, so I'll let you work your last shift without me hanging over your shoulder all night. I'll have the radio on, so if you need anything just give me a call. Otherwise, enjoy yourself. Just get the carpets and the floors done like the old man said."

"Okay." Duke was a permanent resident at the foundation, like the stupid Wilson kid and his stupid streak-leaving sneakers.

"Lock up the labs when you're done, all right? You know how to do that?"

Pete nodded.

"Okay," Duke said, smiling. "Have fun."

As he said this, he placed his keycard on the edge of his desk, pressing it down with an audible click.

Still smiling, he turned and left the monitor room.

What the hell? Pete thought, first watching Duke head down the corridor on the monitor screen, then turning back to the keycard on the desk. What is this, some sort of stupid test? A dare?

Whatever it was, Pete wasn't playing. He was just going to get the floors done, keep his head down, and get the hell out of there, "fully rehabilitated," as the man had said.

But filling up the mop bucket, he started thinking about the thing in the lab, how he could see its spine twitch when he was looking at it.

He added some chemicals to the hot water.

What did Davidson mean by leaving his keycard there? Was he trying to goad Pete into doing something?

He mopped the entrance hall, then vacuumed the carpet in the encounter room. Angela had dropped a few hints about having him sit in on one of their sessions, but that had never materialized. Her legs, and the look of annoyance she gave him when she caught him staring at them, were the only things he'd miss about this place.

He went back to the supply closet, changed the mop water, and did the hallway outside the encounter room and the short hall to Angela's office. The keycard, he realized, would let him into her office as well as the main office, two areas of the building that were off-limits to him after hours. He could use the card to go in and get his files.

Not like she wouldn't have backups, he thought. He went back to get his soda and sandwich from the small fridge in the monitor room. He had one more corridor to do, and then he could watch the clock until it was time to go.

Time to go, he thought. Don't do the crime if you can't do the time.

Well, he'd done the time. He knew, despite the wrist slap the judge had given him, that what he'd done was a crime. And despite appearances to the contrary, he did feel guilty for what he'd done. Adam hadn't deserved to die.

But the zombies did.

They deserved to die, die and stay dead. If it wasn't for the zombies, Adam would still be alive, and Pete would still be in school and playing football and getting an endless supply of tail, rather than getting homeschooled by a balding guy in his thirties who smelled like menthol and started shaking every time Pete reached for his pencil. He wouldn't be spending all of his free time in this cave, listening to Duke's rambling. He'd be hanging out with Stavis and getting drunk and playing Xbox or cruising around the streets of Winford looking for even more tail.

Pete ended up throwing half of his sandwich away. His

mother had made him a salami sandwich. No matter how many times he said, "I hate salami, please give me ham," salami ended up in the bag. The Wimp must like salami.

He saw the keycard on Duke's desk.

He swore under his breath and got up from his chair. Just the lab hallway and he'd be done.

The lab hallway, he thought, looking at the keycard.

He switched off the monitors, thinking that maybe he ought to at least say good-bye.

Phoebe and her friends stopped in their tracks when they saw Pete Martinsberg waiting in the front corridor as they entered the Hunter Foundation. Phoebe instinctively moved in front of Adam, as though by doing so she could rewind the past. She felt Adam's heavy hand on her shoulder. Margi and Karen moved beside them and stood glaring at Adam's killer.

"I don't want any trouble." Pete raised his hands. "I was just leaving. Today was my last day of community service, and I won't be bothering any of you again."

Adam, gently but firmly, drew Phoebe back and stepped forward at the same time, his big body casting a long shadow from the sunlight streaming through the foyer doors over Martinsburg.

"I just want to leave," Pete said, looking at each of them in turn, as though unsure of who was the greater threat. From the corner of her eye Phoebe could see the other girls; Margi looked positively feral, a cat poised to spring. Beside her, Karen was the implacable ice princess, looking as though she could kill merely by narrowing her eyes. Even Kevin Zumbrowski, stand-ing behind them, looked vaguely threatening.

"Can I go?" Pete said. He didn't say "please," but Phoebe thought there was a pleading tone to his voice.

"Go."

The word rumbled up from Adam's chest, and he moved aside, shielding Phoebe, in order to let Pete pass.

"Thanks," Pete said, looking contrite. He ducked his eyes as the Undead Studies students watched him pass the way they'd watch a snake slither through the garden.

He stopped once he had the foyer door open.

"Oh, I almost forgot," he said. "Mr. Hunter said he had a surprise for you, something about one of your classmates being back. He said to meet him at the lab at the end of the east corridor. The one on the right."

He might have smiled as he turned, Phoebe wasn't sure.

"Grrr," Margi said, watching until Pete was out of sight. "I really want to scratch his eyes out."

Phoebe squirmed past Adam, feeling partly annoyed and partly proud of the way he'd tried to protect her. "At least he's done."

Karen was already walking down the hallway. "His kind are . . . never done. Come on, let's go see Sylvia."

"Syl-vi-a!" Kevin said, drawing out all three syllables.

They followed her down the hall, but Margi wasn't done with Pete. She held her arms out in front of her as they walked.

"Look at me, I'm vibrating, I'm so mad. How can you not want to beat him up the moment you see him, Adam?"

"I . . . do."

"Why don't you?"

"Some . . . day . . . maybe."

"I really hope so. I really mean it. Let me . . ."

Phoebe cut her off. "Margi, I really think it's best if we forget about Pete Martinsburg. The sooner, the better."

She started to explain why, but Karen had reached the lab door, which was open. And then she screamed.

Phoebe had never heard a zombie scream before, and she never wanted to again. The shrill noise was the sound of a choking animal being tortured—it rang out and echoed through the hallways of the entire foundation at what seemed an impossibly loud volume.

Phoebe ran the short distance to Karen, and she saw why she was screaming, and then she was screaming too.

Karen was the first to recover.

"Give . . . me . . . your phone," she said.

"What?"

"Your . . . phone, Phoebe . . . give it . . . to me!"

Phoebe went digging, the phone suddenly a wriggling fish swimming at the bottom of her bag, but then she caught it, turned it on, and with shaking hands passed it to Karen.

Margi was clinging to Adam, who stood in stunned silence.

"She's . . . she's been taken *apart*," Margi whispered.

Kevin, distraught, shuffled from side to side, his left leg dragging behind him, his stiff arms waving.

"Help . . . her . . . help . . . her . . ."

Karen held up the phone and started snapping photos. On

the third flash, Sylvia opened her eyes, and Phoebe and Margi both shrieked again. Karen ran to where most of the girl hung, and when she spoke her voice was reassuring and steady.

"We're going to get you out of here, honey. Don't . . . worry."

Sylvia's mouth moved, but no sound came out. It looked like she might have been trying to speak. Across the room, her arm twitched twice and then lay still.

"Phoebe." There was an element of command in Karen's voice now, and Phoebe forgot about her fear when she heard her name. "Help me with these straps. Adam, wheel that gurney over here. Margi and Kevin . . . collect . . . the rest of her."

"Oh, Karen, I don't know if I can . . ."

"Do . . . it, Margi! Phoebe, get that . . . scalpel."

The voice at the door froze them all where they stood.

"I wouldn't do that if I were you."

They turned, and Alish stood in the doorway, the sadness on his face deepening the many wrinkles there. Duke Davidson stood with him, holding what looked to Phoebe like a Taser, or a gun.

"You . . . monster. We . . . trusted . . . you." Karen said.

Phoebe watched Karen walk toward Alish and Duke. She'd plucked the scalpel from Phoebe's hand without even breaking stride. Duke stepped forward and braced himself in front of Alish. The old man waved his hands, one of which still held his cane.

"Please, please," he said. "Hear me out. Please. This isn't what is seems."

"It . . . seems . . . you . . . are . . . *dissecting* . . . her. *Vivisecting* . . . her," Karen said.

Phoebe gasped as Adam and Kevin began to surge forward. Duke's voice was a gunshot, and they halted, as though by supernatural command.

"Not another step!" Duke's body was tense with the promise of easy violence. He was smiling.

Time seemed to freeze, and in that moment, when all eyes were on Karen, Phoebe reached over and palmed her phone. Karen had left it on the table beside Sylvia. She was pretty sure that Duke wouldn't let them leave with the phone—if he would even *let* them leave.

"Please, please," Alish was crying, and Phoebe could hear the tick tick tick of Angela's heels as she ran down the hall. "Please, just listen to me."

Karen held the knife, and there was nothing like mercy in her diamond eyes. There was no fear. When she spoke, her voice was a voice from the grave.

"Speak."

"You can't move her," Alish said. "Not when she's like this. She'll reterminate. She needs the fluids we're giving her."

Phoebe looked behind her at Sylvia, although it was difficult to do so. She saw curling plastic tubes attached to her friend, each pumping a violet fluid into or away from her.

Karen pointed at Alish with the knife. "Put her . . . back . . . together."

"We will. That was the purpose all along, you see. We . . ."

"Now."

Alish looked at her. By this time Angela had joined them in the lab, and Phoebe thought the expression of sympathy on her face was the most hypocritical thing she'd ever seen.

"It isn't that simple, Miss DeSonne. The procedure is a lengthy one, and delicate, and . . ."

"I'll . . . wait."

Alish shook his head. "You couldn't stay. It would be very, uh, unpleasant for you."

"Unpleasant? Un . . . pleasant?" She took another step forward. "I'm . . . dead, monster . . . you don't know . . . what . . . unpleasant is."

Another few steps and she would be within Duke's striking distance, and had settled into himself, as though preparing for her attack. He watched the dead girl, his face blank.

Alish's whining grew louder. "You don't understand," he said. "We're helping her. We're really helping her."

Angela walked forward, shrugging off Duke's hand as she moved past. "Karen, please. I know what this looks like. But my father is right, we really are helping Sylvia. When the procedure is done she'll be better. She'll be like you, able to speak and walk and everything else. You need to trust us."

"Trust . . . you."

"Yes, Karen. Trust us. We've always only had your best interests at heart. Please put the knife down."

Karen looked back at Sylvia, whose mouth still worked soundlessly.

"You expect me . . . to trust . . . you."

"I do, Karen. Put the knife down."

Karen hesitated. "But just . . . *look* . . . at her." The scalpel slid from her fingers and struck the tile with a hollow clink.

The zombies wanted to stay until Sylvia was reconstructed, but Alish, backed up by Davidson, insisted that it wasn't possible. They were actually in the middle of the process, he said, which they expected to last another week. Alish blew his nose on a handkerchief and told them that Sylvia would be returned to them for the next class.

"There won't be . . . another class," Karen responded. "Ever."

Thorny was waiting in the encounter room with Cooper and Melissa, and Phoebe would have found their obliviousness hilarious if she wasn't still reeling from the discovery in the lab. Karen, sparing no detail regarding Sylvia's condition, told them what they'd just seen. She told them that Undead Studies was canceled, permanently. She didn't need to take a vote, the consensus was immediate, if unspoken. She advised Cooper to leave the foundation with them, and the dead boy agreed.

"Can I . . . stay . . . at the . . . Haunted House?"

Karen looked back at the door, where Angela stood sucking on her lower lip.

"For . . . now," Karen replied. "I think we'll need to . . . move. Ms. Hunter, would you please get the van to pick us up? As in . . . right now?"

Angela, sighing, said she would.

"I can't believe it," Thorny said. "I can't even believe it."

"Believe it," Phoebe told him.

The students decided to wait for the bus in the foyer. Most of them were all too eager to get on the bus and leave what they'd witnessed or heard about, but Phoebe hung back so she could hear Karen's parting words, which she delivered with ice-cold brevity right to Alish.

"I'll be back in a week for . . . Sylvia," she said. "I'll be bringing . . . friends."

Alish assured her that he'd have Sylvia ready, and then they joined the others, who sat in a cluster toward the center of the bus.

Phoebe took her seat next to Adam, who looped a heavy arm around her shoulders. Karen sat apart from the others, a few rows up.

"Are you okay, Karen?"

Karen ignored the question. "He got us . . . again. Damn . . . him."

Phoebe was confused at first, wondering how the comment applied to Alish, but then she recalled the ghost of a smirk on Pete's face as he'd exited the building.

Karen punched the seat in front of her, and it sounded like she'd used enough force to splinter bone.

CHAPTER
FORTY-THREE

"All differently biotic students are to report to room one eleven for study hall . . ."

Phoebe was late to the cafeteria, having tried to spend a few extra minutes in the hallway with Adam before Principal Kim reluctantly chased her away. Margi was at their usual table, sitting by herself.

"Just you and me today, kid," Phoebe said, smoothing her skirt. "Anything good to eat?"

"You can have whatever you want, I'm not very hungry," Margi said. "Where are Adam and Karen?"

"You didn't hear the announcement? Zombies aren't allowed in the cafeteria anymore. They have to go sit in a study hall with Principal Kim."

"You're kidding."

"Does that sound like something I'd kid about?"

"Jeez. Actual segregation. Unreal. I think trads should be the ones that get segregated."

"I guess we are, by default."

Margi hadn't really eaten anything, her bag of cookies was unopened, and her sandwich had been picked at, but all of the parts seemed to be present on the napkin spread before her. "You want any of my stuff?"

Margi shook her head. "I used to think being dead might be the way to go."

"Oh, Margi . . ."

"No, no. I mean zombie dead, not dead dead. I just thought it might be cool, you know, never having to sleep, being invulnerable to pain, going out at night and basically doing whatever you want. That's all. That freedom, to be outside of society."

"I don't think many zombies are enjoying that freedom right now, Gee."

"I know, I know. It wasn't like I was going to kill myself or anything."

"That's good, because not everyone comes back. Especially . . ." Here Phoebe was going to say, "especially suicides," but Karen was an exception to that rule. "Especially because you have so many people who love and care about you."

"Ease up, Pheebes. I told you I wasn't really thinking about it. And now, after seeing Sylvia, there's no way I'd want to be a zombie. I still can't believe what they did to her, even if it was in the name of science. Do you believe what Alish was saying? Do you really think he was trying to help her?"

Phoebe thought about it. "I believe that Alish thinks he's helping, that the ends will justify the means. The problem is, I don't think he knows what he is doing. How could he?"

"I thought the needles and the reflex tests were creepy enough, but this—this is just crazy. Do you think . . . do you think Sylvia's the first zombie they've experimented on?"

"I don't know. Probably not."

"Me neither."

Margi looked over at the next table, where a bunch of trad students were laughing and carrying on as though nothing in their world had changed. Phoebe realized that nothing *had* changed—for them.

"Makes you wonder where the ones before Sylvia went."

They ate in silence for a moment.

"Karen sent the photos to the *Winford Bulletin* and a bunch of other places," Phoebe said. "It took us forever to figure out how to get the photos from the phone to the computer."

"I saw them on mysocalledundeath, but I really couldn't look at them. They're too horrible. I was surprised the Web site was still up, though. Doesn't the foundation control it?"

Phoebe nodded. "I was locked out this morning. There's a big ole 'under construction' banner there."

"Nice. How will you get in touch with Tommy?"

Phoebe wondered if Margi could detect the wave of guilt that rose up in her upon hearing Tommy's name. She'd be lucky if Tommy read another e-mail from her ever again after the flame-mail she sent.

"I've got a private e-mail address. Karen and I are going to have to set up a different site. Luckily we have all the photos kids sent backed up." She could tell Margi had more Tommy questions, so she quickly changed the subject. "Hey, that reminds me. Have you heard from Colette?"

Margi smiled. "She called me from Dom's cell phone the other day. She's in New Jersey for a few days, and it sounds like she's having a blast."

"That's great. At least someone's happy."

"Yeah. She sounded so good, Phoebe. So *alive*. She wants us to call her together in a few days." A cloud crossed her face. "Oh, man. We should probably call her today. I don't want her to find out about Sylvia on TV. I didn't even think about calling her I was so upset."

"I know what you mean. I went over to Adam's last night and all we did is watch the news. We never watch television."

"Oh no? What do you usually do?"

She said it casually, but Phoebe caught the evil glint in her eyes. "We take long walks in the woods. We walked all the way to Oxoboxo Lake the other day."

"Long walks, huh?"

"Yes, Margi. Long walks. Very long walks." She leaned back in her chair. "It's starting to get really cold, though. It doesn't bother him, but I can't stand it when it gets cold and windy. I don't know what we're going to when we can't walk."

"You'll think of something."

"Margi! Stop it!"

"Whaaaaat?" Feigning innocence, which she couldn't quite pull off. "I'm just saying, you're very creative, and . . ."

"Margi! Not another word!"

Margi laughed and put her peach pit on her napkin. "Okay, okay. Did you hear the latest? Zombies come back from the dead because of vitamin C deficiencies."

"That isn't even close to true. You're thinking of scurvy."

"You're no fun," Margi replied, pouting. "I know what I'm going to do when I graduate."

"Thanks for that message from far left field, Margi. What do your future career plans have to do with anything?"

Margi cleared a space in front of her and folded her arms on the table, then rested her head on her arms.

"I'm going to work with the undead. Really work with them, *for* them, not like the foundation. I want to be the one to discover how they come back, and I want to be the one that discovers how they can come back even more."

"I think you would be great at that."

"I think I can make a difference. I know that sounds clichéd, but I believe it. Once I got over my guilt and all that yuckiness, I think I really helped Colette. She'd 'returned' quite a bit by the time she left with DeCayce, you know?"

"You were wonderful with Colette," Phoebe told her. "She's happy now because of you."

Margi sat up and rubbed her nose. "I can talk to people, and I'm a good friend. I think I just need to learn the science stuff so I can help people like Sylvia."

She looked out over the cafeteria, where the trad kids talked and joked and ate and were mostly unaware that the zombies weren't present in the lunchroom today.

"I better get cracking, though. I'm getting a C in biology."

"Are you . . . sure . . . you want to go with us . . . tonight?" Tak said to the beautiful girl beside him. They were sitting in back of the Haunted House, alone except for Mal, who had been staring into the sky since Tuesday.

"Oh, I'm . . . sure." Karen said, and he heard it again, the subtle hitch in her speech that conveyed how emotional she was. How angry.

When he first heard her story about Sylvia, a girl he had barely met, he'd been secretly thrilled, his mind leaping instantly to all the different ways that the Sons of Romero could make use of not only the story itself but the wellspring of fury that was flowing from Karen. But the more she told it, the wilder she became. She had so much rage inside her that it almost scared him.

Almost.

"What do you . . . think . . . he thinks about?" he said, nodding to Mal, who was sitting on his rock. Tak had tried many times to recruit the boy, but he didn't seem interested in anything but the sky since Tommy had left.

"Who? Mal?"

"Yes."

"He's praying."

"Really?" There was still an edge in Karen's voice, so Tak wasn't sure if she was kidding or not."

"Really."

"He . . . told you that? He . . . talks to you?"

"He used to."

Tak looked at Mal, at the light frost that covered his body. George shambled out of the woods just then, clutching something to his chest.

"What did you . . . see when you . . . died, Karen?"

Karen looked at him.

"Did you see a white warm light like some of our . . . family? Did you see . . . the faces of those that went before . . . or did you feel . . . an elation, like every happy memory you have . . . ever had was being . . . recalled at once? I have heard . . . our family . . . tell stories . . . like these."

Karen shook her head.

"Or did you see . . . a blankness . . . a void . . . a void that swallowed up your screams . . . without even . . . the gift . . . of an echo?"

He held out his hand to her. She stared at it a moment, then took it. He helped her to her feet.

"Tak," she said, "We don't know what we . . . saw . . . when we died . . . was real. We just . . . don't know. Kevin said . . . he saw a baseball field. Green, the grass cut just so. I saw . . . I saw . . . Mal said . . ."

She stopped for a moment, as though collecting her thoughts, or catching her breath.

"Mal said he saw God. He said that . . . God . . . spoke to him. He's been looking for . . . Him . . . since."

Tak smiled. "Really?"

She surprised him then by laying her hand alongside his ruined cheek. Her face softened, as though the anger had finally left her. She stepped forward and hugged him, tightly.

"Don't do it, Tak. Don't . . . give in . . . to despair. I gave in . . . in life . . . and now I've got a second chance."

"Is that was this is?" he said. His cheek was a chiseled piece of ice next to hers, but he held her as tightly as she held him. "A second . . . chance? Does your friend . . . Sylvia . . . think this is . . . a second chance?"

She held him. "We have to . . . believe it is, Tak. We . . . *have* to."

"Why?" he said. But it felt good holding her. In fact, it felt better than anything he'd experienced since his return.

"Why," he said. "Why . . . didn't I . . . see?"

"I don't know, Tak. I don't know why we all saw what we saw. But we're here now. Isn't that . . . good enough? Maybe next time . . . maybe next time we'll get to see if . . . if there is a God."

"If there is, Karen . . . don't you see how that's worse?" he said. "It's so much worse if He exists."

"What . . . what do you mean?"

"If there is a God," he told her, "if there is . . . he turned us away. We were there . . . and he . . . turned us . . . away."

She held him tighter then, as if for a moment he was the rock that anchored her from spinning out into the universe. She buried her face in his shoulder, and he thought he could feel her lips moving against his neck, like she was praying. He could feel her against him. He *felt*, and the feeling was so strong that it actually made him question, if only for a moment, the nonbelief he'd carried so strongly since picking his broken body off of the Garden State Parkway and limping down the exit ramp.

"You're trembling," he said. "How is it that you can . . . tremble?"

They stood like that for some time.

CHAPTER FORTY-FOUR

PETE FELT STRONG hands grip his shoulder the moment he was swung around into the wall of his garage, and all he could think was "they finally caught up to me."

Half-winded, Pete struggled to his feet, expecting to see the slashed face of the Japanese zombie. Instead he found himself staring into the cold blue eyes of Duke Davidson.

"Oh." His voice was raspy as he tried to regain his breath. "It's you."

"Think you're pretty clever, don't you?" Duke said, shoving him back against the wall. Pete found himself wishing the Wimp was home, at least then he might get the pleasure of seeing him get his ass kicked along with his own. Duke tapped him on the side of the head like he was trying to get his attention. "Don't you?"

"I'm . . . really clever," Pete said, deflecting a second tap to the head with his forearm. He could feel spittle on his cheeks when Duke laughed in his face.

"I've got to hand it to you, Martinsburg." He stepped back and leaned against Pete's car, which Pete hadn't driven anywhere other than the foundation and back since his sentencing. "One impulsive act, and you throw away months of planning. A year, even."

"Planning what?"

Duke made as if to strike him, and Pete flinched.

"What do you think, Martinsburg?" He shook his bald head. "The destruction of the zombie plague."

Pete rubbed his shoulder where Duke had shoved him. "You left me your key. And then you practically came out and said you were going to be distracting Alish."

Duke's grin grew wider, and he spread his hands in a "you got me" gesture.

"Am I in trouble, then?" Pete said. "I figured I was doing something you wanted me to do."

"Pete," Duke said, and reached out to grip the shoulder he'd just shoved. "Relax. You passed the test."

"I did?"

"Flying colors, son. You can follow orders, but you can also take initiative—you'd be surprised what a rare combination that is. You're exactly who we need. The Reverend is very pleased with you.

"The Reverend? Reverend Mathers?"

Duke went on as though Pete hadn't spoken. "Your pals got a real eyeful at the lab. The pictures they posted have really polarized the issue. The war is on, Pete. The foundation, the primary zombie-advocate organization in the country, will be seriously discredited. Funding will vanish. And the undead, once they see what has been happening to them behind closed doors, are going to run wild in the streets."

Pete doubted that. Somehow, the idea of the zombies doing anything beyond lurking in the shadows wasn't something he could picture. There could be a couple, the Japanese guy and a few of his cronies, who might do something drastic because of what happened at the foundation, but Pete seriously doubted that there would be any mass uprising. "The zombies are like undead hippies. There are only a few that are going to do anything about it."

Duke smiled as he reached into his pocket. Pete thought that he was going for a gun, and that in a moment he'd be past the point of worrying or caring what Duke did. He only hoped that Duke put the bullet in his head so he wouldn't come back.

What Duke withdrew was not a gun. It was the mask that Pete had worn on the night they desecrated the cemetery. Duke slammed it against Pete's chest.

"That's where you and I come in, my friend." Duke pressed the mask against Pete's chest with the palm of his hand until Pete took hold of it.

"The Reverend is expecting big things from you, Martinsburg. Big things. You start tonight."

Pete looked at him and then looked down at the mask spread out on his fingers. The knobby teeth jutted out through the molded tear on the latex cheek, and Pete could feel the scar where his stitches had been itching; he tried to erase the thought that he was staring at a warped mirror image of himself.

"What are we going to do?"

"We're going to take it up a level," Duke said. "The time is right to blow the whole idea of zombie rights and peace sky high."

Duke took one of the yard tools hanging from hooks on the wall of the garage, a splitting maul. He ran his thumb along the edge of the blade, and Pete wondered if he knew that the maul was the tool Pete'd used to destroy the zombie that had been staying in his neighborhood. He couldn't remember his name, Evan or Kevin or something like that. The kid's family, who lived a few streets over, had put their house up for sale.

Duke replaced the maul. "Thanks in part to you, Pete, we've got the world believing that the zombies are willing to dig up graves as part of their recruiting mission. The Hunter Foundation scandal, which we also owe to Mr. Peter Martinsburg, thank you very much, makes this a perfect time to show the living world just how serious the zombies are about swelling their ranks. And when we show them, the living will rise up and destroy the dead."

Pete felt chills along his spine. The light in Duke's eyes bordered on fanatical, but there was something else there too. Pete thought it was pride—pride for what Pete had done.

And maybe even affection. It had been so long since someone had looked at him with that emotion, Pete really wasn't sure.

Duke's words scared him, but they excited him too. When

he thought that he might actually have a hand in bringing about the destruction of *all* zombies, and not just the couple dozen worm burgers haunting Oakvale, he felt something beyond mere rage and revenge.

He felt *relevant*.

Duke put both his hands on Pete's shoulders.

"If the zombies are willing to dig up graves to get more of their kind," he said, "how hard is it to imagine them using more . . . *direct* methods of recruiting?"

Pete was smiling as he pulled on his mask.

CHAPTER
FORTY-FIVE

POPEYE WAS actually singing "The Twelve Days of Christmas" as they approached the lawn of St. Jude's. He and Takayuki were far ahead of the other zombies, each of whom was moving even more slowly than usual since they were all hauling bags stuffed with Popeye's gear. His singing was off-key, and lacking in rhythm or melody.

"Will you please . . . shut up." Tak said.

"So I'm not . . . Pâvarotti," Popeye said. "Sue me."

"Your lack of talent I could . . . put up with," Tak said. "It's your . . . song selection . . . that grates."

They stopped about twenty feet from the manger, which was illumined by a pair of bright halogen lamps. Inside the manger a plastic baby Jesus was attended by Mary and Joseph, and they were surrounded by the Magi, a shepherd, two sheep, and a five-foot-high camel.

"The baby is still . . . there," Tak said as Popeye completed a line about lords a leaping. He wished he had an iPod like Tayshawn, who lugged his burden a few steps behind, blissfully unaware of Popeye's singing.

"And it better stay there too," Popeye answered. "The whole . . . effect . . . of this piece will be ruined if . . . there is any vandalism."

Tak noticed that Popeye had begun calling their statements to the beating hearts "pieces" soon after they put up the Undead Army recruitment posters. Or maybe it was the visit from the Hunters that put delusions of grandeur in his bald head, Tak wasn't sure. But Popeye had more of Tommy in him than he realized, because he wanted the bleeders to think.

Tak just wanted them to be afraid.

"Set the bags . . . over there," Popeye was saying. "George . . . how many times . . . do I have to tell you . . . to pick it up . . . not . . . drag it?"

Tak watched Karen cross the road with George. Tak much preferred going in smaller groups when they went into Winford; he thought that for everybody they added, they were doubling their chances of getting caught. But selfishly, he thought Karen's presence made it worth the risk. She was probably faster than all of them, so if there was any trouble, she'd be the most likely to get away.

He set his own burden down and looked at the manger, thinking about Christmases past. When he lived in New Jersey there was a church a few streets over that put out a nativity scene year after year, and year after year the baby Jesus was stolen. One year it was replaced with a dead cat, another time someone demolished the whole scene, going as far as to kick in the pressboard walls of the stable and break the heads and hands off the statues. He remembered, as a boy, looking at a photograph of the destruction in the newspaper and wondering what sort of misanthropic idiots would commit such a senseless act.

That was before he died.

There was condensation on some of the statues, probably caused by the cool mist hitting the painted cheeks and then being bathed in the warmth of the halogen lights. The Magi were bearded, and they were carved and painted with somber, dignified expressions. Tak involuntarily lifted his hand to the space where his cheek used to be, his fingers grazing exposed molars.

"George! Hurry . . . up!" Popeye yelled. The church and the mission were at the far end of a busy street. Three a.m. was not a popular hour on a weeknight, but all it would take is the passing headlights of one car for the whistle to be blown. Tak looked back as Popeye started giving instructions to Tayshawn on how to set up. Karen was already busy.

"How are . . . you?" Tak asked her.

"Better," she said, smiling at him as she tied a knot around one of the figures. "I'm still angry, but I . . . feel better."

"Anger is . . . an energy," he said, but even as he said it he knew that something had changed inside of him after their embrace. Even the meaning of the piece they were about to construct had changed for him.

"Tak, are you . . . helping?" Popeye asked. They'd practiced the setup all week in the backyard of the Haunted House so that they could get in, do the deed, and get out.

"Coming," Tak said, looking away from the manger.

When he died, Tak didn't see loved ones who'd passed on before him or bright lights in the distance. He didn't feel the "warm, womblike glow" that one dead girl described. He'd listened to more than a few tales of a reassuring vision of an afterlife from the zombies that had made their return to the Haunted House, but to him the only afterlife was the one he was "living" now. He died on a busy stretch of the Garden State Parkway, where he lost control of his motorcycle in the rain and broke his neck. He came back three days later with no memory of being gone, just a blankness where so many others reported brightness, love, and joy.

He was convinced that these people were delusional, and that these "visions" were the products of minds desperately in need of some piece of sanity to cling to when faced with the fact of their return from death.

Karen looked up from her task.

"Are you okay, Tak?"

"I'm . . . fine. Why do you . . . ask?"

She shrugged. "I just thought you looked . . . funny. That's all."

Tak looked back as George finally made it across the road, an enormous sack slung over his back.

"I'm . . . fine."

"Okay."

"Hey, look," Tayshawn said, catching sight of George. "It's undead . . . Santa."

"Less talk," Popeye said. "More work. The charred sticks for the fire go here, not over there."

"Hey, Santa," Tayshawn said, "looks like . . . your girlfriend . . . made it."

Tak looked across the lawn to the mission. The girl Karen had brought to the Haunted House the other day, Melissa, was walking in their direction, her white mask reflecting the moonlight.

"Hey, Melissa!" Karen called. Tak was glad Karen kept working while she called to her; he thought that six zombies congregating on a church lawn in the dead of night would be seen by the beating hearts as more than a gathering, they'd think it was an uprising.

Tak watched George, who started walking toward Melissa as she waved, the board that she wrote on under her other arm.

"Let's . . . hurry up," Tak said. "This isn't supposed . . . to be . . . a party."

"You're supposed to be . . . helping, George," Popeye said, managing to sound irritated as he set up one of the gaunt, shrouded figures he'd constructed out of old denim and pieces of the shutters they'd peeled from the Haunted House. Their garments were made from black garbage bags.

"Let him be, just get it . . . done," Tak said, starting to arrange the figures according to Popeye's design.

The work itself didn't take very long, even with Popeye crabbing at George and Tayshawn every few moments. Melissa walked over to watch them, and George tried his best to contribute by moving the figures according to Popeye's direction. Takayuki thought that he might actually be trying to show off for the masked girl. They'd arranged five figures, all smaller and less substantial than the comparatively robust figures of the manger scene. Rather than robes of purple and red, Popeye's figures were all in black, and their stick figure limbs and bodies were visible in the rents of their clothing. Whereas the figures in the manger were all gazing with reverence at the pink-cheeked infant in his straw crib, four of the five Popeye figures, their bony shoulders stooped, were gazing forlornly at the charred remains of a campfire that had gone out. Two of the figures were on their knees, and each wore an expression of abject despair as they stared into the ashes or, in one case, their hands. The faces themselves were spare, Popeye having drawn them with a black marker on beige sackcloth.

The fifth figure stood slightly apart from the circle at the fire. Its back was stooped like the others, but there was something in its carriage, a subtle tilt of the hooded head, that set it apart. It was looking into the direction of the manger scene, and its posture suggested either hope or defiance, or both.

When it was done, Popeye made everyone stand back to look. "Let me explain . . . my work . . . to you," he said, speaking to Melissa, but really to the whole group.

Pompous ass, Takayuki thought, but he also thought Popeye had done a bold and powerful job. The figure looking over at the manger—what was it thinking? Was it leading its people, or considering abandoning them? Did looking at the manger bring it hope, or a more complete sense of despair?

Popeye never got the chance to tell Melissa about his work, not even the title, which he'd told Tak was "The Thirteenth

Day of Christmas." They heard the gunning of an engine followed by a squeal of tires, then they were bathed in red, white, and blue light. The zombies froze, standing as still as the figures they'd just spiked into the earth.

"Oh no," Karen said, rising to her feet.

"Don't move! Police!"

Two police cars had stopped in front of the church lawn, and more sirens whined in the distance. He realized that one of the cars must have been close by, watching them and waiting for backup, as there were only one set of tread marks on the road. The policemen were out of their cars, standing behind the open doors with their guns drawn.

"Get on the ground now!"

Tak knew that the others were waiting for his cue. There was so little cover, and so much ground to cross to get it, but he didn't think getting arrested was an option.

"Tak?" Popeye said. A third car, and then a fourth, sped to the scene in the moment that Tak took to decide, blocking the road.

"On the ground now!" The first cop yelled. "This is your last warning!"

"Tak?"

"I . . ."

He didn't get the chance to speak.

He saw George moving at the corner of his vision, moving with a speed he didn't know George was capable of. The dead boy lurched forward. It looked to Tak like he was trying to move in front of Melissa.

The police didn't see protectiveness in the gesture. They

saw only a shambling zombie lurching toward them, its arms raised and forward, as though grasping for their necks.

Without another word, they opened fire.

The explosive sound of the guns split the night. Tak watched invisible fingers pluck at the back of George's jacket, but the dead boy continued down the hill, closing in on the police. Melissa fell to the ground, her board flying out of her hands as she hit the grass. He heard Popeye swear, and someone went over backward onto "The Thirteenth Night of Christmas," splintering some of the despairing figures. Tak heard the humming of bees and felt—although the feeling was far away, as though through a thick haze of painkiller—a sting. He looked down in amazement as a second bullet slapped against his chest, puffing out his shirt, and causing a thick trickle of dark sludgy ooze to drip out.

He looked over at Karen, standing among the effigies, and as she met his gaze he saw something he'd never seen in the diamond sparkle of her eyes: fear.

"Run!" he yelled, but the word had little power, as the bullet had done something to his lung. He heard one of the spikes on his shoulder *ping* as a bullet snapped it off, and then another bullet hit the soft wood of the manger as he ducked behind it. He ran, and he looked to his left and saw Popeye moving as fast as his dead legs could carry him, going for the stone steps of the church. Popeye tripped, or was knocked over by a bullet, but he got to his feet quickly. Tak thought they might have a chance of getting away, if they could get up the steps and around the wall of the church.

They made it to the wall, but when he looked back he saw Karen running the opposite way. A strangled cry was wrenched from his chest as he saw her lifted up and then thrown to the turf.

She didn't get up.

None of the cops were following, and Tak peered around the corner and saw why.

George had made it as far as the sidewalk. One of the cops shot at him from about ten feet away, but he was either shooting to disable or was unaware that the only surefire way of putting a zombie down was to shoot the head. One of the other cops tried tackling George around the ankles, and he went down in a heap.

Tak knew this would be his best, and maybe only, chance of getting away. Popeye was almost at the wall, and he saw Tayshawn cutting across the lawn to a row of houses. Karen had taken the path with the most open ground, as though she were trying to draw fire.

She still hadn't gotten up.

He looked back. Melissa's fiery red hair was lying in the grass like a tangle of copper wire a few feet away from her, her bald head a ruin of burned and puckered skin. The frame of her white board had splintered when she fell.

She lifted her head, her tragicomic mask hanging askew, revealing the charred skin of her forehead above a fear-crazed green eye. She reached toward him.

On the far side of the field, Karen still wasn't moving.

Tak started back for Karen, ignoring the bullets from the

one cop who wasn't in the scrum around George. He went three steps and felt something tear at his leg, and then he was flat on his face on the stone steps.

"Stop!" Takayuki heard from behind him. "What are you doing?"

It was the priest, Tak realized, the one who had given shelter to Melissa and other zombies like Mal. He was padding across the lawn in bare feet, his bathrobe flapping over his pajamas as he ran.

"Stop!" he cried. "They're human beings!"

Tak got to his feet, but the leg that had been shot wasn't working right. He thought Karen might have started crawling, but then again it might have been the wind whipping her hair and white shirt. He went another step and would have stumbled if Popeye hadn't returned to grab him around the shoulders.

"We've got . . . to go, Tak!" Popeye screamed. "We can't lose . . . you . . . too!"

Tak looked at the carnage on the church lawn. George was being clubbed with nightsticks, and then they tried the Taser. Takayuki saw his friend stiffen and jerk as the current went through him. He had no idea how a weapon like a Taser would work against the undead, but George dropped to the ground, rigid and unmoving.

And Karen . . . was she moving? Was she crawling to the shrubbery that marked one of the sidewalks leading to the church? He struggled in Popeye's grip, but the boy dragged him back, and with his leg disobeying him, Tak couldn't get the leverage to fight.

The priest was at Melissa's side. As he held her, he caught sight of Takayuki.

"Go, son!" he called. "Go!"

"Karen!" Tak yelled, as Popeye pulled him back.

"She's up . . . Tak," Popeye said in his ear. "She's . . . up. They will . . . follow us . . . instead."

Tak looked at Popeye, who'd lost his glasses in the fray. There was no way to tell in the wild bug eyes if he was telling the truth.

He fought back the desire to hobble back down the hill and fight the police, to fight until they disabled or destroyed him. His last sight before Popeye dragged him back behind the stone wall was of George, unmoving and on the ground, and of Melissa huddled in the priest's arms, her hand scrabbling for the wig she'd used to hide her scars from the world.

"We have to . . . go, Tak," Popeye said, quietly.

Tak said a quick prayer in his mind to the God he thought had rejected him.

Then he muttered a curse and limped after Popeye as he ran down the back alley behind the church.

"What . . . was . . . that?" Popeye said. They were standing in a wooded clearing within sight of Lake Oxoboxo, a place Takayuki had picked as a rendezvous point in case they were separated during one of their social-protest runs. Something like being fired upon by the local police. Dawn was beginning to break, turning the clouds above the color of cotton candy.

Takayuki didn't answer. He was thinking about Tayshawn and wondering how long they should wait for him before going on to the Haunted House.

"They didn't even . . . give us . . . a . . . .chance!" Popeye said. "They just . . . started . . . shooting!"

The existence of the Haunted House stopped being a secret when Adam was converted. Tak wondered if there were police—or white vans—headed there now.

"They shot . . . they just started . . . shooting!"

"Something's happened," Takayuki said, his voice a whisper, probably due to the bullet that had hit his lung. Nothing they'd done would have caused the cops to act like this.

"I can't believe . . . this," Popeye said. "I'm lucky . . . I wasn't . . . shot."

"You were," Tak said, "In the . . . ass. Right cheek."

"Really?" Popeye said, running a hand down the seat of his jeans. "Aw, hell!"

"Let's go to . . . the Haunted House," Tak said.

"I can't believe . . . I got shot," Popeye said. "I just . . . can't believe it."

"We all . . . got shot," Tak said, starting to walk. Popeye hurried up to join him.

"You . . . did? Where did you get . . . hit?

"Leg, obviously." Oddly, the leg was bothering him less than it had when the bullet first hit him. He was still limping, but the limp was not as pronounced as before. "Also chest. And . . . stomach."

"Damn. Damn! I can't . . . believe this."

"Popeye," he said. "Did you . . . really . . . see Karen . . . get up?"

"I . . . think . . . so," was his reply, but he didn't look at Tak when he said it.

Tak was angry with him, but he knew his anger was misplaced. The tactician in him knew that Popeye had done the right thing; if the Haunted House community were to lose him, Karen, and Tommy, they'd be decimated in no time. If in fact the police hadn't decimated them already.

He quickened his pace. The human in him, whatever small part that was left, wished he'd died the final death with the others.

"I . . . I think . . . George is . . . dead, Tak," Popeye said. "Like . . . really . . . .dead."

Tak nodded. He'd had the same suspicion. Tayshawn was probably a goner too. Maybe the priest was able to save Melissa, but it was just as likely that they'd knocked him aside and shot her like a dog.

But please, God, he thought, please not Karen. Please.

"Did you feel the . . . bullets, Tak?"

"A . . . little," he answered.

"Why did . . . they . . . do it?"

"Something's happened," Tak repeated. But what it was, he could only guess.

He didn't have to wait long for his answer. When they arrived at the Haunted House after the long walk through the woods, the "something" was on everyone's minds. There were over a dozen zombies in the unliving room when he and Popeye arrived. The boys from the foundation, Kevin and Cooper—

were all waiting for them. Even Mal, who rarely budged from his rock, was there. Many of the zombies rushed at them as soon as they saw them, as opposed to waving, or ignoring him, like they usually did.

The questions and comments came all at once.

"Why . . . did you do . . . it?"

"The . . . police . . ."

"Murderer . . ."

He couldn't make any sense of the undead chorus until Anna, a girl whom he barely knew, made her way to the front and told him without pause, in a clear voice, that he had doomed them all.

"What the . . . bloody . . . hell . . . are you talking about?" Popeye said, sounding exasperated. "*They* shot . . . at . . . *us.*"

The girl trained her pale gray eyes on him. "Because you . . . killed . . . that family."

"*What?*" Popeye said. He looked at Tak, his mouth open wide enough to show gray gums and beige teeth.

"Why do you think . . . we killed . . . someone?" Tak asked.

"It was on . . . the radio," said one of the other boys. "Every . . . fifteen minutes there is . . . an update. They give . . . your . . . description."

"The radio," he said. He had to laugh in spite of himself. "Who did they . . . .say . . . we killed?"

"A lawyer . . . and his family," was the answer. "Children."

Then he did laugh. One lie, one false accusation, and zombies everywhere are instantly discredited. To think that Tommy thinks he can actually make a difference, that he can effect change through discourse and nonviolence, when his enemies have the means to erase everything he's done in the moment it takes for a beating heart to exhale. Power in America, real power, the power to annihilate and erase would always be in the hands of the living.

"Zombies," he said. "We have . . . not done . . . what they are saying we have done. I've always said that death . . . is a gift. But it . . . is not . . . ours to give."

Even as he said it, Tak was reconsidering his position. He looked at each of the zombies gathered around him in turn.

"The beating hearts . . . are lying."

His whispered words silenced them. He knew they wanted to believe—there may have even been some who hoped he *had* committed a violent crime against the breathers, but for the most part the others would take Takayuki's word over that of a disembodied voice from the radio.

"We walked to Winford," he began, and continued to relate everything that had happened that night. His audience was dismayed to hear that George—a favorite around the Haunted House—had been taken, but they were devastated when he said that they weren't sure if Karen got away.

"What . . . do . . . we . . . do . . . now?" Anna asked. "The radio . . . said that . . . the police . . . were searching . . . for three. They gave . . . your . . . descriptions."

Popeye groaned.

"The police . . . will . . . come here," Tak said. "You . . . should not . . . be here . . . when they do."

"Where can . . . we go?"

Takayuki looked at Jacinta, who had been at the Haunted House only a week or so before the Hunters visited. Takayuki looked at her and thought that his heart would break, if he had one.

"I know . . . a place," he said. He turned to the zombies shuffling around. "We will . . . take you . . . there. Bring whatever . . . you think . . . you need. Tell . . . whoever else . . . is here. Be back . . . in five minutes."

Tak went upstairs and checked each of the rooms for zombies, but everyone had been downstairs. He stopped in the room with the wall of the dead. Downstairs, there was a crash and a thump and the sounds of slow, scared people trying to hurry.

He debated trashing the wall, thinking that maybe it wasn't such a great idea for the authorities to get so many mug shots, but then decided that he'd rather leave it. One of the recruitment posters with George fluttered in a breeze of unknown origin.

He found one of Popeye's markers and wrote on the poster, then went to join his people downstairs.

When he got there, Popeye was hugging Tayshawn, who had apparently just came through the front door

"Sorry . . . I'm late," Tayshawn said, shrugging Popeye away.

"Better late . . . than never," Tak said. He was glad Tayshawn had made it, but not glad enough to hug him. "Did you see . . . Karen?"

The look on Tayshawn's face reminded him what a curse hope was.

"I . . . didn't . . . see her."

Tak tried not to let his emotions show. His voice, made

more hollow and raspy by the bullet that had passed through his lung, betrayed nothing. He was aware of the zombies gathering behind him, awaiting his instructions

"Don't get . . . comfortable," he whispered to Tayshawn. There were a few of their people, Anna and a newlydead boy whose name escaped him, standing apart from the others. "See if you . . . can convince . . . the others. If you can't . . . after . . . a few minutes . . . leave them."

"Where are we . . . going?" Popeye asked. He'd found another pair of sunglasses, with big round John Lennon—style mirrored lenses that looked almost comical on his pale white face.

"You'll know . . . when . . . you get . . . there."

Tak turned, and the undead eyes of their community all trained on him. He'd thought of this moment often, the moment they would recognize him as their leader. Tommy's leaving had made it inevitable.

But when he'd thought of it, he'd always done so with Karen in mind. Just as he'd always known that circumstances would force the zombies to his side, he'd known that Karen would realize that Tommy's methods would not accomplish what needed accomplishing.

And now, looking into their faces and not seeing hers, he felt an emptiness unlike any he'd ever experienced before, save that of when he'd first returned from death.

He sighed, air passing in a wet wheeze from his punctured lung, and addressed his people.

"We have . . . to go."

CHAPTER
FORTY-SIX

PHOEBE WONDERED where all the zombies had gone.

She'd taken Adam's hand when they were walking to class, a rare public display of affection, but she was unnerved and a little nervous by the stares they'd been getting, stares that had begun the moment they'd gotten on the bus. She'd have thought everyone was pretty much used to the idea of her and Adam being together by now.

Margi had prattled on during the bus ride as though nothing was amiss, but even she had quieted when she noticed the tense hush that swept through the corridor as they walked.

"What's the deal?" she whispered.

"I have no idea." Phoebe looked up at Adam, who tried to shrug.

Principal Kim ended up pulling him out of their homeroom. Phoebe watched him struggle out of his desk to join the principal and Detective Gray, one of the men who had interrogated them in Undead Studies. Gray closed the door behind Adam once he was out, and Phoebe craned her head to try and see where they were going.

When they were out of sight, she realized that the entire class was silent and staring at her, even Mrs. Rodriguez.

"What?" Phoebe said. "What's going on? Where are all the zombies?"

Many looked away, but Mrs. Rodriguez held her gaze. And then she told her.

Pete sat in the warm cab of Duke's truck, watching the small screen of the wireless television Duke had propped up on the dash. This was the third channel they had tuned in, but the news was all the same.

"Attorney Gus Guttridge, lawyer for the defense in the well-publicized Oakvale zombie murder case, along with his wife and two children, ages nine and twelve, are missing and presumed dead after an apparent hate crime committed by living impaired persons. . . ."

"They're differently biotic now," Duke said to the screen. "Get with the times."

Pete looked over at him over the rim of his Styrofoam cup. Duke took another sip of coffee and winked at Pete.

Pete turned back to the screen just as the photograph of his lawyer was replaced by a close-up of the zombie from the fake recruiting ads.

". . . unidentified living impaired man allegedly responsible for the crimes was apprehended late last night, along with . . ."

"What's going to happen to Guttridge and his family?" Pete asked, not really caring who among the worm burgers would go down for his crimes.

Duke sipped his coffee. "You've heard of witness relocation? It's sort of like that."

"Why would Guttridge do that?"

Pete didn't think an attorney would be all that eager to give up his lifestyle in the name of zombie elimination. The Guttridge home was one of the largest and most opulent he'd ever been in, more impressive even than his dad's place out on the West Coast. Pete supposed he should have felt remorse for all the destruction he'd caused in the home—following Duke's orders, he and the other men smashed furniture and took knives to the trad figures of people in the artwork and photographs around the home. And then came the blood.

"We can be very persuasive."

"I guess you'd have to be," Pete said, watching the video Duke's people had released to the media, which showed a trio of zombies—really Pete and two of the men from the group wearing their masks—shambling from the Guttridge home. "Considering that there weren't any bodies."

The zombies were carrying what appeared to be a body wrapped in a blanket over their shoulders in the grainy, jumpy video. Long hair and a pale arm dangled from Zombie Pete's blanket, which in reality had been a blow-up doll and not Mrs. Guttridge. The "bodies," all four of them, were now deflated and folded in the tool chest of Duke's truck. Pete wanted to think about that even less than he did the buckets of blood that they threw around the Guttridge's bedrooms. Duke had assured him that it had been real human blood.

"Pays to have friends in high places," Pete said.

"The murder and abduction of the Guttridges is considered to be in retaliation for Attorney Gus Guttridge's role in exonerating a minor youth of murder in a zombie-related crime . . ." the voice on the television informed them.

"Zombie-related crime," Duke said, snuffling with mirth into his coffee cup. "You popped that kid."

". . . and for recent developments at the Hunter Foundation, which is alleged to be conducting experiments on the living impaired. Photos depicting an unidentified living impaired girl in a partially vivisected state have been circulating on the Web, where . . ."

"Enough." Duke switched the television off. "Mission accomplished."

Pete grinned, admiring his easy confidence. Duke was a man who was fully aware of the power he wielded, sort of like a coach who could back up his talk with action on the field. After they'd vandalized the Guttridge home, they watched from the safety of Duke's truck as the white vans rolled up. The lead van had the FBI seal stenciled on the door. Duke told Pete about the special "Undead Crimes Unit" of the FBI that would be taking over the case.

Pete had thought that the outside world might think it was a little fishy that there just happened to be an FBI van nearby when the crimes occurred, but Duke assured him that no one was going to be all that interested in investigating those angles.

"Is the whole FBI in on it?" he asked.

Duke held up his hand as he listened to the newscaster rattle off a list of crimes that Oakvale zombies were alleged to have committed.

"Sexual assault," he repeated, plucking the crime out of the ten or so she'd named. "Rumor spreads like cancer, huh? Now, what was it you asked me?"

"The FBI. Is the whole Bureau in on the anti-zombie thing?"

"The 'anti-zombie thing,'" Duke repeated, shaking his head. "You make it sound so respectable. The answer is, of course not. There isn't a single organization in America—governmental, corporate, or otherwise—where all of its members are on the same page. Except, of course," and here he grinned, and switched on the ignition for the truck, "my 'anti-zombie thing.' Put the TV on the seat, will you?"

Pete did as he was asked. "Where are we going?"

"We're going to your house, so you can pack and say good-bye to your mom. The Wimp isn't home, I hope you don't mind."

Pete felt a nervous smile creep across his face. It pulled at the scar he still hadn't gotten fixed.

"What are you talking about?"

"Youth ministry," Duke said, pulling off the shoulder and onto the road. "Your mother took a phone call from a very well-respected and important man last night, Pete. The good Reverend Nathan Mathers. He convinced her that the direction your life was taking was not a good one, and that you needed to fill the emptiness you felt with purpose. The purpose that only Reverend Mathers and his youth ministries can provide."

Pete laughed out loud. "She actually fell for that?"

"Like I said, we can be pretty persuasive. The Reverend especially. Just wait until you meet him, Pete. You've never seen such a commanding, charismatic presence in all your life."

Pete heard him as though from a million miles away. He knew that Duke was laying it on thick about the ministry, but the truth was that Pete *did* feel as if he had found purpose in life. And Duke felt so strongly about him that he was able to have the Reverend—the Reverend!—call on his behalf. The respect these men were showing him combined with the self-respect he had from all he'd accomplished in the past few weeks was an intoxicating mixture. He saw himself reflected in the visor mirror, literally blushing with pride, his face bright pink but for the thin white line of his scar. When he felt Duke's massive hand on his shoulder in a fatherly pat, emotion almost burst out of him.

"Welcome to the team," Duke said, the pat turning into a firm grip. "Son."

The ride home was an eternity, almost as bad as the school day had been. At lunch, Margi had told Phoebe all the rumors she'd heard—zombie murder spree, zombie massacre—so now they were mostly silent, along with the rest of the students sitting on the bus, who all sat far, far away from them.

"We've got to get to the Haunted House tonight," Phoebe whispered.

Margi chewed her lip. "You don't think the cops have been there?"

"Even so. We've got to make sure."

"Okay." Margi looked out the window as the bus rolled up to Phoebe's stop, and the first smile of the day appeared on her face.

"Hey, look! It's Adam!"

Phoebe looked out the window and saw him standing at the edge of the driveway. He waved. She ran off the bus to meet him, knocking him back with the force of her hug.

"I thought they'd taken you!" she said, squeezing him tight. "I was so worried."

"Re . . . manded . . . to . . . custody," he said.

"Remanded to custody? To your mom?"

He nodded. "Zombies . . . with a . . . responsible . . . parent . . . are being . . . freed. Others . . . not."

"Have you watched any of the news? What happened, exactly?

He told her what he knew, that zombies in Winford—and other parts of the country—were supposedly committing crimes in retaliation for what had been done to Sylvia. George was in prison for his alleged role in the murder of attorney Gus Guttridge and his family.

"George is in prison? Margi heard he'd been destroyed. Tak too."

"Tak . . . is . . . at large. America's . . . most . . . wanted. Not sure . . . about . . . George."

"This is awful. I can't even believe this is happening."

"It gets . . . worse," he said, leading her by the hand to her door. "It is now . . . illegal . . . to be . . . undead."

"What do you mean?"

"Martial . . . law. All undead . . . who do not . . . have a . . . parental guardian . . . are to be . . . imprisoned."

He told her about watching the news with Joe, who'd been called from the shop to pick Adam up. The news had shown footage of a police raid on the Haunted House, where a girl named Anna, and Kevin Zumbrowski were taken away in handcuffs. Adam told her that at one point Joe took off his work boot and hurled it at the television, on which the Reverend Nathan Mathers was exhorting lawmakers to "take control of our country . . . before it is overrun with the evil dead!" Locally, Father Fitzpatrick was given much less camera time to explain why he was refusing to turn "an unnamed zombie" over to the authorities.

Phoebe listened to the story with an increasing sense of horror, thinking of Tommy, thinking of Colette and DeCayce, who were all on unfamiliar roads somewhere within the country. Worse, Tommy would probably delete all messages from her unread and unlistened to.

"Have you heard from Karen?" Phoebe refused to believe anything other than that Karen was safe.

Adam shook his head.

"Hopefully she's with her family," she said.

"Hopefully."

"We've got to get to the Haunted House."

"They . . . raided . . . it."

"We have to be sure. Come on, let's call Margi, she should be home by now."

Ten minutes later Phoebe had Margi on the phone, but Margi told them not only could she not take the car, she was grounded. Her parents, no longer influenced by Colette's strange but oddly comforting appearance, decided that she'd been spending altogether too much time with zombies.

"I tried calling Karen," Margi said, "her mom said she didn't come home last night."

By the time she hung up, Phoebe had a sick feeling at the pit of her stomach.

"We've got to go to the house," she said.

"Phoebe . . . it's . . . freezing. Let . . . me . . ."

"I'm going."

"Don't . . ."

"I'm going, Adam! They'd try to kill you if you went alone!"

Adam didn't have anything to say to that, so he waited patiently in the kitchen as Phoebe went to find a heavy sweatshirt and warmer boots.

"They . . . boarded . . . it up."

Phoebe shivered, looking at the plywood sheets that had been nailed across the front door and the first floor windows. It had taken them nearly three hours to trudge through the woods to the house, and the already overcast sky was still darkening.

She looked at the boards, which had been stickered with police crime scene tape. "Let's go around back."

Adam fell in step beside her. Cold and fatigue had slowed her to his pace. She swore when she saw that there was planking over the back door as well. Adam looked at her, then walked up the steps, getting his fingers under the crack between the wood and the door.

"Watch . . . out," he said. He pulled, and boarding tore free, the nails seeming to shriek as they were yanked swiftly from the frame. Adam tossed the big board, sailing it halfway across the yard the way he used to toss a Frisbee.

"Wow."

"Told you . . . I was . . . powerful."

Phoebe'd had the presence of mind to bring a flashlight with her. Switching it on and stepping into the dark, long-unused kitchen, she thought that this was the first time that the Haunted House truly lived up to its name. She could practically feel the spirits of the undead moving in the shadows from her light.

"They're . . . gone." Adam said.

"We need to be sure."

They crept from room to room, finding evidence that people had been staying there—a pile of clothes, a CD, a stuffed bear with the button eyes removed—but no actual people.

"Let's check upstairs."

The stairs didn't seem to mind her, but they groaned in protest when Adam followed. Crime scene tape stretched across the doorway facing the top of the staircase. She shined her light in, cutting across the gloom to reveal the faces of the dead staring out from the photographs still hanging on the wall.

"I'm surprised the cops didn't take them," she whispered.

She heard a light ticking noise against the thin plywood boarding the windows and realized it had begun to snow outside.

"I think . . . they are . . . coming back." Despite this sentiment, he reached out and ripped the tape from the doorway.

"What are you doing?" she asked as he walked into the room. She was thinking of the first time she'd been here, when she and Adam went with Tommy and Evan to meet their zombie friends. Tommy had made her lie down in the darkness so she could understand what it was like to be dead.

Tommy, she thought, suddenly convinced she would never see him again. *I'm so sorry.*

"Saying . . . good-bye . . . I guess." The papers on the wall rustled in the cold wind that blew through the cracks in the shutters.

She played the light over the photos, trying to make it easier for him to see the photographs. He reached out for one, but passed his fingers over it. Then he tore a sheet of paper, the Undead States of America recruitment poster, off the wall and crumpled it in his fist.

"Souvenir." He shoved the paper into his pocket.

"I could have folded it for you."

"It's . . . okay. I'll join you . . . in . . . a minute."

They were back in the foyer, just in time to see the bright lights of a car coming up the gravel driveway through the cracks between the boarded-up windows.

"Out . . . the . . . back," Adam said, taking her arm.

They heard the slam of car doors just as they were disappearing into the woods behind the house.

CHAPTER
FORTY-SEVEN

PHOEBE'S PARENTS were furious when she finally got home. Joe was pretty pissed too but think he understood.

Snow falling heavy now, well after midnight. Look up at her window and think what couldn't say.

Good-bye.

The danger is too great, now more than ever. Nothing to give.

Long walk ahead. Right left smooth enough now, prints streak in the snow. At the Haunted House standing in front of the wall of the dead saw his message, put in pocket. OXO spaced out along the bottom of the poster. Not hugs and kisses. Message. TOOK THE POSTER SO AGENT GRAY WOULDN'T FIND.

Snow falling in darkness. The snow is good, covers tracks.

Lot to think about on long walk. Phoebe, warm in bed and dreaming. The dead don't dream. Tried to think about something else but without dreams too hard. Oxoboxo woods silent but for the sound of snow and left right scraping along.

The lake isn't huge but it isn't small either. Not sure where Tak is but have a hunch, an idea. Where Colette drowned. If Tak knows the spot that's where he'll be.

Snow-covered lake appears all at once, just beyond a last hill. A flat disk empty of trees, glowing blue white in the cloud-streamed moonlight, not like summer when all can see is an elusive glimmer through thick foliage. Crested the hill and then stepped on matted leaves slick with snow.

Slick. Fall over backward like a rotted oak.

Slide. Slide all the way to the icy shore of the lake, stop at the base of fallen tree. Abruptly stop. Glad Phoebe didn't see.

Phoebe.

Flat on back, eyes wide open, moon veiled. Snow pooling in unblinking eyes. Pain worse than death when think of her and think of her all the time. What could have been, what should have been, what never will be.

Stay down.

Didn't move for don't know how long. Should stay down. Should stay down from jump. Football told tackled kids Just Stay Down, should listen to own advice. After taking the bullet should have stayed down, avoided this pain pain worse than death. She we could have been together but dreams die with death and . . .

"Get up."

The voice, like a knife blade in the dark. Clear snow from eyes and Takayuki looms above blotting out what little moon remained. Smiling but not smiling, icicles in long lank hair.

"Get up."

Speak. Takes effort so cold don't know how long stayed down.

"Hey . . . Smiley."

Smiley straightened, bones and tendons creak like birches in the wind.

"Got . . . your . . . message."

"I wish . . . you'd . . . get up." Looks down. Smiling his non-smile.

"Wish I'd . . . never . . . gotten . . . up."

He shakes head and hair frozen clicks and clacks.

"You're thinking . . . about her . . . again, aren't . . . you? What is it about . . . her, anyway?"

"Phoebe." Saying her name hurts.

"She's like a reverse . . . Dracula . . . one that beguiles the dead . . . instead of the living."

"No," Sit sit sitting up takes effort. "I . . . dug . . . her when I was . . . alive too."

Tak, creaking, sits on the fallen tree.

"You're . . . doing . . . the right . . . thing. She . . . would always . . . be . . . in danger."

"I know." Didn't feel right, felt like death. "Where are . . . the others?"

Looks at frozen lake. "Safe."

"Karen?"

Shakes head. Clatter, click. Like wind chimes. Looks sad. Didn't think Tak could look sad.

"George is . . . in prison. Not . . . reterminated."

"Unless the . . . breathers . . . lie," Tak said.

Thought of the video of George, caged. Thought of other video.

"What about . . . the murders?"

"We had . . . nothing . . . to do . . . with that," he said.

"Because you believe . . . in the sanctity of . . . life, right?"

"No. Because I believe in the . . . sanctity . . . of death. I don't believe . . . any . . . of us did . . . it. But they . . . the beating hearts . . . believe we did," he said. "And that is all that matters. They will be coming for us . . . for you . . . and they will not be stopped . . . with words. Or even laws."

Want to tell him he's wrong. Can't.

"The girl . . ." said Tak. "Phoebe. She watched you . . . die . . . once. Do you want . . . her . . . to go through that . . . again?"

Don't. Want her don't want her to suffer through that. Don't.

"What . . . are you going . . . to do?"

Tak showed his teeth. "Go . . . underground. Bide . . . our . . . time."

"George? The others . . . ?"

"We will . . . liberate them. Or . . . avenge them."

Blanket of snow around Tak's shoulders.

"I want you . . . to come with me, Adam. With . . . us."

Underground. Underground, like the grave.

"I . . . love her, Tak."

Saying it out loud to Tak made something snap inside chest. Cold inside cold outside cold like the grave.

Tak half-skull grin not mocking or malicious.

"If that were . . . true," he whispered, "you would come . . . with me."

Tak stood, offering hand. Two gray-white knuckles where Tak was missing a patch of skin, and a row of long tarsal bones, like the bars of a prison in hell.

Took it. Rose.

And then heard her voice on the wind.

Adam.

CHAPTER
FORTY-EIGHT

"ADAM," PHOEBE SAID.

The dead boys turned. She was standing at the crest of the hill, just above the long trench Adam's body made when he'd slid down. She was shivering in black sweatpants and her heavy faux fur–lined coat, a gray scarf trailing from her neck.

"You weren't planning on leaving me, were you?"

She didn't need telepathetic powers to read his mind. Something woke her in the dead of night, a feeling that compelled her to go to her window where she'd sometimes watch him as he tried to master the poses and exercises that Master Griffin had set before him. She'd looked down and saw the long slashes of his footprints in the porch light, already half filled with snow.

Once she realized what Adam was planning to do, she'd pulled on her boots and warm clothes and rushed out the door with her flashlight. At first, his tracks, his dragging feet cutting long runnels in the snow, were easy to follow, but as the snowfall increased, the trail became harder to discern in the poor illumination. Eventually she stopped trying entirely and moved to where she thought he was going, which was the lake.

Just follow your heart, she'd thought.

"Phoebe," Adam said, "it . . . is . . . freezing."

She started down the hill, choosing her steps with care, not sure if she wanted to hug him or reterminate him.

"You think?" Her teeth chattered and she hugged herself for warmth.

"You have . . . to go . . . back."

"I'm not going anywhere without you." She slipped a little but caught herself, and soon was at the bottom of the hill with the snow-covered boys. The flakes fell on Adam's cheeks and hair and didn't melt. She looked up at him and saw what she needed to see in his eyes, something that drove the chill out of her body.

"Phoebe," Adam said, drawing out both syllables, "things have . . . changed."

She clapped her mittens together, telling herself that her fingers weren't tingling and her face wasn't numb. "Have they changed, Adam? Have your feelings changed?"

He couldn't meet her gaze. "No . . . never."

"Then why are you planning on leaving me?"

"You are . . . in danger."

"When have I *not* been in danger, Adam? Do you think I entered into our relationship lightly?"

"No."

"Why would you leave me then? Without even saying good-bye?"

Adam looked back at Tak, who brushed his frozen hair back, an almost sympathetic look on his asymmetrical face.

"My . . . anger . . . with you . . . is spent," Tak said. "I really . . . don't want . . . any more . . . of my people . . . hurt."

"They aren't your people," Phoebe said. "That thinking is exactly the problem. They're just *people*."

Tak raised his shoulder, which Phoebe saw was missing one of its metal spikes. "Semantics. If everyone . . . agreed . . . there would be . . . no issue. I'm bringing my . . . the zombies . . . underground. Somewhere . . . safe. I thought . . . we thought . . . you would be safer . . . if Adam . . . came with . . . us."

She turned back to Adam. "Is that what you thought?"

He raised his arms skyward. "Yes. I . . . want you . . . to . . . be . . . safe. Is . . . that . . . so . . . wrong?"

Phoebe noticed that the pauses between his words were longer than usual, which meant that he was getting upset—or that the cold was affecting him. But then again, she was freezing, and at the same time her blood was boiling.

"I don't want to be safe! I want to be with you!"

"Phoebe . . . I'm . . . dead . . . or . . . hadn't . . . you . . . noticed?"

He might speak slowly, but Adam had no problem with volume. Tak looked skyward and then sat back down on the fallen tree.

Phoebe was so angry she stamped her booted heel. "I thought we'd been through this already? You're still here, aren't you? Why do you still keep bringing something up that I don't care about?"

"You . . . should . . . care."

"No, I shouldn't! I care about *you*. Don't you care about me?"

"You . . . know . . . that . . . I do."

"Then why do you want to leave me?" She held out her hands. "Again."

"I don't . . . want . . . to leave . . . you . . . Phoebe. I . . ."

She held up her hand, cutting him off. "Then don't. *Don't*. Don't go 'underground' or wherever else Tak is taking our friends. Don't do it."

Tak looked up at the sound of his name and stopped picking at the entry wound just above his left knee.

"Not everybody can run and hide, Adam. Some people need to stay and fight. The strongest, the bravest, the best and brightest—whoever—some people need to stand and fight. They need to fight for what's right, and they need to do it for all of those that can't."

Phoebe walked to him and took the frozen lumps of his hands. "Tommy. Karen. *You*, Adam. You don't really have a choice. You are the strongest, bravest person I know."

"Not . . . the bravest," Adam said, looking into her eyes.

But she wouldn't be sidetracked. "You're the most dependable, the most responsible, the most admirable . . . and you're getting stronger every day. Every day. Will that continue if you go underground? Without your example, I don't think the zombies have a chance. Let Tak lead the others for now. They don't need you for that. But they will need you when it's time for them to come up again. Let Tak do his job, and you do yours."

She looked back at Tak, defying him to contradict her, but he kept his own counsel. She'd like to think that it was because he could hear the truth in her words, but she rarely could figure out what Tak was thinking.

"You think . . . they need . . . me . . . above . . . ground." Phoebe knew Adam believed her, regardless of what Tak was thinking.

"I do, Adam. I do. But it's more than that," she said, stepping into him, pressing her cold cheek into his chest.

"*I* need you. I really, really need you."

She felt his arms go around her, gently, as though he were afraid he would break her if he held too tight. It made her feel safer than her own words ever could.

"It . . . will be . . . difficult," he said.

"I know. I know it will." She squeezed him more tightly. "But we'll face it together."

The stood like that for some time, and Phoebe felt as though she were warmer even though Adam generated no heat. She heard the creak of leather as Tak slid off the tree, and she braced herself for whatever snarky comment or mocking rebuttal he would surely throw at them.

"I have . . . to . . . go," was all he said.

She saw that she had been wrong, because he didn't say anything else but instead headed to the frozen surface of Lake Oxoboxo.

"Tak." Phoebe could feel the vibration of the word

rumbling up from Adam's chest. The dead boy, already ten feet onto the ice, stopped and looked over his shoulder.

"Take care . . . of them."

Tak nodded, and the rasp of his voice reached them over the quiet ticking of the falling snow.

"Good luck," he said. "To you . . . both."

They watched as he walked farther out, until he was a dark blot on the bluish landscape. When he was a fair distance out she saw him lift his foot and stomp on the ice, the sound of his boot heels echoing back to them across the distance.

"What is" don't . . . worry. "he doing?"

Tak continued his stomping until finally he leaped straight into the air and came down heavily with both feet. There was a crack like thunder splitting the sky open, and he went down through the hard surface of the lake in an icy spray.

A cry rose up in Phoebe's throat, but Adam, still watching the spot where Takayuki disappeared, pulled her closer to him.

"We have . . . to . . . go," he said.

"But Tak . . ."

"He's . . . fine. But you . . . you . . . are . . . cold."

She *was* cold, no matter how much his words warmed her. And it wasn't going to be easy getting back up that hill.

"You're right, I'm cold," she said, teeth chattering. Then she laughed as they started moving.

The going was slow, but they managed to crest the hill by leaning on each other for support. They stopped for one last look at the Oxoboxo, the dark circle where Tak had gone through like a freckle on the blue-white disk of ice. Phoebe turned back and looked up at Adam. When she spoke, she managed to do so without chattering.

"I love you, Adam."

His smile touched his eyes with real expression

"I love you . . . too . . . Phoebe."

The sky clouded over and soon she could no longer see more than a few feet in front of her, but Adam took her hand and led her through the darkening forest.

CHAPTER
FORTY-NINE

From: PhoebeKendall@aol.com
To: TommyWilliams17@aol.com
SUBJECT: Updates
Dear Tommy,

By the time you see this e-mail, you should have already heard the news about what has happened here in Oakvale and in Winford. I'm sorry that I didn't e-mail you sooner than this, but it has been a crazy couple of days trying to check on everybody.

Where do I even start? There's just so much. The worst thing is that we still don't know where Karen is. We know she was with Tak on the night the police came, but we don't know if she got away or taken or what. The television stations like to run video of incarcerated zombies, but she's never in the shots. No one wants to think the worst, but Tak did say they were shooting at her. I pray every night that she escaped and that she's out there somewhere, maybe looking to catch up with you.

The Hunter Foundation closed its doors, but you probably know that already, just like you know that Sylvia is being fought over in court right now. What you might not know is that Oakvale High went further than disbanding the Undead Studies program—they went as far as to ban zombies from attending school. Principal Kim was crying when she made the announcement.

Not that there are many of them left to go to school. The Haunted House is quiet now. Everyone there left with Tak and Popeye to go "underground." Sick pun I know but those were his words. I don't know exactly where "underground" is, but even if I did, I don't think I'd write it in an e-mail because who knows whether or not our e-mails are being monitored. But Cooper went, and Mal, and just about every other zombie we know except for George and Kevin and a few others who are in prison or worse. Melissa is still at St. Jude's, and that's become a huge controversy too because Father Fitzpatrick refuses to turn her over.

I hope some of the things that have happened are useful to you as you look for help in Washington, but I guess after the Guttridge family murder that's wishful thinking.

BTW, Tak swears he and the old-schoolers had nothing to do with the murders, or the grave digging of a few weeks ago. For what it's worth, I believe him. He's one of the strangest people I know, but he has a sort of moral code, if that makes sense. I heard that he's on the FBI's Most Wanted list. They're calling him a terrorist.

I'm glad Colette escaped all of this turmoil. I don't know if Karen told you, but Colette stayed with DeCayce and the Skeleton Crew. She's going to go on tour with them and maybe try to locate her brother. Margi says she might even try to find her parents.

So now it's just me and Margi and the other trads here.

And Adam. Adam the rock. Strong Adam, Adam who is always there for me.

Adam, my love.

Yes, Adam and I are "together" now. It's really weird, because in some ways it feels as if we've been together forever, but on the other hand, everything—everything—is brand new. It's going to be super weird now that he isn't allowed to go to school anymore, but we'll manage. We'll have to.

I also wanted to apologize to you, Tommy, for all the things I wrote in the e-mail I sent you. It was wrong of me, and I didn't really mean it; I was just hurt and confused because I didn't know how I felt about you, and I didn't know how Adam felt about me, and everything else that was going on. And of course I was jealous because you'd found somebody else, and I have no right to be. You deserve to be happy, Tommy. You're a really great guy and what you do is important, and it might end up being the most important thing for zombies everywhere. Don't stop trying.

Sometimes it's the little things that make the difference in this world, little things like writing a poem or picking up a football when everyone says you can't. Or giving someone you love a kiss.

Sometimes the little things aren't enough, though, and
that's why I wish you the best of luck. If anyone can make a
change you can.

I'm using your private e-mail address because I saw that the
foundation already pulled the plug on mysocalledundeath.com.
I hope my note finds you safe and sound.

So, good luck, Tommy. Give my best to Christie.

Love,

Phoebe

Phoebe hit send and checked the clock. There was just enough time to make a cup of coffee before the bus came. She'd been drinking a lot of hot coffee in the past few days, as though she needed it to keep her body temperature up after that night/morning in the woods.

She was adding the sugar when there was a light knock on the door. She opened it and there was Adam standing on her doorstep, holding a candy cane and wearing a red Christmas elf hat. He was also wearing his enormous backpack, and coupled with the cane and hat the overall effect was that he looked like a goofy undead Santa Claus.

"Morning . . . sunshine," he said, holding out the candy cane.

Phoebe laughed as she took it from him. "Silly. What are you doing over here so early?"

"Couldn't . . . sleep. Besides . . . it's time . . . for school."

She unwrapped the candy cane and stirred her coffee with it, peppermint mixing with the rich smell of the liquid. "Adam, you can't go to school—Principal Kim announced it on Monday, you know that."

He shrugged, the shoulder with the heavy bag rising and falling in slow motion.

"I . . . feel like . . . going . . . to school."

His grin was so much like the old Adam that her protests died in her throat. "That's a first," she said, reaching for her coat.

"Come on . . . it's widely . . . known . . . I love . . . school."

She laughed. "Yeah, I seem to recall hearing that somewhere."

His face grew serious. "I'm not planning on . . . taking . . . things . . . lying down . . . ever again."

She touched his cheek, feeling for the first time as if she really had made good on her promise to bring him back. He gazed back at her with a steady confident intensity that made her think he'd come further than either of them would have expected.

Breath turning to vapor in the cold air, she took his hand and joined him outside, where the bus was just beginning to chug down their street, ready to carry them off to school.